RIPPLES AND SHADOWS

BY

STEPHEN TAYLOR

A CIP catalogue record for this book is
available from the British Library

Paperback ISBN 978-1-907939-26-6

Printed in Great Britain

CUPIO BOOKS LTD
Head Office
27 Sotheby Avenue
Sutton-in-Ashfield
Notts
NG17 5JU

www.cupiobooks.co.uk

Also by Stephen Taylor

A CANOPY OF STARS

NO QUARTER ASKED NO QUARTER GIVEN

THE KING OF BLOGNOGPOTEN

Dedication

For my daughter Helen and for Sian with much love.

Prologue.

History is my passion. No, first things first; my name is James Postlethwaite and I will be your narrator through this story and I am a historian – or is it, I am *an* historian; I never know. Let's get something out of the way to start with – yes I know, Postlethwaite is a bloody stupid name, but it doesn't sound so bad in Lancashire where I come from where you can find Satterthwaites, Utterthwaites, Olthwaites and other such names. Thwaite surnames by the way originate from an old Viking word for clearing, but then that's just me being a historian again (or is it *an* historian).

There's something you need to know about history. When you think you understand it, you probably don't. Look at it this way: if I try to explain *when* I live I can say I live in the present or I could say I live in the now. If I wish to give this a more specific explanation I could say that I live in 1992, 2012 or 2022. But that in itself creates a problem in that the present immediately becomes the past. The now is transitory whereas the past is, well, always the past.

But that is also a deception. If I try to tell somebody in the present, a story about the present, then although they may have a different view to me they still have, in the main, the same points of reference as I have. If they live in my country they will have gone through the same education process and watched the same television programmes, read the same newspapers.

To look back into history, however, you have to look back at a point in time or multiple points in time, and in every one of these points the people will have a totally different set of references. These long-dead people may have been of the same nationality as I, or spoken the same language, but in most other respects their reference points are different. These people did not behave like I do; did not think as I think; did not have the same values as I have; they are not the same people. To understand them we have to be sensitive to the ripples that come down to us through time, look into the shadows of their stories.

Very occasionally we get a genuine glimpse into real people's lives, how they lived, how they thought and the emotions that drove them; ordinary people speaking in their own words from across the centuries. Their own words in their own journals.

Ok; let's start our story; I will narrate, but I will let the two main characters speak for themselves through extracts from their journals.

Chapter 1.

I hate it when the phone rings late into the evening. But on this occasion I was partly culpable. I had dipped into the History Department's operating budget to get myself an outside line so that my calls didn't go through the university switchboard. I looked at my wristwatch, irritated. It was after 8 p.m. and I was working late. I had given out my direct dialling number to only a few colleagues and friends and had deliberately switched my mobile to voicemail so that I would not be disturbed, but now a call was coming through on the university landline. Bugger! This was the down side. The whole point of working late was that there were no distractions. 'Damn!' I held my breath as the phone rang on and on. 'They'll get the message,' I thought. And then it stopped. I exhaled, relieved, but the damage was done; my concentration broken.

My desk was chaotic. I was in full research mode and thick manuals and volumes covered every inch of its surface. I had pulled out the desk drawers and rested other heavy books on them so that I could move my attention from one open page to the other without the need to continually open and close them. It was a somewhat precarious arrangement and the whole lot threatened to tumble to the floor. I had been so engrossed in my work that time had stood still for me. It was as though I was somehow separated by some invisible force field from the outside world. This was how I liked to research. I had been jotting down notes of my thoughts as I worked and now I looked again at the last entry, searching in the chaos for my pen, only to realise that I had stuck it in my mouth – probably when the phone rang – and was chewing it without any conscious thought that I was doing so. I grimaced at myself: it was an unhygienic habit. Wiping the slavered pen on my lapel, I was about to start writing again, when the phone burst back into life.

I threw the pen across the room, grabbed the phone off its cradle and making no attempt to hide my irritation, yelled, 'YES, WHAT IS IT?'

'Wow, Jimbo; take it easy man.'

'Ah, it's you. Sorry, Toby, I'm just trying to get on with something.' My tone was more conciliatory at the sound of a voice I recognised. Toby Fielding and I had been at university together, but his field was Medievalism, while mine was the 18th and 19th centuries.

'Here am I, trying to do you a favour and all you can do is yell down the phone at me.'

I knew he was teasing me, but I just wanted to get back to my research. I was about to tell him that whatever it was, I wasn't interested, but Toby was an old friend, so I bit my tongue and went along with his game.

'A favour, what sort of a favour?'

'Meet me for a pint and I'll tell you all about it.'

'I'm busy, Toby,' I snapped. 'Just tell me what you want will you?' Despite my best effort, my irritation was surfacing again.

'All work and no play makes Jimbo a dull boy, you know. Come on, it's too late to be working. A pint of Bombardier will do you the world of good.'

'Look, I work late 'cause it's deserted and I don't get distracted. It's when I do my best work,' I said pointedly.

'Maybe so, but I promise you that you will thank me for this.'

'Thank you for what?'

'Oh no you don't,' said Toby, 'you'll have to meet me to find out.'

'But I can't, Toby, really. I want to get all this down while it's fresh in my mind.'

'When will you be finished?'

'Oh I don't know, a couple of hours maybe.'

'Ok, we'll me meet for the last one.'

'Last one what?' I said. My thoughts were already drifting back to my research.

'The last drink before closing time, say 10:30 at the Nags Head? That's just round the corner from you isn't it?'

I looked at my watch and tried to work out how long I needed. 'Ok,' I said, attempting to hide my reluctance, '10:30 in the Nags Head, I'll be there.'

Now, as I narrate this story, I know it was the best decision I have ever made, but at the time it was nothing but an aggravation.

The pub was full and noisy, but then it always seemed to be. I liked the Nags Head: it was down an old alley and over two hundred years old, all mahogany and mirrors. Inside it was long and narrow, the room split in two by the bar and a bench with tables in front running its full length, although most of the regulars preferred to stand by the bar. It didn't take many customers to fill it and that added to the ambience. It was the most welcoming place I knew.

I looked around and down the bar and saw a hand go up holding a pint of beer as my enticement. Underneath, the grinning face of Toby, his red hair marking him out like a fiery beacon on a distant hilltop. It had been long and curly at university, earning him the nickname of 'Bubbles', which he detested, but now it was cropped short and was beginning to thin.

'JIMBO,' he yelled, 'over here.'

I pushed my way to the bar, took the glass of handsome liquid held out to me and took a long swig. It tasted wonderful; Toby had been right, I did need it.

'Nobody else still calls me Jimbo, you know,' I complained, 'not since uni anyway.'

'Well, if you think I'm calling you Professor James bloody Postlethwaite you've got another think coming. What sort of a name is Postlethwaite anyway?'

'Nay lad, it's quite common in Rochdale,' I said, reverting to my Lancashire accent.

I took another swig, the froth from the head giving me a foamy moustache. I wiped it away with the back of my hand, saying, 'So what's this favour you are going to do for me?'

'Oh, let's have this drink first,' he said. He just couldn't resist teasing me, dragging it out. 'You know your trouble, Jimbo lad?'

'No, but I expect that you are going to tell me. How's Carol?'

He grinned, 'Don't change the subject. You have become quite the little swot, haven't you? You need a work-life balance makeover, Jimbo.'

'And you're the man to do that for me, I take it, *Bubbles*?'

'Aye, Jimbo, just the man.' He raised his glass ignoring my dig at his old nickname.

He was right of course and deep down I knew it. My social life was non-existent. Toby and I had been rivals for Carol's affection at university, but she had chosen him and since then there had been no one else, well no one special. I had resented him for it at the time, yet our friendship had survived and it was old history now. Indeed, he and Carol were always inviting me to stay with them.

'Your problem is that you've never moved on from Carol,' he said.

I stared at him in surprise. It was not something we had ever discussed. 'I've had other girlfriends,' I grunted, embarrassed.

'Yeah, but they never last do they? The only relationship that has lasted with you is with that bloody career of yours. You're chuffing young to have landed a History Chair, I'll grant you that – I mean, Head of the History Department and still in your thirties! You put us all to shame, Jimbo lad. But come on, you can't cuddle up and spoon with a career in the middle of a cold January night can you?'

'Have you quite finished?' I drawled, but I wasn't offended; once again, I knew he was right. 'Look, Toby, I haven't come here for this. What've you really got for me?'

'Source documentation, Jimbo; source documentation. I know where you can find some juicy personal journals.'

I was always interested in journals. They gave historians an insight into how people lived. Unwitting testimony was as valuable as the formal accounts of great events – if not more so, for official history was often biased, or written politically to hide the truth as much as to explain it.

'Have you read them?'

'Glimpsed them; these are real gems, Jimbo lad, real gems.'

'And why so?' I was playing Toby's game, but I didn't mind.

'Because they are different; like nothing else you will have seen.'

'You think so? I'll be the judge of that if you don't mind. I think you had better start at the beginning and tell me the full story.'

Sometime later I drove to Nottinghamshire with enthusiasm and not a little excitement. It seemed on the face of it that Toby had indeed done me a great favour. He had attended a historical conference at Elloughton Park and after he had lost interest in the other attendees, had spent an evening in the bar talking to the manager. From my own experience, I knew that's what people did at conferences: late nights in the bar were all part of them.

Elloughton Park was an old country house that had fallen into disrepair and had been bought by a hotel chain who had converted it into a country hotel-cum-conference centre. That I supposed was their business plan, to take advantage of the conference trade during the week and the seekers of a romantic country retreat at weekends. It transpired that during the restoration, the manager had made a number of finds tucked away in the attic. These included the old manorial documents, the most interesting of which were a series of journals covering almost fifty years and written, it seemed, by the lord and lady of the manor between 1785 and 1832. They must have been there in the loft for a century and a half, if not more. The manager had no idea what to do with them, and when he realised that he had a conference of historians he had taken the opportunity to quiz one of them. It was my luck that by chance, he picked Toby. Being a Medievalist, Toby could easily have simply referred the manager to another of those at the conference, but good friend that he is, instead he had put my name forward. This was a wonderful opportunity for me: a chance to observe at first hand the life of a country house from the points of view of both the lord and lady who lived there in the Georgian era – my particular area of interest.

The manager had made a room available to me which, I was glad to see, in common with many of his conference rooms, offered office facilities as part of the package. He showed me the way with no little enthusiasm and as we walked I explained briefly why I wanted to look at the journals. He had arranged for them to be placed in my room, he said, and they were there waiting for me. I could hardly contain my excitement.

However, when I glanced down at what was waiting for me, I could see immediately that there was something wrong. The manager's words drifted away from me, I was so anxious to start studying those journals. He must have seen that I just wanted to get at them, for his flow of chatter stuttered to a halt.

'I'll leave you to get on with it, then,' I heard him say.

'Err, yes. Sorry,' I said, a little embarrassed, but distracted and confused by what I saw. 'Er, thank you.'

As soon as I was left alone I knelt on the floor to examine the finds. There were two boxes, the first an old leather trunk, worn and scuffed, but I could see that it must have been fine in its day. Inside was a jumbled collection of leather-bound journals, the author's name, 'Lord Corbyn Carlisle' clearly in evidence. They firstly needed sorting into chronological order of course, and I was eager to read them, but they were much as I had expected. Not so the other box: it was this that was wrong – by which I mean, not of the same period, probably earlier and reused several times.

It was a wooden, rustic construction and oblong; about two and a half feet by one foot. Surely this was a servant's box – wasn't it? The lid wasn't hinged: it just sat inside a groove in the base, with a piece of rope that served as a handle. And then I rejected my reservations. These journals had been gathering dust in the loft for so long that somebody, over the years, must have put them in the only available box they could find. It was the contents that were important! I pulled at the rope to look inside and as I did so I saw some initials carved in the lid – 'GF'. Who was GF? Probably just a long-forgotten servant; I dismissed it and turned to what was inside.

There were a number of leather journals belonging to Lady Virginia Carlisle. VC – not GF? I mused. It seemed that my deduction was correct. I took out some of them to find that underneath were a number of cheaply made notebooks, unbound, each one covered in manila paperboard, or what remained of it. Many were creased, wrinkled, scored, their original beige colour now dirtied to grubby russet. Some were falling apart, the stitching holding them together beginning to unravel. I suspected that the hotel manager, unknowingly, had done some damage when he had found them. Written on the front of them was the name Ginny Farmer – GF. So this is GF, I thought to myself. But who the hell *was* Ginny Farmer?

My first task was to put the pieces together so that each page belonged to its original diary. I lifted them out one by one as gently as I could, relieved when I saw that by doing this the stitching, although loose, had enough connection left to identify its constituent pages. If I had attempted to bring them out collectively I'm sure the pages would have spilled all over the floor. My excitement growing, I spent the next hour carefully reassembling these decaying journals and then putting them all into chronological order. They actually started from 1783 and went through to 1832, as Toby had indicated. I put the earliest on the desk and opened it at the first page. I loved this moment, looking back into a life more than two hundred years ago. I began to read.

But again I was confused. The first few pages contained an inventory of food. It was dated 12th June 1783. It was a cook's inventory of the food in the larder of the household. I surmised that it was kept to keep a check so that any theft of food could be identified. It was full of crossings out, and added entries in the margins. The journal itself started at page 7. I guessed that there had been too many errors and a new notebook had been started by the cook. This Ginny Farmer had perhaps retrieved the discarded book for her journal.

Was this an added bonus? It seemed I had stumbled on not just the journals of Lord and Lady Carlisle, but also those of a surprisingly articulate servant, even if she was little educated and the grammar and spelling were crude; such a journal was rare. History from three different perspectives! Hardly able to believe my good fortune, I read on even more intrigued.

Chapter 2.

The Journal of Ginny Farmer
Bristol 1783

1ˢᵗ **June 1783**. My name is Virginia Farmer but everybody calls me Ginny. I am fourteen years old coming up fifteen and I work in the household of my maister Mr Josiah Holdstock as a cinder maid. Thats a scullery maid really. ~~ee~~ He is a wealthy ship owner and ~~ee~~ he is a bit frightening. I am answerable to the cook Mrs Strabane and ~~er~~ she works me very hard. I was also a little bit frightened of ~~er~~ her when I started nearly a year ago now but I am sure that she sees how hard I work and I rarely drop any of the food ~~er~~ she has cooked so I think ~~er~~ she has now developed a bit of a soft spot for me. ~~Er~~ She has given me this old booklet to write my journal in and allowed me to use ~~er~~ her writing pen and ink, and a candle to see by, although it is tallow and not wax so smells awful. ~~er~~ She gets candle ends from the family as something called a ~~perkwisit~~ perquisite, but I am to make do with tallow. I was brought up in the Foundlings Hospital in Bristol where I was abandoned as a baby. I was raised a strict Christian then put into service when I turned fourteen. Mrs Strabane calls me the little sparrow cause I am so small and thin ~~Ers~~ She's Irish and it sounds so nice in er soft accent. ~~Aa~~ctually I am much stronger than I look and I don't seem to get nearly as tired as some of the other maids but the working days ~~is~~ are long and I am ready for my bed at night. I'm the only servant that does not have a bedroom. I had a bed at the Foundlings Hospital, but here I dont have one and I have to sleep in one of the kitchen ~~cubords~~ cupboards. I have some reading and writing, well, after a fashion. T~~t~~hey taught me some schooling at the Foundlings Hospital and Mrs Strabane says that I should practice it ~~cause~~ because if I wish to gain ~~advansment~~ advancement then I will need to be able to keep kitchen accounts. It was er ~~suggeshion~~ suggestion that I should start this journal. I am writing it at the kitchen table and ~~er~~ she is sat besides me now. She has said that I should start by writing about my life so far which is what I am doing and she is going to correct the spelling and grammar and ~~punchuashon~~ punctuation. Edith is the kitchen maid. I don't think ~~er~~ she likes me very much or should I say that I dont think that ~~er~~ she likes the way Mrs Strabane favors me. Edith is above me but she cant read and write. S~~s~~he also says ohroo~~hr~~ instead of yes. W~~we~~ ~~wus~~ was told not to do that at the Foundlings Hospital. A~~a~~s the cinder maid I am the youngest and the lowest-ranked of the female servants and Edith makes that very clear to me that I am ~~er~~ her assistant as she is the kitchen maid. A~~a~~lthough I report to Mrs. Strabane ~~er~~ she says I am to do that through ~~er~~ her. Edith gets to eat at the servants dining hall table and I am a little jealous of ~~er~~ her for that cause I have to eat on my own in the kitchen in order to keep an eye on the food that is still cooking. A~~a~~lthough I am the youngest and smallest my duties seem to be the hardest in the kitchen. I have to clean and scour the floor the stoves the sinks the pots and the dishes. A~~a~~fter scouring the plates in the scullery I leave em on racks to dry. W~~w~~hile they are drying I then have to clean the vegetables pluck the fowl and scale the fish. Mrs Strabane says I am very fortunate to have a position at all and should not grumble.

I have also to make up the maisters special mixtures and I have to be careful to always get that right. Mr Josiah Holdstock is a big plump man with a big round jowly face and ~~ee~~ he is always scowling. ~~Ee~~ He is quite scary. Mr. Brettingham the butler says that ~~ee~~ he suffers terribly from the toothache and the scurvy of the gums. T~~t~~hats why his face is often swollen. ~~Ee~~ He says that if we see that his gums is swollen then we have to be extra careful to do everything right so as not to annoy him. B~~b~~ut ~~yer~~ you dont have to look at his face to see if it is swollen cause ~~yer~~ you can smell his breath even if ~~yer~~ you are at the other end of the room. N~~n~~ot that I have anything much to do with him. Mr Brettingham says his breath is fetid. I dont know what that means but I know it stinks as much as the outside privy. A~~a~~nyway I have to make up a mouthwash mixture for him of anise seeds mints and cloves sodden in wine. S~~s~~ometimes there is an alternative of honey ~~mer~~ myrrh and juniper root and rock alum. Mrs Strabane says she is grateful that I am not lax in my duties cause ~~er~~ she knows how frightening ~~ee~~ he is when the toothache is bad. I also have to boil his sponges what ~~ee~~ he uses to rub his teeth clean with and they make me gag when I have to handle them.

~~Ee~~ He also drinks heavily when ~~ee~~ he has the toothache. Well, so Edith tells me but ~~ee~~ he seems to me he drinks heavily all the time, specially when ~~ee~~ he is in pain. Edith has been warned by Mrs Strabane to keep away from him when ~~ee~~ he has been drinking for fear of being taken advantage of but ~~ee~~ he dont come down to the kitchen and the servants have their own staircase to the bedrooms so that it is not so much a problem for me. O~~o~~ur morning starts at 5.30 of the clock. I have to clean the clinker in the kitchen grate and then set the fire even before Mrs Strabane gets up. W~~w~~hen she gets to the kitchen we all have to say our prayers for the day with ~~er~~ her. M~~m~~ake me dutiful and obedient to my maister make me ~~temprut~~ temperate and chaste make me meek and patient make me true in all my dealings, and make me content and ~~industrus~~ industrious in my station.

23rd **September 1783.** I have not written in my journal for a long while but I have been practicing like Mrs Strabane told me and my spelling is much better she says, and she will not be correcting it no more.

There has been a great deal of goings on today. Edith has been caught stealing food from Mrs Strabanes larder. She was taken into Mr Brettinghams office and we could all hear his raised voice shouting at er. We stopped to try and hear but Mrs Strabane told us it was none of our business. Have you no work to do she said clapping her hands and we all scurried off to get on with our duties but we were all as quiet as possible while we were working, still trying to hear what was being said.

Edith comes from a village just outside Bristol and her father is a farm labourer. She had told me that ee had an accident when a hay cart drove over his foot and crushed it. The broken foot would not set properly and ee now limps terrible badly. And because of that ee had been dismissed cause ee could not do his duties. She must have been stealing food to take to him. It was to be er Sunday afternoon off this Sunday and er must have been going to smuggle it out then.

When er came out of Mr Brettinghams office er was whooping and weeping all red faced but Mrs Strabane would not let me go to er. We always comforted each other in the Foundlings Hospital when one of us was beaten. Mrs Strabane took er up to er bedroom and er was then escorted from the household by Mr Brettingham. I was not allowed to speak to er.

But I am to be the new kitchen maid. I am sorry for Edith but I am also so excited. Me, little Ginny Farmer from the Foundlings Hospital. My first advancement. I turned fifteen last week and now I'll also get to eat at the servants dining hall table. And I get a bedroom which I will share with Emma Price the underhouse parlormaid. It is right at the top of the house. We are allowed a candle to take to bed with us but I am not allowed to read in bed and nor is there a desk to write on.

The Journal of Corbyn Carlisle
London 1784

15th February 1784· I have decided to write this journal because I am experiencing a severe attack of the melancholies· Yesterday I turned 24; ironic that I should be born on St· Valentine's Day, when the pleasures of Venus are so constantly denied to me· Last night I was taken on the town by my friend and roommate, Richard Standing; he likes to call himself Dick Upstanding because of his prowess with the ladies, but then Richard is no shrinking violet like me· He offered to stand me the cost of a Mabel, the socket money, and a night of wenching and whoring was, I confess, very tempting to me· I said that I did not want to partake of a street whore for they were mostly unclean, and he gave me a dejected look, but then his face beamed a great smile at me and he gladly opened his purse to gain me entrance to Mrs· Pearce's establishment·

'Why, young Mr· Standing,' said Mrs· Pearce enthusing all over him· He had obviously been here many times before and she clearly knew him well· She was, to my eyes, a quite grotesque woman· Her dress was loud – crimson and yellow; but it was grubby and had seen better days· Her hair was worn high, which although I confess is the fashion of the day, was so ridiculously overdone that she towered above Richard and myself, although she was in fact several inches shorter· Her wig was jet black, most likely the result of a chemical dye purchased from the apothecary· I could see that it had been starched, the front curled by curl papers and on top of that great height she even wore two large flumes that rose to very near the ceiling· The whole ensemble had been vigorously scented, as had her body· She set my nostrils twitching she was so overpowering· The entire establishment reeked of a myriad of aromas, sweet and sweat fighting each other for dominance, but all playing second fiddle to the madam herself· The woman's dress was cut low to display her bosom to its full advantage, and this particular bosom was ample, pushed upwards by her stays so that the fleshy masses overflowed and rose and fell in concert with her breathing. I suppose she was what I expected a madam to look like, but this particular madam overwhelmed me.

'Why Bess, and how is it with you today?' said my companion, Richard, taking her hand and kissing it as if she were some fine lady.

'I am well, sir,' she replied, 'and what can I offer your good self, today?'

'Ah Bess, I am not to be the client today,' said Richard, and then he turned and introduced me. 'This is my good friend, Corbyn, who today is four and twenty years. Who would you recommend for this fine young man?'

She looked me up and down and I felt that I was being judged as to my manhood. She must have come to the conclusion that I needed toughening up and recommended a stout young wench by the name of Aida.

'You'll have no trouble getting Aida down,' said Richard, laughing robustly at his own wit, and Mrs. Pearce joined in with a most shrill cackling laugh. He had obviously had the pleasure of this wench himself and for some reason thought her suitable for me.

She was indeed a stout wench, stout being the right word for her. She was not of the kind that many men prefer, large and plump; she was in fact small in height and her flesh was not loose but firm, so firm that I am sure she was as strong as I, if indeed not stronger. Why they thought she would be suitable for me is beyond my comprehension. But when it came to it, my member would not stand and do its duty. When Richard asked me why I had returned so quickly, I blamed it on an excess of John Barleycorn, for we had been drinking heavily all evening, but deep down I knew it not to be true. It is simply that the Mabel overawed me and I now wonder if I am to become one of those men destined always to be a failure in the arts of Venus. I confess that this has happened to me before.

Why could I not have been more like my father and my brothers, but then, I have always known that I was different. I was always the cuckoo in the nest. Father was, I have to confess, a robust debauched man of the country who was known to take advantage of the servants. He had a son by his first wife, my older half-brother, Carlton, and then two girls, my half-sisters. When his wife died he quickly took a mistress and fathered my second half-brother, Cavendish· I am the son of his legitimate second wife· My mother was a demur lady and when I was growing up I thought she was much out of place in the household· Likewise, I am less robust than my half-siblings, but I believe more intelligent, although that was not something very hard to achieve· I spent much of my early life with Mother, despite having a nurse, but I think that was because she saw me as a companion as well as a son· There was little companionship for her from my father and none from his other offspring·

My bastard older brother and his mistress mother always sat at the dining table with us, which must have been a daily insult to my mother, but if she did find it so, she never mentioned it to me when I was growing up· Carlton and Cavendish were like my father, hunting was their preferred pastime, to which they added whoring as they got older· I don't think I ever saw either of them read a book for pleasure·

We all had home tutoring, and great effort was made with Carlton, for one day he would need to run the estate, but he was not at all academic and made little attempt to please Father in that respect· But then, Father was cast in the same furnace and I don't think that he was too upset at his son's shortcomings· I too was tutored and I found learning easy, in fact I was a bit of a swot, but I learned more from my mother than the tutors employed to teach me· In particular she introduced me to poetry and I still have a love of it today· I think I am an accomplished poet myself, but I have never shown it to anybody, certainly not my brothers, who would mock me at the first sight of it·

Mother later insisted that I go to an academy rather than public school and I am forever grateful to her for that· She was totally dominated by Father, but she stood firm in that· Those public schools have a reputation for bullying and brutal punishment regimes and I think mother knew that I was not robust enough to endure them· They also teach little more than the classics, whereas at the Melton Academy I was instructed in writing, arithmetic, languages, merchant's accounts, mathematics, dancing, drawing, music and fencing· Indeed all the gentlemanly accomplishments that I needed for a career in law· Surprisingly, I showed a great aptitude for fencing and won the award as the best fencer in school· I am not an aggressive man by nature, but fencing I found had as much in common with chess as it did with fighting. Strategy is all-important: the parry is as significant as the lunge. It has done much for my confidence knowing that I can defend myself should I be required to do so. I think Father took more pride in that fencing award than he did in my academic achievements, and for the first time my brothers showed me some respect. Fighting, it seems, was something that they could relate to even if poetry and learning were not!

Nurse had been with our household for many years. She must have been in her early twenties when Carlton was born, but passed forty I suppose as I became a young master about the house. She still acted as my nurse, and looking back on it now, it seems a little odd, for her duties were really over by that time, but I had supposed she was kept on as an old and loyal family retainer would be. She had always got into bed with us as children to comfort us if we had a nightmare, and since that was not unusual I was never uncomfortable with it. By the age of fifteen, however, it still happened occasionally when I was home from the academy, although she must have been aware that the signs of manhood were about me by then. In fact, the close proximity of her ample body was more often than not the source of those signs!

One particular night, when I had been tossing and turning unable to sleep, she entered my bed for my comfort, perhaps thinking I had experienced a bad dream. Her ample arms entwined me. 'There, there,' she said, caressing me, her hand moving gently about my torso. She brushed my member with the back of her hand and from that it must have been obvious to her that I was no longer a child. But she took my embarrassment away, behaving as if it was the most natural thing in the world. I relaxed and accepted what was happening to me. Underneath the sheets, cocooned in her warmth, I remember the words she whispered to me.

'This is the sign that you are becoming a man, young Master Corbyn,' she said, 'and you need to learn what to do as a man. I can help you with that if you want me to.'

The bed was warm and safe and I remember feeling a sensation rise within me. I lost my virginity to her that night and it was a very enjoyable experience. She came to my bed many times over the next few months.

I have learned later that all this had happened at the bequest of my father and that it was part of nurse's duties· She had done the same for Carlton and Cavendish, although their initiation was at the age of thirteen· I was obviously the slow starter in the Carlisle family, and Father, it seems, had some worries about me·

Now I look back and lament· I had no problems with the arts of Venus when in the arms of my nurse· So why am I so unable to conquer those arts now? Oh, the melancholies are well and truly with me tonight·

3rd March 1784· I have a letter from my brother, Carlton· I wrote to him two weeks ago to inform him of my dire financial need, but once again he denies me funds· It is not that I am extravagant· If I am to study the law, then there are certain expenses that are to be defrayed· I share rooms with other bachelors, here in the Middle Temple off Fleet Street, which are no more than service lodgings· The rooms look fine from the outside, but are a mess and squalid inside· I eat mostly at Bob's Chop House; the fare is plentiful and nourishing, but by no means extravagant· Sometimes I cannot even afford that and I have to dine at a cookshop where for a few pence I can eat plentifully, but have to take what is offered in sheets of old paper, either at the counter or in the street outside· It is hardly a way for a gentleman to behave· And all the time Carlton dines well from his own kitchen·

I do understand the need to keep the estate together for the benefit of the male heir, and that inevitably means that there is little money available for the second son, or even the other siblings· But does that mean that I should be denied my birthright? When Father died suddenly five years ago, Carlton inherited the title and the estate; the eighth baronetcy, Lord Carlisle of Elloughton· He has the lot and I am now merely in his gift· He is the incumbent member of the landed gentry; he owns the country estate and I know I have to accept that, but with the estate comes extensive land so he is not required to work as I am required to do – well, except on the management of the lands, and he cannot even do that properly· He has the country house, surrounded by rolling Nottinghamshire countryside near the River Trent, 124 acres of meadow, 76 acres of pasture, 1,470 acres of land let mainly to forty-seven tenant farmers· He has the income from the estate, which he is unable to manage properly, as well as the rents from the tenanted farms.

Yet he sends me a rambling five-page letter of how he is unable to provide funds for me because of his other expenses. He says he has even been required to cut his workers' wages. He rambles on about how, when workers earn more money, they inevitably spend it on drink, or some other form of luxury or debauchery. He believes the poor are poor because they are idle. 'It is a fact of life,' he writes, 'that some should be rich and some should be poor, some high and some low. The poor should remember that they are dependent on the rich.' Well, he does more than anybody I know to keep the poor, poor. He spends his time doing exactly what he denies his workers, and I also know that he pays poor wages because he manages his estate so badly. Indeed, he has even denied our two sisters a dowry so that they are likely to remain spinsters. He wastes his money on horses and livery, gambling and wenching. It is a good job that he does not come to London for the season, as I fear he would bankrupt the estate. He is not even good at what he enjoys most: gambling. He seems to be the eternal loser.

He then rambles on about having to pay an annuity to my mother. I do not begrudge her that, as it has enabled her to get away from that terrible household. But Carlton is being disingenuous, of course, because that annuity, along with one for Father's mistress, and the Military Commission bought for Cavendish, are all bequests from Father's will, and a trust fund is set up for that. Carlton is merely the trustee administering the fund, but I would not be surprised if he is even dipping into that. He denies those kin around him their just desserts and yet he indulges himself with his bloodstock, his kennel of hounds, and of course his lavish gambling.

Oh dear, I am beginning to sound like one of those radical chappies looking for egalitarian reform, am I not? Perhaps that is to be my lot in life, to be like John Wilkes. But no, I do not believe the mob has a right to vote, that must be left to good men of property. But Carlton writes that he cannot afford to pay even my current allowance, although will do all in his power to continue to stand the present outlay. So I am to be grateful, it seems, for what I have.

The melancholies stayed with me for some days after my 24th birthday. I have decided that what I need is a wife and that the wenching life is not for me, but what can I offer a wife? Well, nothing, until I have established myself in a profession, but that might take another ten years. Even after I qualify I can't see Carlton purchasing a lawyering partnership for me. I must endeavour to do well in my studies, and then work hard in my new profession, and by the age of 35 I might be able to acquire a wife. Until then I fear that loneliness will be my constant companion.

Chapter 3.

The Journal of Ginny Farmer

30ᵗʰ **April 1784.** It has been all change again this week. Mary Gordon, the head house-parlourmaid, has moved on to be the housekeeper at another house up the street. It is not as grand as the maister's house, but Mrs Strabane says that it is a good advancement for er. Emma Price, the underhouse parlourmaid, has moved up to head house-parlourmaid and Mrs Strabane recommended me to take er place. Another advancement for me and I am still only fifteen.

I am not confined to the kitchen now but I still spend most of my time cleaning scrubbing and setting fires just as before. I have two new uniforms. Black dresses with a white apron and cap and I have to look after my appearance I'm told cause I will now be seen by the family. If I meet a member of the family whilst about my duties then I have to flatten myself against the wall and not speak to em unless they speak to me. In addition to my other duties I have to polish and scrape wax off the candelabras, cut wicks and pour pitch oil. Emma Price is instructing me in the correct methods to be employed in carrying out my duties. There is a lot to learn but I am a quick learner. There are special cloths for different uses. Dusters, china cloths, glass cloths and rubbing cloths. All the dustpans are numbered. I have my own number five, and I have to learn how to hold it together with a candle in one hand and use the brush with the other. That is not very easy but I am sure I will learn. I have also to learn how to polish the metal fittings on the furniture with fine sand. How to polish paintwork with cream dressing. How to sweep carpets with damp tea leaves. How to take off old polish with vinegar and put on new with beeswax and turpentine. How to dust down brocaded walls and rub them over with tissue paper and then with silk dusters. In the bedroom I have to learn how to make a bed properly and to black a grate. I don't like that. Blacking is made from a mixture of ivory black, treacle, oil, small beer and sulphuric acid. It makes my hands black and I cant get it off. Oh, and I have to remember what time the sunlight comes into various rooms so that the blinds can be drawn to protect the furniture. But the best part is that I now have a salary of £4 a year. Four pounds.

I no longer answer to Mrs Strabane. I am answerable to Emma Price and then to the housekeeper but Mrs Strabane is still encouraging me with my writing. When the maister has finished with his newspaper then the butler Mr Brettingham reads it and then it is passed down to the housekeeper and then to Mrs Strabane. She lets me read it after she has finished with it so it is several days old by then. But I am learning so much about the world. I am also learning how to spell better and use proper words not Brissel ones and write in proper sentences. Mrs Strabane also gets for herself the Penny Gazette and I devour that when she has finished with it. The maistress has a fashion magazine delivered to the house. It is called The Ladys Magazine. Mr Brettingham is not interested in that and the housekeeper looks at it for a short time but then Mrs Strabane gets it for me. It is so wonderful reading about all the fine ladies and seeing the coloured fashion plates of the new fashions they follow. I keep all the back copies in my servants box as I dont own anything else to put in it and it is nice to have something that is mine even if it is only a cast off. The only thing I actually own is the keepsake from the Foundlings Hospital, a mother of pearl, heart-shaped pendant with initials A and N, and a scratched third initial M. I dont know what they stand for, but I think the pendant must have been my mothers.

The Ladys Magazine tells of life in London, which seems such a wonderfully exciting place and I would love to visit it one day. There is something called the social season. Mrs Strabane says that this is when the best families in the country leave their big country houses and travel up to London so that they can attend debutante balls and dinner parties. It begins after Easter and ends in August so that the fine gentlemen can get back for the bird-hunting season. I asked Mrs Strabane if the maister ever did it, wondering if us servants would be taken with him but she laughed at that. I always thought Mr Holdstock was such a grand gentleman but she says that he is not so important as these people. HEe is very rich but he is something called a man of commerce. He is not part of the gentry as er she puts it. Oh dear, I must remember to spell he and her right. Mrs Strabane says if I did not drop my aitches when I speak, I would not keep getting it wrong.

17th September 1784. I am sixteen today. Little Ginny Farmer, sixteen! I do not think I will ever be anything else but little. Even so, I have had a bit of a growing spurt and filled out a bit. In a womanly way, can

I say. I think that may be cause I now eat meat most every day. At the Foundlings Hospital we hardly ever had meat and if we did it was watered down to be no more than a thin gruel. Mrs Strabane says that I am turning into a pretty young thing and that I should watch out as the boys will be pestering me. The only boy I know is Martin, one of the footmen and he is at least twenty-two. I do not like him very much. He thinks he is so superior as if I am not worthy of his time but we are both lower servants so I don't know why he should think so.

Tonight at the servants dining hall table I thought that I had got into trouble. After our evening meal Mrs Strabane proposed a toast cause it was my birthday. Everybody lifted their cups and said happy birthday to me and I looked down in embarrassment as they did so. But then I did something stupid. I had always been a good mimic at the Foundlings Hospital and I used to make the other children laugh when I did an impression of Matron. We all used to giggle under our blanket when the candle was put out, trying to keep our laughter in so that she would not come back and unleash her wrath on us. She often threatened us with her wrath as she put it but the threat was enough cause we never found out what she meant by it. Anyway I didn't really think about what I was doing when everyone was looking at me. It just came out of my embarrassment I think. Mrs Strabane got up to fetch another mug of small beer for the table and turning her back she said in her lovely Irish accent, Oi tink we'll have a top up just dis once.

I repeated the line in the same accent. I had not been practicing it. It just came out but it was just as if she had said it herself. Oi tink we'll have a top up just dis once.

Well, it all went quiet and I felt everybodys eyes staring at me and I wanted to just crawl away. Mrs Strabane looked around at the table to see who was mimicking her and she saw everyone was looking at me.

Was that you, little Ginny Farmer she said.

Yes Mrs Strabane I said as sheepishly as I could and looking down between my knees as I did so.

But then she just started laughing and with that everybody joined in. Do it again they all said, and so I did and everybody laughed again.

Do you do anybody else said Mrs Strabane.

I thought a moment and then did Mr Brettingham. It was not as good cause my voice was much too high but they could tell it was him and everybody laughed again. Even Mr Brettingham himself laughed and he is very serious all of the time.

It has been a wonderful day today but I am ready for my bed now. I just wanted to write everything down before I go.

27th November 1784. I really did get into trouble today when I was polishing the furniture in the maistress's room. She was in there talking to her ladies maid, Miss Frost, about her outfit for the Merchants Ball that she is to attend with the maister. She was anxious to wear the latest fashion from London but Miss Frost clearly did not know what to advise. She is a very attentive lady and does everything immaculately. She has been in service for years and knows everything there is to know about being a ladies maid but she knows nothing of the current fashions. She is grey-haired and in her fifties I think, whereas the maistress must still be in her late twenties.

The maistress wanted a gown with a fashionable closed bodice but Miss Frost clearly did not know what that was like. It was none of my business but before I knew what I was doing I offered my advice.

There is a picture in the June edition of The Ladys Magazine I said, If you give it to your dressmaker then I'm sure she will be able to make it up for you.

They both turned and looked at me and I could see the look of disapproval in their eyes. It was as though I had been invisible but suddenly they could see me. Nothing was said for some moments and I did not know what to do. I bobbed a small curtsey whilst looking down at the floor by way of a sorry. I did not know what else to do. The housekeeper had told me so many times that I should not speak unless I was spoken to.

This does not concern you girl said Miss Frost. Finish what you are doing and go and I will be talking to the housekeeper about you.

I felt my face redden and I rushed from the room. Later the housekeeper called me to her room and told me off in no uncertain terms. I have been denied supper tonight. But it has got worse. The maistress has sent for me. I am to go to her rooms after I have laid all the fires tomorrow morning. I fear I may lose my position here. I do not know what will happen to me then. If I am dismissed I would never be able to get another job in service, and for girls like me, there is only one other thing we can do.

28th November 1784. I knocked quietly on the maistress's door, so quietly that I don't think she heard me. I had cried all night into my pillow and now as I stood there my heart was thumping in my chest and my knees were knocking against each other. I was reluctant to knock again in case I had just failed to hear her so I just stood there with my ear to the door not knowing what to do for the better. In the end I knocked again this time a little harder and heard her call COME. I went in and bobbed a small curtsey to her but not daring to look in her face. I just looked down at the floor. She was sat at her dressing table and I saw her knees turn away from it so I knew she was now looking at me.

Come in girl.

You sent for me Marm, I mumbled, the words dying in my mouth.

Yes, she said. Virginia is it not. Her tone was warmer.

Yes Marm I said, bobbing again.

You wouldnt happen to have the back copies of The Ladys Magazine would you.

Yes Marm. I was taken aback. I was not expecting the question. But I didnt steal em, Marm, I added hastily.

I was not suggesting that you did girl.

I felt myself shudder. Sorry Marm. I bobbed again.

Where are they girl.

They are in my servants box Marm.

Can you go and fetch them for me Virginia.

Now Marm I asked.

Yes now Virginia, if you please. Her tone was frosty again.

I rushed away up to my room at the top of the house, took the box from under my bed, quickly retrieved the magazines and rushed back down again. I offered them up to the Maistress but she asked me to find the one with the drawing of the closed bodice. I soon found the June edition and gave it to her and she studied it for some moments.

Yes, this is exactly what I want. She said it to herself more than to me I think, but then she said, Do you have an interest in fashion then girl.

Yes Marm. I like to read about those fine London ladies.

So do I Virginia she said and for the first time I looked up at her face. I was surprised to see it wasnt stern at all.

What sort of gown would suit me for the Merchants Ball do you think she asked.

I gawped at her. I think she was as surprised as I was that she had asked that of me. I grabbed up the other copies and riffled through them and then pointed at a drawing and gave it to her. It was a gown in the French style. Silk trimmed with an embroidered cotton ribbon and fringe, lined with linen. I think that style would suit you very well Marm I said.

Her eyebrows sort of knitted at first but then I saw a smile twitch at the corner of her mouth and I knew that she liked my suggestion. Then she asked me some more questions and soon I almost forgot to be nervous. For the next hour we went through all the magazines together and she sought my advice on the fashions. Me. My advice. Little Ginny Farmer and a fine lady talking about fashion.

Well I never. What a strange day it had been

The Journal of Corbyn Carlisle

5th April 1785. I had a wonderful dream last night. I dreamt that I was married with a pretty wife. Our house was clean; I was in my elegant dining room, light green walls divided by a dado rail, a marble fire-surround, a drop-leaf writing bureau, windows curtained, and with candles mounted in sconces backed by mirrors to reflect the light. There was a fine quality tablecloth freshly laundered, and I was taking tea from delicate porcelain cups, with my sweet wife. She was petite in her stature, her hair was rather inclined to fair than brown, and she had a healthy complexion. She was neat in her person, polite, and delicate of speech. Later we retired to bed and she carressed me tenderly. I felt her soft lips and sweet breath, and her yielding kisses lingered long on my lips. I felt the arousal of Venus within me and I was a true man doing my husbandly duties with full vigour. Afterwards she lay in my arms, stroking my chest and we drifted off to sleep together, warm beneath the clean, freshly laundered sheets.

Then I woke and looked about my lodgings. My room is a shambles, unkempt, my undergarments hanging on a line strung up against the wall. Even though Richard's room is far worse than mine, it is no comfort. My bedding is sweat-stained, for I cannot afford the laundry fees to have it washed more regularly if I am to eat well. My wardrobe is that of a gentleman, but some of it is now threadbare, the cuffs of my shirts being particularly frayed. But it is the loneliness that lays particularly heavy with me. I have no wife to be my constant companion. There are many fellows about, living in the Middle Temple, many of whom are fine companions and the life style is one that they enjoy; there is a whole community of us. They are young rakes about town, unrestrained, but they have allowances large enough to allow them to indulge. They study very little, reading for a handful of hours a week. Marriage is not high on their agenda; should it be so, then there would be too much competition for me to overcome, and without funds I have so little to offer that my chances of finding a wife are almost non-existent.

I am living in a city offering all the pleasures and indulgences that a young man of means could ever want, yet I have neither the income nor the personality to take advantage of it. If Dick Standing is a hero for us young men trying to make our way in the world, then what sort of world is it?

So I have resolved that I must prosper in my chosen profession; I have turned my back on this decadent life style, for it is clear that it is not for me. I have become something of a swot. Or to be truthful, I have returned to that characteristic and I keep myself constantly at study. It also seems to keep the melancholies at bay. For the best part of a year now, I have read at length: in Chambers, where I have the position of pupil, I have prepared legal documents, prepared petition papers for the court, and assisted anybody who will have me. Indeed, I have spent many hours assisting in court and done some of the advocacy myself, if under instruction. If I say so myself I am rather good at advocacy. I seem to have the eloquences and the quickness of thought needed for my profession. I think I may specialise in land litigation as there seem to be endless disputes over ownership, which affords a lawyer so much scope for fees. As I write this, I smile to myself, for no one but I will ever read of my conceit. It was a good idea to pen a journal; it allows me a release from my ill humours and helps me to get my thoughts in order.

Richard despairs of me and cajoles me to come out on the town with him, offering to stand my drink and victuals from his own purse, but my pride will not allow me to keep leeching off him, and besides, he will only finish up wenching, and that, it seems, is not for me.

I went to see my brother last week. I had been assisting at the defence of a framework knitter on trial in Leicester. His name was Ned Biscombe and he was accused of destroying one of Mr. Samuel Compton's fine new machines they call a 'spinning mule'; the mob had broken in and smashed it. These poor framework knitters – they call themselves 'stockingers' – work from home and they fear that these new machines will cost them their livelihoods. He had no money for a lawyer, but his fellow workers had made a collection for him so that he could be defended. We put up a strong defence; there was little evidence against him, as the entire mob wore masks and no one identified him as the ringleader. The richer and powerful employers, however, wanted an example made of somebody, and they got an accomplice, one of the other rioters, to turn Crown's evidence against him. It's a scandal that our judiciary system allows such uncorroborated evidence, but the jury, made up of local men of property, found him guilty and he was sentenced to seven years transportation to New South Wales. Poor Ned, he was a likeable fellow, quietly spoken and of no little intelligence despite his lack of education; I wonder who will feed his family now.

I was not in the best of moods when I arrived at Elloughton Park, feeling that we had let poor Ned Biscombe down, but when the dinner was served my spirits rose, it was sumptuous and I had not dined so well for over a year. We started with a platter of baked fish, the main course being steak pie. I took a large portion of the pie, my plate piled high even before I added potatoes and vegetables, then I copiously doused it with gravy. I dined with Carlton and my two sisters, Emily and Jane, together with that wretched mistress of my late father, Alice Clough. Whatever did Father see in her? She is overweight and lacks any sort of style or fashion! Cavendish, my middle brother, was away with his new regiment. Looking back, I am a little peeved at the lavishness of his table when I am offered only a meager allowance. I have to say that I did not feel that I was made welcome either; I was tolerated I suppose, but I still felt like the outsider, same as always.

I needed to undo the top button of my breeches by the end of the meal I was so full, but I was not going to turn down the cheese course. My sisters and Alice Clough did not retire when the brandy and cigars were brought and partook of the brandy themselves, which is somewhat unusual for highborn ladies, but caused no comment, so they must frequently behave in like fashion· The conversation was coarse and I tried hard to join in, but with little success· I mused to myself that Carlton is now 35 and I was bold enough to ask him if he was considering marriage· Father had two children by that age·

He looked round at me as if I had said something unmentionable· His expression darkened; I watched the candlelight dance on his face, but somehow it was not reflected back in his eyes, they remained dark, empty pools, but then he allowed himself a sour smile, although there was still mockery in his voice when he spoke·

'I have a funny story to tell you little brother,' he said, pausing whilst he sucked on a piece of meat stuck between his teeth· He inclined his head, 'Once upon a time, a man asked a fine lady to marry him, but the girl said, "NO!"' Carlton paused and looked round at the rest of the table· 'So the man lived happily ever after, rode his horses, went fishing and hunting, drank beer and whiskey, brandy and claret, wenched and farted whenever he wanted·'

He sat back in his chair and laughed heartily at his own wit, and my sisters and the wretched Mrs Clough joined him· I too joined in, but it was more out of politeness and embarrassment than good humour·

Carlton leaned forward again and then across the table looking directly at me· 'No, but you are right little brother, I cannot continue to live purely for my own pleasure· I need to produce an heir, I know that, however unpleasant the thought of marriage might be·' He looked round at our sister, 'I have asked Emma here to look for a suitable match for me,' he said· He looked back at me, 'We can't have you inheriting the estate little brother, can we?' and he burst out laughing again· My sisters also seemed to find this thought amusing as though it were the most preposterous thing in the world·

It seems very strange to me that here am I desperate to find a wife but with nothing to offer her, whilst Carlton has everything to offer and does not want one· I feel sorry for whoever he does take though, for she will be no more than his brood mare and nothing else· I fear the poor girl will be offered no companionship in the years ahead of her· To my way of thinking, it is decidedly odd that Carlton is regarded as a good catch·

Chapter 4.

The office desk in my hotel room was becoming chaotic, unable to cope with all these journals. I made myself a huge mug of Kenco instant coffee, Millicano Blend, provided by the hotel, the cup holding nearly a full pint. I liked the taste and read the label; the company claimed that it was 100% sourced from Rainforest Alliance Certified farms, but I just liked that it tasted like roast and ground coffee beans, smelt good and had the full-bodied flavour of real coffee. I would buy this when I got home, I thought. Caffeine was part of my research equipment, it helped me to concentrate.

Even without the coffee, this morning I was on a high. These journals were amazing; even better than I had hoped. I particularly liked this Ginny Farmer, because here was a window into the everyday life of a servant in Georgian England. This was invaluable to me as a historian. Much is known about the rich and famous, but to find the testimony of a servant – and one so unusually erudite for the times – was rare in the extreme. But it was more than that. This young girl seemed so alive to me as I read her journal. The writing may be semi-literate, yet it conveys so much, and so much of her. Her fears, her ambitions were all here shouting at me across more than two centuries. My mind had created a mental image of her as I read her words: I could see her at the kitchen table, pen in hand, before a flickering, stinking tallow candle. As a historian I was trained to be analytical, yet here I was, reacting emotionally – it was not like me at all. I was also intrigued: what was a servant's journal from a Bristol ship owner's household doing in the attic of a fine Nottinghamshire country house? I needed to read on to find out, but there was so much here; there were many, many hours of research to get through. What was clear was that I would only scratch the surface today.

A name sprang into my mind: Grace Farmer. Initially it was just association I suppose, Ginny Farmer and Grace Farmer, but then it seemed to make perfect sense. Grace was one of my best students, on her way to a First, without much doubt in my mind. I tapped into the university records from my laptop. Yes, I had remembered correctly. Her intention was to do her dissertation on social mobility in Georgian England. I could co-opt her onto this project and she could use it as her research also; two birds with one stone so to speak. I sent her a quick email singing the praises of what I had found.

I liked Grace, she was in her early thirties and had a drive that most of the other undergraduates did not share. But then, I mused, mature students usually had that. It was coming to university from a different direction and with more experience of life, I supposed. An answer came back from Grace almost immediately, breaking into my musing. She must have been sitting at her computer.

<Amazing! I'll come straight away> her email said, <where exactly is Elloughton Park?>

<No, don't do that ... > I had keyed before I had chance to think it through. I stopped typing, reflected. This was another downside of being Head of Department: to be always thinking about budgets. My "travel and subsistence" budget was already under strain, my "capital budget" was modest, but I could possibly go back to the Vice Chancellor's office to authorise more. I left my laptop and went to see the hotel manager, to see if I could secure the journals for the university.

'Are they valuable then?' he said, and I could see that I had tweaked the businessman in him. His interest had moved on from one of intrigue to one of commerce when I had used the phrase, *I want to secure them for the university.*

'Only academically,' I said honestly, 'I can't see much of a market from the general public.'

'But they still have some value?'

'Well yes, I suppose.' I didn't like where this was going.

He suggested a ridiculous figure and I scoffed, but looking back he was much more adept at this than I, and I supposed he was testing the waters, looking for parameters. Figures were bandied about until he suggested a sum that I thought I might be able to squeeze out of the Vice Chancellor.

'Ok,' I said, 'subject to the university's approval, but I want all the manorial records from your attic for that.'

'No – no way,' he said, 'we are just talking about these journals. There's all sorts of stuff up there; I don't know what I would be selling.' He was like a different person to the jovial manager that had greeted me, all eager to be of help. This was a hard-headed businessman. I suppose this is what the newspapers mean on their financial pages when they say: "Negotiations had broken down." He wanted more than I thought I would be able to get approval for just for the journals.

I went back to my room and started to finish that email, telling Grace Farmer to come up to Nottinghamshire. I was about to key in directions to the hotel when I stopped again, got up and went straight back to the manager.

'Okay, what do you want for the lot,' I said, 'for the journals and the manorial records?'

This was not like me; I was rational, analytical, and yet I was being irrational, impulsive, but at that moment I wanted these records more than anything in the world. Again we bandied figures about like fish merchants at the quayside, until we settled on a sum the manager found acceptable. 'Okay, we have a deal,' I heard myself say. God, Toby is right about me, I thought. Fancy getting passionate about some old journals; I should save it for a good woman!

I re-keyed my email to Grace to say I was bringing the journals back to uni and would see her later, then I packed up my laptop. The manager helped me put the leather trunk in the back seat of my car and I slotted the wooden servant's box next to it. Finally, I put the seat belt around them as if they were my children. We, Ginny Farmer and I, were heading home to the university.

Chapter 5.

The Journal of Ginny Farmer

25th **March 1785.** I have so much to tell you diary. Miss Frost, the ladies maid has obtained a better position. She is to go and work for the Countess of Howden. She is an elderly lady and I think that Miss Frost will be well suited to the position. She will work out her notice for the next three months.

But that leaves a vacancy and the maistress will be advertising for someone to fill the position. Mrs Strabane has told me to apply and although I was reluctant at first I have drafted an application with her help. I am only sixteen and I am too young I am sure. Ladies maids are not usually so young but I have been granted an interview and I am to see the maistress this Wednesday week. I am so excited if not a little scared

3rd **April 1785.** I have waited all day to write this entry, desperately holding in my excitement. I have been given the position of Ladies Maid. Miss Frost was paid ten pounds a year but cause I have no experience then I will only get six pounds to start with but that is one pound more than I get now as an under housemaid. I think the fact that I will be cheaper than an experienced ladies maid has counted in my favour. If I prove satisfactory then my salary will raise by a pound every six months so that in two years time I will have a salary of ten pounds. I think that is as much as Mrs Strabane gets as the cook. Miss Frost will tutor me in my duties until she takes up her new position and I don't think that she will like that.

I will have to look after the maistresses clothes, hairdressing, jewellery, shoes, wardrobe care, do her makeup, dress her and all related shopping, as well as applying lotions and ointments to her skin, brushing her hair and tying it up in curling papers at night. I can already use a smoothing iron but I have not done any needlework since I left the Foundlings Hospital so I'll have to practice that to make sure I do any alterations right. But the best thing is the new clothes that I will get. I will no longer have to wear the black dresses with a white apron and cap. Mrs Strabane says that the maistress will require my appearance to do her credit so I will get new clothes. Around the house I will wear smart dress blouses but I will need traveling clothes if I am to accompany the maistress so I am likely to get some of her cast offs. Mrs Strabane says that is a perquisite of the job. I am still not sure what that means but it is so exciting. And even better is that a ladies maid is an upper servant. The maistress will address me by my surname and the junior servants must call me Miss Farmer, as they will when visiting in another servant's hall. Oh and I get my own room with a writing table so that I can now write my journal there and not wait for the kitchen table when every thing has been cleared away. Who would have thought it? Little Ginny Farmer a ladies maid with her own room and I'm still only sixteen.

Martin the footman is green with envy. He has looked down on me since I started and now he has to call me Miss Farmer.

26ᵗʰ June 1785. I am so thrilled. Next week I am to accompany the maistress to London so that she can buy materials for her dressmaker. I have been given one of her old overcoats to travel in and I must find time to take it up. I am still growing. I'm not seventeen until next September but Mrs Strabane still calls me Little Ginny, the others have to call me Miss Farmer and I'm getting to like that. I've measured it and I only need to take it up an inch. I was quite surprised at that. I held it in front of me in the mirror and I was shocked at what I saw. In my mind I am still a child but there was a young woman looking back at me. My bosom has developed. There is still not much of it but at least there is something for my underbodice to hold up. But I think I look quite handsome in my smart dress blouse. My hair was tidy and my face clean and I was neat of person. My complexion is very pale but is matched by my china-blue eyes and flaxen hair. I don't think I will let my maistress down.

Oh one last thing. I must now be careful to call her mistress and not maistress, Mrs Strabane says. I thought I already was doing that.

1ˢᵗ July 1785. Oh I am so tired but I can't go to bed without first writing this journal. We took the stagecoach the mistress and me from Bristol early morning, the day before yesterday. It was a fine summer day and it was enjoyable at first if noisy with the iron-clad wheels rolling over the cobbled city streets. But when we left the city and got to the uneven dirt roads I felt like I was being tossed about like a rag doll. I had trouble keeping my new bonnet on and I had to keep hold of it with one hand whilst holding the hanging leather loop with the other. The journey was long and the mistress did not speak to me all the way but I was happy just to look out of the window at the countryside passing by. This is the first time that I have ever left Bristol.

We stopped at a coaching inn so that the passengers could use the privy and then we took some victuals and I was allowed to eat with the mistress and she passed some conversation with me. We talked about the latest fashion in the The Ladys Magazine and she asked my opinion of the colours that were in fashion that would suit her. The ~~maistress~~ mistress has had two children but she is still quite young of figure with a handsome bosom and her stays give her a very good shape. She wants to be fashionable but most of her clothes make her look older than she is. I think Ill try and persuade her not to wear her hair so high as well. She is to attend a grand function at the pump room in Bath. I've heard of Bath cause its near Bristol, but my mistress says Bath is where the fashionable of London come. She must be dressed fashionably for this event. She will not get away with being unfashionable there as she would at the Merchants Ball in Bristol.

During the journey the coachmen several times instructed us to leave the coach as it had become stuck in deep ruts, but he said that at least the ridges were high and hard dry cause in winter they are filled with water and suck the wheels deep into them. I was glad when we arrived in London and I could finally get down from the coach. I ached so much. The roads had been thick with dust and the mistress had kept her kerchief to her mouth for most of it and after a while I did the same.

But London. Oh what a place. The likes I have never even imagined. I can hardly find the words to describe it. It was so large. It seemed to go on forever and so many people and street vendors everywhere. It was late, and we went straight away to the inn where we were to stay at and took supper, but then retired early. I had of course to undress my mistress and remove her make up and apply her lotions and finally tie up her hair in curling papers before I could go to bed myself .

Next morning after breakfast we went about the city. Oh my word, what a place I have never seen anything like it before. Even better than the views from the stagecoach. The well-to-do shops were in somewhere called the West End. We walked down a road called Oxford Street which had fine shops on either side. There were shops selling all sorts of wares from watchmakers to haberdashers, from a shop selling fans and silks to one selling china and glass. You could buy shoes, dolls, silver, brass, pewter, fans, gentlemens clothes ladies clothes. And hats. And each with a sign outside showing what was for sale inside. I smiled at the Adam and Eve sign outside the fruiterer. The mistress went in a shop to look at the silks but she did not buy anything there. The shop windows were all wonderfully set out, the goods neatly displayed. Back at that fruiterers there were pyramids of oranges and grapes and other fruit that I did not recognise. There was this large fruit with knobs on that the mistress called a pine apple. It didn't look anything like an apple.

We found the drapers that was the reason for our journey and I could see at once why my mistress wanted to come here. The shop was so brightly lit and the materials and cloths were all so wonderfully displayed, hung from a contraption so that they hung down in folds so that you could imagine it as a fine dress. It made you just want to go and touch to feel how rich they were. My mistress had the salesman running around showing us endless rolls of materials which were laid out on the counter for her to see and I was asked if they would suit her colouring and her figure. After a little hesitation I was as carried away as she was.

Do you think this will suit, Miss Farmer? she would say.

Oh yes Marm, says I. I said yes to every suggestion at first but then I got a little bolder and started saying, Oh yes Marm, but this other would work so well with this style of gown, showing her drawings from the fashion books on the counter. I think I have a good eye for fashion and my mistress seems to be prepared to take my advice. I think this is why she took me on as a ladies maid when I had absolutely no experience. We looked at the drawings of the latest fashion and took many patterns away with us so that the mistress can give them to her dressmaker. She spent such an awful lot of money. I think that I would have to work ten years to earn that much.

We then went onto a Soho Square and then to Greek Street to the showrooms of a man called Josiah Wedgwood. I dont think I ever imagined that anything could be so beautiful. There were cups and saucers and plates all displayed in cabinets against the walls and room after room with dinner tables all laid for a dinner party. And fine-looking vases on columns. Some poor soul will have to wash all those I thought, probably needing to work into the early hours to finish his labour.

We spent all day shopping, going from shop to shop, street to street.

We returned for a meal back at the inn but the mistress wanted to go out again saying that she didn't know when she would get back to London again. She said that the shops stayed open till ten of the clock, and when we went about all the shop fronts were lit with oil lamps. It was so wonderful.

I was tired when I got back to the inn. So was my mistress, she was so exhausted that she was falling asleep as I tied up her hair in curling papers. When I put her dress away I noticed that the bottom was black with the grime of the street, and I looked down on mine and it was the same. That is work for me when we get back home I thought but I didn't mind. I had not noticed that the streets were just as filthy as Bristol. I had to share a room with another servant but she was a kindly lady. My mind was so full of everything so that I couldn't sleep and it did not help that the other lady snored but it was such a wonderful day. When I did fall asleep I drifted off so contentedly dreaming of all the fine things I had seen. The other lady woke me early and I fear I would have overslept if she had not.

The journey home was just as tiring. I noticed that the other passengers were snoozing and I managed to doze as well much of the way even though I was hanging onto the leather loop and was being tossed from side to side.

So that was London. It was such a breathtaking place and I hope that I can go there again. I am so lucky to be a ladies maid and I am not even seventeen until September.

2nd July 1785. After writing my journal last night I was called to the mistresses room to prepare her for bed. Whilst I was brushing her hair the master came home and he was blind drunk. He told me to go but the mistress said that I had to stay until I had finished her toilet.

I want you in bed now woman, he shouted at the mistress.

I was afraid but the mistress did not seem to be. Sir, she said, fixing him with a steely stare, I take it that the dice box did not rattle kindly for you tonight. Or was it losing at Faro again? I shudder to think how much you have lost. You will bring us to penury with your gambling.

Hold your tongue, madam, he said, his voice harsh and growly like a market barker. His foul breath spread around the room.

You prefer to sit up all night drinking and gambling than spending an evening with your wife and family. She looked back at her mirror turning her back on him.

For some moments he seemed to be lost for words but then he went and sat on his bed and started to undress. I looked at the mistress hoping that she would dismiss me but she just gestured for me to get on with my duties. Out of the corner of my eye I saw him slump down on the bed and then try to take off his breeches. He succeeded eventually and threw them on the floor then stood in just his drawers.

I'm waiting, he bawled, his hand held out towards the bed.

And what of our bargain sir, said my mistress, giving him the full force of her stare. She showed no fear of him at all.

Bargain. What bargain, madam?

That you are to stay at your club when you are soused. That is our bargain is it not.

Huh, he grumbled. Well not tonight it isn't. You will do your duty, madam.

And if I refuse, sir, said my mistress.

What! he exclaimed and then he lurched across the bedroom towards her.

I thought he was going to hit her but she stood and faced him down without flinching. At first he didn't seem to know what to do. I think he expected her to wince but when she did not he just seemed to grunt a purghhh sound, spluttering his foul smelling spit in her face as he did so. He then raised his arm as if he would strike her with the back of his hand but before he could the mistress took the hard bristled brush she was holding and scraped it harshly across his face. He squealed like a frightened piglet pulling his hands to his face and turning away swaying as he did so in his drunken state. But then he turned back and withdrew his hands. One side of his face was crimson with numerous scratches beginning to weep with blood. His eyes were threatening and I was more frightened than ever. I could see that his anger was mounting but there now seemed to be cold intent in those eyes as well.

He walked over to me. Well, if I can't hump you madam, then I will hump your maid. He grabbed me by the arm and pulled me towards him and that foul smelling breath stung me like a hornet. His other hand came up to my bosom and squeezed me like a vice, hurting me, and I tried to push him away whilst at the same time turning my head away from his stinking black-toothed leer.

Let her go said my mistress, and she raised the brush again. He released me to protect himself and grabbed her arm and held it rigid above both their heads. She looked round at me and gestured with her head. Go girl she said, and I fled as quickly as I could. I rushed up to my room and wedged my chair against the doorknob. I sobbed myself to sleep at the thought of what the master would do to my mistress.

This morning the master was all repentant. I overheard him saying he was so sorry over and over again to the mistress. It was the toothache that made him drink so much he said. My mistress had no time for his penance saying that if he were a man then he would let the barber use his pliers on his blackened teeth but that he was as afeared as a whimpering pup at the thought of the pain so that she had then to put up with the stinking of his mouth. He knew she was right cause he then stormed off to his office without taking breakfast.

But I was so afraid last night.

The Journal of Corbyn Carlisle

23rd April 1785. I have some good news. I have been accepted as a junior in Chambers. I am no longer to be a pupil. All that hard work has paid off and I am the youngest to be accepted for such a position in some time. I am getting a reputation as a good advocate and I think I can now look forward to a successful career in the law, and my prospects are now much improved. I will start to earn some modest fees although I'll have to start with minor cases, poor law appeals, vagrancy cases and cases of debt, but perhaps by next year I may be able to move out of these lodgings and take a house, and then, maybe, even look for a wife.

5th June 1786. I have received a very disturbing letter from that terrible woman Alice Clough, my father's old mistress. I am to stay away as there is smallpox at Elloughton Park. It seems there is an epidemic in Nottingham, but that is not uncommon in an industrial town as the people live in such filthy and squalid conditions, but the cook is from there and on her monthly Sunday off she went back to visit her mother. The stupid woman seems to have brought the disease back with her to the house.

Carlton sent for the local doctor, a young man acquainted with modern methods and he recommended something called variolation. He treated the whole house by scratching the skin with a substance taken from a pustule of one of his more mildly affected patients.

Most in the house have in fact recovered quickly, as has Alice Clough, except that is for Carlton and my two sisters, Emily and Jane. The ladies it seemed already had the symptoms and in Carlton's case the variolation seems to have induced a severe course. All three are abed with the fever.

12th June 1785. Another letter from Elloughton Park and that wretched woman, Alice Clough; the fever has broken on Emily and Jane and they are both taking their salts and drinking their broth for supper daily now. She says that their faces have been ravaged though, and even if Carlton will now give them dowries it is unlikely that any prospective husband will take them. They are inconsolable it seems. Carlton still has the fever and the doctor is worried as to the course it is taking.

17th June 1785. Carlton is dead; the smallpox took him 2 days ago. I am stunned as I write this, because even though I knew he was ill, I never really thought he would die because he is such a robust man, so the full consequences had not really registered in my mind. Perhaps it is because I have always been treated as such an outsider and a very junior one at that. I have been made to feel that I was of little consequence in the family. But it has suddenly taken me as to what this means. I am now the ninth baronetcy, the new Lord Carlisle of Elloughton. I have a lot of decisions to make.

Chapter 6.

The Vice Chancellor, having invited me to his office, gestured for me to sit in the chair facing his desk. He then got up from his own chair, went to his cabinet and poured two glasses of sherry – his particular favourite was Fino; too dry for my taste. He didn't ask me if I wanted one, but simply handed me a glass and I knew then that despite the refined nature of the encounter I was in for a bollocking.

'It's the dryness and the paleness I like,' he commented as he sat down. 'Fino means refined in Spanish you know,' he added. I nodded as if it was news to me, but he had told me that each time I had been called to his office.

He stared at his glass, raising it to eye level. 'You have to drink it comparatively young you know, and as soon as possible after the bottle is opened, as exposure to air can cause it to lose its flavour within hours.'

Again I nodded, one eyebrow raised attentively as he gave me the usual spiel. *That's probably why you're always pissed*, I thought to myself.

'How long have I known you, Jim?' he said, sipping his Fino.

'Oh, I don't know,' I said, 'it must be some years now, Vice Chancellor.' I wished he'd get on with the bollocking. The man was grim-faced, his features pale and drawn except for a ruddiness around his nose – the telltale sign of his liking for sherry. He was renowned in the university for his lack of any sense of humour and I knew that I couldn't lighten the mood with a quip. I'd tried that before; it would just sail over his head.

'I've read your request for funding,' he said, steepling his fingers before his face and drawing in his breath to deliver a rebuke.

'Source documentation is the Bible for us historians,' I interrupted.

'Quite so,' he said and then looked down considering the papers on his desk. I saw that it was my request for approval of the purchase. 'You are most enthusiastic in your submission, I can see that,' he said eventually.

I had deliberately overstated the importance of the material and I wondered if he had seen through me. 'This is the best I have come across in quite some time,' I said, still gilding the lily.

'Quite so,' he said again through the steeple of his fingers, 'but this is such a lot of money and I am minded of the fact that in these times of austerity we all have to pull in our belts, so to speak. I would not have approved this but for…' He seemed to drift away for a moment then he sat up straight and said with apparent alarm, 'God damn it, Jim, have you committed the university to this purchase? You should know better, a senior lecturer like you.'

I was taken aback; not so much by his words as that he seemed to have shown some sign that there was a human being inside that caricature of a distant, detached academic. 'I know, Vice Chancellor,' I said, 'but sometimes you just have to think on your feet. We can't just let Oxbridge outbid us all the time. I had a chance to get these documents and I believe them to be a valuable acquisition for the university, so I went for it.' I was lying: I hadn't actually committed the university; I had made it plain to the hotel manager that I needed approval before making the purchase, but I was not going to tell the Vice Chancellor that. I didn't want to give him the opportunity to deny my request. I took a drink of the Fino and pursed my lips, looking down at it and then smiling at him to feign my appreciation of his fine choice.

He forced a nod and a fleeting smile in my direction, but the sour look returned quickly to the old bugger's face. 'Not happy, Jim, not happy at all.' He set his mouth hard and I feared the worst, but to my surprise he grunted his agreement. 'Very well, I suppose you have left me with no alternative but to approve this purchase, have you? But mark my words, Jim, you must never put the university in this position again; is that clear?'

'Absolutely, Vice Chancellor.' I held back a smile that was doing its damndest to escape. A bollocking from the Vice Chancellor was like being savaged by a hamster on valium.

I have been so busy these last few weeks: the third semester is examination time and with that comes hours of marking. I am also the mentor for my students and need to give them guidance on their dissertations, which means I have little time for my own research. If it were not for mentoring Grace Farmer's own dissertation I would not have any time to look at the journals at all.

It seems that Ginny is making her way in the world at a most unusual pace. The perceived wisdom is that servants spent years waiting for a position to become available and advancement was judged over a lifetime, but this very likeable young lady is clearly not doing that.

Grace has badgered me for funds to visit the Foundlings' Hospital in Bristol and I have agreed, but I was so intrigued myself that I decided I would go with her and to hell with the budget.

I picked Grace up at 9 a.m. in front of the college. There was a chill in the air despite it being late spring, a swirling wind carried bursts of rainfall on each gust. I pulled up and she opened the door and dived in out of the rain, pulling her backpack off her shoulder as she did so. She shook her hair and splashed me.

'Hey, steady,' I said, and she looked round and smiled at me, but there was no sheepishness in her expression. I think she rather enjoyed the fact that she had wet her professor. She looked me squarely in the eye and held that look and it was I who broke off the eye contact first. Somewhat flustered, I looked down at my watch for no reason. I should have been the dominant person in this research venture, but Grace was unusually self-confident. She leant forward as she took off her cagoule, her arms behind her pulling it backwards. Underneath, she wore a tight-fitting t-shirt with some words written on it. I tried to read them, but then noticed that she had stopped halfway through the manoeuvre and was looking sternly at me as though I was staring at her breasts, which I then realised I was, albeit unintentionally. I felt myself colour up. 'I was just trying to read the words,' I mumbled, embarrassment taking me hard.

For a heartbeat that stern expression did not change, but then a roguish smile sparked behind her face. That is to say, she was one of those people who smiled through their eyes. There was very little in the way of facial movement, but I knew that she was smiling at me; her piercing china-blue eyes proclaimed it.

'I know,' she said, 'I was just teasing you.' With that she turned to show me the words written on her t-shirt. My gaze dashed to them and I read, "WEAPONS OF MASS DESTRUCTION." I smiled at the wit, but at the same time I took my opportunity and I did look at her breasts. They were not large, but prominent, sitting proud on her lean torso. She was a long, slender girl, athletic in appearance, her fresh beauty was unenhanced by make-up. It occurred to me that I had never seen her wearing any. Her hair was shoulder-length, substantial in natural loose curls. She had a habit of running her hand through it when she was reading, crouching right over the book or document, her elbow rooted to the table and that hand in her curls. Then she would just shake her head to restore them; just one shake and they fell back into place. I had noticed that before. I lifted my gaze and saw she was looking at me, one eyebrow raised. Not knowing quite what to say, I gestured that she should belt up, checked the rear-view mirror and started the car.

As she put on her seat belt I slid the car into gear and drove off. My attention was taken by the road as we drove out of the city, but then I started to muse. This morning had got off to a very strange start. Grace had presented a very different version of herself. Despite the fact that she was fairly close to my own age, our relationship so far had been one of teacher and pupil. This morning… well, this morning she had been, well… skittish I suppose, for want of a better word. Alarm bells were ringing in my head and I wondered what my psychology colleagues would make of this. But then, it was probably no more than being out of the college environment; the rules were different.

While we were stopped at traffic lights, out of the corner of my eye I saw her raise one leg; I looked round, down. She was wearing a pair of well-worn and faded jeans, a slit above each knee. The denim clung tightly to her legs, revealing the contours of her calves, her thighs. I chided myself for once again staring, and wondered if she had seen me. I darted a look to her face, but she was engrossed in rolling a cigarette. She took a Rizla paper, bent over her tobacco pouch, filled the paper loosely with tobacco then licked along the edge. It was somehow sensuous. She leant back in her seat and put the ultra slim cigarette to her lip. Tobacco sprouted loosely from the end and it flamed as she lit it. She drew in the smoke, closing her eyes as she did so, as if it were some magical elixir. I found myself ogling up and down her body, I don't know why, perhaps it was simply cause and effect: her sensuousness and my changed perception of her. Then she opened her eyes and saw my look and perhaps assumed my expression was one of disapproval.

She sat up straight and looked at the cigarette. 'Sorry I should have asked.'

'No, it's OK,' I said. I looked back at the road, realised the lights had changed and that an irate driver was honking at me. 'Impatient bugger,' I muttered to hide my embarrassment.

Grace took another drag and then gestured to me with her smoking fingers, 'Would you like one? I'll roll one for you.'

Oh, but I would have liked one. I had not smoked for over three years and the urgency of the cravings were long gone, but they had just returned with interest. 'No thanks,' I forced myself to say.

For much of the remaining journey we travelled in silence, Grace napping as we drove. But later, she stirred and we started to chat a little about her dissertation, but then mostly about other more disparate, inconsequential things. I realised that I knew very little about her and I tried to remedy that, but my enquiries were met by evasion, so I let it go.

At the Foundlings' Hospital we were met by a Mrs. Saunders, the Curator of the hospital museum. I had made prior arrangements and we were expected. She was an elderly lady, past retirement age I surmised, large of bosom, matronly in appearance with half-moon glasses perched precariously on the end of a button nose. She met us with gushing enthusiasm, approaching me first and shaking my hand vigorously. 'So good to see you, Professor Postlethwaite,' her large jowls quivering as she spoke.

I gestured to my side, 'And this is Grace Farmer; she is researching into social mobility in Georgian England.' I deliberately did not say that Grace was still an undergraduate. I wanted her to be accepted as my equal.

Mrs. Saunders shook Grace's hand, but her expression changed to one of puzzlement. 'Any relation to our subject?'

'No, it's just a coincidence,' Grace replied.

I indicated that Grace should take the lead and she seemed more than happy to do so.

'Have you been able to find Virginia Farmer in your records?' she said, turning back to Mrs. Saunders.

'Oh yes, indeed. The date given by Professor Postlethwaite enabled me to go straight to the right ledgers. She was a red-ball girl and was very lucky to be taken in.'

I knew what this meant, but I saw Grace's eyebrows knit in confusion. 'A red-ball girl? What does that mean?'

'There were just too many of them you see,' replied Mrs. Saunders. 'After the hospital opened they were overwhelmed by the response, so they had to introduce criteria for acceptance. Firstly the child had to be illegitimate, under twelve months old and be the mother's first, and the mother also had to be of "good character", but even that was not enough, so they introduced a ballot system to decide which children they could take in. The mothers would line up with their babies and be told to draw a coloured ball from a bag. If they drew out a black ball they were unlucky, tragically so; they were sent away. If they drew out a white ball the child was accepted subject to medical inspection. If they drew out a red ball they were held in reserve in case one of the white ball babies failed the medical. So Virginia Farmer was very lucky to get admission.'

'Can we see the ledger entry?' asked Grace.

'Oh yes, come, I'll show you. We need to go to the reading room.'

We were led to a wood-panelled room that smelt heavily of polish and leather. There was a large table, but also a reading stand with a large ledger already in place, a piece of paper protruding from the top to mark the place. The Curator heaved at the ledger, which opened with a thud, then she put on a pair of white gloves before running her finger down the page. She stopped at an entry about halfway down, 'This is your girl, I think,' she said.

Grace leaned in, following the white-gloved finger. I could see that she did not understand, 'But this entry is for a Martha Cundy?'

'That's right.' Mrs. Saunders ran her finger across the entry to a column headed "Christening". 'They were all baptised on admission and she was given the name "Virginia Farmer".'

'Oh, I see,' said Grace, reading the rest of the entry. 'So the mother was an Agatha Cundy, domestic servant, and Virginia was only one month old when she was left here.'

'Yes, that's right; it was very common at that time. The "good character" test excluded the street prostitutes and the like. Domestic servants could not support their children in service; they were not usually even allowed to marry.'

'That's ironic isn't it?' said Grace.

'How do you mean?' said Mrs. Saunders.

'Well, it's an early form of recycling isn't it? They recycled the children back into service when they were old enough. A sort of waste-not-want-not.'

'Mmmm,' said Mrs. Saunders, looking down her nose at Grace, 'I don't think they would have seen it that way at the time. Recycling is such a modern concept, but I see what you mean.'

I smiled to myself. This is what I liked about Grace; she had her own perspective on things.

'What's this column mean?' asked Grace, pointing, but being careful not to touch the paper, '"Token" what's this all about?'

'The mothers were asked to put some identification on the child, such as a button, a ribbon or perhaps a coin, in the hope that they could return at a later date.'

'Oh I see,' Grace frowned in concentration, 'they would have no ID in those days, would they. So the trustees would know that they had the right person if somebody came back to claim them. Did that happen very much?'

'Sadly no, and we can see from the last entries that Virginia was apprenticed to the household of a Josiah Holdstock as a domestic servant when she was fourteen.'

'So Virginia was very typical of the foundlings of the time?'

' 'Fraid so,' said Mrs. Saunders, 'the only unusual thing is the "token". They were usually quite insignificant things, but the ledger identifies it as a mother-of-pearl, heart-shaped pendant, with the initials A and N, and a scratched third initial M. That suggests a love token from N, whoever he was, to A, clearly Agatha.'

'But N did not want to marry her, it seems?' said Grace.

'Or could not,' I interrupted, 'we enter the realm of speculation from this point. We could speculate that N was perhaps the master of the house or the son of the house. This is a love token, which would suggest that Agatha was not taken advantage of and so it was a love affair. Or N might be another servant and children would just not be allowed. The important thing to remember here is that it is *speculation,* and we need to be careful.'

'Quite,' said Mrs. Saunders.

'Would Ginny have known the name of her real mother, her real name?'

'As a child here, no; but she could have come back later to find out, had she a mind to, although the trustees' minutes of their meetings suggest that it was discouraged.'

'What about the regime here? Was it harsh?'

'By modern standards very much so; it was regimented, but they had a basic education, were well-clothed in the uniform; I wouldn't say they were well fed, but they did not starve. They were schooled in Christian ethics.'

Grace's eyes widened, 'But hardly a loving environment.'

'No, it wasn't.' Mrs. Saunders drew herself up as though steeling herself to defend the hospital, 'but before you condemn it too quickly, remember the alternative. Before the Foundlings' Hospital was opened such babies were often just left on the rubbish tips to die – as indeed unwanted babies still are in some cultures.'

I saw Grace physically shudder at that thought and she was momentarily silenced. Underneath that self-reliant exterior, I thought, perhaps there's a vulnerable pussycat. But then she collected herself, 'And what about when they left?'

'They were placed in an apprenticeship, but yes they were alone in the world, they had to fend for themselves. But is that so different from orphans of today?'

I could see the waters building behind the dam in Grace's mind, the pressure mounting. I decided that this museum was not the place for her to vent her views on the subject and harangue this poor woman in the process. 'Well,' I interjected hurriedly, 'there's plenty of scope for debate isn't there, Grace? You can cover all that in your dissertation.' I looked at her sternly until I saw that she understood, then I turned back to the curator. 'Thank you, Mrs. Saunders, you have been most helpful.'

During the ride home, Grace took her laptop from her backpack, keen to get it all down while it was fresh in her mind. Her fingers dashed nimbly across the keyboard as I drove, the words just flowing out of her. She'll have my job if I'm not careful, I thought to myself.

Chapter 7.

The Journal of Ginny Farmer

18th Sept 1785. Oh I am so very unhappy I really don't know what to do. Yesterday had started so well. It was my seventeenth birthday and I was feeling so good about myself. I thought I looked so grown up in my smart dress blouse and I was so pleased that I was making my way in the world. My mistress had given me a rare afternoon off. She had gone to visit her sister and said that she did not need me. I have no family to visit of course so I did some sewing alterations that needed to be done and that took me a couple of hours. I then sat down and wrote a long letter to my friend Beth Morris. We had been best friends in the Foundlings Hospital and she too had been put into service at the age of fourteen, but that had been five months before me. The family she went to work for moved to London so Beth and I write to each other every once in a while, but I had not heard from her for some time, but then she was never good at her letters. I felt so proud telling her about my advancements if not a bit guilty cause I think she must still be a kitchen maid. I begin to realise how lucky I have been. Like everyone else in my position I had expected to be a kitchen maid for several years before looking to advance.

The nights are beginning to close in and I needed to use one of the wax candle ends that I get from the mistress. It must have been a half past eight of the clock when it happened. I was just finishing the letter and I was reading it back to myself in that small pool of light cast by the burning candle when I heard a crash outside on the landing. I looked round just for a heartbeat then my door started to thump. Miss Farmer Miss Farmer, are you in there? I knew it was the master and I froze in fear. He started banging on my door and still yelling my name, he just kept on banging. Afraid he would come bursting through it I took up the candle and walked to the door. I opened it slightly and peeped out through the crack.

Yes master I said, trying not to provoke him.

Where is your mistress? he yelled. I was hit by a mixed stench of putrid breath and brandy. He cannot be drunk already I thought but then I saw him sway and knew that he was.

She has gone to visit her sister, I said. She will not be back till later.

He grunted and turned away back towards his own room and I closed my door and leant my back against it. I remember putting my hand to my bosom in relief but I should have had my wits about me and wedged my chair under the handle. I walked across my room to replace the candle on my dressing table when I heard my door open behind me. There was no knock and I knew it must be the master. I turned around and he were there, leant against the doorframe and I saw with dread the lustful expression on his face. He had removed his jacket and he stood there in just his shirt and his breeches his enormous belly hanging over his belt. His jowls hung down below his jaw line and he looked like a slavering hound expecting his dinner.

You are such a pretty little thing Virginia, he said.

Why is he calling me Virginia I thought to myself. I knew at that point I was in danger.

It is late master, I said. Would you like me to get cook to prepare some supper for you. I thought that if I could get to Mrs Strabane then she would protect me.

No it is not food I want Virginia, he said. He came into my room, walked up to me and stroked my cheek. You should be kind to me Virginia. It is in your own interests to be kind to the master. I can be very generous if you are kind to me. Do you understand me Virginia?

I understood all right but I was too scared to say anything. I ducked down under his hand and tried to move away from him so there was about two feet distance between us trying to make it clear that I was not interested in his offer but he just started to follow. Each time I stepped backwards he followed until I felt my bed behind me and I knew I could not go back any further, then he cut me off from going sideways. I was about to try and duck away again but he grabbed my wrists so that I was pinned. I was trapped, my bed at the back of me and him towering above me.

Look at me Virginia, he said. I slowly stared up at him as he had commanded and saw that his great fat lips were wet and pursed showing his blackened teeth and they were coming down towards my face to kiss me. I turned my head away to avoid him but he grabbed me by the chin forcing my face into his. Those great wet sour lips seemed to devour my face and I tried to pull away but he was too strong. When he finished there was a satisfied look on his face. Now that was not so bad was it Virginia he said.

I started to scream as loud as I could. I thought he would put his hand over my mouth but he did not, so I just carried on screaming. Scream – scream – scream. I heard footsteps on the landing outside. There was a commotion and then voices, loud at first but then they hushed as if they did not know what to do. A voice said go and fetch Mr Brettingham. The master just seemed to hold me tight for what seemed like a time without end and I could feel my heart pounding in my chest. Then there was a little knock at the door, and Mr Brettinghams voice said, are you all right in there Miss Farmer.

Before I could speak the masters voice beamed out. That will be all Brettingham and take the others with you. There was a pause and then the sound of footsteps shuffling away. He looked down at me with a satisfied grin on his face. His eyes closed to a narrow slit and I knew then what was going to happen to me.

The master still held both my wrists but now he pushed me back onto the bed laid on top of me so I couldn't move. His stinking breath seemed to be everywhere. He kissed me again but I pulled my face away as much as from fear as the stink. I shouted out NO master, NO master, but nobody came. I now knew they wouldn't. He just let me scream as if it pleased him for me to do so. Then he started to fumble with my skirt. He pulled it up and then pushed my legs apart with his knees. I stopped struggling. He hurt me. I must have cried through it all cause I remember the salty taste of the tears that were running down my face.

Today I told my mistress I was ill. She was put out but she has left me in my room all day. Mrs Strabane came to me this afternoon. I cried on her bosom uncontrollably for a good half hour and she caressed my hair as if I were some little frightened child.

Why did no one come, I asked her through my sobs. She sighed deeply and there was a croak in her voice when she spoke. Cause every one in the house is afraid for their jobs little Ginny – to be dismissed without a reference will mean that they will not get another position. There were tears running down her face as well. I saw her top teeth bite her trembling lower lip. I too started to cry again cause I knew what that also meant for me. What do I do now Mrs Strabane I said.

You do nothing little Ginny, she said, there is nothing that you can do. If you leave you certainly will not get another job as a ladies maid. If you are lucky you might start again somewhere else. Get another job as a cinder maid under another name perhaps in another town. I know how hard you have worked to gain advancement Ginny, but this is our lot in life and we have to bear it.

Should I tell the mistress I said. She will believe me wont she.

No don't do that. She may believe you but that won't save you. If it's you or the master it will be you who has to go.

But what if he tries to do it again I said.

You will be safe around the mistress said Mrs Strabane. When she is not around keep to your room and put your chair up against it each night. And in the mean time we'll just have to spit in his soup every night.

24th December 1785. Its Christmas Eve and all the servants are thrilled. There is excitement everywhere. There will be a special meal in the servants hall after the master and mistress have dined. There will be beer to drink and we will play party games. But I am not looking forward to it. My mind is in such confusion. My flux has stopped and my breasts are sore. I am pregnant I know I am. It does not show yet and I have kept this terrible secret for three months now. Nobody knows, not even Mrs Strabane but it will start to show soon and then it will all come out.

25th December 1785. I told Mrs Strabane last night. I think the bottles of beer gave me courage. She put her arm around me and we both cried. The others looked on at us I know, wondering what was going on but Mrs Strabane took me by the hand and we went to my room to talk. We talked for hours and Mrs Strabane said that she had seen this situation many times before. Sometimes it was silly girls who sought favours from the master. Others were like me. Some had little to give up as junior maids and usually left happy with a pay off, not understanding that when the money was gone they would be penniless with no support. Sometimes the master would have some compassion for the bastard child and find a suitable husband for the girl, again with some inducement for the man to take her.

She told me there were ways of getting rid of the baby, there were women who did this sort of thing. It is very dangerous and I might die, but I was raised a good Christian and I don't think I could possibly do *this.*

She said that although my situation was not uncommon what was different was that I was a ladies maid. Not only was I working directly to the mistress but I had a good position. There was so much for me to lose. She said that I had to tell I was pregnant and that made my skin run cold at the thought of it. The question was should I tell the master or the mistress. She said that if I tell the master then he may be extra generous just so that the truth is kept from his wife but that would mean that I would have to give up my position. If I applied for another position I would have little experience to offer and what would I do with the child. I couldn't continue with a child to look after.

If I tell the mistress she would be less generous but maybe just maybe I would be able to keep my position. Whichever course I take there seems to be no place for the baby. I have decided I will tell the mistress and Mrs Strabane says the she will go with me. We will go together after the new year.

3rd **January 1786**. I went to see the mistress with Mrs Strabane today. The very least I thought would happen was that the mistress would believe me, especially after what the master tried to do to me after our trip to London. But after I told her that I was pregnant her whole attitude seemed to change in an instance towards me. She asked, and pray tell who is the father. I just looked down at the floor unable to find the words. They seemed so hard to actually say.

Mrs Strabane came to my aid. If you please Marm it was the master, she said.

Hold your tongue Mrs Strabane. That cannot possibly be true. Now Miss Farmer. Pray tell me who the father is. I hesitated again but she persisted. Who is the father Miss Farmer she repeated.

I shuddered at her raised voiced. Tis true Marm. It was the master the night you went to visit your sister. He forced me.

But she would have none of it. I was condemned. If it was true then I must have tempted her husband, who was a fine upstanding man of the community. It was my fault. I could not possibly stay on as her ladies maid. I was to be put out. The clothes I had been given were to be taken back. I would have only the clothes I stood up in and my wages to date.

5th **January 1786**. Mrs Strabane has been wonderful. She went back to see the mistress yesterday. It was brave of her. She was risking her own job. She pointed out that nobody else knew anything about my pregnancy. Just me, herself and the mistress. Mrs Strabane told me that she had then deliberately not said anything more just kept quiet. I let the seed take root she said. After a few moments the mistress said, how do we keep it that way. Mrs Strabane then said that she was sure I would be grateful for any help that the mistress could give me.

The Minister was sent for and I was also summoned. He said that he could find a place for me to have the baby and after it was born then it could go to the Foundlings Hospital.

Mrs Strabane then asked the mistress, will Miss Farmers position be held for her.

Hold your tongue Mrs Strabane she said gruffly. Don't be impertinent. But the Minister looked at the mistress. His eyebrows were raised as if asking the same question. It is out of the question the mistress said waving her hand at me as if I had the scurvy. Mrs Strabane told me later that it was only to be expected. If I stayed then it would remind her daily of her husbands lechery.

That seemed to give me courage. I will not have my baby taken to the Foundlings Hospital I said.

Ungrateful girl said the mistress snapping at me. There was hatred in her eyes as she spoke. I had always thought her beautiful but now her face seemed ugly.

I was brought up in the Foundlings Hospital and no child of mine will have the same fate I said. Suddenly the words came easy to me. All those hours reading and writing that Mrs Strabane had me do were coming to my aid. I knew what to say.

The child will be fed and brought up a good Christian said the Minister. It will be for the best.

Do not tell me about the Foundlings Hospital sir, I heard myself say as if it were some other person speaking — a woman of letters, not me. I am from the Foundlings Hospital sir and I know. It is an alternative to starvation and little more. I saw the mistress look aghast at my nerve. She set her mouth hard against me and there was a flash of anger in her eyes.

Ginny darling said Mrs Strabane quietly in her Irish brogue. You cannot bring up a child on your own. You will both starve.

I know that Mrs Strabane I said but even so I will not have the Foundlings Hospital take my baby.

Well the ungrateful girl will have to make her bed and lie in it said the mistress. And don't say that I did not try and do my best for her. She raised her head, looked down her nose at me and turned away scornfully.

I went to speak, to say that I was innocent of any wrong doing that I was the victim of her husbands lechery but I saw Mrs Strabanes eyes flash at me. They were imploring me to keep quiet but I was not going to heed her. But then the Minister spoke before I could say the words that were forming in my mind.

I may have a solution here. I know a childless couple. Regular churchgoers. I believe that they may be willing to take the child.

Everything was quiet for a few moments. I felt tears well up inside me and then they burst and ran down my cheeks, but I forced myself to hold back the sobs.

So we have an understanding then said Mrs Strabane. Ginny and me will keep this secret. She looked at the mistress. Shall we say that she will keep the clothes she has been provided with.

I saw the anger flash again in the mistresses eyes but then the Minister looked at her. It will be the Christian thing to do Mrs Holdstock he said. She sighed deeply then nodded but her eyes told a different story. She resented me with all her being I could see that.

I am the wronged person here am I not. I don't know why she now hates me so.

The Journal of Corbyn Carlisle

23rd September 1786. My rank in life has suddenly been elevated. It is three months now since Carlton died, but I have kept away from Elloughton Park until the threat of smallpox has finally passed. Carlton, it seems, was the last to contract it and there have been no new cases since his death. So this week I have ventured to make my first visit as the master of the house. I noticed immediately that the attitude towards me has changed. Even the servants are more reverent. I had not really noticed their disregard for me before, I suppose that I had grown up with it and after Father died they must have continued to take their lead from the condescending way in which Carlton and my halfsisters treated me. But now that I am the master, my previous status comes into sharp focus to me, like a ship's captain suddenly sighting a ship on the horizon that has been shadowing the vessel· The enemy was there all along but had not been visible·

My first duty was to see my sisters· I had determined that they would each have a dowry, even if I had to borrow the money temporarily, for such a dowry would certainly need to be inflated after the ravages of smallpox· But when I saw them I was shocked· They had been spared the blindness but little else of the pox, their faces, especially poor Jane's, have indeed been ravaged· The puss-filled blisters must have covered her whole face· Both girls have been left with large raised scars; in Jane's case nothing of her face, it seems, has been spared· I fear that no man can love either of my sisters now; they are scarred for life and will never marry· They will be my responsibility for as long as they live·

I had a meeting with the estate manager yesterday· I went through the estate accounts with him, but it is clear that they are not up to date· I suspect that Carlton had never exercised proper control over him and he has been allowed to do as he pleased· The rents from many of the tenant farmers are in arrear· The tenants are supposed to bring their rent to the house on each quarter date, but many have not being collected on time and the farm sales look meagre· I have to conclude that either he is not very good at farm management or that, more likely, takings are being deflected into his own pocket, or he is in cahoots with the tenants· I have made it clear to him that his position here is dependent on turning around the profitability of the estate farm and I sent him away to bring the accounts up to date·

That news must have gone round the servants' hall like wild fire and everybody, it seems, is now running about trying to impress me at every turn· This is all so surprising; I had no expectation that there would be a change in attitude towards me of this magnitude· I think I am beginning to like it though·

I have also been through the household accounts, kept by that dreadful Alice Clough woman· They are worse than the estate accounts· She seems barely literate and as for figures, she is totally innumerate; incapable of adding even the simplest of columns correctly· She tries to ingratiate herself at every turn, but she will have to go· Once again my lack of a wife is troublesome to me· A wife would manage this household, control and train the servants, keep the household accounts, control the family medicines, and entertain my guests. But I need a woman who was brought up to such skills, not someone who has grace and favour merely because she was the master's mistress.

I also have a letter from the lawyers administering the trust set up by Father to pay the annuities to my mother and Mrs. Clough, along with the Military Commission bought for Cavendish. It is as I suspected: Carlton as the trustee has borrowed from the fund and the estate will have to make good that deficit.

30th September 1786. I have today received a letter by return from Mother. I wrote to her last week asking her to act as the mistress of the Hall until I take a wife. She has declined. I am disappointed but not surprised. She says in her letter that Elloughton Park holds too many unhappy memories for her and that she has found contentment living frugally off her annuity. I thought to write back to her, pointing out that the dreadful Mrs. Clough will be leaving, but I have decided to honour her decision.

So this afternoon I spoke with my halfsisters. I have confirmed to them that they can continue to live at the house under my grace and favour. They showed no surprise at my offer as if the matter was never in doubt. I suppose that they are right and that I have that obligation to them. I told them, however, that I expected that they would act as joint ladies of the house and run it in my absence. I discerned a look of derision through the mountain of scabs on Emily's scarred face as if I were imposing the most outrageous obligations on them, but they reluctantly agreed. They were even more disparaging when I explained to them that I would want to inspect the accounts regularly and that any withdrawal of funds from the bank account could only be done through me. But it will do them good to run this house for a while; it will probably be their home for as long as they live. They cannot go on just reading trashy novels during the day and drinking too much cognac over dinner.

5th October 1786. I travelled back to London yesterday. It was so pleasant now to have the funds to take the mail coach. I was able to sit inside with three other gentlemen passengers in far greater comfort than I thought possible, certainly much better than the last time I travelled. That time, in an ordinary coach, I felt I was taking my life in my hands just climbing to the top. I was then required to suffer the whole journey with only a short handle fastened to the side to hold on to and only a one-legged sailor for company, his wooden stump unable to give him any purchase to balance himself. How he managed to stay on I just don't know, but each time he felt himself in danger he grabbed my shoulder and nearly took me with him, even ripped a tear in my greatcoat, damn the man.

Aside from the greatly increased comfort, the speed of the mail coach was most thrilling. I did some quick calculation in my head, dividing the distance between Nottingham and London by the time of the journey and if I have ciphered it correctly then we had travelled at eleven miles per hour. Incredible – Nottingham to London in a single day!

We stopped at an inn for lunch, the coachman shouting out, 'Forty minutes here, gentlemen.' We all got out, were given a glass of purl and were eager to warm our rears against the fire. The table was covered in clean white linen and it groaned under the fare on offer: pigeon pie, steak and kidney pie, ham, cold boiled beef, beets and potatoes, and piping hot tea and coffee. It was indeed a meal for gentlemen. It was such a pity that we had to bolt it down as the mail coach had its strict time schedule to follow.

I was most eager to get back to London, for now I am a barrister in Chambers I have been invited to join a political and debating club, The House of Lords Club. It meets at the Three Herrings in Bell Yard and a meeting is scheduled for tomorrow. Its members are barristers, attorneys and other men of the law. It's a great opportunity to make myself known within my profession. My new status as Baron Elloughton has also elevated me within my profession too and I am anxious to make use of it. But herein is my dilemma. I take great pleasure in my ability as an advocate and the law is my chosen profession, but I am now not in need of the fees that will come my way. I will have to decide whether to abandon the law.

Chapter 8.

The Journal of Ginny Farmer

30th June 1786. My baby was born yesterday. Here in this room that I have lived in for several months now. Alone day after day. I have one room at the top of a lodging house run by a Mrs Coleman a caustic woman smelling of gin that I only see when she wants my rent. The room has only a bed and a stand with a washbasin which I remove when I want to use the stand as a writing desk. The bed is uncomfortable as it is far from well sprung. Each night I need to pull tight what is left of the ropes that support the mattress but by morning they are loose again. It does not help the terrible backache I have. The Minister arranged for the room but I have to pay the rent from my back wages. He has shown me Christian charity I suppose but he clearly sees me as a sinner and I resent that. Mrs Strabane has been my sole visitor. She only gets one afternoon off a month but her visits are most welcome for all that. The loneliness has been so hard to bear. The Foundlings Hospital may have been harsh but there were always people about and of course there were always people below stairs in the masters house.

I asked the Minister if he had any books that I could read and at first he seemed to find that very odd. I don't think he thought that people of my station had much call for reading. But perhaps he saw it as a means of my salvation and he has brought me endless reading material of how people can be redeemed through the love of Jesus. He was particularly keen on Mr John Bunyans Pilgrims Progress, but when I read how the main character Christian was weighed down by a great burden and that was the knowledge of his own sin, I do not see how it applies to me. I do not think I have sinned in having this baby.

Yesterday when the pains started and I knew my time was near, I called Mrs Coleman and for the first time she was pleasant to me and she fetched the midwife, a Mrs Puddy who the Minister had also arranged. She was a very large lady with an enormous bosom and with rolls of fat under her chin and the fat on her upper arms swayed from side to side like bed sheets drying on the line. She looked at me and just said there's nothing on you girl. I think she feared that I would not be strong enough to bear the child but I just told her that I was stronger than I looked. I was being brave but inside I was afeared. Mrs Puddy turned out to be an angel and her kindness helped me through the birth. She was a country lady and I didn't always understand what she was saying but her voice was calming and she sat me on the birthing stool she had brought and showed me what I had to do when the baby was coming. She rubbed my back and held onto my hands then she told me to push and I pushed and pushed. I tried not to scream, but the pain was so bad. It seemed to go on forever and I felt like I was being rent in two, but the strangest thing is that as soon as my baby was born I could hardly remember how bad it had been.

Mrs Puddy took the babe straight away so I didn't see it, but I heard it cry which broke my heart and I cried too. I begged to hold it but Mrs Puddy told me it was better for me and my baby if I didn't. She called Mrs Coleman in and asked her to take the babe away to wash it and wrap it up in the linen she had brought with her and to then send for the Minister. Then she told me I was a good girl and it was an easier birthing than she had expected. She put a bucket under the stool then massaged my belly and said all we had to do now was to wait for the afterbirth. It soon came which seemed to please her and I hardly felt a thing. Then Mrs Puddy washed me and put me to bed. You just sleep now dear she said and I did what she said cause I was worn out and I must have slept for many hours. When I awoke the Minister had been and my baby was gone. I started to cry and just couldn't stop. I bawled my eyes out in my loneliness. I tried to console myself that the baby would have a good Christian home but that didn't seem to help. I didn't even know if it was a boy or a girl. It was better that way Mrs Puddy had said.

4th July 1786. I have been in such pain, so sore in my privates and my breasts are hot and hurting cause they are full of milk. Mrs Puddy left me some strips of linen to bind them and said that they would soon stop making milk and get better and then everything would be as it was before and nobody would ever know about the baby. But I will know. I lie awake at night, my breasts aching for my child and I wonder if he or she is being well cared for, trying not to imagine my babe is crying for me its mother.

Mrs Strabane came to see me today. It will be the last time I see her. It was part of the agreement with the mistress that I stay away from the house and leave Bristol when the baby was born so that the secret would never come out. So I have decided that I will go to London and look for a position there. I have written to my friend Beth Morris and asked if she knows of any positions that are vacant. She did not reply to my last letter, she is probably not allowed to use writing materials but then she was never as good at her letters as I was. I shall go and see her when I arrive and hopefully she may have good news for me. I was given five pounds fifteen shillings as back wages when I left the mistress, and I had another two pounds ten shillings saved up, but I have had to pay the rent and I have eaten well for the baby's sake so that I have less than three pounds left.

I determined to leave for London next Tuesday, but Mrs Strabane said that my lying-in period should be at least a month. I said that I couldn't wait that long and I would go as soon as the bleeding went away and my milk had stopped. I hope I don't get mastitis to delay me, as my rent here is due to run out.

15th July 1786. I can hardly see to write this. I am sat on a dirty bed with soiled sheets in a dark bare dank room in Stukerley Street London. The lodging is owned by a pedlar and his wife whose own bed is separated from me by just an old curtain and for this I am paying two shillings a week. I am writing this resting on my lap in what little daylight remains of this long summers day. It must be nearly ten of the clock. It is squalid but at least the pedlar and his wife have shown me some kindness. This morning they took me down to the fruit and vegetable market at Covent Garden at five-thirty of the clock. I was befuddled by the place at first. It was packed and teeming with people. There were carts and vans and donkeys, the avenues leading to it almost blocked with them. Porters with heavy hampers piled high on their heads their faces strained as they weaved through the crowds. The pavement, even at this hour, was already scattered with rotten cabbage leaves and other waste of the vegetable market. But it was the noise that so startled me. Porters shouting at the throng to get out of their way, women shrieking as they fought to be heard, horses neighing, donkeys braying, boys fighting, street vendors singing their wares and trying to get an early sale. Fresh hot. Penny a lot.

From the market people I purchased nuts and oranges but there were dozens of other girls doing the same, some as young as ten or eleven it seemed. The pedlar and his wife said that being a street vendor was a way of earning a living but today I tramped the hot streets from six in the morning till nine at night and done all this to make sixpence. There is drunkenness everywhere, gin on sale at every street corner. This London is not the wonderland that I thought it to be – it is a terrible place. I have eaten nothing all day but all I can now think about is sleep. I can hardly keep my eyes open to write this and I am so melancholy but even so I want for nothing else but to climb into this foul bed and curl up to sleep. Even my aching empty belly will not distract me from it.

Oh dear I nodded off but I must write all this down. I took the stagecoach four days ago. When I went with the mistress to London we travelled by the mail coach which made the journey in a day but that would have cost me twenty-eight shillings and I could not afford that. My money is rapidly going and so I travelled by the ordinary stagecoach but even that cost me twelve shillings and six pence. The journey was much slower and we had to stop overnight at an inn. It was an awful place. The landlord wanted one shilling and ten pence for a single room but only ten pence if I shared which I decided to do. There was only one bed in the room and I went to sleep on my own. Downstairs I could hear the shouting from the taproom and the drinking songs being sung but eventually I cried myself to sleep. I was woken in the early hours when this drunken woman crashed into the bed and then fell into it beside me, fully clothed boots and all. She snored all night like a night-soil man, her breath smelt like the masters and she scratched my legs with her boots.

When we arrived in London I went straight to the address I had for Beth in Gough Square. I went to the back door and enquired of her but a snooty housekeeper was called and she told me that Beth had been dismissed some time last year. She said she was a dreamy girl who could not concentrate on her duties and had to go. That did sound like Beth I have to confess to myself. They had received my letters but they had no address for Beth to send them on. I went around the front of the house and I started to sob uncontrollably. I just looked round me up and down the square in bewilderment, I didn't know anybody in London, I had no place to go and nowhere to stay. But then I felt a tug on my sleeve. I looked around and there was a young scullery maid who had sneaked out of the house. She reminded me of me when I first started in service, looking no more than fifteen. She had a smudge across her nose and cheek and a curl was escaping from under her cap across her forehead.

Her face was flushed from the heat of the kitchen. I know where Beth is she said and told me the address and how to get there.

It took me a good hour to find it and when I arrived it was a tumbledown lodging house but on enquiry I found Beth's room and I knocked on the door. When it opened I first thought I had the wrong room and I hardly recognised her. Her eyebrows had been plucked and replaced by black painted ones. Her lips were painted crimson red and her face was adorned with powder and rouge. She was always a plump girl but now she was squeezed into a dirty gown that had obviously not been made for her and had not been altered with any skill. The stays pushed up her breasts to overflowing and the exposed parts too had been powdered. She looked at me for a moment and then recognised me and then a huge smile crossed her face but the crimson of her lips made her teeth look faded like button mushrooms before they are scrubbed. She grabbed me, hugged me pinning my arms to my side, and then pulled me inside her room.

Ginny Ginny, she squealed and pulled me down on the side of her bed where we both sat together. What are you doing here.

I've come looking for a position I said but even as I spoke I was welling up and I hardly got to the end of the sentence before I started sobbing. I thought you might be able to help me I blubbed. I told her my story and then we both started to cry together. She looked at me with her big brown puppy dog eyes. They were glistening as her own tears filled them and then they burst and the tears ran down her chubby rouged cheeks. Oh Ginny I can't help cause I was sacked from my last position. The housekeeper, er won't listen to me.

We sat quietly for a while and she held my hand. So what are you doing now I said. I suppose it should have been obvious but I am so like a child sometimes. She just looked at me hoping I think that I would see what was obvious. When I didn't she sighed heavily and then said quietly, I go with men Ginny, for money. I remember that I put my hand to my mouth in shock. Beth, yer don't I said, my Bristol words coming back to me and matching hers. But yer were brought up as a good Christian girl.

Ohrrhr I were, tiss true she said but that didn't seem to mean much when my belly was aching with hunger.

But how can you Beth I said, you know, let men do that to you.

It were difficult at first our Ginny she said but after a while it's not so bad. And the money is gert lush.

But isn't it dangerous walking the streets I said.

Ohrrhr tiss, so I don't do that. I looked at her puzzled. Me and some other girls work the cock and hen clubs and so we look after each other.

Cock and hen clubs. What are they I asked.

They're drinking and dining clubs for young men making their way in the world. They are usually in their twenties from the middling class. They meet in private rooms generally upstairs in taverns to do the cock part. You should see the table of food that is prepared for them. Huge steak pies with bowl after bowl of vegetables and large jugs of gravy. Pitchers of ale and they pile their plates high with pie and potatoes and vegetables then pour gravy all over em. They talk about what young men talk about, you know gambling, wenching, cock fighting, the theatre, executions, animal baiting, but also they grumble about their positions and their wages. And when they have dined that's when we come in, as the hens. They buy us drinks and there is always plenty of food left. We talk to em, listen to their jokes, laugh with them. Its gert lush she said which made me smile cause I hadn't heard that Bristol phrase for such a long time. Then if they want you she went on, you tells them how much you wants and there are cubicles available for you to use.

And how much do you ask I said.

I like to ask five shillings but some of the young gentlemen won't pay that. You have to make them feel like stallions, flatter them. If they only pay three shillings but you have made them feel good then next time they will pay the five shillings that you have asked. I have some young gentlemen that come back time after time. Some of them is nice boys and we have fun together. They have saved up all month for their night out and they mean to enjoy themselves and John Barleycorn he makes them spend their money freely. She looked at me for some moments. You should come and join me Ginny she said.

Oh no I couldn't I said. The very thought upset me. I stood up to go. I have to find lodgings I said.

You can share with me until you finds somewhere she said but I couldn't I just wanted to get away. She gave me directions to where I might find lodgings I could afford and we hugged each other. She smelt of perfume, strong that lingered on me after I had gone. I walked along the streets knocking on doors for a couple of hours until I came to the pedlars house.

He called himself a coster rather than a pedlar. He came to the door in a long cord waistcoat with huge pockets and brass buttons with a silk neckerchief. His trousers billowed out from the knee over shiny shoes. He wore a cloth cap pulled down on one side despite him being indoors. He spoke sort of funny and I didn't always understand him but I think he was concerned cause I didn't have work so may not be able to pay the rent.

I can't say how you will pay me he said, it's nothing to me how you earns a living but that's my opinion. He called his wife who he called my gal and she came to the door as well.

Well she aint no ruffian she said cause you can see that from her clothes.

Aye she looks like a goodish kind of a person he said. I aint had no schooling but a cove can see for imself that that's right enough.

I had my lodgings and I was bold enough to ask them how I could earn a living. He was a tin ware seller. He made them himself, funnels, nutmeg graters, penny mugs and then sold them on the street. His wife sold fish on the street and together they seemed to earn a good living. They ate well I saw, and for some reason they called their meals a relish. Saveloys or meat pies or kidney puddings even on weekdays. They went to the penny gaff theatre once a week and had a liking for pastries and cakes.

There's money to be made on the streets all right young Ginny, he said, I knows that to be true cause I does it seven days a week. But what I also knows is that I was brought up to it and I knows all the angles. When you come to this trade as an outsider you have never learned the trick of it see. I aint had no learning but I understands that all right.

Nevertheless yesterday I determined that I had to do something to earn a living. I had tramped the streets of the fine houses all day asking if there were any service jobs available but I had the door slammed in my face so many times. I told the coster that I was a bright girl and was quick to learn.

I can't say how you'll fare young Ginny he said but you're a game un no doubt for trying.

It was agreed that his wife would take me down to the market this morning at five-thirty of the clock and help me bargain with the traders to get a good price. But I fear the coster is right that I don't know the trick of it. And now I must stop cause I am too tired to write any more.

The Journal of Corbyn Carlisle

15th March 1787· The harvest came in successfully last autumn and went to market where it brought good prices· The estate rents are now coming in on time but I have had to make sure that that tardy estate manager does his duty and calls in the tenants promptly on each of the quarter days to achieve that· The estate coffers are filling nicely now, but it is taking so much of my time· I need a reliable manager, that is now obvious to me·

I returned to London after Christmas and I am now back at Chambers· They seem to be indulgent of me being away for so long, but then it seems that having Lord Elloughton in Chambers brings a great deal of esteem with it· I have decided that I do not need to take on petty cases that will earn me small fees· I am no longer desperately short of money to pay for my lodgings and victuals· I am still strictly a junior and that may upset the senior barristers in Chambers so I have decided upon a strategy· I will learn more and gain more experience from the more complicated cases, but I go into them as the junior advocate· The senior barristers will get the lion's share of the fees and so they seem happy to work on that basis·

I am in court tomorrow representing Lord Lauston in a land dispute· He has an estate in Derbyshire not too far from my own· We have that in common and he is delighted with my attendance on the case and the senior barrister is happy for me liaise with Lord Lauston for him·

23rd March 1787. The case with Lord Lauston was won handsomely and I was allowed to do much of the advocacy myself· I am so pleased with myself and I feel that I deserve a pat on the back, for I was sharp and incisive and I think I can take much of the credit for the victory· There has been an added bonus as well· Lord Lauston has an excellent estate manager by the name of William Cooper, but he has a son, John Cooper, who is now twenty-three years old and looking for a position himself· I went up to see him yesterday and he is a fine and intelligent young man· I have decided that I will not let his tender years deter me and I have offered him the position as my estate manager· I am sure that in the future I will be able to rely on him to take much of the burden off my back.

Elloughton Park is a fine house built by Inigo Jones; I'm only just beginning to appreciate that. It is built in local stone in the Palladian style brought from Italy, a central house with balancing pavilions linked by colonnades. It is built on three floors, the roofline hidden by a balustrade, and each of the terminating wings is crowned by a one-storey pedimented tower resembling a Palladian pavilion. I suppose I have judged it previously from the perspective of it being a place where I spent an unhappy childhood; a place where I could see that my mother was so ill-used. But a feeling is gradually taking hold of me and I am quite surprised by this. I have a responsibility, I think, to my family dynasty. I must leave Elloughton Park in a better condition than I inherited it. But I also want it to be a home; I should love one day to fill it with children. I will anticipate next year's rents and make a start immediately. I have plans for a library, but first, I think, a garden would be a wonderful addition. I will start fairly modestly and perhaps expand as the estate coffers fill. Can there be anything more pleasant in life than to sit peacefully in one's own garden and let the tranquillity of it take one over? A place to read and compose poetry.

I still have to decide whether to give up my lawyering, but I'll give it to the end of the year before making my decision.

Chapter 9.

I got up from my desk and made another cup of coffee. I am hooked on Millicano blend; other instants taste too bland for me now. I took a long swig of the dark brown liquid; it burnt slightly as it went down. Strangely, I was finding the journals uneasy reading, painful even. I cradled the mug as I reflected that whilst Corbyn is prospering, Ginny's life seems to be falling apart. I am making a point of reading the journals contemporaneously so that I can judge what is happening to Ginny at the same point in time as what is happening to Corbyn. She is little more than a child and yet she is facing all the harsh realities of life. I fear for her. What a strange thing for a historian to say, I should be dispassionate; detached. I should approach these journals analytically and unemotionally. My discipline is to study the significance of various events in history, to make a cohesive narrative of given parts of history. Even Grace teased me yesterday on this very subject, telling me I was developing a crush on Ginny Farmer. I am the professor, yet it is left to one of my students to point out that I need to be detached! I need to get a grip.

I had a couple of pints with Toby Fielding last night at the Nags Head.

'How are you getting on with those journals then, Jimbo lad?' he said. I think he insists on calling me Jimbo just to annoy me.

'They're even better than you suggested they were.'

'Told you they were whizzo, didn't I, Jimbo?' He cocked a smug eye at me over the glass he had raised, then he took a long swig of Bombardier as if he was rewarding himself.

'Who do you take the piss out of when I am not here?' I meant to sound sarcastic, but I wasn't really offended. We were friends and it was allowed.

'No, it's just you, Jimbo, I don't cheat on you,' then he laughed at his own quip. 'Come on then, tell me all about them.'

I didn't need a second invitation. 'There is a third set of journals, written by a servant. So we should get a view of the country house in Georgian England from a third perspective, so we have the master, the mistress and now also from below stairs. In fact I have not yet got to the mistress's journal, written at a later date.'

Toby was a fellow historian as well as a friend and I found myself eager to tell him all about it. In fact I think I began to bore him after a while because he started to tease me again.

'What's this Grace girl like then? Is she up for some action, d'ya think?'

I just looked at him; it was my turn now to cock an eye to show my scorn at his suggestion.

'What?' he said, feigning injury. 'Don't give me that look. You don't think you would be the first professor to have his evil way with a student do you? Come on, Jimbo, wise up.'

'Well, apart from the fact that it is absolutely against university policy,' I said indignantly, 'I am quite capable of working professionally with a young woman without letting my libido get in the way; unlike some.'

'Oh, so she's a minger then, is she?'

'And no she's not a minger, as you so indelicately put it, she's a ...'

'Aha!' he interrupted, 'so you *have* cast your evil lecherous little eye over her then?'

I sighed heavily, exasperation making me temporarily speechless. 'What!' was all I could say.

'So I can take it she's a looker, can I? What else, how old is she; twenty-one, twenty-two?'

'She's about *thirty*-two actually,' I replied, and then wished I had not, as it set him off again.

'Even better, Jimbo lad. More experience – but on the other hand more difficult to impress than a gullible young undergrad. You'll have to work harder.'

'Can you hear yourself? You sound like a spotty pre-pubescent youth in the playground.'

'Oh lighten up, Jimbo. Your precious Miss Career is not putting it out for you, is she? Perhaps this Miss Grace will.' He took another swig, one that seemed to gesture his smugness, but I saw that his reference to Miss Grace had triggered something in his mind.

'Shall we get the conversation back to the journals please,' I said, but he was having too much fun at my expense. The amused look on his face intensified.

'Hey, there's a song about her isn't there?' And then he started to sing it, 'Ooh ooh ooh Miss Grace, satin and perfume and lace. The minute I saw your face, I knew that I loved you-oo.' I could have smacked him one.

Sat at my desk at the university I was just thinking about Grace Farmer and

Toby's teasing, but I had to admit she was an inspired choice on my behalf. She has graduated now with a First, as I expected, and the research she has done into these journals added that final something to her dissertation. She is staying on another year to do her Master's, and she has determined to do her postgraduate MA dissertation around these journals and also the manorial records, which were still languishing in the hotel attic until they could be catalogued.

The phone rang and, by coincidence, it was Grace. I had known she was up in Nottinghamshire at Elloughton Park. 'Professor Postlethwaite?'

I thought to tell her to call me James, but after Toby's ribbing I stopped myself. Stupid really; I hate that handle. 'Yeah, how's it going?'

'Well if you like being sweaty in a hot garret, being filthy and covered in dust all the time, then it's going fine. No, actually I'm enjoying it, but there's weeks of work up here just cataloguing everything. It's all just been piled up in this attic gathering dust and mouse droppings over many years.

'It has to be done, I'm afraid.'

'Yes I know, but you're getting it done for free by me, aren't you?'

I knew that and she obviously now realised it as well, so I did not respond to the question. 'If it's not done in the university summer break then the material won't be available for you when term time starts again in September, will it?'

'Suppose not,' she said, 'but is there any chance of getting somebody down here to help me?'

I would have liked to have helped her myself, but the department was down to a skeleton staff, everyone away on their summer holidays. I liked this period; I could get on with my own research. What a sad man I am, I use my own bloody holidays to do my research! Toby is right about me, I thought. When did I become such a swot?

'No can do,' I said, 'I've no one to spare and the students have all gone home, so I can't persuade any of them to help. Do you know an undergrad who would give up their summer to help?'

There was silence for a while, and I waited while she thought. Being older than most of her fellow students she probably had not made close friends amongst them. 'No, don't think so,' she said eventually and then changed the subject. 'I've made a couple of finds that may interest you though.'

'Go on,' I said, putting my pen down and leaning back.

'Do you remember that Lord Carlisle had a picture painted of Elloughton

Park? Well I think I've found it. It's filthy, but I'm sure it's the one.'

'Who's it by?' I was thinking about my budget again. If it had value then I might be able to offset it against the costs of securing the manorial records.'

'Oh I can't make out the signature, it's too dirty to see – why?'

'It might have value. I can top up my budget if it has.'

'But will it count as a manorial record? Does the university own it?'

I hadn't thought of that. 'Maybe not,' I said, but my mind was still working on it. Perhaps I could do a deal with the hotel manager. 'What else?'

'I've found a pendant, mother-of-pearl, heart-shaped.'

'Really? You think it's the token, as recorded in the Foundlings' Hospital's register?'

'Yes, really! I know it is.'

'How?'

'The initials, A an N, and a scratched third initial M; it's the same one all right.'

'Yes, certainly sounds like it', I said, feeling a sudden frisson of excitement.

'But why wasn't it in the servant's box that *you* have? It was in one of the boxes containing paintings and other pictures.'

'I don't think there's anything particularly sinister in that,' I said. 'It's probably no more than as a result of someone throwing everything together, but I agree, it deepens the original mystery as to why a servant's stuff has been kept at all.'

'Mmm,' she said, obviously thinking about what I had said.

'Is there a picture of Ginny?' I asked, failing to keep the hope out of my voice.

'Huh!' Why would there be a picture of a servant?'

'No, suppose not,' I had to say. I don't know why I asked. 'Look,' I added, 'I have some time owed to me. I'll take a week off, come up and help you with the cataloguing. Monday next, how's that sound? Between us we'll break the back of it.'

There was a pause. 'Yes, OK,' she replied hesitantly. 'Bye then.' The line went dead.

I put the phone down and looked at the pile of work on my desk. I had just been impulsive and I didn't know why; I was not an impulsive person. 'Sod you, Toby Fielding,' I found myself saying out loud.

Chapter 10.

The Journal of Ginny Farmer

25th **July 1786**. I've been tramping the streets for ten days now but still I am unable to sell enough nuts and oranges to make a living. I think maybe my quality clothes are putting off the customers as the other vendors look little more than beggar girls. I bought some cheap material from the Jewish merchants in Monmouth Street, not much more than rags but I have made myself something more appropriate, but even so the most I earned was eight pence one day. My shoe leather will not last long with all the miles I am covering. I need I think to look for some other form a work if I am to advance myself.

27th **July 1786**. Yesterday it rained all day. I went to the market and bought my supply of oranges and nuts as usual but as I tramped the streets everybody was rushing around trying to get out of the rain, they did not want to stop and buy from me. The rain was welcome and washed away some of the filth from the streets and London smelt better than it has since I arrived here. All that ash, rubbish, and horse droppings; even the contents of chamber pots that had missed the night soil collectors to be emptied into the street and had lain festering in the summer sun was now washing its way down the gutters on its way to the River Thames. For the first time I did not have to wrinkle my nose at the disgusting smells. It is much worse than Bristol.

At about two of the clock I gave up. I was drenched right through to my skin and I went back to my lodgings and took off my clothes to dry. I spent the afternoon sewing the remaining rags. I have become quite skilled with a needle and thread and I was pleased with what I was able to put together. The coster and his gal were still on the streets, or more likely at the tavern and I had the house to myself.

It must have been about nine of the clock cause there was still some daylight outside when I heard banging on the front door and somebody shouting my name. I was wearing only my underbodice so I opened the door slightly and just put my head and shoulders around it. It was Beth

Morris holding a shawl over her head to shelter from the rain. Oh at last I've found you Ginny she said and pushed her way in.

I wasn't sure what she wanted and she spat words at me that didn't seem to make much sense. Now slow down and start again I said and she took a deep breath. Yer have to come she said to the Royal Oak Tavern, there is a special customer and you are perfect for him.

I just looked at her wondering if I understood her right. But I'm no Mabel I said. I know I know she replied but they have a young man at the cock and hen club there and ee is a virgin. It will be his first time and his friend is looking for a virgin girl for him too. I'm no virgin either Beth I said, Ive had a child remember. Ohrrhr I knows that she said but ee don't do ee. You tell him you're a virgin and you can ask half a sovereign, virgins cost more money see.

I just sat on my bed dumfounded not knowing what to think, what to say. Beth looked around my half room and saw the unsold oranges and nuts. I did that for a while, selling on the streets she said. I never made a sixpence. I finished up eating the unsold nuts and oranges cause after paying the rent I had no money left to buy any proper victuals. Is that what yer wants Ginny. Theres hardly an ounce of fat on yer as it is. Yer'll starve to death when winter comes.

I was thinking about looking for a position as a seamstress or a milliner I said but my words were soft, uncertain, and I think she knew that I did not hold out much hope of such a position. I sucked on my lip and then I burst out crying again and Beth put her ample arm around me and I sobbed against her rain-wet bosom. What is to become of me I blubbed. Now this isnt the Ginny I remember from the Foundlings Hospital she said, yer know the one that mimicked the matron and made us all laugh when we wanted to cry. You were the one that was strong. Little Ginny who mocked the matron remember, you were braver than all of us put together.

I saw some truth in her words. They reminded us every day at the Foundlings Hospital of our lowly position, wanted us to be grateful. We had to say our prayers every day asking for <u>humilitude</u> for <u>gratitude</u> — I never even knew then what those words meant. I could only sniffle a nod against her bosom adding to the raindrops with my own tears, all the time that powerful perfume stinging the back of my throat. Well what is it to be little Ginny Farmer she said.

I pulled back and looked at her. The question was still in her eyes. I twitched a smile, nodded not really knowing why I did so or what I was nodding yes to. I think it was just a sense of hopelessness. Right she said lets look at yer best clothes. I showed her my smart dress blouse but she just sighed. Put that on she said and we'll see what we can find for you.

At Beths lodgings she sat me down on her bed and sent for two of her friends. Penny a young girl of I think our age but maybe nineteen or twenty, and Moll who was older and it seems the mother hen. Molls dress was loud – a swirling pattern in red and emerald – but it was grubby and had seen better days. Her hair was worn ridiculously high and I suspect that she thought it fashionable, but from reading the Lady's Magazine I knew that that it was long out of fashion. She had a musky smell I did not like. She looked down at me and told me to stand up. She then looked me up and down and then nodded saying that for sure I would certainly pass as a virgin. But we will have to do something about the way she looks she added. They were in a great hurry and they quickly dressed me in one of Pennys gowns, a blue-green lustring dress, the silky material lined with white. They put stays on me to push up my breasts, and it did give the illusion that I had a bosom although in truth I have little bosom to display. But then they plucked my eyebrows so quickly that there were droplets of blood appearing, but they wiped it away and then replaced them with black painted ones higher on my forehead. Then they painted my lips a vivid crimson, but mercifully they did not put powder or rouge on my face just pinched my cheeks.

They showed me myself in a looking glass and I could see they had succeeded in making me look older than my seventeen years. I suppose that was to make me look worldlier, more desirable. I didn't like what I saw though. They had taken away my youthful prettiness, and none of it complemented my pastel blue eyes, flaxen hair and pale complexion. It also made me look less like a virgin so I was not sure what they were trying to achieve. But my mind was filled with fear for what was to come and I just let them do this to me.

They took me round to the tavern almost dragging me in their haste. I was hauled through the taproom and then up the stairs to the function room. It was dimly lit by a few lanterns but it smelt of food, I could smell wonderful beef gravy but mixed with the smell of ale and gin. But it was the noise more than anything that hit me. There was a fiddler playing somewhere and there was a buzz of voices like a swarm of bumblebees as if everybody was trying to shout to be heard and then there would be a peel of laughter when somebody said something funny. They pushed me through all this to the far end of the room where two gentlemen were sitting. One was a military man in his uniform and the other a younger gentleman, I thought in his twenties, in a very smart black frockcoat. When I saw them fear took me and I stopped rigid but Moll just pulled me along by the hand. When we got to their table she turned, placed her hands on my shoulders and pushed me forward. This is Ginny she said.

I didnt know what to do or say. I felt my cheeks blushing and I just held my head slightly to one side unable to move just like a rabbit confronted by a stoat. Ginny I'd like you meet my friend Johnny said Moll looking at the military gentleman, and he nodded politely saying your servant Ginny which nobody has ever said to me before. And this is his friend Samuel she added looking at the other gentleman. I bobbed a slight curtsy at him but he seemed too embarrassed to speak to me or even look at me. When our eyes did meet we both just seemed to flush and looked away again. Moll laughed at us both saying, we ave got two bashful lovebirds ere aint we deary. The military gentleman said the best thing was to leave us alone together to get to know each other.

Moll pulled the military gentleman by the arm leading him away saying that nature would take its course. I saw the look on the other gentlemans face and could see the last thing he wanted was to be left alone with me. I was still afeared but I could see that the other gentleman was as well. For a few moments he stared after Moll and the military gentleman like a scolded pup and I just stood in front of him not knowing what do. I could feel my heart pounding in my chest I was so afeared but I took a deep breath and sat in the chair the military gentleman had been sitting in. I felt my dress brush against his leg and I saw him look down at it as if it would somehow sting him. We then sat in silence and embarrassment, both unsure and neither of us confident enough to talk to each other. All the time I was trying to stem the rising fear within me. But then he took a deep breath and said his name was Samuel, Samuel Medina. And I am Ginny Farmer sir I replied.

After another pause, Samuel cleared his throat and said you're not from London then. I hadn't realised that I had such a strong West Country accent. I told him I'd only been here a few days. I'd come to London looking for work, but it had not been easy to find.

He asked me what sort of work but he could still not look me in the face. I told him I was a ladies maid before I came to London and he seemed to understand that the gentry brought their own servants with them when they come to London for the season and work would be hard to find. I could see that he couldn't think of anything else to say so we sat in silence for a few more moments. I like your dress he said eventually.

Thank you sir I replied and I could feel my cheeks reddening but I forced myself to speak. But it's not really mine I said and that my cousin had borrowed it for me. I couldn't afford this. And then she and her friend did my face, I only had a few minutes to get ready after Moll arrived.

Then for the first time we looked at each other. I think we were both feeling some relief that we were in similar circumstances but then we both realised that we were staring at each other and looked hurriedly away.

He mumbled into his tankard and asked me if I knew what went on here.

Oh yes sir I said my cousin has explained it all. I have to be considerate to the young gentlemen. There was another pause when embarrassment suddenly returned to both of us and then he asked me if I would like a drink and what would I like, and I told him I,d been told to ask for gin but to be honest I didn't really like it much.

He offered ale, and when I nodded he reached for a spare glass and poured ale from the pitcher. I took a deep gulp before putting the glass down and I noticed my fingers were trembling and I saw that he noticed too. He picked up his tankard, held it in my direction so I picked up my own glass again and we clunked them together saying cheers and drank again. After that we continued to drink for some time beginning to feel more comfortable with each other.

So why London he asked eventually and I said that I had a cousin here who I thought was in service and could help me find a job. But it turned out that she was not in service at all. Actually she's a...I started to say but I couldn't say that word so instead I said that she entertained gentlemen. He nodded to show he knew what I meant and then asked me if I intended to go back. When I said that I couldn't do that he asked me why not. I didn't know what to say and again I found I couldn't look him in the eyes. I told him that he didn't want to know my troubles but he persisted so I said that my cousin told me not to talk about such things and that I was to talk about him not me.

But he was good with words and asked if I was also told to do what I was told. I seemed to be cornered but then he smiled at me and for the first time I looked at his features. There was something unusual about him. It was his eyes. Large brown eyes that seemed warm and kind-hearted. He wore his hair in a pigtail and his face was clean shaven. He had olive skin quite unlike my own very fair skin. His nose was prominent but softened by those two great soulful eyes. He had one of those faces which while not handsome was warm and heartening. I felt that he was genuinely interested in me. Aye sir I said I was told to do as I was told.

Well then he said I'm telling you that I want you to tell me why you can't go back. I was still unsure. I don't know why I confided in him but I did. I told him it was the master, hoping that would be enough for him but I could see from his eyes that it wasn't. He took a shine to me I said if you knows what I mean and Samuel smiled kindly. I think I do he nodded, so you've run away then have you lass he said.

When I nodded in reply he asked if this was any better and would they take me back if I returned. I said I didn't think so but I could hear the sudden alarm in my voice. I didn't know how much to tell him. He kept asking questions. Are you so sure lass he said are you sure, and then he took my hand gently in his. I looked down at it and started to sob and then blurted out that the mistress had thrown me out. But he was not satisfied with that either and wanted to know why and I froze not knowing what to say, but then I just told him everything. A stranger who I had just met. I realised that tears were running down my cheek and this kind man reached across to try to wipe them away but I turned away and did it myself.

And then he asked me why I didn't go back to my family. Come on lass you've gone this far he said. So I told him everything, about the Foundlings Hospital in Bristol, about being abandoned as a baby, about being brought up as a strict Christian and then put into service. That they would disapprove of me getting pregnant if they knew, that I couldn't get a job in Bristol cause it was part of the agreement with the mistress that I move away. That I thought I'd come to London where nobody knew me.

And then alarm took me when he pointed out that I had said I had a cousin. He had caught me out in a lie. I thought he would think that the whole story was a lie. Oh I don't tell lies sir I blurted, my voice almost squealing. It was important to me that he did not think of me as a liar, why I don't know. But then I saw in those kind eyes that he didn't. I added that it was just easier to say she's my cousin, that we were actually both at the Foundlings Hospital together. She had been put into service in London.

His face broke out into a kindly smile asking how old I was when I got pregnant. I told him that I was sixteen when I got pregnant, seventeen when the baby was born. I tried to change the subject, forcing myself to sound more cheerful, so you see sir I said, I know what to do if we, you know.

When he asked me how much I was told to ask for I realised what I had done. I told him Moll will be annoyed with me. I was supposed to ask for half a sovereign because I'm a virgin, and now I'd gone and told him I was not.

Samuel laughed unexpectedly and that laugh seemed to pierce our embarrassment like a hot knife through butter. I laughed with him and we both drank again. We were relaxing with each other. He said that he was happy just talking if that was all right with me and that I was to call him Samuel. Yes sir I said stupidly and then I giggled when I saw his face and realised what I had said. He asked me if I knew what I was getting myself into and I nodded.

Oh yes. Prostitute is not a nice word is it I said. The Foundlings Hospital brought me up a good Christian girl, and I was diligent with my studies. I'm a bright girl but I have little choice do I, if I don't want to starve. I'll use my looks cause that's all I have at this time. My cousin says we can keep off the streets if we can find a room and attract gentlemen of means. We can make a future for ourselves.

I hope you can Ginny he said.

I told him that I must accept my lot and that he must not think I am unhappy with the prospect. I lied of course and I think he knew it. I confided though that I found London scary, such a very big place.

And then we just talked together. It must have been for another two hours or so, but as we talked, the topics became lighter and more trivial. We ate some of the victuals, giggled together and talked about our childhoods and how different they had been. He was just nineteen but he looked older than that, I thought him twenty-three or even twenty-four. He told me he was a Jew and I have never met a Jew before and knew nothing of Jewish ways, and he told me all about his religion. We were from so different backgrounds but we seemed to get on so well. I asked him what he did to earn a living as I was puzzled cause his clothes were too fine to be from his middling class background. He said that he was a pugilist but I did not know what that was and he said that he was a boxer, a fighter. I looked at him still a little puzzled cause he seemed such a gentle man and he laughed when I said that. He told me that as a Jew he had always had to stand up and fight for himself. A Jew in

England could be set upon in the street at any time without recourse to the law. If he stood up and fought to protect himself that didn't mean he was a quarrelsome man by nature. He said he was brought up to behave honourably. And then he told me to feel the muscle on his arm what he called his bicep. It was hard as a rock and my small hand could not span it. He took my hand and put it on his chest and I could feel his muscles rippling. This Samuel Medina was an unusual man indeed.

But then as time wore on I became agitated again and he saw that. I told him that Moll would expect things of me, she'd expect me to – you know, I couldn't say the word. Samuel reminded me that he had said he was happy just to talk, but of course I was expected to earn some money. He told me not to worry cause he had recently come into some funds, that he had enough for that half a sovereign. You are such a good man Samuel, I said looking at his kind face intently and then I said something outrageous. I don't know where it came from but I told him that I had to learn to do this. Here was a man who was being considerate. It was unexpected, but I was so very pleased to receive it so I said that I would like the first time to be with him, cause it would be easier that way. I held my breath waiting for his reply.

I would like that as well he said and I was so relieved. We smiled at each other and then that smile turned to a grin and then into a beam, as if we were some naughty children about to do something very bad. We both shrugged our shoulders to gesture that feeling to each other, and then Samuel stood up but quickly sat down when he realised he didn't know where to go. Then he stood again and sought out his friend John who I saw smirk, but then they hurried back and he slapped Samuel fiercely on the back in the way men do, teased him by calling him stallion but then directed us to a door leading to several cubicles. Samuel turned to me and put out his hand and I took it willingly, but we didn't speak until we entered a cubicle. It was dimly lit, and furnished only with a small table and a well worn, leather-bound lounger that was open at one end and had long since lost its attractive aroma of freshly tanned leather. In fact it was rather shabby and frayed, but we had other things on our minds than the state of its upholstery.

We sat down together and both breathed deeply in unison, and then giggled when we realised what we had done. I leaned across and kissed him gently on the lips and closed my eyes instinctively as I did so. The kiss was long, but tender rather than passionate. When the kiss ended he put his forehead against mine. He asked me how we would do it, should we lie down, but I just got up and sat on his lap straddling him. I was shocked at my own boldness but even more shocked when I felt his thighs beneath me. So shocked that I had to get up again and look back and I felt his legs sheepishly with my hands this time. They were huge and I realised that I had only really seen him from the waist upwards whilst he had been sitting at the table. I think I must have been embarrassing him cause I felt his muscles tighten beneath my touch and I realised that he was still just as nervous as I was.

I asked him if all Jews were like him and that made him laugh. It was no more than a little giggle but it was so appealing. He was such a lovely man. I suppose I had said something stupid but I didn't mind at all. That giggle just seemed to make everything so much easier for me from that point. He asked if his body upset me. Oh no I blurted out worried that he should think so, and sat down again on his lap and kissed him again. This time it started gently but I felt the passion rising in me and I could feel that his passions were rising as well.

Then we lay together, or rather we sat together. Oh I don't know how to say this. Yes we did it, we coupled. I had expected it to be awful but it was not. In fact it was so enjoyable that I now know why people do it so much I think. I had always thought it something women had to endure but Samuel was so wonderful. At times I felt like a rag doll in his powerful arms he lifted me up and down so easily, at others he was the most gentle of gentlemen. And afterwards Samuel said that he wanted to see me again and I hope that he does come back.

Afterwards Beth was angry with me when I told her all about it. She told me that whoring was a living. Sex was to be my profession and not to be enjoyed. I must not believe anything a gentleman told me especially overtures of love, claims that he would look after me, or even marry me. Even in the unlikely event that the man was serious when he said the words, in the cold light of day he would only let me down. All I know is that Samuel is such a nice man and I believed that he was being honest with me. If he had just wanted to tupp me then he could have done just that. I can still picture us together as I write this, his powerful olive-skinned body, dark hair, large brown eyes, and me a slight, pale skinned girl, flaxen-haired powder-blue-eyed girl. I remember the warmth of his body. It has been so long since anybody has been nice to me. I do hope he comes back to see me again.

So I have become a prostitute, a Mabel. The good Christian girl that I thought I was is no more. I am a common whore. Well if that's what life has led me to then so be it. I cannot even hide behind Samuel not treating me as a whore. For after he left, Moll found me another young man to lie with. He was drunk but he treated me respectfully, well as respectfully as he would treat any whore. He used my body to gratify himself and this is what Beth told me it would be like. I can handle that I am sure, but if I am to be a whore then I am sure that I can be better than just a plaything at a cock and hen club.

The Journal of Corbyn Carlisle

21ˢᵗ November 1787. The Indian summer now seems such a distant memory, but I have that painting of my garden in my office at Chambers· I am quite the envy of my fellow barristers because of it· We had defended a hot-headed young man by the name of William Blake, who called himself an artist and poet, who had been charged with taking part in a riot· His father, a wealthy hosier, was at his wit's end with his brilliant young son who seems to want to change the world all by himself, and was so grateful that we managed to get him acquitted· I did some of the advocacy myself so I took the opportunity to suggest to his father that he paint my house for a small fee· The young man himself was not so keen, claiming that he was neither a landscape nor an architectural artist, but with his father's insistence he agreed to undertake the commission· I put the young man up at the hall for a week and I think his father was happy to have him out of his hair for a while·

I walked to work this morning, the autumn leaves swirling round my feet in the icy east wind, my greatcoat pulled up about my collar and my face huddled beneath my muffler for warmth· This winter weather has brought on a melancholy which I resolved to do something about, so yesterday I joined a fencing club so that I can reacquaint myself with the skills I learned at school· Monsieur Lievremont, the fencing master, seemed quite pleased with my level of competence although I know I was very rusty, but he says that he can turn me into a fine swordsman· That lifted my spirits, but today the weather has dampened them again·

Emily has already arranged introductions to two prospective brides· Firstly I dined with a Miss Georgina Huffington and her parents at a fine house in Dover Street· She was a pretty young thing, but I confess that I found her empty-headed and she could not converse on any subject that I broached. As far as I could ascertain she is proficient in embroidery and little else. Next, I went to a musical evening where I was introduced to a Miss Amelia Woodville who was so timid that she just suffused every time I spoke to her. I left having found out absolutely nothing about her.

I am beginning to suspect that Emily is intent on finding a bride, not for me, but herself; a lady that she will be able to dominate when she comes to Elloughton Hall as the new mistress.

Chapter 11.

I arrived at Elloughton Park just after 10:30 a.m. after making an early start. I checked in and the reception clerk said he had given me the room next to Miss Farmer. I wished he hadn't; Toby's words were still stinging in my mind. I was already wearing an old pair of jeans and a t-shirt so I just dropped off my case and went straight to the attic. It was remarkably spacious and I found I could easily stand, there being at least four feet clearance to accommodate my six-foot frame. It was extensive, probably forty feet by thirty I thought to myself, and there was electricity, so there was ample light to work by. Grace was at the far end, her curly hair tied up and a pen precariously placed behind her ear. There was a rolled cigarette hanging from her lips and she was smoking it with no hands, just letting it hang when she needed to. *'Only me,'* I shouted down to her as she hadn't seemed to hear me climb up the retractable loft ladder, engrossed in a ledger that she was balancing on her left arm whilst turning the pages with her right; she looked up at me.

'Oh hi,' she said distantly, still absorbed.

'Not sure smoking is all that clever up her here amongst these dry old documents,' I said.

She took it out of her mouth with her free hand and looked down at it. 'Probably not,' she answered, but then just put it back in her mouth and carried on. So much for admonishment, I thought to myself. It was a light admonishment from me, but it had clearly been rejected. The pattern established on our car trip to Bristol was being repeated.

There was a dirt smudge on her cheek running across to her nose. I thought to tell her, but decided against it; it looked quite attractive in a cute sort of way. I could see that she had been busy; she had made an impromptu desk out of some upturned crates, and her laptop was open to record the cataloguing. I would have done it on paper and then transferred it to the computer, but then I was a bit anal that way. There was an ashtray in the corner and the remains of a cup of coffee. There was room to put a ledger beside the laptop, but I could not see a chair. She saw me looking around.

'I didn't want to worry the hotel manager by asking for a desk to be brought up,' she said, 'and I didn't want to be carting all these ledgers up and down to my room so I improvised.'

'No probs,' I said, 'I can work this way, but no chairs?'

'Oh, I've been working standing up, but I'm sure the manager can find you a chair.'

'No, I'll see how we go.'

'Right,' she answered awkwardly, looking over her shoulder.

'So how's it going?' I said, as much to fill the uneasy silence as a real enquiry, but then she seemed happy to talk.'

'The manager and an assistant came up with me the first day, and we put all the hotel stuff at that far end and the manorial records are at this end. So this lot is what you have bought for the university.' She gestured with her head to the piles around her.'

'And the records – how are you finding them?'

'There's not much before 1785 and what there is is poor, incomplete entries, not easy to follow; there seems to be a lot missing, unless we come across the missing bits as we go along. But after 1785 they become quite meticulous, cataloguing should be fairly easy; except, of course, for the sheer volume of it.'

'Good, good,' I said, where is this box with the pictures in it?'

She walked across the attic to a sort of halfway point where there were a number of boxes. 'I've put these here as it's not clear who they belong to. The manager put them with the manorial records but I don't think he thought about it too much.' She pulled out a large box made of thick cardboard, probably made specifically for storage. She started to pick it up so I went over to help her.

'I managed before you arrived,' she said in strangled tones as if my help was somehow offensive to her independence.

'But now you don't have to,' I said, taking the other end of the box and together we took it to the desk. 'Which one is the picture of the house?'

'This one,' she said, lifting out a painting in an ornate but very dirty rococo style frame, or what I thought of as rococo in my limited knowledge of the subject.

I took it from her and walked to stand under the light so that I could see as much as possible of it. It was as Grace had said, very dirty but I could just make out the scene – the garden, and the hall as a backdrop. I peered in the bottom right hand corner but the signature was not visible.

'Told you,' she said. I looked up and saw that she had raised an eyebrow, the nuance suggesting I was being condescending, did not trust her, and she did not like it. She struck a pose to emphasise her words; her t-shirt said, GOOD GIRL BAD HABITS. It was apt.

'I've reread the journal entry made by Corbyn,' I said, 'do you remember who he said he had got to paint this?'

'Some young hooligan who he defended in court wasn't it.'

'Yes, but he names him as William Blake. Does that name mean anything to you?'

'No, should it? …Oh – there was a poet by that name, wasn't there?'

'Yep, there was, but I've been on the tinterweb, he was an *artist* as well.'

'You think that this is the same William Blake?'

'Might be; if it is it may have some value. I'll ask somebody at the university to look at it.'

We worked hard for the rest of the day, working well together and making very good progress. She'd clearly done her reading on cataloguing skills and she needed very little instruction from me. I was happy to follow what she had already done, and even told her that she could lead on this, for this week I would be her assistant. I had registered some reluctance when I suggested that I come down and I had put it down to her wanting somebody to assist, not somebody to take over. It was about 4 p.m. when I realised that we had missed lunch, had only had a coffee from the flask that she had brought up. The build up of heat was beginning to get to me and I started to flag, I could feel sweat trails running down my back. 'Phew', I said and sighed heavily, and Grace looked round at me.

'Yeah, it starts to get very stuffy after a while doesn't it?' she said, then looked at her watch. She placed a piece of paper in the ledger she was holding and closed it, the weight of it making a thudding sound. She put it down. She looked back to me. 'Well I'm ready for a swim,' she said, 'do you want it join me?'

That sounded wonderful, but then I realised something, 'I didn't know they had a pool here, I haven't brought my cozzy,' I said.

'I'm sure that you aren't the first to do that.' I was unsure what she meant and she must have seen that in my expression. 'They'll probably have them on sale in the fitness centre.'

When I emerged from the cubicle I was feeling quite self-conscious in my new Speedo's, I would have preferred shorts. I headed for the shower to get the days dust off me before taking to the pool, and I needed hot water and a good shower to do that. When I dived in, the cold water made me shudder, my skin was still warm from the shower. I swam to the edge of the pool and waited there whilst my body acclimatised itself to the cold refreshing water, my back against the poolside. I looked around for Grace but she had not yet arrived. I put my arms over the side, leant back and just closed my eyes, relaxing in the cool water, letting it buoy me, beginning to feel good, invigorated.

Something made me open my eyes however; I became aware of the graceful movement of long limbs walking down the side of the pool; it was Grace Farmer. I turned my head to look up at her, and she nodded slightly to acknowledge me. I was shocked at what I saw; gone was the dress-down, the old frayed jeans, the cheeky t-shirt, the absence of sophistication. She was wearing a one-piece swimsuit, brilliant sunshine yellow. It was cut high around her hips, accentuating her long, slender, lightly tanned frame and the tightness of her buttocks. Her tummy was flat, her torso athletic and firm. She looked like a model on a catwalk; a third Grace Farmer had emerged from her chrysalis. She walked past me to the end of the pool, perhaps ten feet from me. My position accentuated the view of her and the long linear nature of her body. My eyes ascended from her toes, which curved forward and gripped the edge of the pool; they were painted red like two bunches of cherries. Grace was an accurate name for her, I could see that now; she was indeed graceful. Then embarrassment took me, as I realised that I was staring. I looked away, and when I did so I saw a couple of other male faces had also turned to look at her expectantly; she was about to dive in – but not yet. Whether she did it deliberately I don't know, but she allowed the expectancy to increase, to mature in her newfound admirers before she released it. It was as if both men had inhaled together and were holding their breath, awaiting her permission to exhale.

I looked back and allowed my eyes the same indulgence as these other two, moving ever upward, scanning her body. The sight of her, I have to confess, brought lustful thoughts to me.

She stood motionless for a moment, then raised her arms and pulled back her hair and then gathered it in a band. That movement emphasised her breasts and I found myself staring at them as well. Then she looked down at me, I assumed I was caught in the act of gawping and that embarrassment returned to me. But she just smiled and nodded to gesture that I should join her swimming. She dived in athletically and swam up the pool. I set off after her and we swam some lengths together. I struggled to keep up with her and I eventually gave up. I got out of the pool and watched her glide up and down for several more lengths. I felt I was watching a different person.

We dined together in the hotel restaurant. She was back to Grace number 2 mode: jeans and t-shirt, but clean ones; the t-shirt said, ATTITUDE PROBLEM; I had to smile. She was wearing no make-up and her hair loose around her shoulders. She seemed to have made no effort but yet she was never again to be the Grace Farmer number 1 that I knew from the university. I had that image in my mind of her by the pool, athletic, womanly, desirable. Strangely, this made me a little reticent to start with; I was probably trying to impress her, but that in itself made me awkward, ill at ease. But after a few glasses of wine that reticence began to wane and we spoke more easily, well at least I began to; she was at ease all the way through it.

She excused herself and for a few minutes I was left by myself. I mused; how long had it been since I had been with a woman. Some months now; a brief fling with a colleague, Danielle Binoche, a lecturer in French. That had seemed so exotic when I started it, but it had gone nowhere. I think she found me too wrapped up in my work.

After the meal we went to the bar and had a few more drinks. I drank Bombardier from a bottle; they had no draft. I never liked those young guys who drank their beer straight from the bottle in bars, and here I was doing the same; trying to look hip.

'Will we being doing this every night,' she said to me, 'its not conducive to early starts and hard days is it?'

'Maybe not,' I answered, but early starts and hard days' work was not what I had in mind at that moment; I was powerfully attracted to her. She was a student of mine and I had always been careful not to do that sort of thing; but now I didn't care. I viewed her as a woman of my age not an immature student; a colleague not a pupil; I wanted her. We walked from the bar to our adjacent rooms. My conversation had become increasingly personal as the evening had progressed and there had been no signal on her part that I was straying into forbidden territory; I had expectations. We stopped outside her door and she immediately swiped the cardkey, and then turned the handle, but only opened the door a mere inch or so. She lent back against the doorframe, raising one leg, still holding the handle as if she was gesturing that my entry was temporarily barred. I looked at her framed in the doorway and she smiled an amused smile at me. I took it as an enticement, a lure – but then she just opened the door enough for her to slip through it. 'See you for breakfast at eight,' she said before the door closed.

With that she was gone; I stood there bemused for some moments, unsure as to what had just happened. What had seemed so crystal clear to me only moments before was now like a diffused image, out of focus. Then I allowed myself a smile; I realised that although I was the professor, she was really the one in control. She would remain so for the rest of the week.

Toby Fielding was right again. I would have to work harder with her. Damn the man.

Chapter 12.

The Journal of Ginny Farmer

27th **September 1786**. I turned eighteen last week. As I look back on the past year it is amazing how much my life has changed. I thought I was making my way in the world, becoming a ladies maid at such a young age. I had so many plans and such expectations but then I was reduced to being penniless and on the streets. No I will not say that of myself. I must admit now to being a whore but I will not become a street whore. In my short time in London I have seen these pathetic creatures, gin soaked, doing their business for only a few pence on the Strand, risking a beating from their drunken clients. Then those few pence are spent on more gin to null the pain of their pathetic existence. They will sometimes mix the gin with turpentine cause it's cheaper and a quicker way to dull the senses. No I will not become one of those. Old before my time, to be fished out of the river before I am thirty with no one to mourn me.

I have moved in with Beth and it's nice to share with her again. She is not the brightest of girls but she has a heart of gold, although it is also plain to see how streetwise she has become since becoming a whore. I must copy that if I am to gain advancement. What a strange thing I have just written. I was going to cross it out but I will let it be. I am still looking for advancement yet I am a whore. I will leave it there as a reminder to myself. If life has at present cast me in the role of a cock and hen whore then so be it, but I will not settle for that. I will make my way in the world somehow. The Foundlings Hospital always told us that we were lowly and that we should know our place. Why am I so different. Why can I not accept what I am. Why do I always think about advancing myself.

Despite the repeated warnings from Beth about Samuel he has been to see me every week since we first met and each time he has paid me a half a sovereign, which is much more than the four or five shillings I get from the other young gentlemen. He also took me to Marylebone Fields last Sunday as a sort of birthday present. The Fields and Gardens took my breath away they were so beautiful, not at all like the smelly streets of

London. It was a sunny day and there were crowds of people of all ranks. There were many of the meanly clad vagabonds that are so common on the streets of London, but also working tradesman and merchants and even some sporting gentlemen of rank, for there was entertainment to suit the widest of tastes. Ball games and animal baiting were popular and <u>throwing at cocks</u> was a particular favourite. A cock was tethered to a stake, and for a penny anyone could throw a short wooden club at it. Samuel offered to pay for me to try and hit it but I did not like the idea of it. The winner was the man who killed it and took the dead bird as his prize. I felt sorry for the poor bird but everybody else seemed to find it funny every time it was hit.

I loved the cries of the vendors that rang out, and their enticing smells filled the air. Fresh hot, cried the tea vendor. Hot spiced ginger, answered the vendor of another hot drink. It was so exciting to hear it all. Ring bell, cried the muffins man, and Penny a lot, answered the fishwife selling her oysters. If I had have known about this park I'm sure that I would have made more than the measly six pence that I was making on the streets selling my oranges and nuts. The day was wonderful and I walked on Samuel's arm which made me feel so good as well. He bought us both a hot eel pie from the pie vendor and we ate them from our hands. I ate it but I have to confess it was not to my taste, but Samuel devoured his as if it were some delicacy. I said to Samuel that I was surprised that so many people of different ranks were about and he told me that they had come to see the fights. He walked me over to a mound where a ring had been erected surrounded by seating for the rich sporting gentlemen. There was a bill poster pronouncing the contestants, like the ones you see outside the theatres. Samuel asked me to read it.

AT MARYLEBONE FIELDS THIS PREFENT SUNDAY, BEING THE 22nd DAY OF SEPTEMBER, THERE WILL BE PERFORMED A TRYAL OF SKILL BY THE FOLLOWING MAFTERS.

Whereas I Michael O'Connor from Ireland, mafter of the Noble Science of Defence having heard the bragging that the young upstart Samuel Medina has been making, am fully perfuaded that if my proper method be executed against him he will not be able to stand against me. For a tryal of which I now invite him to meet me and fight upon the stage.

I Samuel Medina, from Bethnal Green London, mafter of the said Noble Science of Defence, to give the said Michael O'Connor an opportunity of putting his proper method into execution, will not fail to meet him at the place and time appointed. Hoping the spectators may from thence receive entire satisfaction, affuring them beforehand that the method I shall make use of will be the way of my new style of fighting.

I looked round at Samuel and saw a huge grin on his face. You, you are fighting today I said. He nodded, that grin still stuck on his face. When I asked when, he said he was next on in about half an hour. His brother Solomon came to look after me while he went to change, and found me a seat with a good view. When he came into the ring he was stripped to the waist wearing only a pair of breeches and some athletic slippers, but his skin was all oiled up and I thought he looked magnificent, just like that bronze statue that the master had in his hall. I thought that he looked so much bigger with his clothes off but then I saw his opponent, this Michael O'Connor, and felt a cold fear rush all over my skin. He was a huge man and must have stood five feet eleven with long arms in proportion to his size and must have weighed sixteen stones at least, if much of it carried around his ample middle. Samuel looked like a boy beside him and I feared for him.

Solomon must have seen my fear and told me not to worry, that the big brute was too old and too slow to land a punch on Samuel, and when the fight started, Samuel was indeed too quick for him. Every time the big Irishman threw a punch Samuel just sidestepped to his right or his left. But after a few moments of this I could not watch any more. All I could think of was if that big brute landed a punch it would no doubt kill poor Samuel. So I buried my head in my hands for the whole fight. I could hear the crowd getting louder and more excited and then I heard the referee start counting. This happened two or three times until finally he reached ten and then cried <u>ten and out</u>. I peeped through my fingers expecting the worse but saw Samuel with his arms raised and the big man lying on the canvas floor. Solomon said that Samuel had exhausted his opponent with his agility and then given him a terrible beating. There was blood everywhere. It was on the canvas and also all down Samuel's chest but Solomon said that it was the Irishman's blood and not Samuel's. Despite my dislike of the fight it was a wonderful day out, but I don't think I want to watch him fight again and I told him so.

After the fight we went to a tavern with his brother and his military friend John Campbell-John to celebrate and then to count up his takings. I have never seen so much money. His share of the purse was two thirds as the winner and that alone was forty guineas, but they also had something called noggins. These were the coins that the sporting gentlemen threw into the ring to show their appreciation of a good fight. The coins were stacked into neat little piles to count them and this added another five pounds fifteen shillings to the total. And then Samuel looked at John Campbell-John and asked him how the book had run and he said that it had run hard against him. I didn't know what this meant but I assumed that this was a bad thing but all three seemed pleased with this. I waited until the last moment said John Campbell-John until you were in the ring and the bookmakers could see the difference in size, and they were willing to give me five to one against you. At this he took a bulging purse from his tunic and triumphantly thumped it on the table. He had wagered 15 guineas on Samuel's behalf and one guinea for Solomon. He then counted out gleefully 75 guineas for Samuel and five guineas for Solomon. I now realised why they had insisted that the landlord find them a cubicle to drink in. They did not want the others to see all this money, although it would be a brave man indeed to tackle Samuel for his purse.

And how much did you wager John, asked Samuel. The military man sat back in his chair for some moments gloating before he replied. Everything I had, he then said. I saw Samuel and Solomon lean forward expectantly. How much asked Samuel. Fifty guineas said John Campbell-John. FIFTY shouted Samuel and then looked round fearing that he would be overheard. You have won two hundred and fifty guineas. He just nodded, grinning from ear to ear. I have never seen such sums, they had as much money I should think as the very wealthiest of merchants. They counted everything out and John took another twenty per cent of Samuel's purse as his manager in addition to his betting winnings.

I asked this John Campbell-John why he had wagered everything he had and he told me that it was a once in a lifetime chance. He knew after this fight that the bookmakers would know that Samuel was capable of beating much bigger men even if they were skilled fighters. At the next fight he would struggle to get even money. Even so, to wager your life savings on a single fight seems foolhardy to me. I hope Samuel can trust this man.

Afterwards Samuel walked me home. He started to talk and it was obvious the sweet man was concerned about me becoming a Mabel. He offered to set me up in a business and it is difficult to understand how such a kind man can be such a brutal one fighting in the ring. You can see how much I am earning at the moment he said so I can afford to do so. I didn't know what to say and there was silence for a time, and then he said something that took my breath away. I can't offer you marriage he said cause as a Jew I need to honour my father and mother and that means that I will marry within my religion. Marriage, the very fact that he thought of me enough to even consider it was overwhelming to me. I welled up and he put his arm around me when he saw that. Come on lass he said, there is no need for that.

What about a milliners or dressmakers. I can find you a partner who will teach you all the skills. It was a wonderful offer but I found myself turning him down. I may come to regret that but I felt that I would be taking advantage of his kindness to do so. And he had been drinking and that may have loosened his tongue more than he intended. Yes, I may come to regret this.

31st January 1787. I have some marvellous news. Samuel has rented a furnished house for me and has paid the rent for six months. He says it will only stand empty if I don't take it so I have decided to accept the offer. I now have so many plans in my mind.

8th February 1787. Samuel took me to see the house at 22 Rathbone Place today. It is in a good neighbourhood and is much grander than I expected, being in a terrace of recently built houses, each one symmetrical and built in what Samuel told me is the classical style that he admired, of stuccoed brick to look like stone, with columns, decorative plaster mouldings and paned sash windows. Samuel is very well read I am finding out. The houses on the eastern side are set back in gardens, at the northern end are a pond and windmill, and will be wonderful for a morning constitutional, although you have to pay the miller a halfpenny to walk in his grounds. Samuel himself has bought a house just down the street at number 6 and says that it had always been his ambition to become a man of property. Inside number 22 the furnishing looked as though it had belonged to an independent gentleman of means. It is elegant but it is not what I have in mind.

I have purchased a copy of the directory published by Mr. Jack Morris. It is a directory for gentlemen about town and lists many of the Mabels in London, their addresses and the services they offer. The bookseller was taken aback I feel at my request, but at the sight of my coins he went into the back and when he returned he was willing to accept my money. The directory makes very interesting reading and it seems that the Mabel's of London offer a wide variety of services to suite every taste. I have decided that I will play the role of a young innocent virgin, a cherry ripe for the picking and advertise myself as such. It will be a transparent illusion of course and the gentlemen will realise this if they care to think about it, but my youthful looks will help me maintain the illusion. The quality of this house has put another thought into my mind. If I also play the role of a young lady of breeding and social standing, that will add a spice for the gentlemen clients I am sure. I think I will become Lady Virginia of Rathbone Place. I will have to change some of this furniture to make it more feminine, or I will do when I get the funds. And so that my clients can be entertained from a suitable house I will also offer tea and genteel conversation. I will charge two guineas, or maybe I should start at one guinea and see how it goes. Rathbone Place is on the north side of Oxford Street opposite Soho square so it is a very fashionable area and is convenient for the right sort of gentlemen.

I will need a wardrobe, but it must be fashionable to maintain the illusion, not the gaudy clothes that the cock and hen Mabels wear. I will design them myself and have them made up by the Jewish merchants in Monmouth Street, although I may have to start with second hand clothes from Rosemary Lane and alter them myself.

What shall I do with Beth. I desperately want her to accompany me but she does not really fit in with my plans. I think I will suggest she too plays a role, that of a country wench I think. Yes that will be a part that she can play well, for her Bristol accent proclaims that anyway. So 22 Rathbone Place will be both the address of a virginal young lady and country wench.

25th April 1787. My new business has started well if slowly. Money is coming in and the word I feel is starting to get around about the services offered at 22 Rathbone Place. I took only one guinea in the first week but by last week, our third week, I had taken four guineas. Beth is charging half a sovereign and she has added a full sovereign now to her name. She says that it is gert lush to be able to charge a half sovereign. She will never change and I love her for that, and anyway the words fit in with the illusion of a country wench and if her clients do not understand some of her sayings it all adds to the illusion.

My own illusion, however, I think could be better. I can mimic well a few phrases in a genteel accent. But when I try to converse with a gentleman I struggle to keep it going and my Bristol accent starts to seep through like water escaping from a hole in a bucket. So I have enrolled this week to take elocution lessons and for one shilling and fourpence a week a Miss Pilcher has agreed to instruct me in the finer ways of society. I hadn't realised how bad my speech was, for this lady sighed heavily at our first lesson at my poor grammar. She said that it would be pointless improving my pronunciation and enunciation if my grammar is all over the place. So she is instructing me in that as well.

I have always been used to working so very hard from early morning to late at night but now I seem to have so much time on my hands. I still have that habit of rising early. Beth is so grateful to me that she has taken on the role of maid and cleaner without my asking and will not hear of me doing any of the housework. Yesterday she answered the door to a gentleman and she bobbed a curtsy to <u>me</u> when she showed him into the drawing room. I had to suppress a giggle before I could greet him. But I have resolved to use this free time wisely. I have subscribed for two daily newspapers. I will apprise myself of events of the day so that I can converse with my gentleman over tea. It will be good to have an unwrinkled copy of the newspaper, not the master's old one having being read by several others before me and many days old. Yes I intend to offer my gentlemen companionship as well as the delights of Venus. I also intend to be a regular at the booksellers for the same purpose and I have to confess I am developing a thirst for knowledge. I have already made several visits to Mr. Joseph Johnson's bookshop of St. Paul's Churchyard.

1st **June 1787.** Miss Pilcher is amazed at my progress in just over a month. I had told her at the beginning that I was a bright girl and a quick learner, although I hadn't told her of my talent for mimicry, but she had obviously not believed me before. Today I visited her in a new fashionable gown that I have had made by the Jewish merchants in Monmouth Street. Her eyebrows rose at the sight of me. I had used eau de citron to blanch my face to a delicate paleness, although I did not need much because I am pale anyway, but this set off my new bonnet. My dress looked fashionable and expensive, but tasteful and elegant, and I wore a cape around my shoulders. The neckline was also fashionably low, but there was only a hint of cleavage, the skin on my breasts being equally blanched.

'My, you have the natural poise of a lady of breeding and I do believe that you could probably fool most people,' said Miss Pilcher. Then she must have realised that her fees were at stake and added, 'but you must keep learning to complete the illusion, my dear.' So I am learning more about commas and semi-colons and apostrophes and possession and all sorts of grammatical devices.

At home Beth treats me as the mistress of the house. I seem to have transformed before her eyes and she does it willingly.

The Journal of Corbyn Carlisle

2ⁿᵈ **December 1787.** I dined with Dick Upstanding last evening· He still prompts me to call him that although I tried hard all evening to call him Richard, but he would have none of it· He has stood the cost of many an evening's victuals for me in the past and on one occasion even stood for me the cost of a Mabel· Many an evening's drinking with John Barleycorn were also down to him and it was time I repaid him· I had been putting it off for some time, fearing where an evening with Richard might lead to·

I took him to my new club, Brooks's on St James Street which has a fine restaurant and is one of the highest establishments in London· It is a meeting place for Whigs of the highest social order and I have decided that it shall be the place for me, although I have not really taken an interest in politics before· We dined at seven and I thought that the fine surroundings might rub off on Richard, but his conversation was as ever low and mainly surrounded his exploits with the ladies; he hardly touched on his lawyering studies· He seems to spend as little time at his studies as ever he did and does almost no work at Chambers, still being the lowliest of tutees not trusted with anything of any import· Other than breaking off to ask if it was indeed Horace Walpole dining at the next table to us, his bragging conversations surrounded all the women he has managed to tupp since we last met and according to him there has been a considerable number· Like me he was not the firstborn, but his father has given him a generous allowance so that he can make his way in the world through the legal profession, but he shows little inclination to do so.

After we dined, we both sat back in our chairs and loosened the top button on our breeches, so much had we eaten; I called for cognacs, and we exchanged snuff, though I must confess I found his blend much too spicy for my taste; but then that is typical of the man.

'Will they allow me at the gaming tables on your surety, Corbyn?' he asked, and I could see that his mind was running ahead to some rakish antics for the rest of the evening. I explained that however generous his father's allowance was, the amounts wagered here were too rich for him, and for me if I did indeed stand surety for him. Brooks's club itself keeps a book of all the wagers that are made between members so that there can be no doubt in the sober view of morning what wagers had been made. It is not uncommon here for the gaming rooms to be busy all night with prodigious amounts gambled.

Richard seemed a little crestfallen at first by my explanations, but then after a few moments' thought his countenance changed and a great grin seemed to cut his handsome face in two. He leant forward and resoundingly patted my back making me spill some of the fine cognac.

'But the night is still young, Corbyn my fine fellow,' he said, 'what shall we do; a drinking club or perhaps a music hall?'

I have to confess that both sounded enticing, especially the night's supping, for it is a while since I had such a night. So we went to the Kings Head, an alehouse near to my old service lodgings off Fleet Street. There we met many of my old drinking companions still, like Richard, under instruction at Chambers. I have recently taken a liking to Claret, the landlord was able to come up with a remarkably good bottle of it, and so I abandoned my friendship with John Barleycorn's ale for my other capricious friend the fruit of the vine. Such an evening was just what I wanted and I was beginning to wonder why I had put off such an evening's revelry with Richard. At about thirty after eleven of the clock however, I was thinking of my bed, but for Richard it seemed the night was still young; his thoughts were turning to other entertainment.

'Shall we go wenching, Corbyn my fine fellow?' he said, 'we haven't done that together for such a long time.'

This was what I was afraid of; that I would end up at some disreputable bawdy house run by some gin sodden old madam offering a drink of purl with a poke as the house speciality. 'No thank you,' I said, 'I am away to my bed, my friend.'

But he would not have it and despite my protestations I agreed to go to a very special place that he had found with just me in mind. To my surprise, he took me to a fashionable house in Rathbone Place. I stood outside with him for a few moments; we exchanged glances and I noticed a satisfied smile on his face. 'Is this in keeping with your new status, my lord,' he said.

'Aye it is a fine town house,' I said, 'but who lives here? Where have you brought me?'

'I've brought you wenching, Corbyn, as I have promised.' He paused for a moment I could see, to check on my reaction, but then said, 'But a special form of wenching tonight.'

'So who exactly lives here then?' I asked. I was curious but not a little exasperated with his performance.

'Two fine young ladies, one for me and one for you my friend.' He was becoming more and more pompous in his role-playing. It was as though he was the chairman at the music hall introducing the next act. 'For you, Corbyn, there is Lady Virginia, a beautiful virginal lady of fine breeding, and for me there is Beth the country wench.'

'Oh, this is intolerable, Richard,' I said and then turned to walk away. He ran after me and took my arm. 'How can a Mabel be a virgin?' I said, shaking him off.

'She can be anything you want her to be, Corbyn. You have to enter into the spirit of the fantasy. In mine tonight, I will be the squire accepting the favours of a country wench, and yours – well that is for you to decide.'

I don't know why I agreed to go in, but I did. The door was answered by a plump young woman with chubby rouged cheeks, wearing what I presume was a milkmaid's outfit. She bobbed a curtsy at the sight of us and bid us to enter. Her accent was thick with a West Country twang, but what was clear to me was that we were expected.

'Ah Beth,' said Richard, 'you are well I presume?'

'Aye zir, I am very well thank ee zir,' she said. It was obvious where the girl was from.

We were led into the drawing room and I confess I went with some resistance, but when I entered, it was a delight with a touch of feminine elegance. I looked around me, I confess, in a most ungallant way, but I did not expect that I would need to display my manners that evening. But then I saw, sitting in a corner, the most delightful creature that I think I have ever seen. I was lost for words for a moment as I stared at her. Richard, I think, saw my reaction and a conceited expression betrayed his smugness. He had got the reaction from me that he wanted, but at that moment I didn't care.

'May I introduce my good friend Corbyn,' he said as if addressing a fine lady, 'Corbyn, this is Lady Virginia.'

She nodded the slightest demure nod in my direction, and held out her hand. Without thinking I walked over and took it, kissed it with the very best of my manners.

'Will you take tea with me, Mr. Corbyn?' she said looking up at me with the bluest of blue eyes.

'Why thank you, my lady,' I said in my most gallant voice, 'that would be a pleasure, Lady Virginia.'

'And what about you, Mr. Richard?' she said, turning to look at my self-satisfied friend.

I shot a sheepish look in his direction and he took notice of my unspoken words.

'Thank you, no,' he said, 'I think I will retire with Miss Beth for my pleasure this evening.

'As you wish,' she nodded, 'but do you mind if she serves us tea before she attends to you?'

'Not at all, Lady Virginia,' he gestured with the slightest bow of his head.

To my relief I was left alone with Lady Virginia. She poured the tea and placed the cup and saucer before me. As she did so I took the opportunity to look at her. She was small of stature, slender, but with a natural poise. Her hair was arranged high with ringlets, though not so high as to take the eye away from her face. Her skin was delicately pale, and her expression demure. Her dress was tasteful and elegant, to all intents she was a lady of the finest breeding, and I lamented inwardly wondering what had brought a fine lady such as her so far down in the world that she is now a lowly Mabel offering her services for money.

I was reminded of that dream I sometimes have where I am married to a pretty wife. Our house is clean; I am in my elegant dining room, light green walls divided by a dado rail, a marble fire-surround, windows curtained, and with candles mounted in sconces backed by mirrors to reflect the light. There is a fine quality tablecloth freshly laundered, and I am taking tea from delicate porcelain cups, with my sweet wife. Her hair is rather inclined to fair than brown, and she has a healthy complexion. She is neat in her person, polite, and delicate of speech.

I looked about me in some wonder. There was the fine quality tablecloth freshly laundered, there were the delicate porcelain cups. There was the marble fire-surround, the candles mounted in sconces backed by mirrors to reflect the light. And most of all there was this fine young lady who was just like the wife in my dream. Richard Standing! I thought to myself, do you really comprehend what you have done for me?

And then she astounded me even more.

'Have you read this morning's article in The Times about the Irish question, Mr. Corbyn?' she said.

'Aye I have, and it was most interesting reading indeed,' I replied. And then we discussed it at length and I was most surprised that she supported the call for Irish home rule put forward by Mr. Henry Grattan. I was aghast at her grasp of the problem and I found her arguments most persuasive that the Irish Catholics feel disinherited in their own country, and confess that I have changed my own view on this vexed question. But then the conversation turned to the arts and literature. This lady is so well read and a delight in conversation. Certainly not like the prospective wives that Emily would have me marry, empty-headed, however well bred they are.

Richard came back downstairs and made no attempt to show his irritation with me. Lady Virginia and I were still talking, and he made it very clear, without actually using the words, that I was letting him down by not taking advantage of what he had found for me. I looked at my pocket watch and was amazed to find that I had been talking for over an hour. But I was taking advantage of what he had found for me; I was in heaven without him knowing it.

'It is time that we took our leave, Corbyn,' there was irritation *in his voice.*

'You go, my good friend,' I said, 'I think I will stay a little longer in the delightful company of Lady Virginia.'

He shot me a look that expressed his disappointment in me, but I didn't care. 'Very well,' he said and left us as I had bid.

'You can go to your bed now Beth if you wish,' said Lady Virginia to her maid. We were left alone and we talked for another two hours. I told her that I was a poet and she expressed a wish to read my work. She said that she had little appreciation of poetry, reading mostly literary fiction, but was eager to learn more about it. I gave her a short list of my favourite poets that she might read and she said she would visit her bookseller immediately.

I seemed to lose track of time as we spoke together. I saw her look to her mantle clock and I, too, saw that it was after three of the clock; I was amazed at how the time had flown.

'It is getting late, Mr. Corbyn is it not?'

'Aye 'tis, Lady Virginia,' I replied. I was then taken with embarrassment. This was no low Mabel to casually flick a sovereign with my thumb in her direction. I didn't know how to settle payment. I fumbled with my purse, but she leant across and put her hand on mine.'

'Later, Corbyn' she said. 'I mean the business that you have come here for.'

'Oh,' I mumbled. I had forgotten all about that.

'If you take me abed, then I hope that you will be gentlemanly with me, sir, for I am new to all this.'

'Of course, my lady,' I said. I'd like to say that I was playing my part in the fantasy but that would be a lie. I was playing no part; I was reacting as if it was real; and it was marvellous.

She led me to her boudoir, and it was the most feminine of rooms. The sheets were freshly laundered and there was a fragrance of orange blossom. A fashionable tester bed, with decorated drapes above the head; there was a smart carpet from the new Wilton factory. She then retired to her changing room, but bid me wait for her in the bed, so I quickly disrobed and slid between the cool linen sheets. An apprehension suddenly took me and I felt my heart start to pound in my chest. It had been some time since I had been wenching, and it had never been the most successful endeavour on my part. But then that apprehension subsided, this was so far from wenching that it felt perfectly normal; it was as though this was right for me· Lady Virginia returned wearing her robe; she smiled a demure smile at me, then turned and the robe fell from her shoulders to reveal the merest glimpse of her slender nakedness before she slipped quickly in beside me·

It was as if that dream I had, had come true· She caressed me tenderly; I felt her soft lips and sweet breath, and her yielding kisses lingered long on my lips· I felt the arousal of Venus within me and I was a true man with all my youthful vigour· Afterwards she lay in my arms, stroking my chest and we drifted off to sleep together, warm beneath the clean fresh-smelling sheets·

I stayed until morning; she lay contentedly in my arms· We breakfasted together; hot buttered toast and a pot of hot chocolate· It was no gourmet feast and yet it was like ambrosia to me· I too felt as immortal as those ancient Greek gods· Oh, how I longed to stay all the next day, but I had an engagement at Chambers· Even the indelicate business of payment was lessened by her charm and good manners·

Oh, but I must see this fine young lady again·

Chapter 13.

The Journal of Ginny Farmer

2ᴺᴰ **December 1787.** I had a new client last evening. No, from now on I shall call them my gentlemen, and he was indeed the most gentlemanly of gentlemen. I know him only as Mr. Corbyn, his Christian name I think, but he stayed for hours and we had the most stimulating conversation together. In fact he stayed all night and even in bed and in the throngs of Venus he was at all times still the most perfect gentleman. This is the sort of gentleman that I wish to encourage. He is clearly a man of some considerable intellect, and my reading has therefore not been in vain. I was able to converse with him on several subjects and I am sure that I was a companion to him as well as a whore. In fact I had to encourage him to the bedroom as I am sure that he was so delighted with my company that he had quite forgotten the main reason for his call altogether.

14ᵗʰ **January 1788.** The new year has started well for me. I have another new gentleman client and he is of the very highest of rank; the very highest rank indeed. He is Lord Dalby, the Earl of Holderness. He has an extensive estate in Yorkshire and is also a Member of Parliament and part of the government itself, as well as a personal friend of the Prime Minister. He does indeed move in very elevated circles and if I am to believe what he tells me he is one of Mr. Pitt's closest advisors. But then why should he lie to me, he has no reason to do so to a whore. Oh I do hate that word.

I have to admit that I was stretched to converse with him on political matters, but I did my best and I seemed to have impressed him. I thought I may have overstepped the mark, however, in expressing some of my views. I think I am inclined more to Whig thinking and he is a Tory.

24ᵗʰ **January 1788.** Lord Dalby has been back to see me twice in the last two weeks. I must have impressed him even if my thinking is not in tune with his. He is a tall, slimly built man, but with a natural swagger about him. He is, I think, approaching forty, but has only a touch of grey at the temples which looks most becoming on him. He still has that youthful vigour about him and not that soused pot-bellied look that most of the very high gentlemen of his age seem to have. Such men seem to display their corpulence and endless chins as some sort of badge of their wealth. When he was first introduced to me, there was a condescending tone to his voice, which I accepted without offence for he is such a high-born gentleman, but at our last meeting, dare I say, I was delighted to find that he no longer seemed to patronise me. I flatter myself to think so. His features are angular, a slightly pointed nose and chin which I first thought gave him a haughty look, but that look now seems to have softened, towards me at least, and he is most eager to talk both before and after our couplings. At his last visit he said that I may call him John when we are alone together.

That delightful Mr. Corbyn has been to see me again. He says that he has been up at his country estate in Nottinghamshire, but he had rushed back after Christmas just to see me. He is in fact Corbyn Carlisle, Baron Elloughton. That means that I have now two lords as my gentlemen. My clientele may be small, but it is certainly most distinguished. He is much less grand than Lord Dalby; he, too, insists that I call him by his Christian name and not "My Lord," but he made no stipulation that I only do this when we are alone. Corbyn is very hard to describe. He is neither tall nor is he short, he is neither slender nor is he sturdy, neither handsome nor homely. He is a man that you would pass in the street and not really notice. He is most gentlemanly, however, and a charming companion who seems to delight in my company.

My new profession is going as well as I could have ever hoped for.

18th March 1788. Today has taken a much unexpected turn. Corbyn sent around a note this morning which asked if I was free to accompany him in the early afternoon to his fencing club. The last time that I saw him he was keen to tell me all about his skills with the sword and I mentioned that it would be nice to see him fence one day. It was no more than a politeness on my part, but he has taken me at my word. I sent my agreement back with the messenger and he called to pick me up at three of the clock. I made a great effort not to let him down and I am sure that my appearance was ladylike and elegant. He was keen to take me on his arm and at his fencing club introduced me as Lady

Virginia, and I am pleased to say that I was accepted at face value by all there, both tutor and gentleman athletes alike.

It was the most energetic of places. The gymnasium smelt of sweat, but it was manly sweat and not unpleasant. Corbyn instructed me on some of the moves, lunge and parry. The aim, it seems, is to make a touch on the opponent's torso to score a hit. He showed me his sword, but I was to call it a blade not a sword, and more specifically a foil. This is used for sport instead of the actual duelling sword because it is lighter and faster and was originally developed as a practice weapon. Corbyn seemed so proud of his prowess and most eager that I know all about it. I did my best to be attentive, but much of the terminology was like a foreign language to me, much of it actually was, because Corbyn explained that this was the French style of fencing and used that language. I think it might be good if I also take some French lessons, as well as my elocution lessons, as all these gentlemen seem proficient in it.

Corbyn fought an exhibition with his tutor, a Monsieur Lievremont. Corbyn looked quite dashing in his breeches and linen shirt, open at the neck without his stock, worn beneath a protective jacket, but with his billowing sleeves escaping and flapping as he moved so speedily. It was so exciting; much more so than I had expected. So fast and elegant; lunge and parry. I began to see Mr. Corbyn in a very different light and that mask he wore made him look quite sinister. He seemed much manlier than the person that I thought I knew. I knew him as a refined gentleman, but if I am honest, a slightly timid one. But here was a most virile man before me. So thrilling was the contest that I began to fear for his safety, but afterwards he showed me the blade. The point, or the blossom as he called it, had been blunted by fastening a knob to it so that it would not penetrate the flesh, but it still looked dangerous to me.

He walked me home on his arm, and it was as if I returned with a different gentleman to the one I had set out with.

25th **April 1788**. Lord John Dalby took me out this evening in public. I dressed in my finest clothes and was on my best behaviour, making sure that my Bristol vowels did not seep through, so that I could be the most charming companion to him. I was paraded on his arm and he seemed to be recognised by everyone. They would have known, of course, that I was not his wife, but I was keen to give the impression that I was his mistress and no common whore. I was probably seen as his courtesan rather than a fine-born mistress, but if so, that is a position which I am happy to take on. Whatever, I was treated with respect, even if I was seen as having lower social status than most of the people we met and I could see from the jut of Lord Dalby's jaw that he was happy to have me on his arm.

We went to Astley's amphitheatre on Westminster Bridge Road in Lamberth to see the circus. Mr. Astley himself entertained us with his bareback trick riding skills. I actually saw with my own eyes him picking up handkerchiefs from the ground while cantering, then doing headstands on his saddle, and even riding astride two horses while playing a pipe. I put my hand to my mouth, as I was sure that he would fall off. There were galleries for the spectators, but we sat in a box of our own in the centre of the house and had a fine view of Mr. Astley as he performed in a circular pit in front of the stage. But we also saw clowns and ropewalkers, and the evening finished with fireworks and waterworks to the delight of everybody present who cheered Mr. Astley at the end of the evening. It has been a wonderful evening. Lord John was most vigorous when we returned; he is staying the night and is now sound asleep. I could not sleep myself until I had made my journal entry.

30th April 1788. Samuel came to see me this morning unexpectedly. Mr. Corbyn was still with me, having stayed all night, and we were still taking breakfast and reading the morning papers together. I was a little concerned at first how they would both take to each other, but I need not have worried as they got on like a house on fire. Beth politely asked Samuel to wait and enquired if I was free, but Corbyn said that he would be honoured to meet the famous young pugilist that he had heard so much about. I am so pleased, as they have both become dear to me in the short time I have known them.

They engaged in a heated debate about the merits of boxing and fencing, and Samuel said that he had studied the techniques of fencing in arriving at his new unique style of boxing, moving in and out of range along a diagonal, in order to land a punch and then retreat without being hit. I hope that I have understood that correctly. I sipped my tea and returned to my newspaper after a while, as they seemed happy to converse with each other.

Corbyn said that he knew from his lawyering work that the streets of London were not always the safest place and that a gentleman could be relieved of his purse at any time by a knife-wielding ruffian, but since returning to his fencing skills he felt much safer and happy that he could defend himself if necessary, and he carried a swordstick with him at all times. Samuel, however, advanced the theory that the sword was not a close-quarter instrument and that he should learn also how to handle the cudgel and that he would be happy to teach him. They went off together this very day to start the tuition.

The Journal of Corbyn Carlisle

30th April 1788. I visited the charming Lady Virginia yesterday and again stayed overnight in her delightful company. This morning, as we were breakfasting and reading the morning papers, she had a call from that famous young pugilist Samuel Medina; he is a most remarkable man, not at all what I expected. I have to confess that I thought such fighting men just big brutes that traded their strength against each other until the strongest prevailed. But here was an educated, articulate young man who explained the skills to me that are necessary in his profession. The best of them are given the title of Master of the Noble Science of Self Defence. He has taught a number of the sons of the gentry how to defend themselves and it is one of his ambitions to open an academy for that purpose when his own fighting days are over.

I told him that I was developing my own skills as a fencer for that very purpose of defending myself and the conversation came round to fencing skills. His own fighting skills it seems have been developed from his own study of fencing and we talked at length about such tactics; surprisingly we had much in common. But there were words of warning from him that I should be careful on the streets; the rapier may not be the best weapon of defence as it cannot be deployed at very close quarters. I now see what he means; if I am set upon by ruffians, there may be no space to draw my sword.

'The cudgel is what you need, sir,' he roared, patting my upper arm forcefully, 'and I am just the man to teach you.'

Well we went off this very morning to his gymnasium for tuition. Samuel has taught me that, although the cudgel is a peasant weapon, basically just a stout stick, this does not mean that it cannot be used with consummate skill. The ruffian will use it merely with a clubbing motion bringing it down on their victim's head, but it is a fine defensive weapon, especially when in a confined space. It can be wielded quickly, with both a forehand and backhand motion, particularly aimed at wrists and knees; it can quickly disable one man, giving time to take out a second. Because I had fencing skills I was easily able to convert them to the use of this cudgel. Most gentlemen who favour it would carry a long cudgel, which doubles as a walking staff, but he has provided me with a short cudgel that I can conceal beneath my frock coat and advises that I should have it on me at all times when I take to the streets.

23rd May 1788. Oh but these last few months, I feel, have been the happiest of my life. Since meeting Lady Virginia I am complete as a man. She is such a fragrant creature and the most delightful of companions. I suppose that is an odd thing to say of a Mabel, for I know what she is, but she has become so important in my life. It is so terrible that such a fine-born lady has fallen so low, yet I must also applaud her resilience that she has found a way to support herself.

I have visited my mother today and spent the day with her at her cottage in Newark. She lives frugally, but she was in the best of spirits and commented on my spirits also. I think she saw that there may be a lady in my life and teased me so for it, but I was, of course, forced to deny it. I could not tell her that I am visiting a Mabel regularly. I arrived last night and will also stay over tonight and then travel on to Elloughton Park tomorrow. Mother looks years younger and has taken to painting the local scenes in watercolours, something that she had done before she married, but father discouraged almost everything she did. She also has a gentleman caller, a widowed clergyman by the name of Herbert Millican. He has dined with us tonight and he seems a fine chap; he is well educated and they have intellectual pursuits in common. The conversation at dinner came round to my future. Following my denial, mother was anxious to know if I had thought about marriage and if I had anyone in mind. Stupidly, Virginia came to mind again and I longed to tell her all about her, but of course, I realise that I could not possibly marry so far beneath me and I had to hold my tongue, saying that I had charged Emily with finding me a suitable bride. I don't think she was too enamoured with my plan.

24th May 1788. I arrived at Elloughton Park at just after four of the clock. I had sent word ahead that I would be coming down, but I sensed immediately that something was wrong from the demeanour of the butler as he took my greatcoat from me.

'Is everything well in the household, Whittaker?' I asked.

'Yes everything is well, my lord,' he said, but I could see some awkwardness in his eyes, 'but Mr. Cavendish is at home. He is on leave from his regiment I understand,' he continued sheepishly.

'Is he behaving himself?' I said the words without really thinking about what I was saying, but they prompted Whittaker's expression to harden. He was clearly uncomfortable with something.

'Well, my lord...' He started to speak, but then he seemed unsure of himself.

'Oh come on, Whittaker,' I said, beginning to be irritated, 'I know very well what my halfbrother is like. Out with it man; what's he done? I take it he has been bossing the servants about?'

'Well, – yes, my lord,' he said, 'but that's not it.' I gave him a look to tell him that it was all right to go on. 'He has been here a week sir, but he insisted on having the master bedroom, your bedroom sir. When I informed him that you would be arriving today he told me to have another bedroom made ready for you.'

'Has he indeed?' I said. I found myself rubbing my chin in contemplation. 'Is he at home now?' I asked.

'Yes, my lord, he's in the great hall with Lady Emily.'

I walked straight through to the great hall where I found them before a roaring fire, despite it being late spring, with no concern for the expense; they were both drunk, Cavendish on my port and Emily on my brandy. Cavendish lounged over a high-backed chair in his military uniform with his booted leg trailing over the armrest. It was a position that I had seen Father adopt so many times. I could see Father in him, broad of shoulder, blond hair, square chinned and a gap-tooth grin. Emily sat facing him, just nodding into insensibility. He heard my footsteps and assumed that I was the butler whom he had rung for, not realising that he was attending to me.

'Ah, Whittaker,' he yelled without looking up, 'about time, man. Bring me another bottle of port will you and his lordship's good stuff if you please·'

'And should he bring a glass for his lordship as well?' I said as sarcastically as I could·

He looked up at me, then sat up and kicked Emily's foot, bringing her back into life· 'Look who's here, Emily,' he said, 'it's our little brother come home to play at being lord of the manor·' There was contempt in his eyes; that contempt that I had seen so many times as I was growing up· A contempt that said that he belonged here, but I did not·

Emily started to laugh· He joined in as though it was the wittiest thing he had ever said·

'Go and find what has happened to that lazy butler will you, Corbyn old chap,' he said, his hand gesturing as if to dismiss me·

'There will be no more port for you today, Cavendish,' I said, 'and you will tell Whittaker to move your things to another bedroom if you please; your old room, I think·' I was surprised that there was no fear in me· Both Cavendish and Carlton had bullied me when I was growing up and I continued to be cowed by them even as an adult; but now I felt a different man somehow·

'I think not, little brother,' he said and then turned to Emily and laughed robustly, prompting her to join in· 'Our little brother actually thinks he can order us about, does he?' he said· He turned back to me· 'Just toddle off and get me some of your best port, will you,' he added contemptuously· He made that hand gesture again as if to dismiss me and that set my dander up·

I stood upright before him, legs apart and crossed my arms over my chest·

'You were never the sharpest pencil in the box were you, Cavendish?' I said, the words spitting from my mouth, 'slow witted, and needing a prompt to keep you up with the conversation· Well take this as your prompt· I am now Lord Elloughton, not you· Your allowance is in my gift· If you want to be able to settle your mess fees, and knowing you I assume that they are considerable, then I suggest that you think on that before you say anything else·'

He shot me a fiery stare· I could see that the meaning of my words had not been assimilated; only the insult had penetrated his thick hide· He set his mouth hard· 'And a pitiful allowance it is, little brother· As you suspect, it does not go near to covering my mess bills.'

He went to continue but I interrupted him. 'Well even that pittance is in danger if you do not behave yourself. You should know that Elloughton Park is now a different place. It will no longer be the base for your rakish behaviour. I will not finance your gambling, your drinking, your wenching, as Carlton did. Get that into your slow witted brain if you please, sir.'

He sat up in his chair and gave me a fierce stare. I returned it and for some moments we were locked in a loathing for each other. He went to speak, set his mouth hard, but I could see that words deserted him. I saw his impotence rise, his face suffused when no words came. His eyes narrowed in a flash of anger; if belligerent words were not to be his weapon, then he would resort to belligerent action. He jumped to his feet and marched straight for me, but I did not back away. He was a good two inches taller than me and he had filled out since he had joined the army, but I, too, was not the frail youth that he used to bully. He took me by the lapels of my frock coat and pulled me up to him so that we were eyeball to eyeball. I could smell his liquor-laced breath on my face. I could see his eyes darting to my left eye and then my right, looking for fear in them. I did feel fear rise up from the pit of my stomach, but I fought hard to repress it; I stole myself in the face of his intimidation; maintained our eye contact.

And then he spoke, low, guttural. 'You will not get rid of me as easily as you got rid of my mother. I think that I need to teach you a lesson, little brother. A good whipping is what you need, me thinks.' He yelled to Emily without breaking our eye contact, 'Emily, go fetch my riding crop so that I can administer his thrashing.' Out of the corner of my eye I saw her start to get up, but then she sat back again. Some reason must have penetrated her addled brain. A reason that said she would remain when Cavendish was back with his regiment.

I now knew, however, that he would try to beat me, whether it be with whip or fist or boot. The purpose was to humiliate me, to establish dominance over me. I don't think I reasoned this out at that moment, but my instincts told me I must not submit to this. If he succeeded now, then he would always treat me this way. My right hand slipped under my frock coat instinctively and found the handle of the cudgel. Thank god for that young Mr.

Medina. I drew it, and in one movement brought it down on his right knee. I heard the crack as it struck bone and he let out a painful yell, releasing me from his grip to hold his hurting knee. He crouched, looked up at me, disbelief evident on his face. He lunged at me with both hands as if to take me by the throat, but I brought the cudgel across me with a sabre like slash onto his left wrist and then with the backhand movement of the same stroke dropped it to connect with his right knee. He fell to the floor cradling his left hand to his body and holding his right knee with his right hand whilst shouting out in pain.

'Get up, Cavendish, I have not finished with you,' I said as bold as you like. I knew I could not leave it at that. He had to be humiliated. He was helpless before me, but I could not bring myself to hit him whilst he was down. I am sure that if the roles had been reversed then he would not have hesitated to have brought his crop down on me to complete the whipping, but I waited for him to stumble to his feet. I looked into his eyes; there was still hatred there, but now mingled with some bewilderment as if he did not know what was happening to him.

He gave me a scornful laugh. 'You'll pay for this, you little turd,' he said, but his body was in no condition to make such a threat. He hobbled towards me. I only administered three more strokes; again to his right knee, his right wrist with the backhand and then the left knee again. He fell to the floor crying out in pain. I knew he was a beaten man and at that point, unexpectedly, fright suddenly returned to me from that hidden place that I had banished it to some moments before. I started to tremble.

I took some deep breaths to calm myself. Again I planted my legs apart, but now folded my arms behind my back, the cudgel still held in my right hand and the bulbous head in the palm of my left. I stood dominant over him and he looked up at me, and I could see the acceptance in his eyes.

'WHITTAKER!' I yelled out.

'Yes, my lord.' He answered immediately coming from just around the corner.

I swivelled round. He must have been spying on us. I could see also the face of a footman peering round at me. The loud words must have attracted them both.

'Will you and the footman help Mr. Cavendish to his old room please? If he has any broken bones you can send for the doctor. Whatever, he is to be out of the house by noon tomorrow. Do you understand me?'

'Oh yes, my lord,' he replied, 'by noon tomorrow.' I could hear that there was satisfaction in his voice. I had done to Cavendish what the servants would have liked to do to him.

I then looked back at Emily. There was incredulity on her pock-marked face. 'I suggest that you go and sober yourself up before dinner, Emily, if you please,' I said in a fierce whisper.

'Of course, Corbyn,' she said and scuttled off without saying another word.

I have a fine story to tell that young Mr. Medina when I see him.

Chapter 14.

I mused on Ginny and Lord Carlisle as I waited in the reception room at Brackley's Auction House. Well, well; the journals have revealed that Ginny was never a servant at Elloughton Park. That is, in some ways, a disappointment; it removes that perspective of the place from below stairs which would have been invaluable. On the other hand it is still gold dust for Grace's Master's Dissertation on social mobility.

So, the connection between Ginny and Lord Carlisle is not one of master and servant; she is in fact his whore. I agree with Ginny, the word whore is an unpleasant one and does not accurately describe what she has become. The mystery remains, however, as to why these journals are at Elloughton Park; hopefully further reading will answer that question. I am beginning to warm to Corbyn Carlisle also. He is not the wimp I thought he was.

Grace is still up at Elloughton Park just finishing off the cataloguing. Before I left, we went through the other boxes of paintings as well, mostly named, but still anonymous aristocratic heads similarly covered in years of dirt. They will be easy to research in due course to put into some sort of chronological order. I brought the picture of the hall back with me and showed it to Amanda Davies, the university's senior fine arts lecturer. She has dated it to the late eighteenth century, but could tell me little more about it. As she says, she is not a valuer and advised me that the first step was to get it professionally cleaned, so I have squeezed some more funds out of my budget and had it done. The results are disappointing; well that's not quite true, the picture has been transformed and all the original colours are once again vibrant. Amanda tells me that the painter's hand is unusually dexterous for a journeyman landscape artist of the time and she sees some likeness to William Blake's hand, but the problem is that the picture is unsigned.

'Mr. Postlethwaite?' It was a childlike female voice. I looked up and a lady was walking purposefully towards me with her hand outstretched; I stood and shook it. 'Hello, I'm Jilly Cole, sorry to keep you waiting,' she added. The voice did not match the person; neither did she look like a Jilly.

She was a large woman, standing nearly as tall as me, 5 feet 11 perhaps, broad of shoulder, sturdy of build rather than overweight. She was wearing a pin-striped suit, the skirt of which was mid-length and taught across her abdomen and thighs as if her body was straining to get out. She seemed to be perched precariously on slender high-heeled stiletto shoes, her feet looking small and stressed in relation to her ample calves. She then held out her hand in the direction of a door into the inner sanctum of the premises. She swiped her pass across the security mechanism, we walked through, and she took me to her office.

It was a corner office, had two sets of windows overlooking both roads at the junction, but both had aluminium venetian blinds at them. The furniture was metal, gun grey, and the whole room seemed to be in just these two tones; grey and aluminium. There was an easel beside her desk and on it the picture of Elloughton Park. She gestured for me to sit.

'This is a difficult one,' she said, looking round at the painting. 'Thank you for letting me see a photocopy of the journal entry, that's certainly good provenance.'

She paused, looked down at her desk. I took the opportunity to examine her features. Her face was childlike to match her voice, but again was counterpoint to her size. She was immaculately made up however, her eyeliner accentuating her sparkling eyes and her lips painted a cherry red, but then I'm a man and I don't understand these subtle shades that the manufacturers give them. 'I suspect a *but* is coming now?' I said, interrupting her thoughts.

'Yessss,' she said, drawing out the word. She was obviously sorting out her words carefully in her mind. 'I understand that you have already had an opinion from Amanda Davies?'

'Yes, that's right; is there any more that you can add?'

'Well you know the main problem, the picture is unsigned.'

'Yes, but won't the provenance stand for something?'

'Well yes, as far as it goes.'

'As far as it goes? How do you mean?'

'Well because it is unsigned, can we really claim this is the same picture referred to in the journal? Even if it is, can we claim that it is by *the* William Blake and not *a* William Blake; do you follow?'

'OK I follow,' I said, 'I'm a historian, I know all about interpreting documentation, the dangers of making assumptions.'

'Forgive me, Mr. Postlethwaite, but, with respect, it's not quite the same.

You, as a historian are required to make an interpretation, but I cannot sell something as genuine on an interpretation. I need much stronger evidence to authenticate than that.'

'Then where do we go from here?'

'Well I've already been busy,' she said. 'Firstly I have looked for labels, stamps or written notations that might give you some history, provenance or other indication of authenticity.'

'And?'

'And nothing; there's absolutely no labels on the back at all. The brass plate at the front just identifies the subject, Elloughton Park.'

'This doesn't sound good, does it?'

'Well no, but the back can still tell you things.' She must have seen from my expression that she needed to explain further. 'It still has fingerprints; you just have to read them. The frame is of solid Baltic oak. It's right for the period – it's also chamfered in the right places.'

'So that's good?'

'Well yes, but it gets worse. The standard reference work on Blake is Alexander Gilchrist's biography of 1860. Blake was more famous as a poet, as you know, but there is this evidence that we can consult. Unfortunately, there is still no mention of this painting.'

This wasn't going well, but there still wasn't finality in her tone. She went on.

'So I've been to the Witt Library. It's an essential resource for anyone looking to attribute a work; they have information and images of over a million pictures. If any picture has ever been in an exhibition or any public auction or a public collection, you have a chance to find an image there.'

'That sounds a wonderful research facility,' I said, enviously.

'Yes, it's absolutely brilliant. They have a collection of reproductions of paintings, drawings and prints of western art, covering the period 1200 to the present day.' She paused and that brief burst of enthusiasm just seemed to evaporate like a campfire at dawn. 'But I've been through everything they have on Blake and there is nothing about this painting. Probably because it has always been at the hall and has never been to market.'

'So the painting is worthless?'

'Now hold on a moment; there are other things that I can look at. The canvases usually have a stretcher and it helps you judge age and authenticity. Paint also has its own character, its own pigment and we can look at what was available at the time. You can see the flow of paint on a surface, how much it stands up on its own and how its colour adds to others around it. You can feel paint with your fingers, rough or smooth, with a tactile sense to it.'

I didn't know there was so much to this authenticating lark. 'And what does all that tell you?' I asked.

'It tells me that this is not a reproduction. This, in my opinion, is a genuine eighteenth century painting, a period piece.'

'As Amanda Davies thought, but can you go any further than that?'

'If this is William Blake, then he is only a very young man of 22 at this time. His later style and expertise will not have developed. I can see, however, some similarities of style in the brush work. But if you hold it up from the back to the light, the paint is thin.'

'I'm not sure what you are telling me?'

'I'm telling you that my gut reaction is that this is genuine. I suspect from the journal entry that what he was doing was just sort of *jotting off a quicky* to use a modern phrase; you know, doing the minimum to satisfy the client and his father, and because of that he was not prepared to sign it.'

'That's great,' I said enthusiastically, 'so you'll attribute it to Blake?'

'No!' she said, shooting me an irritated look, 'no, not at all.' She must again have seen the confused look on my face and knew she had to explain. 'This is an auction house and we have to be cognisant of the law. We don't want to be sued for breach of contract, so we have to be wary of material misrepresentation. We don't want buyers to claim that we duped them with our attribution just to turn a profit. We cannot falsely represent a material fact.'

'I see,' I said. I suppose this made perfect sense.

'This painting is in no way representative of Blake's work, and neither can it be said that it has any great quality, but nevertheless, I think I can still value this at between seven and twelve thousand as an eighteenth century oil on canvas landscape, *possibly* by William Blake.'

Chapter 15.

The Journal of Ginny Farmer

28th May 1788. Corbyn came to see me unexpectedly today. I like nothing better than his company, but I had to impress on him that he needs to send word ahead to see if I am free to receive him. But he was gushing and bursting to tell me of his exploits back in Nottinghamshire where his country home is. He seems to want to confide in me his most personal secrets and he really ought to have someone else in his life to open up to like this; but if he hasn't, then I am happy to see that as part of my services. He has stood up and bested the brother who had bullied him as a child; well done, Corbyn, well done.

The Journal of Corbyn Carlisle

19th June 1788. ~~The spectre of the hangman haunts my dreams.~~
4RJ6 7M88T4   9SVC2   33FAV6...

Chapter 16.

What is this all about? Corbyn Carlisle is an inveterate diarist, that is so abundantly clear, but the diary entry of the 19th June 1788 suddenly goes to code. And what does that opening sentence mean, which has been crossed out heavily: *The spectre of the hangman haunts my dreams* – why the hangman for goodness' sake? From what I have read of the man so far, he is the most unlikely of men to trouble the hangman. This is all very puzzling.

I emailed Grace. <What did you make of the diary entry of 19 June 1788?>

She replied immediately. <Yes strange isn't it, reverting to code like that. I thought we'd discuss it when you got to it. You free now?>

<Yes, come on up.>

'You know what I think?' Grace sat on the corner of my desk, her left knee raised, resting her chin on it. 'I just think it's his legal training kicking it.'

'How do you mean?' I was not sure where she was going with this.

'Something traumatic has happened and he needs his diary to confide in. That's what he does. He is always the outsider, the cuckoo in the nest at home; he is not comfortable drinking and wenching with his fellow student lawyers, so it's his diary that he turns to. He pours his heart out to *it* rather than a trusted friend.'

'I'll go along with that,' I said.

'But he knows what he's like, and he started to do just that. So he starts, *The spectre of the hangman haunts my dreams*, but then suddenly realises that he could incriminate himself, so he crosses it out and reverts to code to protect himself.'

'But why not just tear out the page, and start from scratch in code? Why leave that entry at all?'

'I thought the same, it worried me until I realised something, but I'm not sure if you'll buy into this.' I looked at her, gesturing her to explain. 'Paper was expensive.'

'Oh come on, Grace!' I said, 'so he spoils the ship for the cost of three ha'pence of tar.'

'No you don't understand, James; look at his journals, see, they are neat, super neat.'

'Yeah, he's fastidious, that comes across clearly; we know that of him.'

'But look at the number of words?'

'Again, we know that, he spews his guts to his journal most every night.'

'No, the number of words on each page; when he started the journals he was skint remember?'

'Oh yeah, I see what you mean, so he gets as many words on the page as he can. There are probably four hundred per page, if not even more.'

'Ah but more importantly he uses both sides of the page, see?' she said.

I turned back as Grace had pointed out, and yesterday's entry was there – on the reverse side. 'So he would have had to rewrite six hundred words or so, if he had torn it out.'

'Exactly!'

I leant back in my chair and cradled my fingers before my face, Grace's reasoning made sense to me. 'And so we have a mystery to solve. We need to crack the code to find out what he has done, don't we? What do you make of it?'

'Well I thought I'd crack it easily, but I haven't as yet. It's a mixture of symbols and numbers, but old Corbyn was a bright cookie it seems.'

'Well keep working on it,' I said, 'I may have a go myself, but let's not waste too much of our valuable time on it. It's not our first priority.'

'And *you* need to read Ginny' s journal entry of the 18th June 1788,' she said, 'she is being careful, but it gives us a clue about what happened to Corbyn.'

Chapter 17.

The Journal of Ginny Farmer

18th June 1788. Corbyn and Samuel arrived late this evening and Corbyn in particular was in a terrible state. Samuel had Corbyn's arm across his shoulder holding him up, and they both staggered into my house; luckily I was not entertaining Lord John. Samuel set him down on the armchair by the fire and he slumped into it and fainted. I called Beth for the smelling salts and she rushed in with them. He was slumped forward, and Samuel, with his strength, set him back upright, so that I could put the bottle under his nose. His head shot back as the salts stung his senses and then he quickly came round.

With his head back I noticed the wounds on his face, there was a gash two inches long on the right side of his forehead weeping blood, running down the side of his face. The cheekbone below his left eye was bruised and already beginning to turn purple, swollen so that his eye was no more than a slip. There was a lump on his head as big as an egg, growing through his hair like a new daffodil emerging in spring. There was just a splash of blood on his stock collar, but his grey frock coat was covered by a huge crimson stain where blood had steeped into it; at first I thought he had been stabbed. We removed his frock coat and then his linen shirt, but thankfully I did not found any stab wounds, but he held his ribs throughout to reveal more contusions, the skin blackening in several places with the imprint of the weapon that had hit him. It was his body that had taken the most punishment. Beth brought a basin of water and some lint and started to clean his face, but I took over.

I told Beth to bring me some bed linen and I tore it into strips so that I could bandage poor Corbyn's chest, and then we put him to bed. I sat with him holding his hand and that seemed to calm him.

'You are a sweet angel, dear Ginny,' he said to me through swollen lips, and I saw that his teeth, too, were bloodstained.

'Close your eyes,' I told him, 'sleep will be good for you, help your body heal,' but he tried to sit up instead, then drew a sharp intake of breath that whistled across his teeth as the pain in his chest took him.

He fell back on the pillow, gritting his teeth.

'Sleep, Corbyn,' I said again, adjusting the pillow beneath him with my free hand to make him more comfortable. He squeezed my other hand and looked fondly at me.

'Yes I will, sweet angel,' he said in and uncertain voice and then closed his swollen eyes. I could feel the tension quickly leave him and he gently gave way to sleep as I had hoped. I sat with him for a few minutes still holding his hand, but then I went back downstairs to talk to Samuel to find out who had attacked him. The streets of London are never a safe place are they?

29th June 1788. Lord John Dalby has stayed with me four times this week and I have accompanied him as his companion on two of those evenings. The social season is well underway and on Tuesday we went to a cards evening and on Friday a dinner party. My impression of a fine lady is now, if I say so myself, almost perfect. There are no grammatical mistakes to indicate the fraud that I clearly am. I am now wondering if the visit to the circus was some sort of test set by Lord John, but if it was a test then I must have passed with flying colours.

But going to a dinner party was much more demanding than going to the circus, for much of that evening we sat together enjoying the show and I had little socialising to do. But on Friday I was thrust into the heart of London's society people and my heart was pounding when we arrived, but I calmed; there was a reverence displayed to Lord John by everyone present and that was, somewhat illogically, extended to me, and that seemed to reassure me. I spent most the evening on Lord John's arm whilst the conversation surrounded affairs of state, politics, economics and the Irish question. I confined my conversations to small talk during this time, keeping my opinions to myself, which I believe was the right thing to do and was appreciated by Lord John. But when it came to talking about the arts, I saw my chance and gave my opinions forcefully. I quickly realised that I was as well read as most of those present, in fact better than most, even if I say so myself. As I relaxed I became more expressive, and my wit was found to be most humorous and the people laughed most generously, well at least the gentlemen did. I am unsure what the ladies thought of me, as they seemed, in general, to have little conversation, confining themselves to merely laughing in the right places, but I could see the look of disapproval on their faces. In fact we gathered quite a little crowd around us and the more I talked the larger that crowd became.

I think that I will become rather good at this.

4th July 1788. Corbyn came to see me last night. His face has almost healed, there just being the merest hint of bruising below his left eye. He says that his chest is still troubling him but that, too, is healing. We spent a very pleasant start to the evening and perhaps we drank a little too much wine. When we do, Corbyn seems to pour his heart out to me. All his successes in life and all his failures are paraded before me without any restraint. I don't think he is looking for approval from me; it's just that he sees me as his confidante. I suppose I should be flattered, but I also find it an obligation.

But this need to unburden himself on me led me to reciprocate last night; the wine, I fear, may have had something to do with it as well. So I told him my full life story, from the Foundlings' Hospital to my life in service, from my bastard child to my becoming a whore. Foolishly I thought that he would think well of me, be proud of my struggles to better myself, but later in bed he just turned over and went to sleep, and this morning he was very distant with me, we hardly spoke. He picked at his breakfast and took his leave after just a perfunctory look at the morning papers. We had always taken so much pleasure in reading them extensively and discussing them at great length. I am sure he will come around though; we seem to enjoy each other's company so much.

12th July 1788. I have not heard from Corbyn for over a week now; not a word or a message. The social season is coming to an end now and the country gentlemen will soon return to their estates for the hunting season, and Corbyn may have already gone back up to Nottinghamshire in preparation for this.

No, I am deluding myself. Corbyn does not follow the social scene. He is a lawyer and he comes to London to follow his profession, not for the social season. I fear that he has taken offence at something I have said or something in my past. This is most distressing.

I need to tell him more about that particular task Samuel undertook on his behalf, to put his mind at rest, but that cannot be committed to paper. I should have told him when we met on the 4th, but I sought to protect him, at least until everything died down; how do I now tell him?

The Journal of Corbyn Carlisle

20ᵗʰ June 1788.
    FSV67 88N4   9GTK2 33YK6...

4ᵗʰ July 1788. Oh, I have such a sad, heavy heart this evening, disagreeable thoughts have been swirling around in my head since last night; my mind is a whirlpool. Last night Virginia told me her life story; it was so very far removed from what I had thought. I expected her to tell me that she was a high-born lady whose father had gambled away her inheritance, left her penniless; or perhaps she was the illegitimate child of a fine gentleman who had paid for a governess and her education, but he had now died and his widow had cut off the allowance. Or even the daughter of a gentleman who had cast her out after she fell in love with a person of whom he disapproved.

But I didn't expect to be told that she is the produce of the Foundlings' Hospital. How does one respond to that kind of information? She is no fine lady fallen on hard times at all, she is of the lowest of the low; I feel deceived, lied to. Last night after we retired to bed I feigned sleep to avoid intimacy; suddenly she was no longer that fragrant lady that I longed to hold in my arms. But sleep did not come to me for many hours and when it did it was fitful. Round and around my head swirled, as this feeling of betrayal took me, it has been with me all day, dominating my thoughts to the point that I could not concentrate on the legal brief that I was examining.

She even told her story with a misplaced sense of pride, as if she has achieved something notable, but I see nothing to be proud of. I am sorry that she has been so terribly wronged by her master, but what right does that give her to deceive me in this way? She is so very far beneath me and yet I have opened up my heart to her, she has led me to be so very indiscreet. Oh the betrayal, the duplicity, the treachery. These are such strong words I know, but that is the way I feel this evening. I know the melancholies are coming on me again. I feel as though I am now looking at the world through a bubble-paned, mullioned window, nothing is clear to me any more. The candlelight dances on the page as I write, so that the words seem to disappear momentarily, then reappear, but with their meaning now imprecise, subtly changed, not quite what I intended. I feel like a dupe, like a dupe with the foul smell of the Thames in his nostrils.

It was all a deception. The education no more than some elocution lessons from a tutor around the corner, the fine clothes made up in the Jewish market, the fashionable design taken from plates in The Lady's Magazine, the debate on issues of the day just the regurgitation of articles written in the newspapers; its all an illusion; an illusion designed to deceive the likes of me.

I must be away to my bed and hope that sleep comes more easily tonight and that the morning will find me less downhearted. With this other matter also preying heavily on my mind, I feel like a man running from a hue and cry.

Chapter 18.

The Journal of Ginny Farmer

12th August 1788. I still have not heard a word from Corbyn. I find that I miss him most terribly and I feel that I have lost a good friend. Beth admonishes me for allowing myself to feel this way. She says that she told me at the very beginning I must never get too close to a gentleman and especially never ever believe anything said to me in the heights of passion. But our conversations were at their best when we just talked long into the night or over a relaxed breakfast, not when Venus inflamed us. Perhaps she was right after all; I should have taken more notice of her.

Lord Dalby has gone back to his country estate in Yorkshire. Parliament is in recess and he will spend the summer with his wife and children. I wonder if she knows that he visits me, or the others before me. I expect that she will put such thoughts to the back of her mind; there will be an acceptance on her behalf. It is expected of such elevated men. Perhaps I should feel some guilt for my part in the deception, but I do not.

I have always found Lord Dalby's strangled vowels his most unattractive feature; there is such a condescending tone to his voice, the way he uses his wit as a stick to beat people, but now I find I even miss his voice, no matter how unattractive; even if he is not a warm man like Corbyn, something of a cold fish if I am honest, I still miss him also.

Perhaps it is just loneliness that I feel at the moment. If it were not for visits from Samuel, I am sure that I would hardly see a soul from one day to the next. Oh, my apologies to dear Beth for saying that, she is a good friend. I also discount most of my other gentlemen, as they do not converse like Corbyn and Lord John.

I worry about Samuel too. He is now a man of considerable means from his exploits in the prize-fighting ring, but he is becoming quite the rake about town. I would hate it if all that money were to change his generosity of spirit. I blame that friend of his, that soldier boy, Captain John Campbell-John. He leads poor Samuel astray, introducing him to all the debauchery that London has to offer. Oh, I have just seen the irony in what I have written; it was because of John Campbell-John that I met dear Samuel; I myself am part of that debauchery. But I am right nonetheless, Campbell-John will gamble on anything and will finish up in the debtors prison, I have no doubt about that, and if Samuel is not careful he too will be penniless at the end of it all.

And yet I am in Campbell-John's debt myself. That distasteful incident with Corbyn; but no more of that here.

Well if my special gentlemen will not be visiting me for the foreseeable future I will make the best use of my time, I will study French, I think.

5ᵗʰ October 1788. Lord Dalby has been to see me today and his visit has left me shocked and bewildered. He has proposed that I be his permanent mistress, exclusive to him. I ought to be thrilled, yet I have misgivings and I am racked with uncertainties. This is what I wanted when I moved to Rathbone Place, to find advancement for myself; courtesanery is so much more preferable than prostitution and it has come much sooner than I could have expected. The role of a courtesan must be an improvement on my present life, no matter how genteel the specialised services I offer.

I think I fully understand what life as a courtesan will mean for me. I will have no social standing in my own right; I will take all that from Lord John. I will be expected to provide charming companionship, no matter what my own frame of mind might be at the time. I will be totally at his beck and call, but all that is understandable and I am prepared to accept it as part of my advancement. There will be religious disapproval of course, but I already live with that on a day-to-day basis because of the immorality of my current profession.

I will also lose my independence, the only source of income available to me will be in the gift of Lord John; I will become wholly dependent on him and that is what troubles me. If he tires of me, what can I look forward to; he could pass me on to another high-born benefactor as a favor to me, or set me up in an arranged marriage to someone not so high-born. But if I angered him in some way, I would just be jettisoned like some piece of flotsam with only the street as my destination. On the other side of the coin of course, a whole new lifestyle will open up to me . I will move in the very highest of social circles, if on the arm of Lord John. I should put these feelings of vulnerability to one side and grasp this opportunity with both hands. This was the advancement that I dreamed of when I moved to Rathbone Place and now that opportunity opens up to me; me, little Ginny Farmer, an orphan from the Foundlings' Hospital, and I only turned twenty last month.

But Lord John is such a cold fish. I know there will be no tenderness from him. I will not be one of those mistresses who has found love and affection from a man so far above them that marriage is not an option; that will not be my role. Even when making love, Lord John seems to only want to be vigorous like a rutting stag, to come to his satisfaction as quickly as possible. I suppose it is part of his character, his sense of superiority is so total that it invades everything he does. Even his proposal left no room for my acceptance, a fate, a comply. 'I propose that I take you as my courtesan,' were his exact words, 'I will look around for a suitable place for you to entertain me from.'

I was stunned into silence for a few moments, but I don't think he interpreted my silence in that way. He is used to people being in awe of him. Actually my own vulnerability was, surprisingly, the first thing that sprang to mind, and I wondered how to broach the subject without upsetting him.

'Is not Rathbone Place a suitable address?' I said uncertainly. He cocked an eye and looked down on me; he was warming his backside in front of the fire at the time. I continued equally as uncertain, 'My gentlemen know to send word in advance, so I can send a written note back advising them that my services are no longer available. I am sure that you will never be disturbed by an unwanted caller.'

'Well there you have it,' he said dismissively, and at first I was unsure of what he meant. He turned to face the fireplace to warm his front, 'I will purchase the freehold for you,' he said over his shoulder.

I saw an opportunity. 'In my name, Lord John, you are most generous indeed,' I said as demurely as I could, feigning diffidence by looking down at the floor.

He looked around at me and I resolutely kept my eyes on the floor as modestly as I could. It was only a heartbeat, but it seemed like a time without end. 'What!' he said, and I held my breath, 'well yes, as you wish, I'll have my lawyer sort it all out, and he can also make arrangements for an allowance for you. I will need you to look presentable at all times.'

I let out a long breath as silently as I could. I should have been relieved, as I would not now be so vulnerable, but yet that feeling of unease did not leave me.

I must write to Corbyn to advise him of the change in my

circumstances. Perhaps it will spur him into making contact with me, as I hope we can still be friends.

The Journal of Corbyn Carlisle

10th October 1788. I have received a letter from Lady Virginia. Lady Virginia indeed! The hypocrisy of the woman. She writes as if I am her equal; an old friend to converse with as intimates. The over-familiarity of the woman is quite overwhelming. I wonder at times who she thinks she is.

She writes to tell me that she is to be the exclusive mistress of Lord John Dalby; as if I care a jot. I've never met the man, but I know of him of course, a very powerful man. I wonder if he knows the truth of her background as I do. I am sure that he would not be so eager if he knew. I shall write back and congratulate her for her elevation, for she is certainly flying high, so very high above her station.

15th October 1788. It is six of the clock and the sun has not yet risen; there is darkness all around, it matches my disposition. Oh, but I have been suffering from the melancholies for over two months now; they will not seem to lift. I know the root cause of it, that dreadful woman, Lady Virginia; ever since that evening when she told me her life story and the deceit it contained. I have tossed and turned all night long, sleep elusive with only the endless, slow, rhythmical ticking of that damnable clock to punctuate the silence and to keep me company. Its uncomfortable beat was like a demon stealing my slumber and breaking into my consciousness. Each long pendulum swing, backwards and forwards, inscribed an imaginary arc in the dark night that seemed to dampen further my sad, heavy heart.

But in that gloom I have taken stock. I have contemplated my folly, for that's what it is; my pompous and pretentious folly. I realise now what a stupid man I have been. The truth is I miss her dearly; I have missed her every day for the last two months. I have missed the sight of the candlelight dancing on her fair features. I have missed her soft lips and sweet breath. I have missed her expressive, inquisitive eyes.

I have just read again her letter to me. I must have previously read it with vindictive blinkers covering my eyes. But now, as I read it again, there is a nuance to her turn of phrase. I see now that she is unsure. Was she looking for guidance from me? I do believe that she was.

But as I recall my response, I see the coldness of it. I took pleasure in finding the words to congratulate her, but those words were also laced with sarcasm, with irony, with undertones of my own irrational loathing of her. Yet I now realise that this fair creature has done nothing to deserve my wrath. She has merely played the bad hand that life has dealt her with dexterous skill, and none of that has dampened that generosity of spirit that she so sweetly displays. I fear it is too late for me. Have I lost her forever? I fear that I have.

And my ungratefulness passes all comprehension. When 65HIM87 happened it was her that I turned to, her that toiled on my behalf, it was her insightful plan that brought about my deliverance; she saved my life I am sure. I must now face up to my own immense ingratitude alone; that is to be my punishment.

Chapter 19.

I woke early; it was still dark; I looked at my bedside clock. The large red digits glowed in the dark proclaiming 5:22. My heart was pumping, I had just had an erotic dream and I had an involuntary erection. I should have been pleased, enjoyed the imagery before it faded like a figure walking in the night to be swallowed by the darkness, I should have abandoned myself to it, relished it. But it was a bitter-sweet feeling because the subject of the dream was Ginny Farmer. *What was that all about?* I thought, *this is adolescent.* In my dream I was at 22 Rathbone Place, I was a punter visiting this fine lady. I was on my best behaviour, my manners impeccable. We took tea together, chatted. In my dream she asked me what my profession was and when I answered that I was a historian I was amazed to find that she had knowledge of it. Later she took me to her boudoir and I swear that I could smell the fragrance of orange blossom. She stood at the side of the bed with her back to me; her nightgown fell to the floor, revealing a slender alabaster body, delicate shoulders, small rounded buttocks with a dimple above the rise of each mound, slender legs. She slipped between the sheets and then looked round at me, puzzled as to why I did not join her in the bed. But I seemed incapable of moving; I desperately wanted to, but my legs just wouldn't work. She held out her arms in invitation, but I was transfixed, as if my legs were wood and screwed to the floor, I just couldn't move. Panic then began to take me. The bed and this beautiful creature began to recede, moving away, slowly at first and then it accelerated and all the time she held out her hands imploring me to come to her. It was then that I woke, heart pounding, sweating. I rolled over on my back as rational waking thoughts slowly returned to me. My heartbeat began to return to normal. *I'm working too hard*, I thought to myself. I rolled back over onto my side and closed my eyes again, to capture those few hours left of the night in sleep.

I opened the fridge door, took out a bottle of Bombardier, and drank from the bottle. I had just showered and thrown on an old pair of jeans and a clean t-shirt, but my hair was still wet. I opened the fridge door again as an afterthought, looking back in to decide what I could have to eat. It was 5:30 p.m. and for once I had finished work early; last night's dream had prompted me to do so. I had time to prepare myself a proper meal; I was having too many ready meals and I knew it. The trouble was, there was little in the fridge to choose from, a little boiled ham, some Emmental cheese, but I had eggs so I reluctantly decided to settle for an omelette. I shrugged my shoulders; it was only one rung up from a ready meal. A chance missed.

I heard my mobile phone go off in the distance; I patted my jeans stupidly to see if it was mine, but then realised it had to me mine, I was the only one in my apartment. I ran through to the bedroom, grabbed it from my bedside cabinet, but the caller had just rung off. 'Why does that always happen?' I said out loud, annoyed. The *missed call* function showed that it was Grace Farmer. I rang her straight back.

'Hi, it's Professor Postlethwaite.'

'Yes I know,' she answered.

'Huh!' I was put off; she had taken the wind out of my sails.

'It says so on the phone display, silly.' She was teasing me and I had fallen for it. *She plays me like a fiddle*, I thought.

'Have you been trying to find me?'

'Why, have you been hiding?' she said. I heard her giggle.

'OK, OK,' I said, 'shall we start again?'

'Oh I'm sorry professor, but you're so easy. You're like a tease magnet; I just can't stop myself.'

I thought of Toby Fielding; *he* was always teasing me. Perhaps it *was* me; was I just a stuffed shirt to her.

'Hello, you still there,' she said, 'I haven't upset you have I?'

'Is that how you see me? A pompous, over-inflated academic balloon to be pricked, burst?'

There was a pause. 'Well, sometimes,' she said hesitantly. There was caution in her voice though, I could tell.

'There's another side to me, you know?' I must have sounded wounded, feeble, because she obviously thought that she needed to explain.

'I sense that, and that's why I tease you; to get past the professor that I have to deal with at the university. You should take it as a compliment.'

I made an effort to snap myself out of this self-pity; I didn't want her to see me as some pathetic figure. 'Yes, maybe. OK, what can I do for you?'

'Steady, tiger,' she said teasing me again, turning my simple comment into an innuendo.

'Yeah, yeah, very funny. What do you want?'

'I've just got back from Nottinghamshire, I'm at the university, but you're not in your office. Are you still here somewhere?'

'No I'm at home.'

'Oh – never mind, it'll wait.'

'What will?'

'I've finished the cataloguing, but the last thing I did was identify the portraits. You know, which head belonged to which baronet.'

'And?'

'Well there's one of the ninth baronet with his wife.'

'What, Corbyn, C.C. and V.C?'

'Yes, they're old in it, but it's them. According to the date he's 58 in it.'

'Oh interesting. It does no harm to see an image occasionally; it brings historical research into focus.'

'I thought you'd say that 'cause I've brought it back with me.'

'Oh good,' I said, 'bring it round. I'd like to see it.'

'Where? I haven't enough money to waste on taxis. I'm on a grant, remember?'

'It's only around the corner. I have a flat on Curzon Street – Curzon Place, flat 4F. Just buzz me.'

'You live in those posh trendy flats?'

'Yep, posh and trendy, that's me.' I bit my lip after I spoke; it wasn't the wittiest thing I had ever said. I realised I was trying to impress her.

I looked round. The place wasn't so bad because I was never there, but I quickly tidied up anyway, and then gave it a quick hoover round. Why I thought I needed to I don't know, but I did. Then I sought out a clean pair of jeans and towel-dried my hair some more, put on some deodorant. The door intercom sounded and I buzzed her in to come up. When I opened the door she smiled a playful smile at me, leaning against the doorframe, the picture under her arm. She was dressed as usual, faded jeans ripped at the knee and a t-shirt. I looked down at the words and she saw me and helped by puffing out her chest so that I could read it better. "IT ONLY SEEMS PERVERTED THE FIRST TIME"

'Good, yeah?' she said as she came in before I asked her to.

I nodded a sort of grunted *yeah*, but my smile was genuine. It *was* funny.

She looked around my apartment nodding her head, gesturing her approval. 'Nice,' she said, 'very impressive. You should see the student hovel that I have to live in.'

'Been there, got the t-shirt,' I said, without realising the humour. She looked at me with those smiling eyes as if to congratulate me; the penny dropped and I gestured with a returned smile to accept the non-verbal, undeserved compliment.

'So,' she said, putting the portrait on my table. She stood back a pace and I went closer to have a good look.

'It *is* filthy, isn't it?' I said.

It was a standard pose, a gentleman and his lady, dated 1818. Grace was right; Corbyn Carlisle would have been 58. I peered through the dirt; the image of Corbyn was clearer than that of his wife; her image indistinct.

'Why's he wearing a wig?' she said.

'It was a fashion, but also a badge of social status,' I replied whilst still studying the canvas.

'No; why in 1818 I mean?'

'Oh yeah, wigs were out of fashion by then weren't they? But older conservative gentlemen continued to wear them; and the portrait reflects his formal wear, remember?'

'Oh that's probably it then,' she said.

It took a few seconds for that comment to sink in; I was still studying the picture, but then I looked up at her, 'Huh!' I said.

'He's a lawyer, remember; the law, ceremonial wigs and all that. The tossers still wear them today, don't they?'

She was right of course. I looked at her and a smug smile entered the corner of her mouth. She was staring at me; there seemed to be a challenge in her look.

'I was just going to eat; do you want to join me? Just an omelette I'm afraid.'

She continued to look at me, as if calculating consequences. 'Yeah, why not,' she said and then her whole outlook seemed to change, it became skittish again as if a hurdle had been jumped.

We went through to the kitchen. I opened the fridge, damn there was no wine. I offered her a bottle of Bombardier and she took it eagerly. We chatted as I made the omelettes, both drinking from the bottleneck occasionally.

'So, Ginny Farmer is to become a courtesan then, to Lord Dalby?' I said, putting butter in the frying pan.

'I'm ahead of you; I've read much more than you. There're more surprises to come.'

'Don't tell me, Grace,' I found myself saying, 'I want to see how it unfolds.' I suddenly realised how illogical this must have sounded. 'Contemporaneously with Corbyn's journal,' I added eagerly.

She still looked at me as if I was bonkers though. 'It's not a novel you know, it's historical research!'

I was whisking the eggs, but I stopped at her comments. I knew immediately she was right. 'I know,' I said, 'its just that Ginny is such a fascinating character.' It was a bit weak as a justification.

'Why James; I think you're falling in love with a woman who died nearly two centuries ago,' she was making fun of me again. '*James and Ginny sitting in a tree, K I S S I N G*,' she sang.

I laughed it off, but *ouch*, that struck home like a rapier after last night's dream, I struggled for some words to make me sound rational. 'Yes, it's a bit unprofessional, I know, but I do seem to care about her. Isn't it amazing that she has managed to manoeuvre Lord Dalby into signing over Rathbone Place to her; good for her I say.'

'You should care more about Corbyn; he needs it. What a plonker! He's found the perfect woman for him and he rejects her.'

'Any progress with the code by the way?'

'No,' she said, 'but there are some clues in what Ginny says, although *she* is very circumspect as well. *"And yet I am in Campbell-John's debt myself. That distasteful incident with Corbyn; but no more of that here."* '

'Yeah, we know he's been the victim of an attack. That might be the origin of the phrase, *"The spectre of the hangman haunts my dreams."* '

'I'm not so sure,' said Grace, 'he keeps referring to *this other situation*. Doesn't that suggest something ongoing? If he was attacked in the street, well that's what happened *then*. He was injured, but it was over. If he killed a ruffian, no magistrate is going to charge a baronet with anything, especially if he was protecting himself. So why would that be preying on his mind?'

I nodded, her argument was sound.

'So I repeat, Corbyn is a bit of a plonker, isn't he?' she added.

'And that must be part of your Master's to explore that,' I said, being the professor again. 'Social conventions get in the way even today, but back then – well it was so much more important. The idea of romantic love as a basis for marriage was a long way off in 1787. He is *gentry* remember, a baronet; he would have been required to look for an alliance of families. And the woman was expected to bring two things to that alliance; her dowry and her virginity. That's why debutants *"came out"* you know, they were taking themselves to market. Look for some quotes on that, I think Defoe said something along those lines, check it out.'

We ate and drank the beer and talked around Corbyn's dilemma. 'So you are saying that there is just too much of an abyss between their stations?' she asked.

'Exactly, don't be too hard on poor Corbyn. Ginny is an illegitimate foundling and certainly not *virgo intacta;* she fails both requirements – and he is of the highest social class. His whole world had suddenly come crashing down on him.'

'The noble and the peasant, hey,' she said. 'Yeah OK then, but I'm sure I've read of exceptions. *Money* certainly bridged that abyss; impoverished aristocrat and the daughter of a wealthy merchant; so why not some cases of love?'

'OK, research that too; see what you can find. The exception that proves the rule, so to speak,' I said.

'I suppose there is a parallel with you and me. I'm the impoverished undergrad and you're the rich professor of history living in your expensive bachelor pad.'

I darted a surprised look at her. Her face was serious, but her eyes told a different story. I knew she was mocking me again; we exchanged glances, but I was unsure of her meaning. *Was that a come-on,* I thought, my mind running ahead of itself. I made an effort to rationalise the situation. 'The comparison falls down 'cause we're not lovers?' I raised my eyebrows to show that that was a question. I was quite pleased with myself; I felt I was gaining some control of the conversation.

'But that's so easily remedied,' she answered. It was the response I was manoeuvring for, but now I felt uneasy. At Elloughton Park I also thought that she was interested in me, but there she just literally shut the door in my face. Was this about to happen again? And then she said something even more confusing to me.

'You know what I'd really like to do now?'

'What?' I said, playing my part in her game.

'I'd like to take a shower; I've been on buses and trains all day.'

'OK, no probs,' I said, 'there's an en suite off my bedroom.'

I took her through and got her some towels. She went to go to the bathroom, but then stopped at the doorway. 'Don't go away,' she said over her shoulder.

I lay on my bed, still unsure of what was happening; was I interpreting the signs, the words correctly? I knew she was deliberately teasing me, but was it part of a sexual foreplay?

When she emerged from my shower she was wrapped in one of my large white fluffy towels, with another being used to towel-dry her hair. She stood at the foot of my bed and I watched her intently, my eyes somehow glued to her, running up and down her from head to foot or as far as I could see from my position. She then shook her head and her hair fell into place; still damp, but the natural curls already returning. It was as though she was giving a performance and I was the solitary member of the audience; a private and intimate viewing. She looked up at me lounging on my bed; saw that I was fully clothed; a look of incredulity crossed her features.

'It tends to work better if we are *both* naked,' she said.

There was now no doubt in my mind. 'Is this a good idea, we have to work together, remember?'

'I can handle it, if you can,' she said matter-of-factly.

I sat up on the side of the bed and pulled my t-shirt quickly over my head, and then I thought I might look too anxious, too desperate, so I deliberately slowed my disrobing. She slipped in behind me as I did so and I felt cheated of the sight of her nakedness. But I need not have worried; when I too slipped under the sheets she moved over immediately and straddled me, the bed sheet falling away to reveal herself fully to me; naked; magnificent. She leant forward and kissed me. Words came in to my mind, *I felt her soft lips and sweet breath, and her yielding kisses lingered long on my lips.* These were Corbyn's words and they were coming to me in the midst of my own passion. *Damn you, Toby Fielding,* I thought, I *am* obsessed by my work; I decided that I would just yield to this passion that was rising within me; I needed to cast these other thoughts from my mind.

I put my hand around the back of her neck, pulled her closer to me, and returned her kiss harder, more passionately, but she pulled away when I did so. 'Gently, James,' she said.

There was an incongruity here. I did not rationalise that thought, but it was there nonetheless, instinctively, a confusion in my mind. Grace had clearly been the instigator of this encounter; she had immediately straddled me as soon as I had got into bed with her; the action of a young sexually confident woman, but now she wanted tenderness not fervour, or more probably gentleness to go along with the ardour. This was an enticing mix; it was the perfect mix for me. In my dream, Ginny Farmer receded, went away, but now there was no doubt that Grace Farmer was coming boldly towards me.

'Why now and not at Elloughton Park?' I said to her.

She sat up on me, contemplating, 'I don't know; you were lusting after me then, I saw you leering at me in the swimming pool. Not the most attractive thing for a woman. But since then I've got to know you; I liked our time cataloguing. And I've made it my business to find out about you.'

'And?'

'And you're not one of those lecturers who uses his position to screw as many of his students as he can. In fact you don't seem to put it about very much at all do you; the last one was Danielle Binoche, the French lecturer, wasn't it?'

I was gobsmacked; I thought I had been discreet, but she had found out about my sex life. I was about to respond but she put her finger over my lips.

'Condoms?' she said. I reached awkwardly into my bedside cabinet, uncomfortable on my back, my arm stretched, my fingers rummaging. She bit my nipple as I did so.

Chapter 20.

The Journal of Ginny Farmer

31st July 1789. Parliament is in recess and Lord John has gone back to his estate in Yorkshire. It is a year now since I became his exclusive mistress and it is a good time to take stock of my life. It has been a strange year, but a wonderful one for all that, and so much of it is what I had expected. I am under no illusions as to what Lord John wants of me; a woman who is pretty, well mannered, socially acceptable, intelligent, witty and discreet. It is a long list, but I think I have succeeded in being all those things, yet strangely I long to offer more. I am amazed how my own intellect has developed; I have a thirst for knowledge, on current events, politics and the sciences. I know this is the last thing that most men would want of a courtesan, but Lord John is such a gifted man himself and with that superior attitude of his he is not threatened by an intelligent woman and he just seems to stand above it all. At the start of the year I confined my opinions to subjects such as the arts and fashion, but as the year has progressed I have tested the waters, so to speak, carefully at first, and expressed my personal views on more weighty matters. Lord John did not reprimand me for it and so I have done it more and more. It's hard to explain, but I think he sees himself as such a superior man that it is within his compass to have a clever woman on his arm. But he never debates my views with me, either in public or, more surprisingly, even when we are alone, and that is most exasperating; he just looks down on me in that way he has; it's not an attractive characteristic.

I move in circles that I never dreamed I would, or to be truthful, never even knew existed. It is so stimulating; all the entertainment, the social season, and the powerful people I meet, the expensive clothes that I am now able to buy. I use the fashionable shops in Oxford Street, but I work with the designers and have them made up to my specification. I don't think they like me very much for that, but they are coming round to accepting that I have an eye for this. I still design some of my clothes from scratch and have them made up by the Jewish merchants in

Monmouth Street, but I don't tell Lord John that. The Jewish merchants cannot do enough for me and their seamstresses do excellent work. I do believe that some of these fine ladies of society, who at first looked down on me, now look to me as a leader of fashion. There is so little of little Ginny Farmer left in me.

If I say so myself I am something of a success at courtesanery, I seem to be the one in demand at social gatherings, constantly surrounded by men, and my opinions are sought on so many subjects. It gives Lord John time to talk of matters of state and I am his diversion to do so; I think he likes that because his work at the centre of government seems to be constantly with him.

What I did not expect, however, were the long days of inactivity. I know that other courtesans whose patrons have rank, wealth, but no responsibilities, live a life of constant socialising, but Lord John is such a busy man that such a life is not open to me. But I do not miss that life, as so much of it is debauched and profligate, and having been a foundling and penniless I know the value of money; to see it squandered in such a way is obnoxious to me.

A few weeks ago, we attended an evening at Sir Thomas Kettel's. Sir Thomas has the knack of mixing the ladies and gentlemen of rank with those of the lower sort who would bring entertainment value to the evening, just so long as they adopt the manners becoming their humble status and neither offend the ladies nor frighten the horses. These words are condescending of course, but I repeat them as spoken to me; they are the words of intolerable snobs. Not that it is easy to say what might offend ladies from the upper echelons of society; I know they customarily visit lunatic asylums, public executions and other such delights merely for their sheer entertainment. But so long as coarse language is kept to a minimum and outward appearances maintained, then virtually anything is acceptable at Sir Thomas's house parties. The dining and drinking started in mid-afternoon and went on late into the evening. Gluttony and over-indulgence was the order of the day, for by providing a cornucopia of luxurious fare, Sir Thomas was able to display his own wealth and rank — I am told that it is all illusionary; it is said that he has serious gambling debts.

There are few, if any, restraints at these house parties, especially gluttony; obesity among these gentlemen is a badge of their status. Not so for us ladies however, our waists are expected to remain sylph-like even without the confines of our corsetry.

At ten of the clock, the dancing was interrupted and two small tables were erected in the coffee room, each table having four lace-edged napkins, one placed on each corner. It was all very genteel of course, the napkins had little purpose, merely an expression of style and a statement of wealth. It signalled of course, that the card playing was about to commence. The games were watched by an audience who were mostly skilled in the games themselves and they applauded politely when a good hand was played, but it is essentially about gambling. I find this passion for gambling most baffling, there is many a young gentleman brought to ruin because of it, and I was upset to see Samuel Medina and his friend, that awful soldier Captain John Campbell-John, take their places at the tables. I had spoken to Samuel earlier and his invitation had been acquired by Campbell-John; Samuel now has some celebrity and he was there merely for entertainment value I am sure. They both lost, luckily Samuel modestly, but Campbell-John began by winning and then lost heavily as his inebriation increased. I suspect he is like these young gentlemen of wealth and power who believe themselves to be accomplished card players, whereas in reality they are nothing of the sort. A life of debt and losses do not shake them from this belief.

But what I did not expect of the coutesanery is the boredom, days on end when parliament is sitting, but weeks on end when it is not. I see little of Samuel and I have not heard from dear Corbyn for over a year. At least I was able to do that one last good deed for him. But I am making good use of my time; my French is coming along easily, although having just learned all those English rules of grammar, I now have to learn new ones for the French. My teacher, however, says that I have a gift for languages.

15th **August 1789**. Lord John had promised to take me to Paris, but the papers are full of the events in France and he says that it is now too dangerous for him to travel there. Last month there was the storming of a prison there and according to him our government is in a state of panic, lest all the unrest spreads to Britain. What strange times we live in.

30th **August 1789**. I am back in Bristol; it has been a bitter-sweet experience. It's been on my mind for some time now to try and find out who my real mother is, and the absence of Lord John has given me an opportunity. I will be twenty-one next week and it seems like a good time to do so. I took the mail coach yesterday, which made the journey in a day. I have taken lodging at the best inn in town and I sent a note straightaway to the Foundlings' Hospital saying that I wished to see one of the trustees to discuss one of their former foundlings. I said I would arrive at eleven of the clock the following day (today). I signed myself as Lady Virginia Dalby.

I hired a fine carriage to take me, and dressed in my finery to give the impression of a fine lady. I was met by one of the trustees, a Mr. Ezekiel Bates, who obsequiously offered his hand to enable me to get down from the carriage. I took it graciously, but with just enough irreverence to suggest that I was far above him in status. I was led into a wood-panelled office that I did not know even existed, despite living at the institution for fourteen years. I was offered tea, and this was brought by the matron, Mrs. Smiley who, Mr. Bates said, would also attend the meeting, as she would hopefully remember the child in question. Smiley was a most inappropriate name; she was as hard faced as I remember her, but now with a sour sycophantic smile that replaced the snarling, twisted lips that I remembered. I have to confess that I took some pleasure in seeing her cringe before me.

We took tea in silence, but then Mr. Bates put down his cup, 'And how can we be of service today?'

'I'm looking for information about a Virginia Farmer,' I said, my grammar and pronunciation perfect and with all the authority of a fine lady, 'she was born in September 1768 and left your establishment aged fourteen in 1782.'

'We normally require proof of the "token" before we discuss these matters,' he said, 'but in your case that will not be necessary. Perhaps I should explain the purpose of the token, it's...'

'No matter, Mr. Bates,' I interrupted, 'the token is a mother-of-pearl heart-shaped pendant, I have it here.'

I passed it to him and he examined it. 'A most unusual token,' he said contemplatively, 'they are mostly just buttons or other worthless trinkets, a piece of cloth perhaps.'

'I understand so,' I replied, my tone expressing some impatience.

'If you'll excuse me, Lady Dalby, I'll go and consult our ledgers.' He scuttled away equally respectfully.

As I waited, I shot a look at Mrs. Smiley. She stood to the side of me; wore a grey uniform with a white pinny, her greying hair tucked unevenly into a cap, with some escaping from the side. I remembered the beatings. She was not a handsome woman, tall, well built, unfeminine, but what was most dislikeable about her was her expression, it was hard, grim, and deceitful. I suspected that she fawned over the trustees, but then showed her true face to the foundlings, but if she did she probably fooled no one; it was impossible for her to be two-faced, as that sour expression proclaimed what she was. Even fawning before me she was unable to remove that look of malice.

Mr. Bates returned with the information from the ledgers. 'Virginia Farmer,' he said, sitting down opposite me, 'was originally named Martha Cundy before she was christened here as Virginia Farmer.'

I raised my eyebrows involuntarily; I was not even called <u>Virginia</u> it seems.

Mr. Bates must have seen my expression. 'We always christen the children,' he said, 'the institution is run on strict Christian principles.'

'And the mother's name?' I asked. I could see that he was puzzled by my request.

His eyes widened. 'Well, an Agatha Cundy,' he replied and then turned to Mrs. Smiley. 'Do you remember Virginia Farmer, Matron?'

'Oh yes,' she replied. 'A very wayward child, was always disobedient. Punishment never seemed to remedy her. Has she stolen from you, my lady, and then run off?'

I fixed her with a steely look. Her eyebrows knitted at first, but then the realisation that she had said something wrong took her and she looked down at the floor. I turned back to the trustee, put back my amiable superior smile, 'And do you have an address for Agatha Cundy, Mr. Bates?'

'No, I'm afraid we don't keep that information. Many of our mothers do not have an address when they come here; that's one of the reasons they leave their babies.'

'So you can tell me no more about Agatha Cundy?'

'Only that she was in service.'

'Would that be in Bristol?'

'In all probability, yes, Lady Dalby,'

'Well that is somewhere to start at least,' I said more to myself than Mr. Bates.

'May I ask the reason for your enquiry, my lady? I would hate to think that one of our Christian girls has wronged you in some way.'

'No nothing like that, Mr. Bates,' I said, 'I'm merely trying to find my mother.'

I looked at him intently, willing him to understand, but I could see by his expression that he did not. I looked round at the matron and saw the same bewilderment. I suddenly realised why I was so successful as a courtesan; if I'm convincing in the image I depict then I am accepted at face value as to whoever I want to be.

'Yes, <u>my</u> mother, Mr. Bates; I am Virginia Farmer.'

Disbelief was still at first evident in his expression, but then the realisation took him. I stood to take my leave, looked round at Mrs. Smiley. 'And I remember you as well Matron, oh, but I remember you very well indeed,' I said.

31st August 1789. I am now back in London after my bitter-sweet trip to Bristol. So I am really Martha Cundy. It is a name that I like and I think that one day I may reclaim it. But for the time being Virginia Farmer is who I think I am; it is also a name that I like. I have not given up on finding my real mother. I have appointed a lawyer in Bristol to use his contacts to see if he can trace her whereabouts.

The Journal of Corbyn Carlisle

2nd July 1789· Work has been my salvation this last year· I have kept myself busy and taken on many briefs, both as a junior advocate and latterly as leading advocate· My melancholy lifted slowly as the weeks passed, much helped by my incumbency of Elloughton Park; I am beginning to love the place greatly, and I no longer expect that every visitor will be the constable· My sister Jane, is turning into a fine lady of the house, a task that she should be sharing with Emily, but I'm afraid that Emily has been found wanting· I spend hours talking to my estate manager, young John Cooper and he has so many wonderful ideas· The estate under his stewardship is prospering dynamically and I now have funds to think about upgrading the hall· It is an exciting time for me, but I still have that feeling of loneliness; I desperately need someone to share my life with·

Last evening I went to a house party given by Lord Kettel· It is not something that I normally do, but I was persuaded by George Burgess, one of my fellow advocates at Chambers who had done some work for Kettel and had received an invitation as a perquisite. We were dining at our club, Brooks's on St James Street when he asked me to come, and he told me all about Kettel's house parties; they are the place to be, as his invites extend not just to the people of rank but to others of interest. It was also a chance for us to gain work for our chambers. But it was the mention of the name Samuel Medina that swayed me; he is becoming quite a personality. I have never attended a bare-knuckle pitched battle, but by all accounts he captures the acclaim of all who see him. He is so small compared with the other pugilists, but he seems to embody that right of an Englishman to strip to the waist and fight for what he believes in, even if it is against a more powerful foe; it is something that I can relate to in my own advocacy. I know him personally of course and I thought it would be good to make his acquaintance again.

The evening started fine, we dined well and I had a long talk with Samuel, he is such a stout-hearted fellow, so likeable. I had just thanked him again for 4RJ6 7M88T4 , but then I saw his face light up and I looked round to see who it was that had excited him so. There was a late arrival; it was Lord John Dalby and Ginny on his arm. At first I was transfixed; the sight of her taking my breath away. She lit up the room with her mere presence; beauty, elegance, style; they all radiated from her, yet her expression was still temperate without any sense of aloofness. I could sense that the mood around the room was lifted by this dynamic couple. People flocked to them instantly, but I could see at once that all eyes were on her rather than that powerful but remote Dalby — he is so superior, he merely lowers the lids of his eyes to signal his acknowledgement of people. It was like bees to honey and Ginny was certainly the honey.

'Let us go and renew our acquaintance,' said Samuel, his manners impeccable as always, but I was frozen to the spot. He looked at me puzzled. 'What is it, my friend?' he added.

At first I was unable to come up with a sensible response. But then I just looked at him. 'I have wronged that fine young lady,' I said, 'she will not want to see me. But you go; she will be pleased to see you.'

He nodded slightly to gesture that he would and started to walk away from me. I took his arm to stop him temporarily.

'Please, Samuel,' I said, 'don't tell her that you have seen me.

It will only distress her· Will you promise me that?'

'If you wish,' he said over his shoulder, but that look of bewilderment was still writ across his face·

I made my apologies to George Burgess and left with my tail between my legs·

15ᵗʰ August 1789. *Ever since catching that glance of Virginia at Lord Kettel's house party I have felt the melancholies creeping up on me again· I have thrown myself into my work to try to keep the monster at bay, for that's what I feel it is; a monster that comes and takes me· I am presently engaged in my most high-profile case and I am the lead advocate representing Lord Applecote in a complicated land dispute· The other party is also a noble, Lord Northton, and the two families have been linked together by marriage; the dispute surrounds several parishes and their livings, and whether they should revert to Lord Applecote following the death of Lord Northton's uncle, the previous baronet who died in a hunting accident a year after his wife (the sister of Lord Applecote) had died of scarlet fever· It is a complicated case, the point at issue being whether the disputed parishes are entailed with the estate of Lord Northton, or not· It is generating some notoriety in the newspapers because of the high profile of the parties· I expect the judge to give his ruling towards the end of next week and that gives me an opportunity·*

I have decided to go on the grand tour of Europe; I am a wealthy man now and I can afford it; I am twenty-nine and if I don't do it now I probably never will· I am sure that travel and culture are what I need to regain my good spirits·

Chapter 21.

The bar of the Nags Head was full, but then it did not take much filling. I leant in on one elbow, claiming a spot for myself and ordered a pint of Bombardier, and a pasty. There was a buzz of conversation all around me, natural, the way pubs release words from their clientele, effortlessly, as if they had been stored up for those very moments. They tumble out like welcome visitors, wanted, and embraced, ending in anticipation for an appreciative response. But it was wasted on me. I nibbled the pastry, my thoughts faraway, swigging the Bombardier without thinking, without savouring it.

I was thinking about Corbyn. The pain in his journal was palpable; he has lost his love. But all good love stories follow the same route; boy meets girl, boy loses girl, boy finds girl again. Perhaps there would be a happy ending, but then I admonished myself for my stupidity, I was reading a historical journal not a love story.

'Is that your evening meal?' said a voice behind me; it was Grace. I was expecting her, but I had been lost in my reverie.

'Oh hi,' I said, standing. She squeezed in beside me, but there was little room and we were squashed together uncomfortably. I liked it.

'You don't eat properly, James,' she said, looking down at my pasty.

'I know, but it goes with the beer.'

'I invited you out, to get you away from your office and to get you to eat a proper meal, not a pasty.'

I shrugged my shoulders. 'Yes, you're right,' I answered, 'next time. But we can't eat a proper pub meal and listen to the entertainment, can we? What can I get you?'

She sighed gently. 'Go on then, I'll have what you are having.'

We talked easily. The pasty was surprisingly good and we both had a second. The Bombardier was also good, it always was, and Grace was a keen convert. We had moved from being lovers to a couple in a few very easy weeks. She spent several nights a week at my flat, but I didn't feel threatened or pressured in any way, in fact it all seemed so natural. I had stopped trying to impress her after that first night of passion, and from that moment on I had been myself and she had responded to that. We had not tried to keep it a secret; I was still her professor I suppose, but she was not a twenty-year-old, she was my age, well almost. I may have to get someone else to grade her written work, but I did not see that as a problem.

'What have you been doing today?' I said; it was small talk but it was easy.

'I've had a good go at that code again, but I've been googling all about cryptography to help me.'

'Any luck with it?'

'Not really, it's a lot more complicated than I thought. If I understand it all correctly, what Corbyn has used is not really a code.' I raised my eyebrows gesturing her to explain. 'A *code* has a more specific meaning; it means the replacement of a word or phrase with a code word. You know, where say the word *picnic* replaces the *name of the spy* in those spy novels. But Corbyn uses symbols and letters.'

'So what's that mean then?'

'It means he is technically using a cipher. It's encryption, so he converts ordinary information into unintelligible nonsense.'

'So how do we break it?'

'It's all about finding the algorithm and, in particular, the cipher *key* that he used.'

'And that *key* is two centuries old, isn't it?'

'Absolutely, it's a tough ask to decode, sorry *decipher* it from this distance. It's probably a dead end.'

'Oh I don't know,' I said, 'you won't be the first historian to come up against coded source material. Let me use my contacts to see if I can get a cryptographer to look at it.'

She smiled at me; there was a skittish twinkle in her eye for some reason. 'What?' I said.

'I think I like being called a *historian*. I've only been a student up to now.' She reached up and kissed my cheek.

It was Halloween. The pub had hired a couple of professional storytellers to come and tell ghost stories. The bill on the door said – "Tis The Season To Be Scary." They did this every year, but I had never come before. The first storyteller stood at the end of the bar and began his tale. Within seconds the noise level fell. Even those who were not immediately interested, one by one, broke off their talking and listened in. The man was charismatic, and the audience hung onto his every word. We both leaned on the bar, facing him, and Grace cuddled into me as the pub became even fuller. There was also history in this tradition, that verbal tradition of telling stories rather than that of the written word, the novelist. The stories themselves sometimes went back hundreds of years, but the man told me afterwards that I should be careful with that because storytellers felt no obligation to tell the original story and adapted their stories to suit themselves or their audiences; it was about telling good stories, not preserving history. But it was still about times gone by and I loved that.

'You staying over tonight, Grace?' I said after the storytellers had finished.

She nodded enthusiastically. She was the best thing to happen to me in years.

Back at my flat, I brushed my teeth vigorously in the bathroom. The shower was pumping out water and it ran down the glass shower door, the blurred naked image of Grace within enticing me to look. The glass was steamed, but that did not seem to diminish the appeal of her nakedness. Through the blur I could see her statuesque body, her head thrust up and backwards to receive the refreshing, cascading water. Her allure was self-evident, I wanted her physically at that moment, and I knew she was a willing party. I found myself grinning like an adolescent.

I slipped in between the sheets of the bed and waited for her; I didn't have to wait long. Her body was still warm from the shower, contrasting against the coolness of the sheets; she felt wonderful against my own naked body. We made love easily, without lies, without any dishonesty, as if it was the most natural thing in the world; or at least that's what I thought.

I laid back afterwards, my arms behind my head, a little smug in the afterglow, and she snuggled under my arm, her head resting on my chest. For some reason I wanted to talk.

'You know, I think we're good together?' There was a question in my tone.

'Down, tiger,' she answered.

It was meant as a bit of fun, and I should have left it at that, but I suppose I wanted her to agree with me, to confirm that we were in the same place. I wasn't looking for any commitment, just agreement I think. 'No, I think we *are* good, don't you?' There was now insistence in my tone.

'Will you and your ego go to sleep please?'

At first I closed my eyes and snuggled down to comply; she turned off the light, but as I lay in the dark a thought took me. She was always evasive whenever I asked anything about herself. I had noticed it before but just let it pass. I didn't want it to get in the way of my pursuit of her. But now the pursuit was over and as I lay there it began to bother me. I needed to know how far she would take this evasion.

'What's your accent?' I asked, fishing, 'I've never been able to pin it down.'

'I haven't got an accent.'

Another evasion, I thought. 'So where do you come from?'

'Go to sleep, James, its late.'

Another evasion. 'No, come on what's your home town?'

'In the morning, James, please.'

'Everybody has to come from somewhere. Where do your folks live?'

I heard her sigh, and then there was a pause as if she were calculating what to reveal. 'Beverley,' she said.

'Beverley, East Yorkshire, you don't sound like a Yorkshire lass.'

'Well I am, now go to sleep.'

'What did you do before you came to university?'

She spoke without moving her position or opening her eyes. 'I was a soot juggler, its very popular in Yorkshire; they even have championships for it.'

I laughed, it was a funny line, but I knew it was another evasion.

'No, come on; tell me what you did before you came up to university. You are a mature student, you must have done something?'

'Oh leave it, James, will you,' she said, turning her back on me, adopting the foetal position at the other end of the bed.

But I couldn't; I knew I was entering dangerous territory, but I just couldn't stop myself. It wasn't normal to be this evasive unless she was hiding something, a husband, children perhaps. I wanted to know.

'Why won't you tell me, it's a perfectly reasonable question?' With hindsight I still think that it was, but her response overwhelmed me, it went past exasperation.

She got up, turned the bedside light on, knelt on the mattress. There was anger in her gaze and I felt the full force of it. 'What is this, an MI5 interrogation?' There was belligerence in her voice, but she was not finished, she held out her wrists to me in a strange gesture that at first I didn't understand. 'Would you like to wire me up to the electric supply and torture the information out of me?' she said. She got out of bed and walked up and down the room, seemingly unaware of her own nakedness, but her rant continued. 'Jesus Christ, but you can be such an arsehole at times, James.'

I looked at her, dumfounded. It was only a few moments, but it seemed like a hundred years. I thought I had found this wonderful person: but now she had morphed into someone completely different, wild, a feral ranting creature, with eyes full of fire. I opened my mouth to speak, but no words came out. I waited for her anger to subside, but it didn't, she just kept prowling, vindictive words spitting from her mouth like bullets from a machine gun and there was no doubt as to her target; it was me. Then she picked up her clothes and went into the en suite, all the time the tirade continuing until she emerged a few moments later, dressed, well sort of, her collar half in and half out of her fleece top. My head was full of questions, but at that moment I dare not ask them.

She stormed through to the living room and then I heard my front door slam with such a force that a picture fell from the wall to the floor. And then there was silence, a silence that rang as loud as a clanging bell. Her words seemed to have remained, even though she had gone. I was stunned, not really comprehending what had just happened. I got out of bed, pulled on a pair of boxers and a t-shirt and went through to my kitchen. I put a heaped spoon of Millicano coffee in a mug and turned on the kettle. I opened the fridge door to get the milk, but then saw a bottle of Bombardier and I took that instead. I sat on my sofa and supped out of the bottleneck, contemplatively; what had just happened? Had it been my fault? It went round and round in my mind, but I couldn't come up with a rational reason for her reaction; to say that it was disproportional was an understatement.

I took my mobile and inputted a text message that said that we needed to talk, but then I decided not to send it. No, the ball was in her court to explain herself, I thought; I didn't sleep much that night. After a week, there was no contact from her and when we met unexpectedly at the university she cut me dead.

Chapter 22.

The Journal of Ginny Farmer

5th June 1790. The social season is at its height. There is a frivolity about; no, it's more pronounced than that, somehow the season is different from last year, more unrestrained. Not that there is much restraint anyway, but this year it is even more evident. I think the whole thing is fuelled by the terrible happenings in France. I believe that all these privileged people fear that everything may be taken away from them if the unrest was to spread to England. They are intent on enjoying themselves to the full whilst they can. No matter how genteel the events are at the start, they now all seem to degenerate into something depraved. It is no longer just at Lord Kettel's that these things happen. But it is something I have noticed since my first ventures on the arm of Lord John; the grace and good manners are only a veneer and underneath there is little Christian morality.

17th June 1790. I have finally received a letter from the lawyers in Bristol; finding my mother has proved difficult. I know from their previous letters that their runners had failed to locate an Agatha Cundy and I was beginning to lose heart, but now it seems that a cook to the Dean of Bristol Cathedral remembers her and who she was in service with. That set up a trail to be followed and they believe they have now traced her present whereabouts. She is in London; the address given is Grosvenor Square in the city of London's affluent West End. My heart was in my mouth as I read the letter.

18th June 1790. Today started unpromisingly, unseasonably cold, a grim, dank day, rain falling constantly. I needed my cape and a bonnet. I had arranged to take Lord John's carriage; a nervousness took me and the din of the ironclad wheels and the clatter of the hooves on the cobbled streets hardly registered in my mind. I looked out of the window, but I didn't really take in what I was looking at, but then I noticed there seemed to be a depression hanging over all the good, and not so good, citizens of London as they went about their daily business. They seemed to be doing so in silence, and this is so unlike the streets of London which normally resound with the sound of voices crying out, singing and chattering. It was a dreary, depressing day to match the weather and my apprehension.

When the carriage arrived at Grosvenor Square, I stepped down and looked at the house before me. I had to shield my face with my hand to avoid the drizzle that was blowing in my eyes. But the drabness of the day could not disguise the grandeur of the magnificent town house before me; it stood commanding, looking out onto the central garden of the square. I approached the two great and imposing wrought-iron gates of this London residence, its splendour proclaiming to the world the status of its owner. I stood for a moment; head and eyes raised, trying to ignore the rain, and looked through the railings to the lavish property. This was London's fashionable new West End, and this property was part of the very beating heart of it; a three-storey building with attics atop, seven bays, and Corinthian columns. There were few, if any, residences finer than this and I wondered who lived here. The lawyer's letter said that Agatha Cundy was in service to a Mr. Nathaniel Coker. I had not expected it to be so fine a residence. The name was unknown to me; I had not come across him as part of the social season. What was clear was that I could not merely knock on the front door, uninvited, as I had expected to do. I would need to make an appointment. I was taken by a profound sense of anticlimax; I had prepared myself for a meeting with my mother and now I had to go home, my task incomplete.

19th June 1790. I have made enquiries of Mr. Coker. He is a Quaker banker and runs the London office of his family bank, and by all accounts he is one of the wealthiest men in England. He shuns the social scene, because of his Quaker religion. I have sent him a note asking for his permission to interview one of his servants on a private and personal matter. Again I have signed myself Lady Virginia Dalby.

25th June. 1790. I have a letter from Mr. Coker's secretary granting me permission. Mr. Coker will be unavailable on business, but his butler will make all the arrangements. I am to call on the 1st July.

1st July 1790. I announced myself as Lady Dalby, and then I followed the butler's white-gloved hand as he beckoned me to enter the house. I saw his look as he appraised my fine clothes and, despite my extreme nervousness, I stole myself to again play the fine lady with all the superiority that that entailed. He responded to me, as I knew he would, and I was shown into the library. I'm not sure if that room was his original intention or whether he made that decision when he saw me, but it was an impressive library, an impressive room, large with a great array of books. I took a seat by the reading table and looked at him questioningly. He nodded a servile nod at me and said that he would fetch Mrs. Cundy.

<u>Mrs</u>. Cundy! I thought to myself; is she married? I had played the scene in my head so many times over the last few days, but that thought had not occurred to me. I frantically tried to reassess what I would say; I suddenly felt unprepared and panic took me. I felt my heart start to pound as if it was trying to escape through my mouth: and then the door opened. The butler, tall, towering above my seated position, entered, he nodded a brief servile nod, turned and he was followed by a lady. He did not introduce her.

I tried to look at her features, but she kept her eyes on the ground as all good servants were taught to do. I looked up at the butler, apprehensive that my extreme nervousness would be apparent in my voice if I should speak. I just gestured dismissively with my hand instead and he bowed and left, closing the doors as he did so. There was an uneasy silence for some moments.

The lady before me was not dressed as a maid. She wore a smart dress blouse with a brooch at the collar. She was slender of frame, not unlike me, perhaps taller and with a more ample bosom. I bid her to sit next to me and she bobbed a curtsey and did so, still not offering me any eye contact, but when we were at the same level I could see that she was pretty of face, a warm and friendly expression. I looked at that face for some moments and a feeling of relief took me; I could sense kindness of character, and then relief coursed through my whole body. Her hair was blond beneath her cap, but there was greying starting at the temple. I noticed that she was starting to shoot up quick looks at me and I realised that the silence was making her uncomfortable; she didn't know if she was supposed to speak or not.

'You wanted to see me, ma'am?' she started to say, but the words caught in her throat.

'Yes, Agatha,' I said, my voice as soothing as I could make it.

'Ma'am?'

'Did you live in Bristol previously, Agatha?' There was something wonderful about saying her name and I just wanted to keep doing it.

'Aye, I did, ma'am.' I could see perplexity in her face.

Words deserted me at that moment, but then I took my bag and rummaged in it and took out the token, the mother-of-pearl, heart-shaped pendant with initials A an N on it. Perhaps this would explain things far better than I could. 'Do you recognise this?' I said, handing it to her, my fingers trembling.

She looked down at it; then her fingers, too, began to tremble. She looked up at me, her eyes closed to a narrow slit. I think her mind was full of questions, but she was too afraid to ask them. The harder she tried to rationalise the situation in her mind the further it receded from her. I tried to help her.

'You had a baby, Martha,' I said, 'and you left it at the Foundlings' Hospital.'

I saw tears begin to well in her eyes, they glistened in the morning light coming softly through the window, and then the dam burst and they teemed down her cheeks. She pushed them to the side with her hands, as if they embarrassed her. I knew that servants were not supposed to show their emotions to their masters; she was breaking a basic rule. I understood her for that and felt so very close to her.

Then we exchanged a long look, there was disbelief in her eyes. I knew she was wondering how I could possible know that. She suddenly sat upright, arching her back as if that would reinforce her resolve. 'Why do you want to know, ma'am?' she asked stoically, returning her eyes to the ground.

'Do you ever wonder what happened to Martha?' I said in an uncertain voice, willing her to understand, but I could see that she couldn't. She could not see past my fine clothes. 'It's me, Agatha,' I said, 'I am Martha.'

She darted me another look and this time I held it for what seemed like a time without end. She ran her eyes up and down me, then she put her hand to her mouth as the realisation took her. I felt the tears well up in me as well and I rushed to her, throwing my arms around her. At first there was no response, she was too afraid I think to embrace this fine lady. A stiffness took her, but bit by bit I felt it soften, her arms came up and around me and we just held each other for several minutes, tears flowing and receding and then flowing again. She reached into the pocket of her skirt and took out a handkerchief, and I followed suit, taking a handkerchief from my sleeve. I sat back on my seat, but I did not let go of her hand.

'We have so much to tell each other,' I said. She nodded that she understood and then, for the first time, a smile of joy entered the corner of her mouth.

I told her about my life, the helter-skelter of my first twenty-one years. I saw the different emotions in her face as my story unfolded. I saw pain, hurt, tenderness. I saw anger, disbelief, and resentment. But most of all I saw affection, I saw love.

And then she told me about herself. She worked for Mr. Coker as a nanny, looking after his three children of eight, five and eighteen months. She said that she loved it, as she had no children of her own; then realised what she had said and she started to cry again. I squeezed her hand and asked her to go on. She had never married; Mrs was only a title that went with the position of nanny. She had only been twenty years old when she had me. She had worked as a Maid-of-all-work in a not very grand house, which meant that she was the only servant apart from the cook. Her master was a clergyman, a canon at the cathedral where he had responsibility for helping to run it. The house was modest and was in the precinct of the cathedral. The master had a small private income, but he was far from a man of means.

'And who was "N"?' I asked.

She drew a breath, looked away, distant for some moments. I saw her thoughts drift away. 'Ah, Nicholas, I have not thought about him for many years.'

'Nicholas? Are you able to tell me about him?'

She turned back to me. 'There were four children in the household, three girls, and then Nicholas; he was the son of the household – he was the eldest. There was not much to him, he was slight of build, his face smooth, he hardly ever needed to shave. The three girls were robust, but he had always been a sickly child. But he had a boyish handsomeness, and a gentle wit. He could make me laugh with his words and that twinkle in his eye.'

I could see the affection in her words. The way her thoughts drifted away to another place when she thought of him. 'He liked you, then?' I asked.

'Oh yes, I know he did, but he would get me into trouble for not completing my work.'

'You were not conscientious?'

'Oh, I was, but he would distract me. He was studying to become a priest like his father, it was expected of him, but I could see that the loneliness hung heavy on him. He sat for hours every day in his room at study, and when I came to clean, he would stop and just talk to me, for hours if I would let him.'

'You liked him too?'

'More than that, I grew to love him. I would rush my other duties to find more time to spend in his room. The mistress would admonish me, but she was harder on him, and his father was too; such a solemn man, his father.'

'So what happened?'

'I was eighteen and he was twenty-two when our relationship started to change. It was high summer and he asked to meet me on my day off. I was undecided at first, but I agreed, and he slipped out of the house and we met down by the river. We walked and talked all day, took a meal in a tavern. It was a wonderful day. And then every month on my day off, we met regularly, and I would look forward to those wonderful days. Even when winter came, we still met, and he wouldn't stop even when the cold went to his chest and forced him to his bed afterwards. When spring came the following year, we were deeply in love. We had our place, a secluded spot down by the river; it gave us some privacy, away from prying eyes. We had our first kiss as the weather started to get hotter, and then each month our passions grew more fervent.'

'But your position as a servant prevented him marrying you?'

'You don't understand. I had no expectation that he would be allowed to marry me. I know his love for me was genuine and that was enough for me. Then one afternoon down by the river, we kissed, and...'

I looked at her; the questioning must have been obvious in my eyes. I wanted her to tell me what happened. I wanted to know that I was a love child, not a child born from a master's evil will as my own had been born.

'And,' she said, I could see the love in her eyes, 'and at that moment I didn't care what was right or wrong. I just loved him so much, and it seemed the most natural thing to do.'

'How long did it last?' I asked.

'All that summer, but by September I knew I was pregnant. I told Nicholas, and to my surprise he was overjoyed. He started to make plans for our wedding as if there were no stiles to climb; he was such a kind man.'

'So what happened?'

'One morning he was just gone. He had been sent away to theological college, his father no longer to tutor him at home. I was called to see the mistress and admonished for my sin. I had somehow brought evil into her household, taken advantage of her weak unworldly son. I was to be thrown out, told to go and pack my things.'

The tears welled up in my eyes again. I recognised the wrong that had been done to her; it had been done to me as well.

'I took lodgings,' she continued, 'but my savings quickly ran out. I was at my wits' end, but then I had an unexpected visit from the mistress. A position as a nanny had been found for me in Bath, but I had to give up my child to the Foundlings' Hospital to be able to take it. They would pay my rent until my confinement and then after the child was born I would go to take up this new position. I knew that Nicholas's hand was in this somewhere and I said a little prayer for him. Giving you up was so very difficult, but the alternative was starving – we would both have starved,' she blurted out, her tears now uncontrollable, her shoulders hunched in convolutions.

I rushed to her again, put my arms around her and we both sobbed uncontrollably again for some minutes. Then I heard a knock on the door; I ignored it, but it rapped again, and then a third time. Then the butler came in, saw me embracing Agatha. I saw distaste in his expression. I was breaking the rules of hierarchy; his own place in that scale was not so high, but he saw himself as well above a nanny, and a nanny did not warrant my consolation. I turned and snapped at him.

'Will you bring us some tea,' I said, belligerence in my tone.

I could see that he was dumfounded; it was not his position to serve tea to a nanny. 'Now, mister, if you please!' I shouted. For a heartbeat he did not move, but then he jumped to it, bowing as he left.

The Journal of Corbyn Carlisle

7th **July 1790.** Mr. Edward Gibbon, a grand tourist himself, has said very wisely that foreign travel completes the education of an English gentleman. I now know what he means; there is so much of the world that I was ignorant of. My scholarly guide on this tour is a Mr. Andrew Cruickshank, a Scottish gentleman who is actually a year my junior. He has trained to be a doctor of medicine in

Edinburgh, but has forsaken that profession to be a full-time guide, or my bear-leader as he likes to call himself. He is a sort of tutor, chaperone, and guardian, all rolled into one. He is a large, robust man; he wears his reddish hair in a ponytail at the nape of his neck and is quite the standout man. You cannot easily miss him; he can also drink prodigious amounts of wine, ale or whatever beverage the locals have to offer. He is the most vigorous of men and all this alcohol does not seem to slow him down in the least.

And yet he is also so knowledgeable on all the scholarly pursuits, from architecture to painting, from literature to poetry, and he seems to know almost everybody, so that he gains me access to view even antiquities that are held in private collections.

He advises me that it is incumbent on me to be a studious observer, and that I must keep a detailed journal of my travels, to record all the antiquities I see and the foreign persons I meet, as this will be invaluable to my fellow Englishmen who have not had the privilege to take the tour. He says that I should also think about publishing such a journal when I get back. I have resolved to do this, and that will mean that there will be fewer entries in this, my personal journal.

My tour has been rearranged by Andrew in view of the troubles in France, and we are not taking the normal route. We began three months ago in April, leaving Dover, and sailed to Ostend in the Spanish Netherlands, (avoiding Calais) where we purchased a carriage to take us on our journey through Europe. Andrew advised that we did not need to hire a French-speaking guide, as his French was sufficient, which is a modesty on his behalf, my own French is sufficient, but his is excellent. French, of course, is the language of gentlemen throughout Europe and my education in the language was not left wanting. I am disappointed on missing out on Paris, as this would have afforded me the chance to witness the manners of French high society and courtly behaviour, whatever is now left of that. I have also missed the opportunity to test my skills in the French style of fencing.

I am writing this entry in Geneva, Switzerland. After visiting Flanders, we skirted rural France as quickly as we could. The intention is to go from here to Lausanne and then traverse the Alps to the German-speaking parts of Europe and will visit Innsbruck, Vienna, Dresden, Heidelberg, Berlin and Potsdam.

Then we will go south to the Italian cities of Milan, Turin, Pisa, Venice, Padua and then to Rome. I am so looking forward to seeing all those high renaissance paintings and the Roman sculptures. We will then stay some months in Florence where there is an Anglo-Italian community I am told. Finally, we will take a boat to Spain and visit Barcelona, Madrid and Seville and then home.

Andrew is keen that I see the trip as more than a scholarly one and advises me that I should take in all that the tour has to offer, even the decadent parts. I should use all my external senses, he says; in particular there is an opportunity to sample the most beautiful women that the world has to offer. I fear that I will be a dull companion for him, but yet I am determined to come back from the tour having learned to dance much better, to fence better, to understand the foreign fellow and be a more knowledgeable fellow myself.

Chapter 23.

Reading the journals contemporaneously shows that Corbyn and Ginny's worlds are diverging, but they both seem to be advancing in life and they make satisfying reading; it's just a pity that they could not have progressed together. They seemed good for one another. Their words, of course, are written in a different time in a different world, and it is my job as a historian to be wary of assigning my own values as a modern man to their own. Nevertheless, they both seem so real to me, and I have never before reacted so emotionally to any source material. I am genuinely interested to know what becomes of them.

These thoughts passed through my mind as I waited outside the office of Joan Fisher, who heads up the University Student Administration and Records section. I know her slightly from faculty meetings, she has been at the university much longer than me. I suspected I was having these thoughts because I was compensating for my own feelings of loneliness. It's coming up a month now since Grace and I last spoke, since that evening in my flat. I felt that I had been the wronged person, and that the ball was in her court to make the first move, but she hasn't. She hasn't even talked to me as her professor about her course work. We are both reading the same journals, she is ahead of me, but the journals disappear from the press in the history department, and then reappear when she has read them. I never see them go; she must wait for me to leave my office to do this, just to avoid speaking to me. Part of me tells me that I have had a lucky escape; that she is unbalanced and it was lucky I saw that side of her before I got in too deep. The last thing I need is a relationship with an unstable woman. But then I have to admit to myself that I miss her so very much; we were only a couple for a few weeks, but that does not seem to diminish the pain I feel. Sitting there, I was also feeling guilt, that I was somehow betraying her, snooping in this way.

The door opened. 'Come in James,' it was Joan. She was a mature lady in her middle fifties, but with a natural elegance set off by her smart business suit. I sat in the chair facing her, following her hand gesture. 'What can I do for you today?' she asked, giving me a gentle, genuine look.

'I'm wondering what information you have on one of my students?'

'Which one?' she said, swivelling her chair round to her computer and opening a programme.

'Grace Farmer.'

She turned and looked back at me; that look of kindness disappeared. *Damn*, I thought to myself, she knows about us. She cocked an eye at me over her half-moon glasses.

'Can't you ask her yourself?' she said.

'Why do you say that?' I feigned ignorance of her meaning.

'James, you may think that the university is a large monolith of an organisation, but I promise you that it is not; in reality it is a very small community, a very small community indeed.'

'So you know about us, then?'

'I know about everything that goes on at the university, James. I've had to have words with the Vice Chancellor on many occasions, so that he can put a stop to the *inappropriate* activities of some of the lecturers.' She gave that gesture with her fingers at the word *inappropriate* to indicate speech marks.

I looked down at my feet; I wondered if this had been a good idea after all. 'So my behaviour is regarded as inappropriate is it?' There was resignation in my tone.

'Well, you have never come up on the radar before, James; you are certainly not one of our, shall we say, *troublesome* lecturers. And the lady in question is not an undergraduate anymore, and not some young impressionable girl, or the opposite, some streetwise siren looking to enhance her grades by offering sexual services; unfortunately they exist, I promise you.'

'I'm not sure what you are saying?' I said, looking back up at her.

'I'm saying that the university exists in the twenty-first century; and on the face of it your relationship with Miss Farmer is not deemed to be *inappropriate*.' She gave the finger gesture again.

'So you will give me information about her?'

She leant forward. 'I repeat, James, why can't you ask her yourself?'

'She won't talk to me,' I said vaguely, giving her a sheepish glance.

'Really, James, I don't think the university records are there to deal with a lovers' tiff, now are they?'

Her eyes moved over my shoulder to her door as if gesturing me to go. I took the hint and stood and went to the door, then looked back. 'Sorry,' I said, as if I were a schoolboy who had been royally told off by his headmaster. I opened the door and started to leave, but I stopped, looked back at her. I saw the condescension in her eyes and that stung me. I shut the door angrily instead of leaving.

'Look, Joan; for goodness' sake, woman, if I could speak to her I would.'

She sighed, gestured with her hand for me to sit down again. 'Come on then, make your case and then I'll tell you whether I consider if there will be any impropriety in giving you this information.'

I sat down hurriedly, leaning forward. 'Well, Grace Farmer has always seemed to be one of the most grounded students I have ever had. She's mature and controlled, but there has been an incident, where she has been…' I struggled for the words, '…well her whole attitude has been irrational.'

'And was this incident a university matter?' I must have pulled a face, and she read my reluctance. 'No, don't answer that question,' she said, 'let's just say that it *is* a university matter and that you are concerned, as she is one of your students.' I nodded appreciatively. 'So what is it you want to know?'

'Well, I wondered if there were any psychological considerations that I should know of?'

'Mmmm,' she said, fixing me with a hard stare, her eyes narrowing. Then she turned to her computer and tapped into it. She read, engrossed, looking over at me from time to time. I waited impatiently. Then she turned back at me.

'Miss Farmer's initial registration for her course was delayed.' My expression must have told her that I needed more. 'Because she was part of a drugs rehabilitation programme in Manchester before she came here. She is still part of it as far as I can see.'

A junkie, that was the last thing I expected; she certainly didn't display any of the indications of that. But then I am not the best person to judge, am I? It must have been a painful time for her, and I had pushed her into revisiting it. I think I now understood why she had been so evasive with me.

I had already sent her several text messages and emails asking her to meet me so that we could discuss things, but all had been unanswered, but what was now clear to me was that somehow we had to talk. The problem had to be brought out into the open, however painful it was for her; until we did, we couldn't go forward. I left my office and walked about the history department, looked in all the rooms, but there was no sign of her. I repeated the tour an hour later, but still she wasn't to be found. I did this for several days, the same routine on the hour, but each time, nothing.

And then I got some course work from her by way of email. It said no more than – <here is my latest work for evaluation> and then an attachment. She had used the minimum of words with nothing that would invite me to respond. But it told me that she had not taken off somewhere, or gone home to Beverley. She was probably working from her flat. I had never been there, so I rang Joan Fisher for the address, but she wouldn't give it to me, saying that if she didn't want to see me then she was perfectly entitled not to. I cursed her after I put the phone down, even though I knew she was right. But then I put my mind into investigative mode; I am a historian damn it, I should be good at that. If she was still working on her course then she would need to research, she must be using the *university library*. I extended my hourly search to it. It was vast and in a different building. I sweet-talked one of the receptionists into telling me what books she had taken out, and especially *when*, and when she had last worked online at the library computer terminals. The problem was that the library was open 24 hours a day and Grace had been working there late into the evening.

I was not making much progress, I needed to rethink. Where did students go? And then I cursed myself for my stupidity. Where was the most obvious place to find students? Students like to drink, and the cheapest place for them to drink was the SU, the Students' Union bar. I spent the next three nights propping up the bar, they didn't even have Bombardier and I had to drink some keg swill, but there was still no sign of her. I was beginning to think that I was wrong in my reasoning; Grace was not an undergrad and not a twenty year-old; perhaps the SU was not one of her haunts. It was just after ten-thirty on the third night, and I was draining my glass, ready to go, thinking that I had struck out again; then I saw her out of the corner of my eye. She was approaching the bar, getting her purse out of her shoulder bag; she was looking down and had not noticed me. She looked up at the barman and was about to order when I said:

'You take some tracking down, Grace.'

She darted me a look. She obviously thought that the SU was a safe haven, well, safe from me at least. She jumped, startled as if she would flee, and I responded the same way as if I would run after her if she did. Our bodies both juddered.

'This is stupid, Grace,' I said, 'we have to talk.'

She looked at me like a cornered animal, I saw the whites of her eyes as they widened in astonishment – but then, then the rancour dissipated from her features as the realisation took her that I was right. 'OK,' she said, 'but not here.'

'Where?'

She thought. 'Neutral ground?'

'Where?' I repeated. I could see that she could not think of anywhere. 'Shall we just walk?'

She nodded.

We walked out into the night. Vapour trails flowed from our mouths in the chill of the early December night air. I felt myself shiver, but it was probably as much from nervous tension as from the cold. The Christmas lights were shining, dazzlingly; the streets were full of late-night drinkers enjoying their evening out, but they all seemed to disappear like images going out of focus as the tension mounted. She made no attempt to say anything, so I spoke first.

'I thought we were good together?' I said, and then cursed myself inwardly. It was the same question that I had asked at my flat that had started all this trouble.

'*Umph!*' she answered derisively; and then more silence.

I decided to stop dilly-dallying around the problem. I stopped and looked directly into her eyes. 'I know all about your drug problem.' I stole myself for her response.

She looked back at me intently. Her eyes widened again, but this time as if she was assessing what I actually knew. 'How?'

'Universities have records.'

'So you think you know all about me, do you?' she grunted.

'No,' I said, 'but I think I have the right to know.'

'*RIGHT?*' There was belligerence in her eyes, but she left the sentence hanging for a heartbeat. 'Why have you a right to know all about me? I only offered you a sexual dalliance, nothing more. That should have been obvious, even to you.'

What was that supposed to mean, I thought to myself. I let it go.

'Surely we had moved on from that?'

'Then that's *your* problem if you think so.'

'*My* problem, yes I suppose it is. And I have another problem, and that is I miss you more than I expected to. I want us to get back together again.'

'You wouldn't want to if you knew the truth.'

'Try me?' I said, holding her eyes with my stare. I was genuine in my desire to know all about her, but I was not prepared for what she now told me.

'OK then,' she said, 'the *whole* sordid truth. I started this degree course once before, twelve years ago, at a London College. I was nineteen, and in my first year I used to go to the SU like everybody else. I met a man there; he wasn't a student, but he hung around the bar. He was tall and good looking and he had money and a flash car and I sort of, well, I fell for him. I saw him as my boyfriend, but *he* saw himself as something else, my dealer, my pimp, I was a source of income to him. He introduced me to drugs, crack cocaine, divided into lines and snorted up the nose. I thought it was cool, but I didn't realise just how highly addictive it was, and then he showed me how to prepare a solution of cocaine for injecting; it gets to your brain quicker that way. He was fast tracking me to dependence.

'Within a few months, I was hopelessly addicted and he had total power over me. I stopped attending lectures, or submitting any written work for evaluation. I tried to sign on, but the welfare state does not finance coke, and anyway I had not paid any stamps as a student and didn't qualify for benefit. So I took minimum-wage jobs, but that didn't pay enough to feed my habit either. So he suggested that I turn to prostitution, well when I say suggested, he beat me until I agreed. I turned my first *trick* when I was still nineteen. I learned how to lurk around the dark streets in a desperate need for cash. I charged only £30 for a blow-job, and at first they paid because I was attractive, but then my complexion began to break out in blotches, I didn't look after myself, my hair became lank, and then most men didn't want to pay more than £20. I was in a vicious spiral of degradation, all to get enough money for a fix.

'You'll have heard stories like that before, but you can't know what it actually means. I'd look for punters first thing in the morning on their way to work, then during lunchtimes, then 4 to 5 in the afternoon. After that, it was mostly other dealers who tried to pick me up in return for crack rocks. If I took *their* coke, I would get a beating from my pimp if he found out. Every day, I faced the possibility of being jailed, raped or killed, just in order to raise the quick cash I needed to support my drug habit. I would prowl the dark streets at night waiting for men to flag me down, and I traded in cars and urine-soaked alleyways. Men who smelled as if they never bathed, and I would suck their stinking dicks for a few pounds to feed my habit, and after a while I smelt just as bad as they did, I was like a walking sewer myself, my complexion gone, my arms like an Ordnance Survey map of punctured veins. I became hard, I knew to get my money up front, but sometimes I was then beaten up for the money they had paid over, or for my stash of coke and money, and if I fought back I was raped for my trouble.

'Within a year, I was at rock bottom: sharing needles and syringes, running the risk of catching or spreading HIV or hepatitis C; or perhaps damaging my veins with abscesses, or even blood clots developing. I was a total mess.'

She stared at me and my reaction. I was stunned, bewildered at her story, and I knew that she could see that in my features. There must have been desperation in my eyes, but that desperation would not convert into rational thoughts or words. I had played this scene in my head many times over the last few weeks, but it had never gone like this. It was as though she was talking about a different person, not the Grace Farmer that I knew. She allowed herself a sour smile; she had got the reaction from me that she wanted. Her intention had been to spare me nothing of the degradation that she had sunk to, and she had succeeded. My mind was a whirlpool and we were locked together for some moments in unspoken words.

'So what happened?' I said, words eventually coming to me.

'I was found unconscious in an alleyway early one morning. It was summer; if it had been winter I would have frozen to death. I was taken to hospital and I was then referred to social services who put me on a drugs rehabilitation programme. That would have been hard enough, but my pimp was not going to have that. My addiction was his power over me and he soon had me back on the streets, feeding my habit. One of the workers on the drugs programme guessed what was going on; it was a known pattern that he had seen many times before. He begged me to get away from him and I knew that he was right. So one morning I fled to Manchester to a place on a rehabilitation programme up there, which he had arranged.'

'So how long have you been clean?' I asked, nervously.

'How do you know I'm clean?' She gave out a scornful laugh.

I felt myself shudder; I didn't know how to respond.

'Never believe a drug addict who tells you they are clean,' she said.

'But are you?'

'Yes I'm clean; over three years now.'

'Well, at least that's good to know,' I mumbled, unsure of myself.

'I've just told you never to believe a drug addict. They'll sell their grannies for a fix.'

She was playing with me, I could see that; she always did, but this time it was more caustic; glances were exchanged, but what could I do? We seemed to have reached an impasse; there was an uneasy silence between us. My head was full of questions I dare not ask, and then the traffic noise and the chatter of the people on the streets suddenly came back into focus. I looked around myself; there were happy faces all around me, the town was buzzing with pre-Christmas revellers, and yet my face was not one of them: I was bewildered.

'I've given you a lot to think about,' she said. She also seemed reluctant, unsure what to do, then she turned and walked slowly away. She looked back over her shoulder, but my feet seemed to be glued to the pavement, I was unable to move, frozen like a rabbit in the headlights, bewilderment etched in my features. I watched in anguish as she walked away until the darkness spitefully swallowed her.

Chapter 24.

The Journal of Ginny Farmer

3rd **September 1790.** Finding my mother has somehow given me a place in this world. I feel that she will now remain in my life forever. The loss of my friend Corbyn has been painful, but hopefully my mother will now always be with me. I have asked her to come and live with me, but she has declined, she will not even come and work for me. Perhaps it is for the best as I would have had to deceive Lord John. She says she is happy bringing up her master's children; she would feel that she is betraying them to leave. I have sent her some money, but she has returned it, but I am pleased to say she has accepted some gifts from me.

8th **November 1790.** Lord John is angry with me. He came to me this evening, but he did not stay, his purpose was to admonish me. He stood, in that way of his, with his elbow on the mantle, the fire warming his backside. He gave me that cold-fish stare, his lips curled into a slight snarl; I could see the disapproval on his features, but I could not at first think of any reason for his displeasure. He looked haughtily down that pointed nose at me and I frantically racked my brains as to what I could have done.

'You have been using my carriage, madam?' he sniffed, and then turned his head sideways and upwards as if to reinforce his superiority.

'Why yes, Lord John,' I answered, still confused, 'but if you remember, I asked your permission before I did.'

'Yes, Yes,' he snapped, 'but on what business, madam?'

A cold chill took me. Suddenly the conversation had moved into difficult waters. 'I had some private business to take care of.' I chose my words carefully. I then frantically tried to think what I would tell him if he asked me the nature of that business; but surprisingly he didn't.

'And what form of address did you use on this… business?'

'Form of address, Lord John? I don't understand.' I was still confused.

'Madam, have you or have you not been masquerading as my wife; is that clear enough for you?'

I breathed an inward sigh of relief; somehow he had found out about my impersonation, from the coachman in all probability, but I would not have to tell him of my history; but as I looked back up at him I saw a flash of rage in his eyes. I felt myself shiver. 'This is a misunderstanding, Lord John,' I said. 'I was in your carriage with your coat of arms on the door. It seemed the natural thing to do to call myself Lady Dalby. It was not my intention to masquerade as your wife.' I looked away from his fierce stare. 'I am sorry if I have overstepped the mark,' I whispered timidly as diffidently as I could.

'Madam, you should understand your place,' he said in a fierce whisper, 'and not forget that your place in society is at my discretion. If you want to return to whoring then that is easily arranged.'

The arrogance of the man stung me. ''At my discretion,'' he had said, but he was ignoring his own motives. The taking of a mistress was making a statement to society, that he was still a virile man; a courtesan was, in part, to enhance <u>his</u> own reputation, a sign of his masculinity. A man's infidelity was not grounds for divorce even if a woman's was. I would have loved to have debated this with him, but this was a time for guile and not debate.

'You are right, Lord Dalby,' I said apologetically, 'you must forgive a silly young girl for her pretensions.'

'Well, there you have it,' he said, raising that pointed nose in the air again.

I saw a smug expression appear on his face. It was not the most attractive sight. 'Will you be staying with me tonight?' I asked sweetly.

'No, I will be away to my club,' he said.

I was not sorry to see him go.

10th January 1791. The new year has passed and it was a lonely time. Beth tries to help; bless her, she is kind, but there is no intelligent conversation between us. Lord John is with his family in Yorkshire, but he was cold towards me before he left; he has been ever since he found out that I had been using the name of Lady Dalby. He has always been detached from his emotions, flying high like an eagle above such irrelevances, but that manner of his has been even more apparent. In some strange way, I suppose it does show that he has emotions somewhere deep down inside of him to be so offended by my taking his wife's name. Perhaps, deep down in that armoured chest of his, he does not have a totally cold heart after all.

Mother is in the country with her employer, they have gone there for Christmas. I do not see as much of her as I would wish, she only gets one day off a month. There is so much that we have to catch up on, but we are relaxed together when we meet and we seem to just talk of inconsequential things instead.

Meanwhile, I am working hard on my French lessons, trying to keep myself busy.

28th February 1791. I know Sir John is back in London, but he has not been to see me. My allowance is still being paid, but as times goes on I wonder if he will ever forgive me my indiscretion. The social season will begin again after Easter and hopefully there will be dinner parties to attend; that will give me the opportunity to show how useful I am to him.

15th April 1791. We attended a party last night in Grosvenor Square. I felt quite odd stepping down from Sir John's carriage in my fine gown, knowing that my mother was just a few doors away at Mr. Nathaniel Coker's residence. The season is just getting going, and we dined well. I was on my best behaviour, trying to show Lord John what an asset I am to him. I strained every sinew to play my part as convincingly as I could. I nodded gracefully and displayed all those barely perceptive gestures of body language that pass for refinement – a minute nod here and a raised eyebrow there. I uttered little snippets of wit when they were called for. We attracted a crowd, but then we always do, but my wit was especially sharp and I showed that I could converse on almost every topic; but Lord John hardly said a word, whatever I said I could not get him to join the conversation. I know that he and the government are extremely worried about the events in France, but I feel it was more than that. I fear that he just did not want to be with me.

He excused himself from the others, saying that he had matters of state to discuss with another at the party, which was always part of the arrangement between us, but this time I fear that this was just an excuse. I tried so hard all evening to be the perfect companion, but the only person who did not see that was Lord John and we drove home in silence; he did not spend the night with me. We have not slept together for months now.

3rd May 1791. My allowance has not been paid; it was due on the first of the month from Lord John's lawyers. I have sent a letter of enquiry to them.

5th **May 1791**. The lawyers have advised that the allowance has been stopped on the instructions of Lord John. I feared that something like this may happen, but I have heard nothing from him direct. I must find the courage to write to him.

10th **May 1791**. I have received a short note from Lord John. It says very little, other than that our arrangement has been terminated. It is so like the man, no explanations; I am sure that he feels so superior that he is under no obligation to give one. I wouldn't say that he despises people, but if he ever deigned to think about them, then perhaps he would. But then he has never offered any love or affection towards me, so I should not be surprised. I must assume that taking his wife's name was something that he could not forgive, I presumed too much.

Hey ho, my life seems so full of ups and downs. But I am not penniless and I own the house I live in; I will now have to think of how I am to support myself in the future.

Chapter 25.

'Another pint of Bombardier,' I said to the barman. He bent his arm, a long slow pull of the pump and I watched the amber liquid start to fill the glass. It was normally a sight that I loved, a precursor to that first swig of fine ale, but today I looked and didn't really see. My mind was elsewhere; I was obsessing, I had been for several days now. All I could think of was Grace.

But now there were two Graces in my mind; the one that I was falling in love with, denim-clad but still elegant, witty, self-assured; but now another, a foul creature who lurked in dark urine-reeking alleyways. I had this horrible image in my mind that I just could not get rid of; on her knees sucking cock for the price of a fix. It was a poison that was polluting my adoring thoughts of her until they were withered, emaciated like a summer flower that a tomcat has sprayed. This thought had been with me as I had tried to lecture this afternoon, and then it followed me home and stabbed my psyche as I tried to prepare a meal. I had come to the Nags Head to try and get away from it, but it had followed me here too. I was distant, these thoughts whirling crazily in my mind.

And then as I drank, these thoughts began to morph in my mind. The alcohol seemed to cultivate belligerence. I began to foster a feeling of betrayal, it started to fester. *How could Grace have done this to me? She had led me on, led me astray. She had been deceitful, pretending to be something that she was not. It was all her scheming, devious fault; wasn't it?* The more I drank, the more antagonistic I became, and I drank so very much.

I staggered home and fell drunkenly into my unmade bed. I fell asleep immediately, or to be more precise I passed out. But I was wide awake some hours later. I looked at my alarm and the red numbers lit up – 4:10 a.m. I lay on my back; it was still several hours to dawn, and then the night-nadges really got to work on me. My ambivalent thoughts about Grace returned to me, the anaesthetic of the Bombardier having worn off, to be replaced by a throbbing head and pounding, relentless thoughts. I still missed her terribly, but negative thoughts were dominant, I knew I had to get over her; I had to move on.

Chapter 26.

The Journal of Ginny Farmer

26th June 1791. Beth has urged me to return to whoring, but I am in no rush; I have some savings and the house is in my name. I called on Samuel today and we spent a pleasant afternoon talking together. His fame spreads, and he told me that the Prince of Wales himself attended his last set-to, that's what he calls a fight. I told him that Lord Dalby had abandoned me, and to my surprise he was pleased, saying that I deserve better than him. He suggested that I send a note to dear Corbyn; after the incident and the service we rendered on his behalf three years ago, he said that he owed me, but I cannot of course do that.

He did, however, also suggest something very surprising, and I find the idea so very intriguing. Samuel regularly gives exhibitions of his fighting skills and these take place in theatres. The theatre owners are keen to engage him as they know he can fill the theatres to the rafters most anywhere in England. Because of this he has become acquainted with the owners of several companies of actors. He says that with my ability to mimic, I would make a fine actress. I know that the reputation of actresses is not far above that of whores, but then that particular stagecoach left quite some time ago.

8th July 1791. Today Samuel introduced me to a Mr. Jeremiah Cotton, the manager of a travelling theatrical company. His company have a summer season in London at the Coburg Theatre on the Corner of the Cut. He was a strange man who talked in an affected plummy voice. If he was trying to mimic a fine educated gentleman then he was not succeeding, it was little more than a pretentious way of speaking. He took my hand and bowed extensively, but his grip was limp and his hand clammy, not at all manly. He was a large, rotund man with ruddy cheeks that were interspersed with pronounced spidery red veins. He was, plainly and simply, a fat man, yet his movements were those of a slim and nimble ballet dancer, a most odd combination. His clothes were garish, but he had outgrown them so that all the buttons pulled against their holes as if they were holding on for their lives. He was <u>player</u> a and it was hard to tell if the image he now presented was the real Jeremiah Cotton or whether he was playing the part of a theatrical manager.

Samuel, bless him, was a bit naughty and introduced me as Lady Virginia Farmer and I let Mr. Cotton think I was a fine lady fallen on hard times, and I am sure that was the reason for his own plummy voice.

'Will it not be beneficial to have such a fine lady in your company, Mr. Cotton?' There was a twinkle in Samuel's eye as he spoke.

'I have to confess, sir,' said Jeremiah, 'that when you first broached this arrangement, I was somewhat dubious, but the lady, as now presented to me, is of such beauty that I can see the possibilities; but can she act sir, that is the question?'

'To quote the bard, Mr. Cotton,' said Samuel.

'Huh?' said Jeremiah, not at first realising what he had said. 'Oh Yes, the bard, sir,' he added, 'very droll, sir, very droll indeed.'

'Ohrrohrrr zir,' I said, reverting to my Bristol accent, 'but yer do say the nicest things about me.'

''Pon my soul,' said the fat man, looking at me dumfounded, 'you are a mimic, my good lady,' and then he burst out laughing, 'you mimic a fine West Country accent indeed.'

'Do I indeed, sir,' I said reverting to my fine lady voice, 'are you so sure that the West Country accent is the mimic?'

'Well, of course it is, however well it is performed. I pride myself in being able to spot a performance.'

'Well then sir, you are wrong this time,' interrupted Samuel, unable to contain himself, 'it is the fine lady that is the performance.'

Jeremiah looked at me again, he was silent for a heartbeat; his eye widened as he took in the deception. 'Well I never,' he said, 'can you do other mimics, madam?'

I gave him a French accent, and he applauded after it. Then I spoke in a cockney accent just like the costermonger and his gal had spoken to me. Then an Irish accent like Mrs Strabane had spoken. He applauded after each.

'Oh she will be capital,' he gushed, then added quickly, 'well, after some tuition from myself.'

'Then we can come to an arrangement?' asked Samuel.

'Oh I think so, sir,' he said, 'but, of course, I can only offer an understudy's salary to begin with. How old are you, my dear? Perhaps we can start you off with juvenile parts, you are young enough to carry them off, I feel.'

'Oh I think we can do better than that,' said Samuel, trying to look after me, 'and anyway, you already have a juvenile lead, do you not?'

'So what do you propose, sir?' said Jeremiah.

'Your female lead, Mabel Royale; is she not getting too old for the roles that she plays?'

'But she is my wife, sir,' he answered, 'and my good lady will not willingly give up her roles. And I know what's best for me if harmony is to be maintained in the Cotton household. And besides, I have other actresses keen to take on leading parts.'

Samuel thought on the matter, but I saw an opportunity. 'Mr. Cotton, I know that if I join you, I will be no more than a Johnny Raw to begin with. What if I offered to come and join you for no salary at all, but I take, say, twenty percent of any additional ticket sales; what would you say to that?'

Samuel looked at me; I could see that he was unsure.

'No salary indeed,' said Jeremiah, rubbing his chin in contemplation. I could see that he was hooked, believing that he had a fine bargain; an attractive new actress for no extra cost. 'Very well,' he said, 'I think we have an arrangement between us.'

'Capital,' said Samuel, but I could see some concern in his eyes, 'but you must let me see your ledgers before we shake on it, so I can see the numbers of paying customers that you have had so far in your engagement.'

'You do not trust me, sir?' said Jeremiah, as if offended.

'I am only looking out for the delicate lady,' answered Samuel, bowing politely.

'Very well, sir,' he said, his feigned affront melting away.

Afterwards, Samuel expressed his concerns as to the arrangement, but I convinced him that if I have no talent for this I will be the first to depart. If I have a talent, then I hope to make more than a meagre wage, with the prospect of some fine gentleman in the audience to take me as a prize. I have already walked down that particular alleyway, and another stroll down it is not my immediate plan. It may be the dream of many a young actress, but it is certainly not mine. So I start tomorrow, learning the ropes. Me, Ginny Farmer, an actress.

15th July 1791. I have just completed my first week as an actress in the company. The Coburg is considered a minor theatre and therefore does not have a licence to perform serious drama, but that fits in nicely with what Mr. Cotton has to offer.

We play and sing songs, especially patriotic ones, a little light opera sometimes. And we perform playlets and other entertainments such as scenes or excerpts from major plays. The second half is always a melodrama, a combining of spoken recitation with short pieces of accompanying music. Sometimes the music is also used to accompany the non-speaking parts of the drama. The orchestra rises to a great crescendo to emphasize the most dramatic parts. The current one demonstrates the evils of drink; Mr. Cotton himself is a confirmed abstainer and he performs it himself with great gusto. Unfortunately, most in the audience are inebriated themselves and I don't think that they actually see the evils performed before them. They jeer and applaud in the wrong places, but it doesn't seem to deter him.

I have found that I have a good singing voice and can hold a tune, but my voice is a little weak at the moment. I have to practise something called projection to strengthen it, and sing from my <u>diaphragm</u>, that's just below my ribs.

I must confess that when I first walked on the stage I was almost overcome with nerves. Although the theatre itself is neat and tidy, the same could not be said for the audience, they looked a meanly clad bunch. I looked up at them, the auditorium was only about a third full, but I could smell the pungent odour of stale ale and gin in the air; they did not seem friendly at all. I felt like a rabbit frozen before a stoat. I had had little opportunity to learn my lines but, luckily, in the excerpt that was being performed I had only one line to utter. When I opened my mouth to speak it however, my voice let me down. The line escaped in a whimper as if I were a mouse cornered by the cat. I heard jeers and whistles and I looked around at the other players for some indication as to what I should do. I saw Jeremiah Cotton's eyes bulging wide, his arm was stiff by his side, but his hand was waving at me, and I took it that he was gesturing me to say the line again. I stole myself, took a bold step forward and boomed the line again as loud as I could and the audience cheered, but I think there was some irony in their enthusiasm. I stole a look at Mr. Cotton and I saw him nod covertly to me.

After that, my nerves just seem to fall away from me. Reciting lines is not at all like ordinary speaking, and you have to make sure that the person at the very back of the hall can hear you, and if I forget a line I just make one up. I realised that playing before a crowd was not so different from the masquerades that I had been undertaking for the last few years. It was about performing a role with confidence and I was used to doing just that. I have only been required to play minor roles so far, with very few lines to learn, but I also have to help build and move the scenery. All the players, it seems, must help; be prepared to roll up your sleeves, so to say.

Backstage is an exercise in ordered chaos. There is obviously some rationale to the hive of activity, but it is hard to see it. Things seem to get done, however, or only just get done in most cases. Only Jeremiah Cotton and Mabel Royale have their own dressing room. Our changing room is cramped and filled with semi-naked bodies frantically trying to change their costumes or applying their make-up. It is a room of hustle and bustle, of commotion, of goings-on and of sweat. It is poky and overcrowded, but it is vibrant and alive; it pulsates with emotion and passion. I love it; I have had the most wonderful week.

30ᵗʰ August 1791. The engagement of Jeremiah Cotton's travelling theatre company at the Coburg is coming to end. We have only three more weeks to go. He moves from here to Plymouth and then on to Exeter. I will have to decide whether to go with him.

I have so loved my few weeks here. Most of the costumes were too big for me and I took to altering them so that they would fit me. I seem to be in demand now as a seamstress, as well as a player and scene-shifter. I get along with everyone, even the other young actresses. We are all in competition for roles, but they seem more interested in finding a wealthy gentleman than being jealous of me. I say everyone, well except for Mabel Royale that is. She should have given up the lead roles some years ago; even with the heavy make-up, her painted face cannot hide the lines of age on it, and her ample figure is bursting out of her costumes. I offered to alter them for her, but she has refused my offer. She glares at me even when we are on stage together. For the last two weeks I have been playing the second lead in the melodramas, and I have my own solo song in the first half. The word seems to be going round of the new pretty young actress, and the audiences are growing. It seems that the young gentlemen around town, the adventurers, are coming out to see me. Jeremiah can see this of course, but I know that he is in fear of his wife.

There was an amusing moment at Friday night's performance. We had nearly a full house, and the audience was of a much better sort than usual, the middling classes, even some fine gentlemen and their ladies. In the melodramas there are always stock characters. There is the hero, the villain, and the heroine, involved in themes of love and murder. The hero is required to save the heroine from the villain, to rescue the damsel in distress, so to speak, to represent a triumph of good over evil. But when Jeremiah rescued Mabel Royale, a wag in the audience stood and shouted out, "Leave the old bag, guv'na and save the young filly." Well, the whole audience to a man burst out laughing to a point that it interrupted the performance for nearly a full minute, until Jeremiah and Mabel carried on, with the audience at first taking no notice of them.

Afterwards, in the changing rooms, it was the only topic of conversation, and the looks I got from Mabel would have frozen the devil in hell himself.

20ᵗʰ September 1791. Jeremiah has begged me to come with the company on tour; he can see that the audiences are growing, and has offered me a fine fee. The problem is my own ambition; I know that I am the newcomer, but I want the lead roles. He returned after speaking with his wife; I say speaking, the whole cast could hear the row from their dressing room. She was saying the most terrible things about me, using the crudest of language. His compromise offer was that I alternate with his wife taking the lead roles. I am looking favourably on the offer; I wonder if he can take Beth in some minor role.

21ˢᵗ September 1791. Out of the blue I have been approached by a Mr. Jack Brown. He runs the travelling theatre company that is engaged at the Coburg after Mr. Cotton's contract expires. He saw my performance of Friday night and said the most charming things about it and my beauty. He says that he has a number of very beautiful actresses in his company, and he knows that they are responsible for bringing a large number of gentlemen to the audience. He says that I will fit in well, and that he can offer me a number of leading roles. He changes the performance twice weekly, and there will be many an opportunity for me.

The Journal of Corbyn Carlisle

5th August 1791. *Andrew Cruickshank, my bear-leader, has returned to England from Seville where my grand tour effectively ended in June. But I have not returned home with him. I am writing this entry in Florence, or Firenze as the Florentines call it. I have returned here on my own; it is a wonderful city and I feel that it is my spiritual home. I have never felt so at ease in any place before. I had thought of myself as a typical Englishman, but now I realise that I am not. They are a narrow-minded, intolerant race, believing that the sun rises and falls in London. There are ideas abroad in this community that I have never heard discussed anywhere in England. The English society lies in its bed at night fearful that the revolution in France will cross the Channel. Well instead of putting up barriers, they should think about embracing some of the new ideas. The English community here is most stimulating, and they have also introduced me to many fine gentlemen and their ladies from continental society. There are many young artists keen to understand the skills and techniques mastered here centuries ago, and to encounter such different people and views is, I confess, most stimulating.*

I am developing a love of theatre and the opera, and I had become a regular visitor when we stayed here as part of the grand tour. The intention was to stay for three months, but it was extended to six months at my behest. I have to confess that the attraction was not all cultural; there is a fine lady who I have made the acquaintance of. She is Maria Elena Viscontessa di Castiglioni. She became my guide in the city, taking me to literary salons where I was bold eno ugh, with her encouragement, to recite my own poetry. She also was kind enough to take my arm on many visits to the theatre. I am unsure of her age, I do not like to ask, but I suspect that she is in her early thirties, though she is much younger than her husband, the Visconte di Castiglioni, who, although a grand impressive man, must be well into his sixties by now.

Chapter 27.

I find that reading about Virginia takes my mind away from Grace, somehow it is cathartic. Reading about her lonely new year was so like my own. I stocked up with a few cans of Bombardier and never left my flat, I didn't want to socialise, and the thought of spending a crowded evening with colleagues and their wives held no appeal for me. I say a few cans; there were a lot of cans. I normally only drink modestly, but I have been drinking to excess for some weeks now. I am getting to work, still hung-over, and I am not functioning properly until at least eleven each morning.

But I am trying to move on. I have not seen Grace since that awful meeting in early December; other than her work that comes via email, which I have to evaluate, I have no contact with her at all. I wonder if she thinks about me all the time, the way that I think of her.

So Ginny is now an actress; well, good for her; she is such an attractive character. She has now turned twenty-three, an accomplished and enterprising young woman. It's so unbelievable what she has achieved when you look back at that semi-literate first journal entry of that fourteen-year-old child with her er's and ee's. She's like a bird in an abandoned nest, but instead of dying, she learned how to fly on her own, tentatively at first, but now she soars. There I go again; it is not professional to be so involved with this woman. She has been dead for nearly two centuries for goodness' sake; I need to get a grip. But this change in her life is propitious; I know the theatrical profession has left behind excellent records for historians and that gives me an opportunity to do some independent research. The V&A archive have a record of every performance on the London stage between 1660 and 1959.

The archivist introduced herself as Megan McCarran, shaking my hand unconvincingly as if it was a skill she had never learned; she offered me little more than three fingers to hold. She was very small and slight. A pretty face with piercing green eyes and raven-black hair greeted me with a smile. I had made an appointment and I was expected. She took me to a reception area and we sat at an interview desk large enough to display records, with a computer terminal on the corner.

'Have you brought all the information I asked for when I emailed you?'
Her words had a lilting Scottish accent that I could not place. It certainly
wasn't Glasgow or Edinburgh. 'The more we know about the person we
are researching the better. Registration documents, parish records, wills
and census returns are the best source of crucial information about an
individual's whereabouts at a specific time.'

'I can provide a name and an address at a specific point in time, but little
else,' I said.

'Is the subject a lady or gentleman?'

'It's a lady.'

'Then that makes our search more difficult,' she said. 'Where women
are concerned, stage careers could be very short. The theatrical life was not
suitable for a wife and mother. There were some exceptions, but actresses
usually retired when they got married. Did she have a stage name?'

'If she did I don't know of it.'

I saw her pull a slight face as though the prospects were not looking
good.

'Are we looking at serious acting roles or music hall performances?'

'I think we are looking at something closer to the latter.'

'That's a pity,' she said. 'The British Library holds the Lord Chamberlain's
papers, plays and daybooks which contain play-texts, readers' reports and
correspondence. But that did not extend to popular forms of entertainment.
That is more difficult, especially as many performers changed their names
all the time.'

'This isn't going very well, is it?' I said.

'We wont give up just yet, Professor Postlethwaite,' she said, reassuring
me, 'what is the name you have?'

'Virginia Farmer,' I said, 'she took to the stage in July 1791.'

She looked at me for a heartbeat, and then I saw a small smile enter the
corner of her mouth. 'You are in luck, Professor, I know all about Virginia
Farmer.'

'You do?' I didn't hide my elation. 'Was she so very famous then?'

'Well no; well I say no, she was a headliner, but her career only lasted for
a couple of years or so.'

'So how do you know of her?'

' 'Cause I spent quite some time researching her only the other week,
for another enquirer.'

Grace! I thought to myself, *Grace, of course, Grace.* She was a bright girl; she was ahead of me. 'Grace Farmer?' I asked.

'Yes, you know of her?'

'Yes, she is one of my students.'

'Oh, then you will have access to all the information I gave her.'

'Well…yes,' I said hesitantly. I didn't really want to approach Grace for it. 'What can you tell me now about her?'

'We have many thousands of playbills covering the London Stage; they are our best source of information. She is first named in October 1791, but she has top billing by the end of the year; it was quite a meteoric rise. There are newspaper reviews and it seems that she was a young beauty with an aristocratic background; she styled herself, Lady Virginia Farmer. She quickly became a star of the stage, not so different from pop singers of today who become overnight sensations.'

'And yet she was from the Foundlings' Hospital in Bristol.'

'Was she, well I never,' she said, 'well she must have been some actress to fool so many people.'

'Yes, she seems to be a remarkable woman, but I had not realised that she was so famous in her own time. What else can you tell me?'

'Well, according to the reviews, she had a sweet singing voice. Many of the female singers sang vulgar songs or songs with obvious sexual innuendo, but it seems that this was not her style. Her songs, it seems, were engaging and charming, as was her own image. She seems to have been one of those entertainers that *everybody* liked, the old and the young, the rich and the poor, male and female. The word got around and people flocked to see her; the Prince of Wales himself was a fan.'

'And her acting, what did the reviews say of that?'

'Well it's hard to judge from this distance, acting styles were so different than today; *we* would probably consider it overacting. But the reviews are all positive; if she was playing the damsel in distress, then it seems that she was convincing enough for every man in the audience to want to save her.'

I smiled to myself inwardly. I inclined my head and that inwards smile must have escaped to my features and I saw that she noticed.

'Does this fit in with your own research, Professor Postlethwaite?'

'It adds to it,' I said, 'but I am not surprised by what you tell me. This lady appears to be a most remarkable person; she had universal appeal it seems.'

'That's probably a good way to describe her from what I have read. She even crossed over to major licensed theatre to perform serious acting roles and I *have* found her name in the Lord Chamberlain's papers. Her reviews from that are all positive as well. She seemed to have the ability to take on many different roles.'

I continued to smile and I drew a smile from her as well. Then she went on.

'And then it all seems to end abruptly. I can find nothing about her after September 1793. She seems to have left the stage at the height of her fame.'

'Do you know why?'

'No I don't, I'm afraid, but I can take a good guess. I suggest that she either married or was taken by a high-born gentleman to be his mistress. A great many actresses saw this as their ultimate objective.'

'I hope she found a husband,' I said unprofessionally and I saw Miss McCarran raise an eyebrow at me, so I knew I had to explain. 'She had been a courtesan once before,' I said, 'to a very high-born gentleman, but he dumped her and that's why she turned to the stage.'

'Ah, well then let's hope so,' she replied uncomfortably.

'Do you have a picture of her?'

'Not as yet, but I wouldn't be surprised if there is one in our archives. Would you like me to continue looking?'

'Yes I would, it would be good if you can find one.'

Back at my desk I stole myself and sent Grace an email, asking if I could see the research from the V&A. I know I was chickening out, but I didn't want to meet her. I got an immediate response. <I'll put the papers in your press with the journals.> it said briefly, but there was a PS. <James and Ginny sitting in a tree, K-I-S-S-I-N-G.> She had said it before to tease me, but this time it was more caustic; it stung.

Chapter 28.

The Journal of Ginny Farmer

5th **February 1792.** Mr. Jack Brown is not at all like Jeremiah Cotton as a theatrical manager. He has no interest in performing himself, and little interest in tutoring his cast in the acting profession. He tells me that his father ran a travelling menagerie, exhibiting strange creatures from Africa around the country and that is where he learned his profession. His style is very much that of the showman, but he seems to know his business because the theatre is mostly full.

He is also a much younger man, I would say about thirty years. He dresses like a gentleman and his frock coats are obviously well tailored, but he makes no attempt to hide his pronounced accent. It is difficult to place where he is from; probably because he moved around so much as a child with his father's menagerie. I detect North Country at times and then there are Midland vowels and sometimes even cockney. He is not what you would call a handsome man, a slightly bulbous nose and his skin is pock-marked from, I assume, adolescent mange, which he manages to cover to an extent by his large, curly sideburns. But he has a fine head of dark, curly hair tied at the nape of the neck. But it is his mannerisms that make him stand out, his chest is always thrust out in a military bearing, which I assume came from his posture whilst barking at the menagerie performances. He is a very manly man indeed.

The actresses are clearly the stars of his company, and they are all young and very beautiful, although, I have to say, they are not the most sophisticated of girls. Some cannot even read and write and have to be schooled through their lines; the prompter is the busiest man in the company, I think. If they are unable to master some lines, Mr. Brown has no compunction in rewriting them so that they are easier to say or easier to remember. I seem to be different from them and I spoke with Mr. Brown today about what he wants from me. He says that it is that difference that attracted him; he wants to catch the fancy of some of the finer gentlemen and their ladies, as well as the <u>young bucks</u> about town, as he puts it. I am to get my name on the bill posters too and

I will take the title of Lady Virginia Farmer; it is an image that I am happy to continue with.

I am to take my first lead role next week in a melodrama, and the heroine's role is being rewritten as a titled lady. It is a role that I have already mastered, I think.

10th February 1792. I have my first reviews as a performer. I have read the ones in The Globe and the London Morning Penny Post; they are most flattering, describing my performance from charming to engaging, from forceful to passionate. Mr. Brown clearly understands his profession, as by casting me as a Lady, my distress connects with the higher orders of society, whereas the lower orders are equally concerned that such a fine lady should be in such danger. It is a strange thing, is it not, that an English lady should be respected so by the ordinary folk; not like the French at all. There is even a review in The Times, which says that my performance made every man in the audience want to be my saviour. I will remember that; that is what I will aim for from now on. The performance will change from next Monday, as Mr. Brown offers a twice weekly programme, but the current performance has been such a success that he is to bring it back from Thursday of next week by popular demand as he puts it, and he is having new bill posters made up saying just that. He has told me that he will have all my parts rewritten now for a fine lady; that will be my draw. If I speak to a reporter I am to speak to him as Lady Virginia, a fine lady that has been forced to take to the stage. I am to maintain that illusion at all times; strange that Mr. Brown should be the first person to recognise that the part of a fine lady is an illusion.

There is even a report in the Penny Gazette. I know Mrs. Strabane reads that journal and I wonder if she will realise that it is her Ginny Farmer that they are talking about. I will write to her, I think, to confirm it. I should have kept in touch with her anyway, but I did not want to tell her that I was working as a Mabel.

Mr. Brown has negotiated an extension to the company's contract at the Coburg; we have another three months engagement, due to the excellent ticket sales.

8th June 1792. I have taken the lead role in all the performances for the last 3 months. I know it upsets the other actresses in the cast, but Mr. Brown sees only the financial success at the box office and will hear none of their demands. I offered today to step aside and let one of the others take the lead at the next change, but he refused and instead offered me a substantial rise in my salary, that is the third rise since February. I am astonished the audiences seem to love me so much, even though I basically play the same part in each of the melodramas. They stand and applaud me at the end of each performance, sometimes even during the performance, and the other actors have to wait until they have stopped cheering before they can say their next lines.

I am now corresponding regularly with Mrs. Strabane. She is most interested in my acting career and I have been sending her programmes and the cuttings from my reviews. She, in turn, keeps me informed with everything that is going on at Josiah Holdstock's house, although nothing seems to have changed very much. She has been most mischievous though; she has shown my cuttings to the mistress's new ladies maid, who of course knows nothing about me or why I left, knowing that she was bound to mention it to the mistress. The mistress, apparently, had a face of thunder for days afterwards.

28ᵗʰ June 1792. Mr. Brown has moved the whole company to the Sanspareil Theatre on The Strand; he has a three-month contract and the theatre is much larger than the Coburg. Tonight was our first night and the theatre was full to the rafters. There are more dressing rooms and I have been given my own. When I arrived, there was a bill poster outside with a likeness of me at the top, proclaiming me in large letters as LADY VIRGINIA FARMER. I stopped to admire it; it is a full-length depiction, the gown is off my shoulders, voluminous, as if I were attending the most prestigious of balls. The artist that Mr. Brown brought in has done a wonderful job, but once again it is Mr. Brown that is the genius behind all this, he also seems to have that eye for deception that I have discovered in myself, but with him it is on a much larger scale.

12ᵗʰ August 1792. The most surprising thing has happened. I have been offered the role of Helena in Shakespeare's A Midsummer Night's Dream. It will be at The Theatre Royal Haymarket, a patent licensed theatre and will be proper acting. I have read the play of course and have now studied it again to refresh my memory. I know why they want me of course; I will be a big draw at the box office for them. But I want to play Oberon, the king of the fairies. I quite see myself as Oberon come to the forest outside Athens, feuding with his wife, Titania, the queen of the fairies. I know this is a male character, but for some reason it is always played by a woman.

Let's see how much they want me to bolster the box office; yes, I think I will ask for the part of Oberon.

28th October 1792. I have just finished my first week at The Theatre Royal Haymarket playing in A Midsummer Night's Dream. Mr. Brown was most upset and pleaded with me to stay with his theatre group, offering me much more money that I am receiving here; but I wanted to find out if I could do some proper acting. I wanted to find out if I could play a part other than the fine lady in distress. The run will take us through to Christmas and I have promised him that I will return in the new year.

In the end I was offered any part that I chose, but I found that my legs were too slender for the part of Oberon; I realised that my physique is too delicate to masquerade as a man. So I have chosen Titania, the queen of the fairies. I am learning so much about acting, but then I always was a quick learner. The theatre owner Mr. George Colman, an elderly gentleman, but much respected as an actor and playwright himself, says Titania should embody all the mystery of femininity, all wrapped in an extraordinary beauty; elegance, lightness, intelligence, humour and passion. That is a lot for me to accomplish. My costume is wonderful; it is a brilliant lilac of colour with a purple banding. The bodice is made of silk, but there are flowers sewn on to it. It then billows from the waist in several layers of chiffon, again with flowers sewn on to it, and I know that the stage backlighting gives the audience a glimpse of my legs through the delicate material. My slippers, too, are of purple, and as I flit about the stage, they seem to punctuate my movements. My hair is worn high and held by a headdress of flowers, and on my back I have two little wings of gold with the veins again picked out in purple. With this costume, I don't think I can fail to be everything Mr. George Colman wants of me.

3rd December 1792. Oh but this has been such a disturbing day. It had started off so wonderfully, we had a full house; about twenty minutes before we were due to go on stage, a rumour spread around the dressing room, like a man running from a hue and cry. The King himself was due to see the performance. We were all so nervous and excited, but old Mr. Colman told us that we should be on our best behavior and concentrate on our performances, and try to ignore the King and Queen Charlotte. That was easier said than done, but the performance itself had a sort of spark and was the best we have done so far. Queen Charlotte in particular seemed to love it.

We were in the dressing rooms afterwards all chattering away, thrilled, when the news started to come through. First of all it was just that there had been a crush. Then, it was that there had been a great crowd, all eager, and pressing to see His Majesty. And then we learned that people had been crushed to death at the side door. Twenty people at the last count, some had actually died standing up, with their lips blue as the air was squashed from their lungs, some were well-known ladies and gentlemen of society.

We all left the theatre in silence, our elation drained away like water escaping from a hole in a barrel. Life is fickle it seems.

The Journal of Corbyn Carlisle

15th February 1792. Last night was St. Valentine's night and, of course, my birthday. I dined with Maria Elena Viscontessa di Castiglioni at her villa. There was the smell of jasmine in the room and I felt it intoxicating, but then I was also intoxicated by Maria Elena. We lingered over the meal and talked of architecture, of painting, of literature. She told me of the new Italian writers who had a love of liberty and equality, who sought to free their country from political and religious repression. They wanted to reestablish the ideals of ancient classicism, a second renaissance. I found these ideals equally intoxicating. Are there no such writers in England?

We then took cognac before a large open fire. I sat in an armchair and Maria Elena sat on the floor beside me, resting her arm on my knee, holding her cognac. Her perfume entered my senses and I closed my eyes momentarily at the delight of it. Then I opened them and took in her beauty; long, wavy dark hair, pale skin, a delicate oval face. The firelight danced on her features and her eyes seemed to change colour from green to a vibrant blue velvet with each flicker of the flames. It was at that moment I admitted what I had denied to myself for several months now. I was in love with Maria Elena.

I reached down and took her hand gently. There could be no doubt that I was being intimate, I stole myself for her reaction, but she did not pull away. I took the glass from her and then took her hands in both of my mine. I lent forward and pressed my lips gently against hers; they were sweet, and delightful. Somehow I was not now apprehensive that she would reject me, in fact I was not apprehensive at all. I was right, our lips touched tenderly for several moments. Then the passions of Venus engaged within me; I knelt beside her and took her in my arms.

We retired to her bedchamber. We both disrobed in front of the fire and I wondered at her alabaster skin in the dancing firelight. I threw some logs on the fire, and the sparks flew and then disappeared up the chimney. I took her hand and led her to the bed and we slipped between the sheets; I felt as though there was an invisible hand guiding me, as though everything was preordained. I heard the trees swaying in the wind outside. The candlelight danced on her face and the words of love came easily to me; we became lovers.

Chapter 29.

My phone rang; I was hard at work, but I was not researching, so I'd didn't mind so much. Doing the quarterly budget was not my favourite task.

'Hello, its Megan McCarran from the V&A,' the voice said.

'Oh hi, do you have good news for me?'

'I think I do, Professor Postlethwaite.'

'What have you found then?'

'A bill poster with a likeness; large letters at the top proclaiming Lady Virginia Farmer in The Marquis of Banbury. She was clearly the star attraction; there's hardly a mention of anybody else in the cast.'

'Oh that's wonderful,' I gushed, 'can you scan it and then email it to me?'

'No problem, Professor, I'll do it straight away.'

I tried to return to my budget spreadsheet, but I couldn't concentrate. I opened my email folder, but there was nothing there from Megan yet. I got up and made myself a large mug of Millicano coffee, sat back in my chair and sipped the hot, dark brown liquid, the aroma satisfying in my nostrils. Then I saw the email come thorough with a ping and I quickly put the mug down. In my haste, it spilled onto my desk, but I didn't stop to mop it up. I opened up the email, but didn't read Megan's words; I just opened up the attachment.

And there she was; a full-length depiction, the gown off her shoulders, capacious. It was indeed a picture of a fine lady with all the prettiness of youth, but there was more. Maybe it was the way she held her head, or set her shoulders, I don't know, but there was clearly elegance, sophistication, about her bearing. It wasn't the arrogance that a lady of good birth might have acquired; there was no superiority in her pose. I knew that she was a mimic, a masquerader, and yet I was just as taken in as everybody in her own time had been. It was only a likeness, and yet it spoke to me.

'You silly bugger,' I said out loud to myself; I hit the print button, then opened my budget spreadsheet again, 'it's only a bill poster, the artist has probably made her look more desirable than she actually is.' Then I realised that I had said, *IS*, I corrected myself, '*WAS*,' I exclaimed. I was having a conversation with myself.

But after a few moments I went to the printer and took off the image. I sat back down at my desk with it, savouring the picture, holding it as if it were a precious piece of porcelain. It was just a black and white sketch, it didn't depict her blond hair or blue eyes and yet it crystallised the picture of her that I carried in my head.

And then my email pinged again on my screen. I opened the email folder again and there was an email from Grace. I quickly reopened the email from Megan, and saw that she had copied in Grace; DAMN.

I opened Grace's email and read her message. <Something to keep you warm at night James?>

Chapter 30.

The Journal of Ginny Farmer

6th December 1792. The mood at the theatre has been one of sadness for the last couple of days. There is a gloom about the place, and all that elation from the success of the production and the visit of the King has vanished overnight; everybody is crestfallen. All those people who have lost their lives make our efforts somehow irrelevant. Old Mr. Colman told us before we went on stage last night that the theatre helped take people away from the troubles in their lives. Unexpected tragedy is so very hard to bear, but we should see ourselves as healers and give of ourselves the best performance that we can do, to honour those that have died. We all tried so very hard, but many of the audience did not turn up and those who did were inattentive, distracted by the terrible events, I think.

But then something unexpected happened this morning. I was taking my breakfast with Beth, reading the morning papers which were again full of the tragedy, page after page of obituaries of the eminent people who had died, when there was a knock at the door. It was a messenger, and Beth returned with a note for me. It was an invitation to call; the sender was Sir Joshua Lazenby. I, of course, had heard of him, he is one of the most famous portrait painters in England; a well-accepted man in society, his patrons of the very highest echelons within it, and a renowned exhibiter at the Royal Academy. Dear Corbyn once took me to see his work. I sent a note back with the messenger to say that I would call at twelve of the clock; I was intrigued.

I put on my finest outdoor clothes; a refined new bonnet, a fashionable and expensive dress, tasteful and elegant, with a velvet cape around my shoulders. When I arrived, I was shown into his study where I was met by a very tall distinguished old gentleman. He was an imposing figure; sixty-four years old, I later found out, with a shock of white hair swept back from his forehead, but not tied at the nape. He had a large hooked nose so that in profile his features had a biblical look about them. He could have been his own model, portraying Moses. Although age had

191

bowed him, he was still an imposing figure. A pair of spectacles pinched his hooked nose, to assist his fading eyesight.

I greeted him with my fine lady performance and he responded by taking my white-gloved hand gently and kissing it with all his finest manners. He offered me tea and I accepted, and he gestured for me to sit, which I did, still in character. We drank the tea almost in silence, punctuated with only the occasional pleasantry. I was beginning to feel a little uncomfortable, so I took the initiative.

'You wanted to see me, Sir Joshua?' I asked.

'Oh do forgive me, Lady Virginia, but I fear that I have been a foolish old man.'

'How so, Sir Joshua?'

'Well, I thought to ask you to model for me.'

'And why is that so foolish, sir?'

He paused and sighed before he went on. 'I am not a theatregoer, but the artistic community is a very narrow one, and gossip has reached me of a new and very beautiful young actress with the face and body of an angel. And then one of my models, the pugilist Samuel Medina, said he knew of your address.'

'You know Samuel?'

'Yes, he modelled as John the Baptist for me. So I thought I would make it my business to see for myself. I won't be the first artist to covet your services, my good lady, but I am clearly the first to insult you in this way.'

'Why should that insult me, Sir Joshua?'

'Well, because you are such a fine-born lady.' There was incredulity in his tone.

I was still not sure what he meant and he could see that he had to explain further.

'You must be aware of the very lowly status of an artist's model. I only have to pay a man a few shillings to sit for me because there is no social stigma in that. But I have to pay a woman at least half a guinea because they are regarded as little more than...' He did not complete the sentence.

'Little more than common whores,' I completed the sentence for him.

'Quite, my good lady,' he said, 'it would be quite scandalous behaviour for you to sit for me.'

I thought to tell him that I had been a whore, though I like to think not a common one, but somehow I wanted his respect, the respect of such an eminent gentleman.

I chose a different strategy. 'I have seen your work, sir, when you exhibited at the Royal Academy in '89. I was most taken with it; your reputation is well deserved.'

'Why thank you, good lady, you are most kind.' He bowed his head lightly to acknowledge my compliment.

'I am not sure how to describe your style, Sir Joshua,' I said in an uncertain voice, trying to pick my words carefully.

'The art critics call it neoclassical, but I am not taken with such labels,' he said.

'But that makes sense to me,' I replied, 'the women in your pictures seem to be dressed in gowns derived from ancient Greek and Roman clothing styles.' Corbyn had explained that to me.

'That is true; you are most perceptive, Lady Virginia.'

'If I were to sit for you,' I said hesitantly, 'the gowns would be equally revealing, gossamer, almost transparent.'

'That is what I had in mind, I use directed light to define texture and the simple roundness of faces and limbs. But it is out of the question, you would be scandalized.'

I mused for a heartbeat, and then a mischievous notion came to me. 'What if I were to commission you, to be your patron, so to speak.'

He cocked an eye at me, but I then saw that his thoughts were of rejection. 'Such a major work as I had in mind would be outside your pocket I fear, and I already have a patron for it.'

'No, no,' I said, 'I have in mind another commission, for you to paint me as Titania, in the costume I wear on the stage.'

I saw his eye cock again and this time I could see that he liked the idea. He liked the idea so very much.

10th December 1792. I had sat in the pose that Sir Joshua had arranged for me for over two hours; I didn't think that it would be so difficult. My muscles ached and cried out for relief. It was December and it was bitterly cold outside, but the bright winter sun, which had shone for many hours, warmed me through the expansive skylight, supplementing a rigorously burning fire inside. But now I began to shiver as the warmth of the sun began to fade, the long hours of holding this unnatural pose was taking its toll on me; I longed to exercise my arms and legs.

'Sir Joshua, I wonder if I might just stretch my legs for a few moments.'

'Just a moment longer,' he muttered vaguely without looking up.

I set myself again in the pose; I looked at him sideways without altering my stance. I could see that he was meticulous in his pursuit of accuracy. If that meant extreme discomfort for his models, then that was the way of it: they were paid to put up with this discomfort. I smiled as I looked at him; his long, thin, gaunt face seemed to show permanent irritation, and a deep furrowed forehead and rounded shoulders supplemented this expression – the result, I should imagine, of many hours spent concentrating over his easel. The glasses pinched his hooked nose, like a butterfly with its wings set, but he still hovered only inches from the canvas.

'Very well, you can move now,' he said into his canvas in an uncertain voice. Then he looked up at me and I saw that reality was returning to him, he had been in some place of his own, an artistic place of technique and brushwork and perspective. He looked at his pocket watch and I saw that his forehead furrowed deeper as the realisation that I had been posing for two hours took him.

'Oh my good lady,' he said apologetically, 'how remiss of me. You have taken no sustenance for so long, some tea perhaps, you must be parched.'

I nodded, 'Some tea would be most refreshing.'

'I eat frugally, but I can offer you some bread and ham or perhaps some cheese. I am sure that my man can find us some cake.'

'A little cake will be sufficient,' I said.

He gestured me to sit, but I was interested in the picture. 'Am I allowed to see your progress, Sir Joshua?'

He gestured for me to come round and see it and I did so. I saw that he was attempting an elaborate background, but that was still in a charcoal sketch.

'Will this be the forest outside Athens?' I asked, and he nodded appreciatively. I think that he was happy that I understood his intention.

But he had made fine progress on my likeness, and my costume was already appearing in paint. 'I notice that you use such very long brushes, Sir Joshua?' I asked, 'what is the reason for that?'

He was keen to explain it to me. 'Long brushes and thin oil, my good lady. It's a technique that I use to achieve that shimmering effect of your lilac Titania's costume; the silk, the layers of chiffon, and especially the little wings of gold with the purple veins.'

'You are a genius, Sir Joshua,' I said genuinely. He inclined his head to acknowledge the compliment.

I sipped my tea and nibbled at the cake, as Sir Joshua took a cognac with his bread and ham. I felt comfortable with him.

'What is the commission that you have a patron for?' I asked.

'A large canvas work, my good lady, a portrait of an archbishop. I thought to depict him with keys; an allegory that he has the keys to heaven. There would be an angel hovering above him inviting him to enter. You would have been the model for the angel.'

'I wonder, sir,' I said cautiously, 'if there is scope for a negotiation between us.'

He cocked an eye in that way of his. 'How so, my lady?'

'As payment for the picture of me as Titania, could I pay by being your model for the angel?'

'I will never before have paid a model such a handsome amount,' he said, but his tone showed that he had not taken any insult at my proposition.

'And I sir, will have to live with the scandal.'

A broad smile traversed his wrinkled, gentle face. 'Very well, I accept, let it be so.'

'You know, of course, that I will deny that it is me.'

The smile on his face broadened.

Chapter 31.

The revelation that Ginny had been a model for Sir Joshua Lazenby has thrilled me no end; I feel like a child on Christmas Eve overcome with delightful expectation. These journals just get better and better. Not only is there an insight into two lives from the Georgian period, they are intermingled with some of the great names of the period, Samuel Medina, Lord John Dalby, and now Maria Elena Viscontessa di Castiglioni and particularly Sir Joshua Lazenby. He is such a famous painter that his catalogue will be, I am sure, on record somewhere. I will need to research this, but those pictures that she sat for will surely be traceable.

I mused in my mind the best place to start; should I go to Amanda Davies, the university's senior fine arts lecturer; or perhaps Jilly Cole at the auction house. Alternatively I could go straight to the Witt Library. Jilly Cole told me it's an essential resource for anyone looking to attribute a work; they have information and images of over a million pictures. If either picture has been in an exhibition, any public auction, or a public collection, I should find an image there.

But then I remembered that Grace was ahead of me in the reading of the journals. She must know of these paintings. I needed to speak to her; this was uncomfortable for me.

I opened my email page; I thought I would keep it simple and professional – <Grace: I have just been reading Ginny's journal and I see that she sat for Sir Joshua Lazenby. Have you researched this?>

There was a reply almost immediately. < James: Research? What sort of research?>

Damn! She was playing those games with me again, I could see that. <Grace: He's such a famous man that there is scope for verification, don't you think. I just didn't want to duplicate any research that you have already done.>

<James: tell me what you have in mind and I'll see if I have already covered it.>

I had been right to feel uncomfortable about contacting her; she was clearly still extremely angry, to say she was pissed off with me was an understatement and she was making no attempt to hide it. I opened up the work she had sent me for evaluation. I had scheduled it for my review later in the week, but now I brought it forward and looked at it. After an hour, I realised there was nothing about Lazenby. I emailed her again.

<Grace: Can you just tell me please what research, if any, you have done?>

The reply was again immediate. <James: Yes, I've been down to the Witt Library and you'll be pleased to know that both pictures are catalogued. The standard reference work on Lazenby is Thomas Pine's biography of 1904. Amanda Davies has ordered a copy for me through the university library.>

She was still playing games with me; there was no mention of images of the paintings. <Grace: have you tracked down where the paintings are now? >

<James: What do you want to know that for? Is it relevant?>

Oh sod the woman; she was playing me like a fiddle. Grace: <It would just be interesting to see how Lazenby depicted her.>

<Oh James – this is so cute. It's just the classic love story isn't it? Boy meet girl, boy loses girl, boy finds girl again. NOT!!! SHE'S BEEN DEAD FOR TWO CENTURIES JAMES!!!>

The worst thing that you can do in an argument is to be right. I knew she was right and at that moment I hated her for it. She had also made me spell out my folly, picking at me like a vulture on a carcass until I did so. I conceded defeat. <Grace: Just answer the question please.>

<James: The portrait of Titania is in a private collection. The portrait of the archbishop is in the National Portrait Gallery.>

The National Portrait Gallery; I was just contemplating a trip to London when my email pinged again – Grace.

<James: before you book your train ticket to London. Don't bother – I've got colour images of both paintings from the Witt Library.>

She must have just sat there at her laptop, counting the seconds before she sent that last email, like a comedian with expert timing. I imagined the smug smile on her face, sat by her screen, waiting for me to play her game. I *was* her plaything and I didn't like it, but I felt useless to resist.

<Grace: can you put them in my press with the journals please?> I tried to be as detached as I could, as if my request was purely professional.

<No James, come and get them.>

It seems that she wants to see me squirm.

Chapter 32.

The Journal of Ginny Farmer

14th February 1793 Today is Corbyn's birthday. St. Valentine's Day has made me think of him for the first time in so long. I wonder what the dear man is doing now; I still miss him after all of this time.

Since I returned to Mr. Jack Brown's company in January, he has put on bigger and bigger melodramas for me. He wanted me to sign a contract so that I would not be able to accept other offers, but I refused. It has had a strange consequence; he offers me more and more, much more that I can get with a licensed theatre in a proper acting role. I think it is his alternative strategy; he hopes to bind me to his company by money.

But it means that I prosper and my savings are growing propitiously to the point that I may soon be a lady of independent means. Yet I find that I have found a love for this profession and I long to play other parts, and now a new possibility has presented itself. A new play is to be performed at The Theatre Royal Haymarket. It is to be a dramatisation of the legend of Tristan and Iseult, and I am wanted to play the fair Irish maiden, Iseult. It is, of course, a most passionate story. There is valour, for after defeating the Irish knight, Morholt, the Cornish knight, Tristan, goes to Ireland to bring back the fair Iseult for his uncle, King Mark, to marry. There is passion, for the two take a love potion which causes them to fall madly in love. She marries King Mark who is Tristan's adopted father, but they deceive him with their love for each other. This sounds so wonderful to me and I am most taken with the idea of it. There is fervour, obsession, rage and fury. I know they only want me to ensure the success of a new play, but I cannot conceive of such a part coming my way again.

The Journal of Corbyn Carlisle

15th February 1793. This last year has been the most wonderful of my life. My love for Maria Elena has not diminished but I am connected intellectually as well as romantically, she is all things to me; my love for her has so many interwoven strands· She has made it clear, however, that she will never leave her husband as she still loves him, and all she can offer is to be my mistress· A strange word, mistress, in England it has undertones of something seedy, but here in Florence, well it seems to have a fragrance all its own· Such an arrangement would, I know, satisfy most men; it would be perfect for them, but I find it hard to share her in this way· And then there is the jealousy, I have to confess to that unwanted interloper, it consumes me at times; it fights a never-ending battle with its companion, guilt, a fellow intruder· Maria Elena says that she admires her husband Lorenzo, the viscount, more than any man she has ever met and I too can see all that she sees in him· I count him as a friend also; I wish he had been my father, my mentor as I grew up, a sage and a role model through my adolescence, rather than my own drunken, lecherous, little-educated father·

Last night I was invited to dine with her on my birthday, and initially I was a little put out that Lorenzo joined with us also· But the evening was delightful; the food was so well prepared, the conversation stimulating and the décor at their town house exquisite· I remember looking around with my cognac cradled in my satisfied hand, imagining Elloughton Park decorated in an Italian style to match its Italian-styled exterior· And then Lorenzo excused himself and retired to his apartment, leaving me alone with Maria Elena, and lustful thoughts quickly entered my mind· We retired to her apartment and I took her to bed· I was a little nervous, as we had never before been intimate with the viscount just down the corridor, but she calmed me saying that she had no secrets from her husband· I had not realised before, the extent of that openness; I assumed that he suspected, but that he did not know for certain·

We coupled for longer than I thought myself capable of and then we lay exhausted in each other's arms, then talked easily for an hour or so· But then she took me by surprise with what she said·

'Do you think much about an heir?' she said in French, we always spoke together in French· 'Does the responsibility lay heavily with you?'

I was aware, of course, of this responsibility, but in my newfound love for her I had put it to the back of my mind. I now had to admit to myself that I am still a man in search of a wife, but I had done nothing about it since I started the grand tour in April 1790.

'No,' I said matter-of-factly, 'the responsibility is no great burden, but it is true that I have an obligation to my family line to find a wife.' I was being honest.

She raised herself on her elbow so that she could look directly at me. 'I cannot be that wife, you know that, dear Corbyn, do you not?' I saw in her eyes that she was searching for my confirmation, my acceptance.

'Yes, I know it,' I lied. In my heart I had not given up the hope that I could one day take her back to Elloughton Park as my wife: but I denied it.

'Good,' she said, lying back down beside me, resting her head on my chest. She slowly drifted off to sleep in that position with my arm around her, as though that confirmation was somehow a relief to her, something that needed to be understood. It felt wonderful with her so close, her perfume in my nostrils, her soft body entwined with mine, and I expected that I too would find slumber, but my mind began to go over the implications of what she had said. Sleep did not come easily, but by this morning I had reached a decision, and that was that my future is not here in Florence.

I talked with Maria Elena over breakfast about my decision and was surprised that she accepted it so readily.

'I've always known, dear Corbyn, that one day you would go back to England. Parting will be painful, but our time together here in Florence has been spent in love. We will have those precious memories.'

There seemed to be finality in her words that I did not expect, and now, as I write this entry, I realise that she is prompting me to face my responsibilities – I must accept that prompt. I have decided that I will not make this a long goodbye as that will only make my heart heavier.

I will leave as soon as possible.

Chapter 33.

I caught up with Grace at the university library. She was busy at her laptop making research notes. This was good; there were people about, it was less personal, I could hide behind my professional image; I was the professor after all.

'Do you have those pictures?' I adopted an urgent tone as if I needed to be somewhere else.

She looked up at me and smiled, but I could see that it was a hard smile; there was no kindness in it.

'Pictures?' She inclined her head in mock innocence.

'Yes, pictures,' I snapped, raising my voice, irritated, then saw people look round at me. *Damn*, I thought to myself, *only one line and she has me dangling already.*

'Which pictures do you want, James?'

'You know which pictures, Grace, the images of Victoria Farmer,' I said in a fierce whisper, leaning in to her so that others could not hear.

'Oh those; why didn't you say?' she said, again feigning ignorance.

I had started off playing a part; that of the man in a hurry, but she had been too good for me. My strategy had been negated as if I were a rooky chess player whose opening gambit had been easily rebuffed by a chess master. I was now playing her game according to her rules and that realisation angered me. I looked round and saw an empty chair; I took it, pulled it up and sat next to her, leaning in for the illusion of privacy.

'Where are they, Grace? I really haven't got time for this,' I grunted.

She sat back, sucking on her teeth, now feigning contemplation. 'Now where did I put them?' she said as if to herself, staring up at the ceiling.

'You really are intolerable,' I said gruffly.

And then I saw that look, the one that said more than words and I felt myself shudder. I knew I had opened a door and that she would burst through it with all her pent-up resentment.

'Don't talk to me about being intolerable, you insufferable wimp,' her voice was guttural, emphasising every word.

I looked around me, partly afraid of what was to happen next, partly embarrassed because this was not the place for it.

She went on: 'You would rather have a virtual girlfriend than a real one, you silly, silly man.'

I was taken aback by the venom in her voice, her face. Glances were exchanged, but for a heartbeat I was unsure what to say, what to do.

'Do I really deserve all this,' I said eventually, 'what exactly is my crime?'

'Crime? – Well I suppose that *is* the right word for it. Yes, you should think about your *crime;* think on it, James, think on it long and hard.'

'You are not making any sense, you know.' I was now totally confused. 'I really don't know what you are so angry about. For God's sake, it was you who walked out on me, remember?'

She looked at me, staring intently into my eyes, focusing on one and then the other as if trying to tell if I was being serious. It was as though she were looking right into my soul. I waited for her anger to subside, but it didn't.

'Your crime is one of deceit, James, treachery and dishonesty.'

'*Me?*' I said, flabbergasted, '*me* deceitful? Kettle-pan-black Grace, kettle-pan-black.'

'It's true that I didn't tell you about my past, but I didn't tell you any lies either. I offered you only a love affair, a sexual dalliance, but I didn't offer any commitment. It was all going fine, but then it became clear that you wanted to move on, so I was honest enough to end it.'

'But you left me without any explanation.'

'Yes, and I am sorry for that, but the signs were all there for anybody with an ounce of sense to see – but not you; no, not you, James. You pursued me, endlessly, and at every turn I avoided you, hoping that you would finally give up.'

'But why avoid me?'

'Because I was afraid that you would not be able to accept my past; I would have rather lost you that way, than have you reject me when you found out.'

'But not knowing why was tearing me apart.'

'And do you remember what you said to me when I told you that you wouldn't want me if you knew the truth? You said *try me. Try me*, James, that's what you said.'

'But I had fallen in love with you – that's what you do when you are in love; you think nothing can shake it.'

'Yes, I realised that when you finally tracked me down at the Students' Union bar. It made me think that your love for me just might be enough for you to accept my past. So I took a chance on you. I revisited all those terrible times that I had locked away in a dark corner of my mind; all those dreadful, horrifying images of that despoiled me that I'd become. You forced me to tell you of them, because you *loved* me, and you wanted to know. But that *love* turned out to be such a fragile little thing didn't it, James; puny, brittle, it snapped at the first sign of pressure. Oh what a fool I was to trust you, James.'

I shuddered at her stinging words, looked down, bit my lower lip. But then I looked back up at her and faced the full vengeful force of her gaze. 'But how is that being deceitful or treacherous?' I said feebly, twitching a smile.

'Oh yes you were; you said that you could *handle* it, but when it came to it you *couldn't*, could you, James? You pretended to be one person and then turned out to be another; a silly little boy who just thinks he is a grown-up.'

'Is that how you see me?' I said, crestfallen, 'but...' the words were left hanging.

'Oh don't you see, James; it was a test; a test that you had set for yourself. *Try me*, you said. And so I did; I tried you; and then you failed it. A big fat *not graded* James – zilch, zero, nothing, sod all, James, sod all.'

I looked down and considered my feet. I could not look at her. I suddenly became aware again of those around me in the library; I looked around as they came back into focus. Eyes were staring at me, embarrassed looks matched by my own embarrassment. But my embarrassment was overlaid with anguish. Deep down I knew Grace was right. Words formed on my lips, but I did not speak them, as I knew how inadequate they were. I could feel her eyes burning into me, waiting for me to speak, but I didn't. I just sat there contemplating my folly. I felt in an ever-shrinking place.

'Oh James, you *are* hopeless,' she said, turning to her briefcase on the floor beside her. She opened it and took out the images of Virginia Farmer. She threw them on the desk and then she stood, grabbed her briefcase, put her laptop under her arm and started to walk away. She stopped and looked over her shoulder back at me. Those china-blue eyes held my gaze and they were full of belligerence. She opened her mouth to speak, but no words emerged, just a sour smile at the corner; she ran her hand through her loose curls in that way of hers, and then she walked away.

Chapter 34.

The Journal of Ginny Farmer

6th May 1793. Mother came to the play at the Haymarket yesterday. It was a matinee performance and we took tea afterwards and I could see the pride in her eyes, and that pride rubbed off on me. It was the first time that she had been to a proper licensed theatre, and she said that when Tristan died of grief, thinking that Iseult had betrayed him, and then Iseult herself died grieving over his corpse, she almost fainted away herself, she was so taken up by the play.

We only see each other once a month, but we exchange letters regularly and I tell her all about my career. I wrote her about this play and it was she who finally persuaded me to take the role of the Irish maiden, Iseult. It is such a success; the crowds are flocking to see it. We are in our fourth week and there is talk of an extended run when it comes to an end in June.

The Journal of Corbyn Carlisle

30th April 1793. I arrived back in England last week and I have spent my time at Elloughton Park. I have inspected the ledgers of my estate manager, John Cooper, and the estate coffers are in fine order, in fact I am wealthier than when I left. The revenues from the estate have increased fourfold since my brother's time. The garden that John Cooper had prepared for me is now matured and is a wonderful sight to behold. The spring flowers are in full bloom, so colourful in their display, it's as if they have bloomed to welcome me home. But he has also planted that orchard we talked about and it so compliments the garden. High fruit trees, pear and apple at the far end from the house and garden, and then smaller ones, cherries, plums and apricots nestling in the foreground. The trees need to grow, of course, but there is already a fine display of blossom in the spring sunshine; it is wonderful to behold.

Jane has kept the household accounts in fine order too, mostly within budget, except for the wine merchant's account which is growing quarter on quarter I see. My two sisters have had the run of the house for three years now and I suspect that my return will be a shock to them. Jane seems to be fine, but it looks as if Emily is as lazy as ever and that her taste for wine and brandy is not diminished. She is a soak, I fear.

I cannot help feeling guilty that I have neglected the place whilst I have indulged myself abroad. From the hall, I would be expected, as part of local society, to run balls and entertainments, suppers and fairs for the tenant farmers at harvest time. I have done none of these and nor did my father and brother before me. It is time that these conventions were resurrected. That is something for Emily and Jane to get involved with, although I fear they will resist as they do not want society to see their pock-marked faces.

And I can now afford more servants. The hall has been run for too long on a minimum entitlement for one of this size — one groom, one butler, one footman, one cook and her assistant, one gardener and a few maidservants are clearly not enough. Servants were shed by Carlton in consequence of his gambling, but I have done little to replace them. In particular, one groom cannot really run a livery yard. I know that carriages are enormously expensive to run, but I feel that I can now afford it and I therefore need a coachman and a second groom. More house servants too if entertaining is to become part of life at Elloughton Park. I also have plans to refurbish the house; when all the antiquities that I have collected arrive from the continent, I will draw up a proposal. My head is full of ideas.

7th May 1793. I came up to London yesterday for a meeting with my fellow barristers at Chambers. It was agreed that I return to work very much on the terms that I did before. My advocacy skills are appreciated it seems and the esteem of having a baronet in Chambers is still compelling.

Later, I dined with my old friend George Burgess, one of my fellow advocates, and afterwards he suggested that we go to the theatre to see a new play about the legend of Tristan and Iseult. With my newfound love of the theatre I was keen to take him up on his offer. When we got there I saw that the bill poster proclaimed the actress playing Iseult as Lady Virginia Farmer. No, it couldn't possibly be, I initially thought to myself, but when the performance started I borrowed George's theatre binoculars to get a good look at the actress, and, well blow me down, it was Ginny. I was keen to ask George all about her, but he was intent on watching the play, and all he would say to me was that she was new and everybody was flocking to see her.

The Journal of Ginny Farmer

8th **May 1793**. Today I have received a most wonderful surprise. A messenger called this morning with a note from dear Corbyn asking if, should he call, would he be welcome? I sent a reply immediately with the messenger that he should call this very day, and not extend our parting a moment longer.

We took tea this afternoon. I was so nervous before he came, my heart was in my mouth, and when Beth showed him in, I am sure my heart missed a beat. He stood before me and he held my eyes, but his manners failed him, he seemed unable to speak. His bearing was upright, stiff like a soldier on parade. He has filled out, his stature is more solid, but then those rigid shoulders seemed to slouch, he physically drooped and I could see the anguish in his features; we seemed locked together in unspoken words; then finally he spoke.

'I was not sure that you would want to see me; I wronged you so, the last time we met. You did not deserve it.'

'Let us not speak of that,' I answered, 'let us just turn a new page.'

He bowed his head slightly, his manners returning. I smiled at him, and gestured for him to sit beside me. 'We have so much to tell each other,' I said.

Beth brought us the tea and we ate cake greedily, as if a great weight had been lifted from our shoulders. And then we just talked; we talked for hours, as if a sluice gate had been opened. It was as if we had never been parted from each other. I realised that I missed all this stimulating conversation that had been denied me by Lord John Dalby. I told him about my venture into the theatre and was not surprised to find that he is knowledgeable about my profession; he has acquired a love of opera it seems. And then he told me about his grand tour of the continent and everything that he had seen.

'You embroider more than an old widow woman, Corbyn,' I said to him capriciously, but he assures me that all the wondrous things he has told me about are true.

I had not known that he had been out of the country for most of this time, and likewise he had not known of my acting success. I suddenly noticed that sparks were flying in the fireplace. Beth had put a new log on the fire, but I had not even noticed her coming in, we were so engrossed in our conversation. I sensed a new found maturity in him, more self-reliance; his travels have been good for him I think.

And then he told me that he had found love with a very grand lady in Florence. I was so pleased for him, he is such a kind and generous man that he deserves it, but alas, it seems that he has left her behind.

Chapter 35.

I suppose this is what they call a moral crisis. Grace's words have stung me like the angriest of hornets. I *am* obsessed by Victoria Farmer; deep down I know that, but I can't seem to stop myself. I study these images of her endlessly. I can see what all those theatregoers in Georgian times saw in her, there is something magnetic about her, and Sir Joshua Lazenby has clearly caught that in his picture of her as Titania.

I have let things slide, I know, my fixation with Ginny and my manic wrestling with Grace's past have been dominating my life, but I have resolved to once again give my students the support that they are entitled to. The only research project that I currently have is the journals, and I will now endeavour to complete it. I have spoken to Colin Milner who is a mathematics professor here and he has given me the name of Sebastian Silver, an Oxford man who specialises in cryptography. I have emailed him to see what he can make of the ciphers used by Corbyn Carlisle.

I have his reply today; he seems most interested in it, saying that it is an interesting cipher and has been invented by a man of considerable intellect. Nevertheless, he has seen this sort of thing before, but the difficulty for him is finding some time to work on it. Grace, it seems, was right, the problem is to find the cipher key and that won't be easy. Without knowledge of the key, it is near impossible to decrypt the resulting ciphertext.

Chapter 36.

The Journal of Ginny Farmer

26th June 1793. Corbyn has been a regular visitor these last few weeks and his company is most welcome. My life is blessed by knowing two of the finest of men in Corbyn and Samuel Medina. They are so different, but both, in their own way, are honourable of character.

Last night we talked of Corbyn's future. One of his reasons for returning to England was an obligation he felt to his family line to produce an heir, and that, of course, means finding a wife; he is 33 now and is well into marriageable age. He tells me that his sister Emily is once again drawing up a list of potential brides for him, but he does not relish the thought of meeting all these prospective young brides.

I suggested to him that he arrange a house party; they are all the rage when it comes to finding a match. Indeed Samuel was hired to attend one such house party to give lessons to the young gentlemen in the science of self-defence. The party could last for say ten days and I suggested that three other eligible young men and four eligible young women could be invited. The whole purpose of the house party was matchmaking, presided over by a hostess, and that would be his sister Emily who would take charge of the gathering. Her job would be to keep the party respectable, within the rules of society, but her main role would be to find a match for Corbyn.

All the girls, I suggested, would need to be chaperoned, but each chaperone would be trying to get a match for her charge and would be looking after the interests of her own girl. Not only would it fill the house with people, it would give Emily and Jane the chance of entertaining. I am told that there is an edge to these house parties, as the chaperones vie with each other to put forward the cases of their charges. It should be fascinating.

The Journal of Corbyn Carlisle

30th June 1793. I spoke at length to Emily earlier this evening on the patio, raising the idea of the house party. The sun was going down on a fine summer's day and there was now a gentle evening breeze to cool us down; there was also the fragrance of the flowers to please us. I was enjoying a glass of port after dinner and Emily joined me, never one to see it as an unladylike drink. I told her of my idea to hold a house party and asked her what names she could put forward as possible marriage candidates for me, but to my surprise she proposed none, saying that she could not suggest anybody suitable. I remember looking at her confused, as she had seemed to be throwing herself into the task of finding me a wife with such enthusiasm; yet now there was not one name to be put forward.

'But you had a list only the other week, Emily dear, you showed it to me,' I said, raising an eyebrow.

'They are not suitable,' she replied in strangled tones, but I could see in her eyes that this was a lie.

'They seemed eminently suitable the last time we spoke, Emily, you seemed so positive,'

'No, they are not suitable,' she repeated. She now stared at the ground, not meeting my eyes.

'What about that Gwynne girl, Florence was it? You seemed keen on her.'

'No, she is not suitable,' was all she would say again.

Her words were vague and she was still avoiding my eyes. I could see that something was wrong and I should have realised the answer immediately, but I have to confess that the obvious did not occur to me.

'It's a wonderful opportunity for you and Jane to do some entertaining,' I said, but I was making matters worse.

And then I saw her shoulders start to rise and fall. There were little sobs coming from her as she continued to stare at the ground. Emily and Jane have never been sensitive souls and I was taken aback; in fact they are rather thick-skinned and opinionated, in the mould of our father. I might go as far as saying unfeeling and callous. I was not used to a display of emotion from her.

I adopted a gentle tone. 'Something is upsetting you, Emily dear; tell me what is it?'

She looked up at me and I could see tears cascading down her cheeks, her pock-marked cheeks, and then the answer was so obvious to me. She plucked her handkerchief from her cuff, started to speak, but no words came. She just stood, and then ran away sobbing.

I sat back in my patio chair and poured myself another glass of port. I was pondering what to do next when Jane came thundering out onto the patio. She plonked herself down in the seat that Emily had vacated, her back straight with resolve, her face carved with a belligerent expression, her jaw jutted and her lips snarling and twisted. I knew what was coming.

'You dunderhead, Corbyn!' she thundered. 'Good grief man, what were you thinking?'

'Yes, I'm so sorry,' I said contritely, 'I thought she would relish the idea of entertaining, it's been so long.' My words tailed away, knowing how useless they sounded.

'Look at us!' she bellowed at me, pointing her finger at her face. 'We would curdle the milk at table. We would give your house guests colic before they had even finished breakfasting. Is that what you want, for your guests to have the bellyache?'

I sat and took my punishment; I deserved it. 'I'll have to think of something else,' I said into my port as Jane railed on at me.

I'll write to Ginny straight away.

7th July 1793. I have a letter from Ginny. She is most charming, as usual; she has never seen Emily and Jane, but she seems to understand their reluctance to act as hostesses for the house party. But she has put forward a very tempting and intriguing alternative. Her current production comes to an end in six weeks. She has volunteered to act as the hostess for the gathering, so long as Emily and Jane agree. I will put the proposal to them at once.

The Journal of Ginny Farmer

10th July 1793. I have a letter from Corbyn, accepting my invitation to host the house party to find him a wife. I am quite excited about it all. Emily and Jane have not yet decided whether to go to a neighbour for the duration of the event or to stay in their rooms. Emily, however, has agreed to draw up the list of guests, make the sleeping arrangements, and order all the victuals and wine. She says that she will also arrange for some entertainment for the evenings, which is a splendid suggestion.

Whilst Emily takes care of all the practicalities, I must go to work on Corbyn. He is no extravert, but he must take it upon himself to give of his best. There will be other male suitors there and he must not be outshone by them. For this house party, he must appear in his finery; must be seen as a man of means; must be charm personified. And this must be repeated with his fellow guests, both male and female. I must make sure that he will be all things to all men — and women. He must keep a special welcome for the chaperones, for they hold the key to any success in the matchmaking stakes; he must especially charm them.

I know that he is a fine swordsman. I will ask Emily to arrange for the entertainment to include a fencing exhibition, so that Corbyn will stand out and appear manly to these privileged young women.

But what of myself? I must once again, I think, play the part of Lady Virginia to the full. I am really far too young to be such a hostess, the role normally falls to a much maturer woman. It is a part, however, that I will see as a challenge.

Chapter 37.

I have received an email form Sebastian Silver. <Hi James. Just a quick update. Making some progress with this ancient cipher; it's not as bad as I first thought. I have run it against some computer programmes that I have put together myself and the results are encouraging. What we have to remember is that this cipher was constructed with pen and paper, not a computer, so it will never be as complicated as a modern cipher. I'm pretty certain what we have here is a simple *substitution* cipher. All that means is that it is a method of encryption by which units of plaintext are replaced with ciphertext, according to a regular system; the "units" may be single letters (the most common), pairs of letters, triplets of letters, mixtures of the above, and so forth. The receiver deciphers the text by performing an inverse substitution. Seb.>

<Hi Seb. Glad you are making progress. You say simple, but it's gibberish to me. Please continue to keep me in the loop though.>

< James – Sorry if I confused you. Think of it this way – in a substitution cipher, the units of the plaintext are retained in the same sequence in the ciphertext, but the units themselves are altered. So we are looking for substitution over a single letter – simple substitution. So we need to find an alternative alphabet in some order to represent the substitution. This, as it suggests, is termed a substitution alphabet. The cipher alphabet could be shifted or reversed or scrambled in a more complex fashion, but let's hope not. Seb.>

<Seb. I'm afraid it's still another language to me, but thanks for the explanation anyway.>

<James. OK, but don't be frightened by my explanations, I promise it's not as complicated as you think, don't give up just yet. Look, using this system, let's say that the keyword is "polar" and that gives us the following alphabets:

Plaintext alphabet. ABCDEFGHIJKLMNOPQRSTUVWXYZ.
Ciphertext alphabet. POLARBCDEFGHIJKMNQSTUVWXYZ.

So we still have to find the keyword. Can you let me know what your guy did for a living and what he was interested in? Seb.>

<Seb. Ah, I think I'm beginning to get it; the mists are clearing a little.

His name is Lord Corbyn Carlisle, Baron Elloughton. He was a lawyer. He was interested in the arts, especially the theatre, and was a competitive fencer. Does this help? James.>

I settled down to my work again, but then I stopped; a thought occurred to me. What would be his *keyword* – I wonder.

<Seb. The keyword? Just a long shot. Try Virginia Farmer, or Ginny. James.>

I went to get myself a Millicano coffee, poured the hot water on the granules. The aroma hit my nostrils and I added the milk. I took a sip and it burned my lips, but I couldn't wait so I drank again. I sat down at my desk again, cradling the mug in my hands. The photocopier outside my office was making a racket, someone had left it on multiple and it was churning out endless copies of something, clattering with each sweep of the light mechanism. It was irritating, but then I heard the computer ping. The din was instantly cast from my consciousness. I lunged to open my email folder. It was Seb Silver again.

<James. Bingo! Keyword is Ginny. Seb>

Chapter 38.

The Journal of Ginny Farmer

5th September 1793. 'We are approaching Elloughton Park, M'Lady,' the words of the carriage driver rang out from above me.

I took hold of the hanging leather loop and peered out of the window, holding the sill with my other hand. The late summer sun bathed the landscape, the fields lush with produce and the field-hands busy at work bringing in the harvest. I suddenly felt guilty. I had pushed Corbyn into arranging this house party at short notice, never thinking that it would be harvest time, and he may have other business to take care of. I then looked to the horizon and got my first sight of the hall; it took my breath away.

Corbyn has told me that Elloughton Park is a fine house built by Inigo Jones, and the name of that fine gentleman should have prepared me for its splendour, but I am now taken by sweet surprise. I see now what he meant by the Palladian style brought from Italy, a central house with balancing pavilions linked by colonnades. As we drew closer, I saw that it is built on three floors, the roofline hidden by a balustrade, and each of the terminating wings is crowned by a one-storey tower.

When the carriage pulled up at the front of the hall, Corbyn, the dear man, rushed to meet me, and instructed the footman to take my bags up to the master bedroom.

'But is that not your room, Corbyn?' I asked, not wanting to inconvenience him.

'Aye,'tis,' he said gallantly, 'but it is yours for the duration of the house party. Would you like to see it and freshen up?'

'No,' I said, 'right now I want you to show me the garden that you are so proud of.'

We walked through the hall and out into the rear and sat in the sun; he asked the butler to bring us some cordial. Corbyn pointed out everything to me – the absence of walls so that the eye is taken to the furthest part of the estate, all the tenant farms, the village of Elloughton Vale over to the left of the vista, and the estate lands rolling down to the River Trent.

It is informal, delightful; there are terraces, shrubberies, flowerbeds and gravelled walks to enjoy. And as one looks back to the house, it is so complimented that it stands in its full grandeur. I have seen the painting that Corbyn had commissioned, but fine as it is, it does not match this piece of paradise that Corbyn has achieved. Roses, primroses, violets, gillyflowers, peonies, marigolds and lilies all abound. There are pinks and carnations, and Corbyn was keen to point out some flowers called nasturtiums which are new from the Americas. And then there is the orchard, this the first year that it is laden with fruit; pear and apple at the far end from the house, then cherries, plums and apricots nestling in the foreground.

We sat and sipped our cordial. There were finches chattering playfully above us in the fruit trees and sparrows around my feet, in anticipation of some titbit that I might throw them. It was so refreshing after the long drive, but I was enthused by the task ahead of me.

'Have all our guests arrived?' I asked.

'All but Captain Thomas Cadogan,' he answered, 'he arrives this evening; he will be here for dinner. Mr. Piers Mortimer and Mr. Soames Lambton are already here.'

'That is good; you will be the gentleman of the highest rank, the best catch. But I want you in your finery at dinner tonight, Corbyn.' He looked at me as though I were a fussing mother hen, but I ignored him. 'And the ladies?' I added.

'Lady Amanda Derby, Miss Paulette Walters, Miss Lydia Heslop and Miss Elvira Hart.'

'And they all come with fortunes?'

'According to Emma, Lady Amanda is of the highest rank, but the father has gambled much of his estate away, mortgaged to the hilt I understand. The others are likely to come with fine dowries, especially Miss Elvira Hart whose father is a wine merchant. Trade I know, but well educated and very rich. Her father is intent on using his wealth to find her a marriage in the gentry.'

'And who is the prettiest?' I asked.

'Oh, I don't know. I hadn't really noticed.'

'Corbyn! Stop being so coy with me; if I am to help you find a wife, you have to be honest with me.'

'Lydia Heslop.' he said sheepishly, 'a delicate, pretty little thing.'

'That's better, Corbyn dear. If a wife is to be found, then I need to know your preferences.'

The Journal of Corbyn Carlisle

5th September 1793. *I introduced Ginny to my sisters this evening before dinner; they were in Emily's room where they are taking their meals. They had the opportunity to go and stay with a neighbour, but they were too ashamed of their appearance to even do that. I introduced her as Lady Virginia Farmer and I thought they readily accepted her as a fine lady. There was an undertone, however, especially from Jane, who I saw at once resented her. The only thing I can say in her defence was that she was acting in her sister's behalf, believing that she was the rightful hostess of the house. The fact that Emily had turned down the opportunity to host the house party was, somehow, disregarded in her hostility.*

I saw Ginny flinch slightly at the sight of their pock-marked faces, but she quickly regained her control and greeted them warmly.

'You have selected the young ladies, Emily?' she enquired.

'Yes, with the help of the Widower and Bachelor's Directory,' Emily said, 'it's amazing how much one can find out about a person from it.' There was heavy emphasis for some reason that I didn't, at first, understand.

But then I realised when Jane interrupted, 'We couldn't find your name in it, Virginia?' There was an accusation in her tone, but then Jane always did have a caustic tongue.

She held Ginny's eyes, trying to gauge her reaction, but Ginny returned the look and held that gaze for several seconds, all the time just effusing charm and good humour. She held her head slightly to one side and then smiled affectionately at her.

'I'm not surprised, dear Jane,' she said eventually, 'my family's fortune is long gone; I am certainly no rich catch for anyone.'

'And how are you acquainted with our brother, Miss Farmer?' Jane was obviously in an antagonistic mood.

'I am reduced to being an actress,' she said, 'fol derol, but that is my current circumstance. Corbyn, as you know, is a keen theatregoer. We met at an "after performance" party. We have become firm friends.'

'Friends?' she sniffed, then cocked an eye in my direction to indicate that she knew the word friend was a euphemism for something more carnal. She looked as if she had the smell of the Thames in her nostrils.

'Actually, we <u>didn't</u> know that Corbyn was a keen theatregoer,' interrupted Emily. She was taking up the baton from Jane; there was suspicion in her eyes too.

I suppressed a shudder at my sisters' behaviour; I felt that I needed to come to Ginny's aid; it was ungallant of me to let her face this inquisition on her own. But Ginny must have sensed this of me, and she just gave me the briefest look to tell me that she was in full control; I recognised that she was.

Ginny then turned to me. 'You should be more forthcoming with your sisters, Corbyn; they need to know what you get up to in London,' she said nonchalantly, 'they have so few visitors; they must be desperate for news of you and good conversation.' Her words were carefully chosen, and were said with the sweetest of tones. Nevertheless, the pity they represented hit home like the straightest of arrows. The eyes of both Emily and Jane narrowed, and gave flashes of anger. They both sat up, held their backs straight. Ginny just held her head high.

There was an uneasy silence for some moments, and I felt I must speak.

'Come, Ginny, we are expected at table. If you are the hostess, you must not be seen to be late.'

I offered my arm and she took it, and we turned and walked to the door. Emily called after us; there was still rancour in her voice.

'I expect you to come and give me a report every evening on how things are going,' she sniffed. There was desperation in her eyes, as if she knew that she had unexpectedly lost control, been toppled from her pinnacle, which, of course, she had.

Ginny stopped and looked over her shoulder, firstly at Jane and then at Emily. She gave them both an amused look. 'Oh I don't think so, dear Emily, not now,' she paused, 'no, not now.'

When we left, I am sure they were screaming in their heads.

The Journal of Ginny Farmer

5ᵗʰ September 1793. Corbyn introduced me to his sisters this evening. They tried to bully me, but I was having none of it. They are clearly anxious about the new mistress of the hall; they have no income of their own and nowhere else to go. Their faces make it impossible to find husbands. I feel for them, although I have to say that they are not the most likable of ladies.

At dinner I hosted, and I strained to give my most charming performance, but the evening, surprisingly, turned out to be most enjoyable. There were thirteen of us, which is, of course, an unlucky number, the four young ladies each with their own chaperone, the three young gentlemen, and then Corbyn and myself. In the superstition it is said that one of the party will die within the twelvemonth. It is a silly superstition for old women; we are all young people; nevertheless, I will get Corbyn to throw an old shoe after me for the sake of good luck. Listen to me; I will be putting my stockings on inside out next for the same reason.

I have made my first assessment. As far as the young ladies are concerned, Lydia Heslop is a pretty little thing, as Corbyn describes her, but she is timid and hardly said a word all evening. Emily and Jane would devour her whole if she was to marry Corbyn. If she doesn't come out of herself, I see no future for her as far as Corbyn is concerned.

Lady Amanda Derby is empty-headed, good for embroidery and riding out and little else. Apart from her title, she has little to offer.

Miss Paulette Walters is a plump girl and a clumsy, dreamy creature. She lagged behind in all the conversation at table.

Miss Elvira Hart is the only one with any personality it seems. She is bright and not without wit. But she is unfashionably tall with slightly drooping shoulders, and poor skin.

I suspect that Emily has selected wisely, so that Corbyn will be taken by Lydia's good looks. She is <u>her</u> choice I am sure.

As far as the men are concerned, Mr. Piers Mortimer is the oldest and a little on the stout side. He is listed as a gentleman, which means that he is probably idle and overeats, overdrinks and gambles, but he is keen to tell all the chaperones that he has £2000 per year. He is no threat to Corbyn. My first impressions lead me to think he will be a good partner for Miss Paulette Walters.

Mr. Soames Lambton is the youngest. He is slightly built with a round, expressionless face, a blank canvas of emotion and difficult to read. But he also has an anaemic face with milk-white skin and is far from a robust man. Again I see no threat, although he comes with an impressive £5000 a year.

Captain Thomas Cadogan, on the other hand, is a different kettle of fish. He wore his military uniform to dinner and he stands a fine figure of a man. He is also a silver-tongued scallywag. His wit was sharp at table and the eyes of the young ladies were glued to him. He flirted with each of them in turn and then with their chaperones, and then even with me. I think he sees this house party as an excuse to bed as many women as he can. I consider him a rogue. He is the second son of a country gentleman with an income of a mere £800 a year and the lowest of rank, but I also suspect that he is a profligate, and his £800 easily spent, and looking for a wealthy wife to refill his coffers. Nevertheless, he is the challenge for Corbyn to overcome. He, of course, has to work the hardest, and to his credit he dominated the conversation over dinner. He was clearly by far the wittiest of the young gentlemen and the most handsome, and the young ladies giggled at his yarns. If wealth and status did not matter, then he would be the leading candidate in the marriage stakes. The night belonged to him.

The Journal of Corbyn Carlisle

6th September 1793. After dinner last night when the ladies had retired, the gentlemen repaired to the games room. I had arranged for a well-stocked tray of refreshments on a side table and my finest cognac was the main attraction. We started with a game of billiards, but then Captain Cadogan proposed a hand of cards and we retired to the card table and played whist. He was a very good card player and took money from all of us. During a break in the game, Cadogan leaned back in his chair, cradling another glass of my cognac. I'm not sure what sort of discussion goes on in the officer's mess, but his manners quickly deserted him and his conversation descended into the coarse. The others did not seem to mind and joined him in his crudeness. They shared pinches of their own blends of snuff as they talked, and an air of rowdiness quickly took hold.

Cadogan talked about the young ladies as if they were livestock: who had the best bosom, who had the best rear and who had the best thighs for the marriage bed. Bosoms were on display, of course, but legs were not, and quite how he managed to judge these things I don't know. With extreme vulgarity, the young ladies were now openly and rudely compared with each other and Mortimer and Lambton joined him.

But then Cadogan turned his attention to the chaperones, and of course he had gone out of his way to charm them too. Two of them were over sixty, but one of the others was a mature lady in her forties, and the last somewhat younger, I presume in her late thirties. Cadogan boasted that he would bed both of them before the party was finished. Seeing that he is sharing a bedchamber with Mortimer, this will be a difficult task for him.

Mortimer then changed the subject, obviously taken with Cadogan's superb horse. 'You arrived on a fine black stallion, Captain Cadogan?' he asked.

'Aye,' he said, puffing on a cigar and blowing the smoke into the air extravagantly, 'it was a lucky acquisition.'

'How so, sir?' asked Lambton.

'Well,' he said, leaning forward conspiratorially, 'I was walking along only last week, minding my own business, when a beautiful woman rode up on that fine stallion, jumped down to the ground and took off all her clothes and said, "Take what you want." '

The other two also leaned forward as if to join the conspiracy, knowing that humour was to follow.

He paused, waiting for the tension to be established. 'So I took the horse,' he said. They both laughed and I did too, it was a first-rate tale, but he was not finished.

'It was a good choice,' he added, 'her clothes probably wouldn't have fit me anyway.'

Well, we all laughed again. I may have initially misjudged him; he is probably a stout fellow, despite his coarseness and dubious manners.

The Journal of Ginny Farmer

6th September 1793. When we ladies retired to the drawing room after dinner, the conversation quickly turned to the young gentlemen. The two older chaperones representing Miss Paulette Walters and Miss Lydia Heslop spoke politely about Mr. Mortimer and Mr. Lambton and their prospects, but as I suspected, their charges had paid little attention to them. The problem was that the conversation was not about Corbyn either. The only person that they wanted to talk about was Captain Cadogan; even the two elderly chaperones had been sent all of a flutter by this dashing young soldier.

I pondered why Emily had selected him and it is not at first sight clear to me, but I assume he is part of her plan. I still think that her aspiration is to pair Corbyn with Lydia Heslop, but I can't see where Cadogan comes in; I know he was a last minute addition. Perhaps his function is to avoid a match with Elvira Hart. If she comes with the biggest fortune, then Cadogan would want her to fund his profligacy.

But then I too can see the attraction in Cadogan. He is an outrageous flirt and, of course, wit is a much-prized quality in a man. He certainly has that in abundance. He has turned the heads of all the ladies present, including their chaperones. Let us hope that before the party is finished they make their recommendations on a much more studied basis.

7th **September 1793**. Yesterday evening, we were entertained after dinner by a silhouettist, who skilfully cut out our images in black card. The evening was genteel and both sexes played their part by behaving with the best of manners; even Captain Cadogan.

This evening after dinner, Emily had arranged a musical evening. A pianist played some delightful Handel and Mozart pieces. Later, a young lady sang for us with songs by Mr. James Hook and Mr. George Frederick Pinto. The servants had arranged the chairs around the piano so that the facade of a small theatre had been intimated. The pianist played the piano delicately and with refinement, and was much appreciated, except, that is, for Captain Cadogan, who I saw was bored and making no effort to hide it. He perked up when it was the turn of the young lady to sing. I understand that she is local, the daughter of the minister and not a professional singer. I felt for her and could see how nervous she was. She was such a slip of a girl, a delicate creature of about sixteen. She cleared her throat deftly behind her white-gloved hand, in preparation for her first song. The first notes sounded pure, but her sweet soprano voice had a quiver, betraying the nervousness that she felt at appearing before her audience. But after a few couplets, the young woman's voice strengthened, the quiver disappeared and her fine voice resounded around the room, its purity being enjoyed by all present; even Captain Cadogan.

Corbyn asked me to join her when she had finished and I reluctantly agreed, but it was most pleasant, singing a duet with her. As I was singing, however, looking out at my small audience, I saw the chaperone for Miss Elvira Hart, the lady in her late thirties, surreptitiously pass Captain Cadogan a note. The matchmaking is beginning to move at a pace I see.

8th September 1793. I was awoken in the early hours of this morning by a knocking at my door. I had extravagantly fallen asleep with the candle still burning, but it was not yet burnt out, there was still a small flame burning at the pinnacle of a congealed blob of molten wax. I held it up to the ticking wall clock and the flickering flame danced, revealing it was twenty minutes after two of the clock. I sat up and swung my legs out of bed and was about to go to the door when I realised that it was not my door that was being tapped. I was still half sleep-dead and not really wakeful, but gradually I realised that it was the next bedroom to mine. And who was in that bedroom? The chaperone for Miss Elvira Hart. I tiptoed to my door, and as quietly as I could, opened it a half-inch to peep out. There, swaying outside the next bedroom door was Captain Cadogan. Ah the note, I thought to myself, it was not about matchmaking after all, it was about more lustful matters. She had told me that she was Miss Elvira Hart's cousin, but clearly she wears a wedding ring and is also a married woman. I was not shocked; my experience has educated me to the goings on of people of society.

Cadogan obviously had an invitation to a tryst, but he had also wanted to drink and gamble, I presume, before he undertook his mission. His problem was that the lady was now asleep and not answering her door. I smiled to myself as I peeped through the crack; he was drunk and he now turned and leaned against the door, his back resting against it to give him support, his befuddled mind trying to work out his next manoeuvre. He turned back and started to call out the lady's name through the keyhole, his arm raised above his head, still tapping, until he unbalanced and fell forward, his drooling mouth now pressed against the door.

I heard a muffled "go 'way" come from within, but now having woken the lady, that was the last thing on his mind. Eventually, the lady came to the door, I think to tell him to be quiet, but as she opened it to what she must have thought was just enough to talk to him, he fell into her room, the door no longer supporting him. The lady then shut the door, shushing the inebriated captain as she did so. He did not emerge again until this morning when I heard him take his leave, again without much discretion, his military boots clip-clopping on the landing floor, but with, I suspect, his lust sated for the moment.

The Journal of Corbyn Carlisle

6th September 1793. *This afternoon, we all assembled in the garden. There was to be a fencing exhibition and two gentlemen from a fencing club in Newark came to show us their skills. They were no way as accomplished as Monsieur Lievremont, my own fencing tutor, but they were proficient enough. We all clapped politely at the end of the exhibition and then took refreshment in the form of lemonade; it was as much for the fencers as the houseguests, who had worked up quite a sweat.*

When they resumed, they suggested we gentlemen come forward and try it ourselves. Both Mortimer and Lambton had never fenced before, but they both put on an energetic display under tuition. Then it was the turn of Cadogan and myself. The two fencing instructors assumed that the captain was proficient with a blade, but I told them that I was too. I took off my grey frock coat, and Cadogan his military jacket, and we stood just in our breeches and linen shirts open at the neck without stock. We were fitted with the protective jackets and the masks to protect our faces. The blade I was given was slightly heavier than I was used to, but I quickly got used to it. The tutor was surprised at my level of skill and I am confident enough to say that I would beat him in a proper contest. I exhibited at the same time as Cadogan, however, and my mask did not give me the opportunity to see his level of skill against the other tutor.

When we concluded, there was appreciative applause all round, but then Virginia suggested that it would be good sport if I fought Cadogan. The other ladies applauded expectantly and the two tutors looked at each other with some alarm. But then they bowed their agreement, saying that it must be fought under strict competition rules, they would referee and keep their own blades ready to intervene if necessary.

We took up our "on guard" positions, side on, our blades in our right hands in a ready position before us, our left hands held high behind us. On the command: "fence", he took an aggressive strategy, lunging forward at me, looking for an easy hit, but I just stepped backwards and parried. What was clear was that he was fit and had speed to accompany his undoubted skill. But I had skill too. He lunged at me again and I parried, but this time I also then countered and my blossom hit home, the foil bending almost double against his protective jacket. The tutor yelled out "hit" and Cadogan acknowledged it. I heard a little cheer from Virginia at my achievement. We resumed again and the fencing was as thrilling a contest as I have had for some time. Cadogan now adopted a more cautious strategy, realising that I could counter his all-round aggression and we exchanged hits for some minutes. The contest was to be brief, the first to five, and I led by four hits to three when we took guard again.

He now unleashed his full repertoire of moves upon me and I felt that I would be overwhelmed, but my instincts protected me and I countered each of them, but he had me on the defensive, he was determining the course of the fight. I parried again and then lunged at him, but he also parried. It must have been thrilling for the onlookers; speed and elegance, lunge and parry, the blades flashing in the air like lightning speeding across the sky. And then I thought I sensed him slightly off balance, and I went in for a hit. The blossom hit home on the edge of his jacket, but it skidded off on to his unprotected arm. The point, or the blossom, had been blunted of course, by fastening a knob to it, but nevertheless it scratched his flesh and drew blood. The tutor called "hit" and then rushed to Cadogan.

He took off his mask and looked at his wound, but declared it of no consequence. 'Bravo, sir,' he said, turning to me. I could see that he looked at me in a different light. I think the young ladies did also.

The Journal of Ginny Farmer

15th September 1793. Corbyn came to my room last night. The clock had not reached midnight, but it was approaching it. I answered the door, but I didn't cross the threshold, deliberately; but he just passed in front of me and came into my bedroom. No words were spoken and he slumped down into a chair beside my bed. I sat on the bed so that we could talk; we talked for over an hour.

It was clear to me that he is unsure about these young ladies. He plainly rejects Lady Amanda Derby, and Miss Paulette Walters. Lady Amanda has a title, but then so does Corbyn, but he sees her as I do, empty-headed, and she will not make a good companion for him. For some men that would not be a problem, but for him an intellectual companion is preferred.

The same is true of Miss Paulette Walters, but he also finds her unattractive.

So it came down to Miss Lydia Heslop or Miss Elvira Hart. My choice would be the latter, bright and not without wit. She will make a good companion for him, as well as a wife. But Corbyn, it seems, is put off by her height, she is ever so slightly taller than him, and he finds this hard to handle. So, after much soul-searching, his preference is Miss Lydia Heslop. I agree that she is a pretty little thing, but I tried to impress on him that I felt she too would not make a good companion, she has hardly said a word all week. He conceded that and so I pressed him for a reason; after some prevarication, he admitted that she reminded him of me. She has my height and stature I had to admit but, other than that, I don't think we are at all alike.

I now have to admit also that I have probably made a mistake; I allowed Corbyn to stay the night with me. It seemed a natural thing to do at the time, and I readily agreed to his suggestion without much consideration. I wanted to console the dear man and the thought of him in my bed again was pleasing to me. But then, in the cold light of day, I have probably complicated his decision.

Tomorrow is the last day of the house party, and the guests will go home after lunch. Before dinner tonight we were treated to a fireworks display, but later, at table, there was a nuance; there was a tension crackling in the air just like those fireworks, I presume because decisions were in the making. After dinner, when we ladies repaired to the drawing room for the last time, it was the turn of the chaperones to make their representations. The only firm liaison was an agreement between Mr. Mortimer and Miss Paulette Walters. He has declared his admiration for the lady and they have reached an agreement. The chaperone has recommended it and both parties have agreed. There will be a series of further meetings with a view to marriage.

After that, the discussions took a surprising turn; to put it bluntly, it descended to the level of horse-trading. Captain Cadogan has made it clear to the chaperone of Miss Elvira Hart that he is interested in her. Miss Hart, too, it seems, is interested in him, but the chaperone will hear nothing of it, saying that he is a cad and his name Cadogan well given; in no way is he a suitable husband; she could not recommend him to the girl's father. I smiled inwardly; Cadogan has sawn off the branch he was sitting on by bedding this chaperone, but his real mistake, however, was not the bedding, but then shunning her to spend his time pursuing other conquests.

But then things got ever stranger. The chaperone for Miss Lydia Heslop turned to me sheepishly and said: 'My opinion is that Lord Carlisle would be a good match for my charge.' She then turned and looked awkwardly at Miss Heslop. Glances were exchanged between them, I saw that there was belligerence in the young woman's eyes; this little timid mouse, who had hardly said a word all week, did not want Corbyn. I smiled inwardly to myself, as it was one in the eye for his sister Emily.

'You know my feelings, Judith,' said Miss Heslop to her chaperone in a fierce whisper, her eyes flashing with anger, 'my preferred choice is Captain Cadogan.'

'But you are not really suited, my dear,' said Judith; she then held her breath.

The little mouse then unleashed a tirade against her chaperone. We were all taken aback, and looked on as the words spat from her mouth.

'But what about your father, dear...? An uncompleted sentence was all that the chaperone could say in response.

I sat back in my chair, pondering what had just happened. Miss Lydia Heslop had set her cap at Captain Cadogan, a man totally unsuitable for her. I knew he would jump at the chance; she was not as wealthy as Elvira Hart, but much more manipulative. Emily's strategy had backfired in two directions, Cadogan had been brought in to match with Miss Elvira Hart I am sure and leave the little mouse as the only prospective new mistress. Thanks to Cadogan's lust, neither will now happen.

I learned afterwards that the chaperone has paid Captain Cadogan £50 not to pursue Miss Heslop. He took it readily I understand, as it will go some way to paying off his debts, or more likely he will just return to the card table with it.

It is my birthday the day after tomorrow and Corbyn has asked me to stay an extra day and celebrate it with him. I will like nothing better.

Chapter 39.

I looked up at the wall clock in my office; it said five minutes to four. It was Friday afternoon and I had a pint of Bombardier on my mind; I had not had a drink all the working week and it was to be my reward. The phone rang and I looked at it ringing in its cradle and thought to ignore it; calls on a Friday afternoon usually meant late nights. Then guilt got the better of me and I picked it up.

'Yep – Postlethwaite.'

'Oh hello Professor Postlethwaite – it's Seb Silver. Just thought I'd put a voice to the name, so to speak.'

'Yeah, no problem,' I was being polite; 'I hope you have good news for me?'

'Actually I have. I've done a full decipher now; luckily the numbers just turned out to be a substitution for their alphabetic letter sequence, so what we have is that simple substitution cipher that I told you about. But I think the result will blow you away.'

'Blow me away; what do you mean?' I said, sitting up in my chair.

'Well I'm no historian and I don't know anything about your man, but I wasn't expecting to read such intrigue, such brutality. I'll certainly look at you historians in a different way from now on; to be honest, I thought you were all boring old farts. You should have given me the heads up as to what to expect; I thought we were dealing with an ordinary guy?'

'But we *are* dealing with an ordinary guy; the research project is into lifestyles, not intrigue, as you put it.'

'Then you are in for a big surprise, my friend.' I was stunned for a moment, not sure how to respond. 'You still there?' he said.

'Yeah, yeah,' I replied, but my thoughts were running ahead of me. 'Ok, I need to read it obviously; when can you get it to me?'

'I don't want to keep you late at your desk on Friday afternoon, James, how about if I email it to you first thing on Monday morning?'

'No, I'd prefer it now if you don't mind.'

'No probs, I'll do it right now.'

I put down the receiver and just looked at it for some moments, but not really seeing. Then I emailed Grace. <Spoke to cryptographer. He has

cracked the cipher, and is emailing it to me. He says it is full of intrigue and brutality. Not sure what he means but I'll let you see it next week.>

I hit the send button and sat back, waiting impatiently. Before the email from Seb Silver came through, there was a knock at my door and Grace came in, not waiting for my response; she had her laptop under her arm.

'Oh no you don't,' she said, sitting down at the other side of my desk and placing her laptop down, commandeering a portion of it.

'Oh no I don't *what?*' I said, confused.

'I'm not waiting till next week for this; I want to read it now.'

I didn't know where she was when I sent the email, but she must have been in the building. Then my email pinged.

<James. As promised – see the attachment. It's long but astonishing. Seb.>

I opened the attachment and started to read.

'No you don't,' said Grace again. I looked up and saw the curiosity in her eyes. I knew she was still mad at me, but that inquisitiveness was overriding it. Those eyes, those piercing china-blue eyes proclaimed that she was not going to wait until I had finished. 'Email it to my laptop, if you please,' she commanded, all the time her eyes speaking for her as much as her words. She ran her hand through her hair in that habit of hers, still holding my gaze. I had been here before, I was treading ground I had previously trod; I knew she would not break off eye contact before me. It was part of her control mechanism, her self-assuredness. For a moment I was speechless because I suddenly realised how much I had missed her. Just being here together was thrilling.

I didn't answer, I just looked down and clicked the forward button, and she eagerly opened the email on her laptop, opened the attachment and began to read. I followed her.

The Journal of Corbyn Carlisle (deciphered)

20th June 1788. I have tried to write this several times; words and phrases composed in my mind and then abandoned, burned from my thoughts, drafts and lines left hanging, trying not to write something that others could use against me if found. So I have determined that it will be in code as a protection. I am in considerable pain as I write, but I know it is important that I record what happened two days ago.

I remember it was at thirty minutes after ten of the clock in the evening, I walked briskly from my fencing academy on Gt. Store Street at the north end of Bedford Square. There was a full moon, and it was a fine summer's evening and I swung my cane intrepidly, feeling good after some strenuous competition. I walked down the street onto Tottenham Court Road and looked for a hackney to take me south to my club on St. James Street near the river. In retrospect it was not a sensible decision; I should have sent out a runner to bring back the carriage to the fencing academy. It was quiet on Tottenham Court Road and I thought I would walk down onto Oxford Street; it would be busier and easier from there. Foolishly, I thought I'd cut the corner by taking a shortcut through Black Horse Yard and onto Oxford Street via Gresse Street. As soon as I entered Black Horse Yard the overhanging buildings cut off the bright moonlight. I was halfway down the passageway when I thought I heard the sound of footsteps following me, echoing off the walls of the narrow alley. I stopped and looked behind me, but my eyes had not yet adjusted to the darkness, but if I was being stalked then I could not go back the way I had come. I quickened my step, reached into my frock coat, and put my hand onto the handle of the cudgel that Samuel Medina had given me.

I was also reassured that my cane was a swordstick. This cane-sword was a handsome piece, made of Malacca wood, the handle made of horn with ivory decoration, but it has a brass collar that twists and unlocks the blade; it was a second weapon. But then that reassurance drained from me; a rapier-pointed blade was no match for a firearm I thought.

I felt that if I got to the end of the yard, then I might get some protection from the bright moonlight being more conspicuous. My pursuers obviously thought the same, and I heard their steps; they were now running after me. I was a dozen yards or so from the corner when the first one fell on me. He, too, was brandishing a cudgel and when I swung round I saw it high in the air above me to be brought down on my head. I had my cane in my left hand, I raised this over my head to protect me, and it took the force of the blow. I then drew my own cudgel and aimed it low at his knee as I had been taught. I heard a crack and a cry of pain and the man went down. If he had been alone I would have fancied my chances, but I looked up and saw two other distorted shadowy faces bearing down on me. I could now see a little more in the darkness; they were soldiers, infantrymen, one wearing corporal's stripes. They were not the normal ruffians, the low street life of London; was I just a casual victim of drunken soldiers wanting more coins to continue their evening's drinking?

The first of them had his cudgel raised and I swung my own in a much smaller arc so that I delivered my blow first, hitting his wrist and deflecting the blow, but the second man hit me severely across the forehead and I staggered back, dazed. Then I thought I heard a guttural voice from further down the yard; a fourth man.

'Get his cudgel,' it said. There was urgency in the tone.

The first man then got up from the floor and held me in a bear-hug from behind. My arms were now pinned to my side and I could not defend myself; I feared the worst. The blows now rained down on me, and then I was allowed to fall to the floor so that the first man could join in my beating. They concentrated on my body as if to maximise the beating, blow after blow to my ribs and stomach, so I would remain conscious throughout it. I should have realised that this was not normal for a street robbery where quick disablement was the object.

I was lying on my back; I discarded my swordstick and my hand searched frantically into my frock coat, I took out my purse and held it up for them. 'Here! – take my coins,' I boomed out, 'here, my purse.'

It was grabbed by one of the soldiers and the three stood over me whilst he shook it to gauge how much was in there. Then I heard that guttural voice again. 'We haven't come here for that, you have been paid already, remember, you scums.'

I was now bemused, as much from these words as from the beating, this was obviously not a random attack. The pain now took me, but my instinct for survival was still keeping me alert, focussed, casting away that dizziness. I looked to the end of the alley as if it represented safety, although now I understand that it clearly did not. There was a diagonal of bright moonlight piercing into the alley, making a triangle of light at the entrance. I shuffled backwards across the dirt floor, trying to get into it, but the fourth figure came over to stop me. He was limping, but he swung his good foot at me, kicking me in the ribs when I was a yard or two short.

'Stay where you are, Corbyn,' it said.

Corbyn! He knows my name; how does he know my name?

And then the figure itself shuffled into that triangle of moonlight, I think deliberately. My God it was Cavendish. He was intent on taking his revenge, I could see the vengeance in his eyes and I knew that my beating was about to get worse. But now that I was disarmed, he was going to be the perpetrator. He stepped forward, brought down his own cudgel time and time again and I struggled to hold off the blows with my raised arms. The beating was not to be like for like as I had administered to him, I thought; he would not play the gentleman and desist when his opponent was beaten.

I scampered backwards across the dirt floor, my back pinned against it, my legs pushing me away from him as the blows rained down, trying to escape his reach. But it was futile, he just limped after me continuing the assault. I felt my head brush against my sword-cane on the ground behind me; I reached up, took hold of it with my left hand, brought it up in front of me, and parried some of the blows.

The other soldiers cheered at this as if it was good sport for their entertainment. I continued to block the blows, but I knew it was only a matter of time until enough blows got through and I was knocked senseless, unconscious; if that happened, I might never wake again. I knew I had to get to my feet.

I scampered onto my knees and looked up at Cavendish. He was coming at me again. I jumped up on to my feet, reeling backwards away from him, but one of the soldiers pushed me back forward towards him, and he raised his be-cudgelled arm to hit me again. I let the blow fall on me, but continued my momentum so that I ran into him. I took him by the collar of his uniform as the blow hit me, but I was so close to him that it negated its power. I swung him round by the collar, and when I felt him off balance I let him go and the momentum sent him scampering to the floor. I then twisted the brass collar of the swordstick to unlock the blade, drew it, and held it in front of me. I let Cavendish stand up before me, expecting him to draw his own sword and fight me like a gentleman, but he didn't, he drew a pistol from his cross belt instead.

I saw him move his left hand over to cock the pistol and I knew that I had only a split second to save myself. I lunged forward with my blade just as his arm was coming up to fire it at me. I felt, through my hand, the blade penetrate, first his jacket and then his flesh just above his heart. 'Arghhh!' he cried out, long, anguished, fearful.

The powder in the pan flared and the pistol went off with a crack. I smelt the acrid, demonic smell of the gunpowder. But the shot flew low, behind me, a plume of dirt rising as it slammed into the ground. I looked round at it, fear taking me at the closeness of it. The smell lingered, sharp in my nostrils, a toxic metallic mixture; in those fractions of a second I smelled sulphur and burnt hair, and then chalk and burnt paper. That smell is still with me as I write this; it is the smell of the devil I am sure.

But then I looked back and saw Cavendish slump to his knees. He was still impaled on my blade; I tried to withdraw it, but the suction of the blood and flesh held it tight. He now fell sideways onto the ground, a sharp intake of breath shrieking across his teeth in pain. He pulled my blade down with him. Again I struggled to withdraw it; in the end I had to put my boot on his chest to give me leverage to pull it free. As I did, blood started to spurt and I knew I had severed an artery.

One of the soldiers then ran to Cavendish. He dropped on one knee and cradled his head. 'Are you all right, sir?' he said in an anxious voice.

But Cavendish did not reply. I saw his eyes leave the soldier and search out me. I felt myself shiver, but then all that belligerence disappeared from his face. He smiled at me for some reason, I know not what, then he gritted his teeth as another spasm of pain took him, but all the time he held my eyes.

The smile returned. 'Well well, little brother, little bookworm Corbyn of all people...' He did not finish the sentence, blood bubbled in his throat and he coughed to spit it out.

The soldier holding his head looked up at his cohorts. He made a knife-cutting gesture across his throat to signal that he was dying. 'He's dun fo',' he added frantically.

'He sez to do it an' we dun it,' said a second soldier frantically at the third, as if to say that an officer had ordered them to do what they had done and they had no part in a murder. They looked at each other, fear taking them as much as shock. The first soldier jumped to his feet, letting Cavendish's head fall to the ground, and then all three ran off back up Black Horse Yard towards Tottenham Court Road, taking my purse with them.

Dizziness now returned and I must have fainted. When I came to, I was lying on top of Cavendish's body. His blood had seeped into my own frock coat; there was a disturbing sickly smell to it that was unknown to me, now mixing with the lingering smell of the sulphurous gunpowder, and I felt a wretch rise up from the pit of my stomach. It forced me off his body and I vomited beside him.

I staggered to my feet; my brain addled, not knowing what to do. I felt as helpless as a rudderless boat bobbing on a vast ocean. But then I realised that I was just around the corner from Rathbone Place; that one thought sustained me and I staggered off, using the walls of houses as my prop to keep me upright. Ginny lives at No. 22, I thought, but as I passed No. 6 I thankfully saw a candle burning in Samuel Medina's window. It was Friday, thank God, I thought, it is his Sabbath, he is home.

I rapped wildly on his door, and when he answered I fell into his arms. I told him what had happened as best as I could. I don't know how lucid I was, but he saw that I needed help.

'I'll send out for a doctor,' he said, 'you need help, my friend.'

My friend! If ever I needed a friend, it was now. I think he thought that all the blood was mine, but I pleaded with him not to send for the physician for I feared that he would alert the magistrate.

'We'll take you to Ginny's, then,' he said, taking my arm across his shoulder and pulling me to my feet. I grimaced as the pain stung me again. 'Sorry, old friend,' he said kindly.

Chapter 40.

'How far have you got?' I said, looking up at Grace from my computer.

'Where Samuel Medina is helping him – you?'

'The same.' I leaned back in my chair; I was bursting with questions. 'Well, well, well,' was all I could say, though.

'So Corbyn is a killer?' she said, raising an eye-brow at me.

'I know, and a most unlikely one at that,' I replied. It was hardly a professorial analysis, but at that moment I was just a surprised observer. I could see that Grace was the same. 'I wonder if that explains why he upped sticks and went on his grand tour,' I added, 'perhaps fearing that he may have been found out.'

'Maybe,' she answered, 'but I've finished all the journals, so I know how it ends. I think his decision was a combination of things.'

'You've finished the journals?'

'Yep.' She gave me an amused look.

'Well don't tell me, I still want to read everything contemporaneously.'

That amused look turned to one of patronising. She held my eyes, I felt foolish. Somewhere I heard a light switch being turned off. I looked at my watch; it was two minutes after six. We were the last in the building, I assumed.

'Shall we get on?' was all I could think to say.

*

At Ginny's, she and Beth cleaned up my wounds and bandaged my chest. She believed that I had broken several ribs. She put me to bed and bid me to sleep and for some time I did so, but then the pain woke me. I could hear Ginny talking heatedly with Samuel down below, and then I heard their footsteps coming up the stairs towards me. She peeped in and I told her I was awake. They came and sat on my bed.

'Where is the body?' she asked.

'Are you sure the man is dead?' added Samuel before I could respond.

'I think so,' I said, trying to sit up, but the pain stopped me. 'It's my brother Cavendish, his body is in Black Horse Yard where he fell.'

'Is Cavendish the one that you had the fight with at the hall?' she asked me.

'Aye,' I said, ''twas him all right.'

'Now, you told me about the fight at your home,' said Samuel, 'and you also told Ginny. Now think hard, Corbyn, who else did you tell?'

'I told the sportsmen at the fencing academy and my colleagues at Chambers.' I knew immediately what he was getting at. The same thoughts had been going through my mind. I had been bragging about my besting of Cavendish, letting my arrogance run away with me. If this had been a street robbery, the magistrate would have readily accepted my story of self-defence, but this was my brother. He could interpret the killing as a family feud; he might think that it was me stalking him down the alley; I might be charged with murder. The soldiers would certainly not come forward to verify my story.

Glances were exchanged between the three of us; we had all come to the same conclusion I am sure. It looked bad for me.

There was an uncomfortable silence for some moments. 'I must go to the magistrate in the morning,' I said eventually.

'I am not sure that will be wise,' said Ginny, looking down pensively. She then shot a look at Samuel. 'No man can be charged with murder without a body,' she said insightfully.

But there was a look of horror on Samuel's face. This brave man who is afraid of nobody is the most principled man I know. 'What are you suggesting?' he said, 'I am not sure that I could...' the words caught in his throat.

Ginny put her hand on his. 'I know you couldn't, dear Samuel,' she said, 'you are far too honourable for that. But your soldier friend, Captain John Campbell-John, well he is another story. Would you know where to find him at this time of night?'

'Oh yes,' said Samuel sardonically, 'he'll be gambling at Molly Jasper's Rooms; that's where the highest stake games are played.'

'Then we must send him a note, asking him to come immediately,' said Ginny, 'I'll have Beth deliver it.'

'I'm still not sure about this,' said Samuel, troubled.

I drifted into disturbed sleep, my mind swirling, terrible images of blood, Cavendish impaled on my sword, and no matter how hard I tried, I couldn't extract it from his taunting smiling corpse. Then I became aware again of raised voices below. I did not know this Captain John Campbell-John fellow. From what I could hear, he was annoyed that he had been called away from his night at the card table. Then the voices got quieter, and I heard the front door slam. I drifted off into disturbed sleep again.

I was awoken again by Ginny gently shaking me; I don't know how long I had been asleep, but it must have been a few hours, the dawn sunlight was beginning to softly fill the room. Ginny was sat on the bed, but Samuel and this Campbell-John fellow were stood above me.

'Corbyn, are you awake, Corbyn?' she said gently. I opened my eyes, the pain immediately took me and I grimaced. 'No, don't try to move,' she added. 'This is Captain John Campbell-John, he has been helping us.'

I looked up at this tall, blond military man. He was not wearing his military uniform, but a worsted maroon frock coat, with delicate lace cuffs, he looked as if his clothes were the finest that could be bought in London; but then I had heard of Molly Jasper's Rooms, they were the pinnacle of elegance for the gentleman of means about town. Those cuffs were now bloodstained however, and the frock coat too, although camouflaged by the maroon colour. He saw me looking at the stains and he, too, looked down.

'Yes, sir, I think you owe me for a new set of clothes at the least.'

'We owe him much more than that, Corbyn,' said Ginny.

'What has happened?' I said anxiously.

Campbell-John took up the story. 'I found the body; he had crawled a few yards, just onto Gresse Street. I would say that it had taken him a quarter hour to die; there was a trail of blood across the dirt floor. I checked and the body was, by then, quite cold, so I dragged him back into Black Horse Yard out of the moonlight so that I would not be observed. I stripped the body so that he could not be identified and brought his clothes back here and told Beth to burn them.'

'I am most grateful to you, sir,' I said, holding out my hand for him to shake it. He did not take it; his story was not yet finished.

'I was still not happy, sir; the body would be just around the corner, much too close. I had the problem of moving it without attracting attention.' I looked at him, urging him to explain further. 'Ginny and I wrapped the body in a blanket and I carried it back here over my shoulder and we came in the back entrance past the privy.'

'The body is downstairs?' I said with alarm, again trying to sit up.

'Calm yourself, sir,' said Campbell-John, 'Ginny has a plan.'

I looked at her, my eyes pleading with her to explain.

'We have put the body in a travel trunk. I will summon a hackney at dusk this evening to take me south to the river. We will ask the driver to drop us at the rear of the Sanspareil Theatre on The Strand; that will not look suspicious. Captain Campbell-John will accompany me and help the driver secure the trunk. Samuel will meet us there and together, under cover of darkness, they will carry the trunk down Dirty Lane to Mr. Capper's Wharf.'

'Will you not be seen?' I asked anxiously.

'Dirty Lane has no houses,' said Campbell-John, 'just warehouses, and it will be deserted at that time of night.'

'And you are happy to do this for me, Samuel?'

He looked at me shamefacedly, I could see the anguish in his face, but Campbell-John spoke for him.

'Carrying the trunk to Mr. Capper's Wharf is the only commission that he has to undertake. I will take care of the rest. Be assured, sir, the body will be in the Thames by midnight tonight, weighted down with bricks. If it should ever surface, it will be decayed and unrecognisable, and anyway, bodies are recovered from the Thames every day; no one will worry too much about another one.' There was an everydayness about the way he spoke.

I squeezed Ginny's hand with relief and rested my head back on the pillow. I confess that I started to cry with relief. I saw Campbell-John look at me; there was condescension in his eyes, as if my tears were unmanly, and I tried to quell them but my body would not let me. I had to look away from him.

'There, there,' said Ginny, and she brushed the side of my face with the back of her hand. 'You will stay here with me for a few days until you are recovered,' she said. 'I will have Beth bring you a little breakfast and then you must try to sleep again.'

Chapter 41.

I looked up from the computer screen, I'm sure there was bewilderment on my face. Grace was still reading, but she, too, finished within a few moments. I leant back, cradling my fingers before my mouth, but then I searched out her eyes. They widened as they met mine and mine did the same.

'Whoa!' I said; it had been pulse-racingly good and then I saw that incredulity in her eyes turn to amusement.

For some unknown reason, that amusement spread to me and I started to laugh uncontrollably. It was the strangest of reactions, but then she joined me. We laughed together as though, for the first time in a long while, we were singing from the same song sheet, and in perfect harmony.

'Whoa!' she repeated, as if to confirm my own reaction, 'so Ginny, Samuel and Campbell-John are his knights errant; well, well, well.'

'Yeah,' I said, 'and a secret told for the first time in two hundred years. It's moments like this that make history worth while.'

We started to talk about what we had just read. We reassessed everything that we had previously read, based upon it. But it was more than that, without thinking about it we were reconnecting. The rancour had gone from her eyes, to be replaced by only inquisitiveness, her enquiring mind now dominant. After an hour, she suddenly looked at her watch; I looked at mine too; it was coming up eight o'clock. I think we were both shocked that time had run away with us.

'I'm hungry,' she said.

'Me too,' I replied without thinking too deeply, just taking the phrase at its face value.

'A Bombardier and a pasty at the Nags Head?' It was just a throwaway line; she wanted, I think, just to continue to talk about the deciphered journal. It was no more than that.

I stood up from my chair, this piece of body language standing as my acceptance. Like her, I did not think to deeply about it.

We talked and drank in the Nags for the rest of the night until closing time. The conversation was not about us; it was about Corbyn and Ginny. Afterwards, we went our separate ways home. I slept so well, the best I had slept for so many weeks. It was so good just to work side by side with her again.

Chapter 42.

The Journal of Ginny Farmer

17th **September 1793.** Tonight I dined with Corbyn and his sisters, Emily and Jane. Corbyn wanted it to be a birthday celebration for me; it was a wonderful meal and he also put out his finest claret. We started with a syllabub of cider, sweetened and flavoured with nutmeg, milk and cream. Then a pease soup made of dried peas, simmered in stock with celery, onion, and seasoning. The cook was particularly proud of this, Corbyn told me. This was followed by oysters with cayenne pepper.

The main course was venison or a chine of mutton served with excellent potatoes, smoking hot and accompanied by melted butter and the luxury of fresh buttered asparagus from his own farm and prepared with a butter/flour mixture. Then a wonderful pudding made of flower, milk, eggs, butter, sugar, suet, marrow and raisins; Corbyn was eager to tell me everything that had gone into it.

The dessert was accompanied by a particularly fine sweet wine and then there was cheese and port. I did not partake of the port, but both Emily and Jane did.

Dear Corbyn had gone to so much effort, but his sisters did not enter into the spirit of it. It was just a pity that the mood was so prickly, Jane in particular, sniping at virtually everything Corbyn or I said. I tried not to let this spoil my enjoyment, but I could see Corbyn getting more and more irritated, and he threw hard, reproachful stares in their direction: they were ignored, especially by Jane. I had made an effort and I had saved my best gown for this occasion, a red plum fabric decorated with pale green oak leaves and white lace at the collar and cuffs. Emily and Jane, however, looked as if they had not even changed for dinner.

Corbyn talked of poetry and politics and the theatre, and I joined him enthusiastically, but the sisters seemed to have no interest in these subjects. They wanted to talk only about a possible bride for him, and eventually we gave in and let the conversation come round to that subject.

'Have you selected a preference from the young ladies?' There was claret running down Emily's pock-marked chin as she spoke, and partly chewed cheese visible in her mouth as she slurped another drink from her glass.

Corbyn was evasive. 'They all have their merits,' he said gallantly.

'Oh Corbyn, don't be such a milksop,' said Jane. She was further along the road to inebriation than her sister, the words slurring from her mouth. She was also being offensive and she clearly didn't care. What was clear was that it was a two-pronged attack on poor Corbyn.

'And who would _you_ favour?' I said, turning to Emily.

She made a pretence to consider the matter, chewing on a piece of meat in her teeth. 'I saw from my window that Miss Lydia Heslop is pretty of face and would suit, I think.'

I smiled at her knowingly, holding her eyes, making sure that she saw me. The look on her face darkened. She knew immediately that I had seen through her little ploy, saying, 'And what is wrong with her, pray?' she said to me pointedly.

'Why, nothing,' I replied, but paused for a heartbeat, 'if what we want for Corbyn is a timid little mouse who will not utter a single word from one day to the next.'

'A fine dowry and a good family is not to be sneezed at,' added Jane, trying to retrieve the situation, 'and she is of a good family and the right child-breeding age; an heir is the prime consideration here.'

'Oh I see, we are looking for a brood mare are we?' I couldn't resist myself; 'I think we can do better for dear Corbyn than that.'

'So who do _you_ suggest?' Jane returned to the fray.

'Miss Elvira Hart has much more about her. She will be a much better companion and _mistress of the house_.' I emphasised these last words whilst looking directly at Emily. I think I rendered her speechless.

'My understanding is that she has set her heart on Captain Cadogan,' interrupted Jane.

Aha, the trap was sprung I thought to myself, and I allowed myself a satisfied smile. She had shown her hand. I already knew that she had set the servants to report back to her. I, in turn, had set them to report back to me on what they had told her. They had been my keen allies, neither sister being liked below stairs. But the servants had not been at the final meeting to hear the chaperone's views.

'Ah yes!' I said and looked at both of them before I went on, 'Captain Cadogan.' I held the moment. 'In retrospect, not a wise choice to have invited him.'

I saw Emily's eyes flash at me, 'And pray, why not?' she asked.

'Because he bedded Miss Hart's chaperone, that's why not; she now knows him for what he is, a silver-tongued profligate without prospects and a gold digger to boot just looking for a rich wife. She will never recommend him to Miss Hart's father.'

'But she is from trade,' interjected Jane snobbishly.

It was all that was left for her to say and I knew it. But your sister invited her?' I said, feigning puzzlement; 'Emily must have thought her suitable? And besides, we both know that new money and old families such as yours have always been eager bedfellows.'

Jane spluttered, unable to respond, and then took a gulp of port as it seemed the only thing left she could do.

I looked back at Emily with an inquisitive eye, inviting her to comment. She looked at Corbyn and I could see that the words dried on her lips.

'And is Miss Elvira Hart your choice in this matter, Corbyn? That tall, gangling girl?' She spluttered.

She had unwittingly stumbled on the one problem I had; he did not like her height. I held my breath, but dear Corbyn was not going to let Emily think that she had won.

'I trust Lady Virginia explicitly in these matters,' he said, turning and giving the slightest of bows to me, 'I can see the merits in her choice.' He inclined his head at his sister as if to mock her.

Emily sat and looked back at him. There was a darkness in her expression, but there was also frustration. She stood up forcefully, knocking her glass of port over as she did so. 'HUH!' was all that she could exclaim. She threw down her napkin and stormed off. After a few paces, she turned. 'Are you coming, Jane?' she said over her shoulder.

Jane was equally as melodramatic, throwing down her napkin. Before she stormed off, however, she had to have her own two pennyworth. 'If Lady Virginia is so damned wonderful, then perhaps you should marry her instead.'

The Journal of Corbyn Carlisle

18th September 1793· Is it so outrageous? That thought had been swirling in my mind all night· It was still there as I sat at breakfast; I was distant, consumed by it· The footman brought me a draft of ale, I took it from the silver tray without really thinking about it, I sipped it, inattentive, lost in thought. The side table was set out with the breakfast fare: oatmeal with sweet cream, smoked herrings, sardines with mustard sauce, and enough bacon to feed all the house party had they still been here. Bread and rolls, spreads including butter, honey, marmalade, jams of raspberries, cherries and apples. Fresh apple cider, tea, hot chocolate and coffee – yet this fare did not tempt me; I had my feet on the ground, but I was floating in some other distant place. A decision hung over me, a heavy burden weighing me down like a collier holding up the ceiling of his tunnel so that it would not become his tomb. Yet, in some place, at the very core of me, I knew that it was the most important decision I would ever make.

'Morning, Corbyn dear.' Ginny disturbed my reverie; she bent and kissed me on the cheek, then sat beside me. 'Are you not eating this morning?' she said, looking at my empty plate.

I looked down at it, surprised, her words snapping me back to reality. 'Yes, I will try a little something,' I said, twitching a nervous smile.

'Are you feeling a little liverish this morning?' she said whilst going to the side table with her plate and helping herself to some bacon and rolls, then some apple jam. The footman brought her some hot chocolate as she sat again beside me. She looked at me, awaiting my response, she gave a little lopsided smile. 'Too much port was it, my dear?'

'No,' I mumbled, 'I am fine, really.' I followed her to the side table and took a little oatmeal and some coffee.

'Will Emily and Jane be joining us?' she asked as I sat down again.

'No, it is much too early for them.' I took my watch from my waistcoat pocket; it was fifteen minutes before nine of the clock.

We ate quietly for some minutes, occasionally some small talk from Ginny, but my responses were short and no conversation developed.

'What time will you be leaving?' My words were uncertain.

'If your coachman can have me away for ten of the clock will that give me time to catch the mail coach from Nottingham at thirty after twelve?'

'Yes, that should be ample.' My words were still distant. I felt like a sailor who knew his position on the map, but was still lost.

Ginny put down her buttered roll and looked at me for a heartbeat. 'What is it, Corbyn? You seem troubled, my sweet. Did your sisters' behaviour last evening upset you so?'

'No, no' I answered eagerly, 'I enjoyed the way you handled them. They would bully you if you let them; I know, they try to bully me. It's just that...' I didn't complete the sentence.

Ginny looked at me and I knew I had to go on, but the words dried on my lips.

'It's just what, Corbyn?'

The footman cut in to fill my glass again with another draft of ale. I put my hand over it and then wafted him away with it. 'You can leave us now,' I said. I then leaned in to Ginny.

'Well, do you remember what Jane said last night just before she stormed off with Emily?'

Ginny looked down at her napkin in thought. I could see that the words had not stung her as they had stung me.

'She said that if I thought you was so damned wonderful, then perhaps I should marry you instead.'

Ginny laughed, 'Oh yes, I remember now. And when she got up she stumbled, having drunk too much port and brandy. It spoiled her dramatic exit.'

'Yes yes, she was soused all right, but I have pondered all night whether those drunken words were not, in some way, actually prophetic.'

Her laughter stopped immediately. She looked round at me; there was incredulity in her eyes.

'You can not be in earnest, Corbyn dear?'

'Oh but I am, my dear Ginny, I'm in deadly earnest.'

She was lost for words for some moments. I saw her face suffuse and then that redness travelled down her alabaster neck and under the collar of her dress.

'Oh fol derol,' she said, trying to pass my words off as foolishness, she picked up her roll again, but I could see that her hand was trembling.

I took the roll from her, put it down and then held her hand gently in mine; she tried to look down to evade my stare and I took her chin with my other hand so that we exchanged eye contact.

'But Corbyn, when you found out I was a foundlings' child, that

was enough for you to feel betrayed; to never want to see me again. And now you propose marriage?'

'I know, and you speak truthfully. But that was my folly, my silly, silly folly and I missed you every day from then on; that was the penalty I paid. But wisdom comes with age, and I am now a much wiser man.'

'But sometimes age comes alone, dear Corbyn; are you sure that this is not also folly. You are nobility and I am merely nothing.'

'No, never say that of yourself; 'tis true enough, that is how society will see it, but I will not be the first lord to marry an actress.'

'But this particular actress has also been a Mabel and a courtesan. What will your friends think?'

'They will think that I am marrying the actress Lady Virginia Farmer; the fine lady who has fallen on hard times.'

'But others know the truth; what if it comes out?'

'Then so be it, and be damned with it,' my words rang out.

I saw her lower teeth bite her upper lip. Her chin trembled as she tried to hold it all together. She took a deep breath and then leaned in to me, she released her hand from mine and then caressed my cheek with it.

'Corbyn, dear man that you are; we have talked about finding you a wife for the last ten days. Perhaps we have all been too preoccupied with this endeavour, to find you a wife. I know that you have responsibilities to your family line, but are you sure that I am the answer to that?'

'Aye, I think you are the perfect answer.'

She looked away, mused for a heartbeat then looked back at me, studying my intense expression. 'When do you come up to London next?'

'I am due in Chambers next week.'

'Then think on it this next week. If you see that it is folly, then we will not speak of it again. If you are still of the same mind, then ask me again and I will give you my answer.'

Chapter 43.

In my new regime, Sundays were now alcohol-free days. I rose late, having slept well again, and then spent three hours on the Sunday paper with a Millicano coffee, toast and honey for company. The coffee was refreshed several times, as was the toast, and this stood as my lunch as well. In the afternoon I watched the rugby international, a six nations' match between England and Ireland. England won by five points, but Ireland were by far the most attractive side to watch: nothing changes, I thought.

In the evening I took time out to make a proper dinner, preparing all the vegetables myself and roasting a small chicken. I took a long soak in the bath with a detective novel for company, the steam making the pages swell, but I didn't mind. I put on just a t-shirt and a pair of boxers and then lounged on my sofa with the next of Corbyn and Ginny's journals in the chronological sequence.

I smiled to myself at the machinations of the house party to find Corbyn a bride. The manoeuvres and counter-manoeuvres; the far from gallant Captain Cadogan swaying drunkenly outside a chaperone's bedroom, too pissed to stand properly, his lecherousness overcoming the last dregs of discretion left in him. And in the morning, without any care for the lady's reputation, he clip-clops in his military boots, his lust assuaged. Lust and young men is, perhaps, one thing that does not change, I thought to myself. What is that coarse northern phrase – oh yes; a stiff cock has no morals. Uncouth, I know, but it seems that it was just as true in Georgian England.

And then I read of the breakfast meeting between Ginny and Corbyn. I have to admit I was taken aback; this was a chasmic step for Corbyn to take, to propose marriage from his noble high perch to a child of the Foundlings' Hospital. '*Good on ya, Corbyn lad*' I said out loud. I flicked ahead through the pages to see if she accepted his offer, but it was not in the journals I had brought with me. I considered calling Grace to find out, but I then thought how stupid I would seem to her, I would once again open myself up to ridicule.

I had slept so well for two nights, but Sunday night was fitful, vivid dreams taking me and then waking me in alarm. Each time I went back to sleep the same theme reoccurred; somehow I was Corbyn and Grace was

Ginny. I was desperate not to lose Ginny/Grace, but she had run away from me. I couldn't find her, I was panicked. I looked in dark alleys, in dank cellars, in crowded taverns. Each time I thought I saw her I ran to her, but then she turned and it was some wrinkled, bloodshot-eyed, painted face. That harridan face sat atop enormous blanched bosoms thrust upwards by stays; they seemed to invade my vision, the fleshy masses overflowing the bodice; an outrageous piece of felt on one of the blanched breasts masquerading as a beauty spot.

'I'm not Ginny, deary,' slithered two scarlet-painted lips that seemed to cut the grotesque face in half, 'I'm Annie, will I do for ya?' The face laughed and I saw that the florid lip paint was all over her teeth, making a patchwork of yellow and vermillion like a mash of cherries in custard.

I turned and ran way in horror. I shouted out, 'Where are you Ginny?' as I stumbled from place to place, trying to push my way through crowds of faces all joking and laughing at my dilemma.

And then I heard a small voice: 'Help me, Corbyn, help me please?' It seemed to be coming from down a long corridor. I dashed down it, but everybody was coming the other way barring my passage. I ran and ran, but the corridor just seemed to go on for ever; then there she was, she was side-on to me but looking away, Grace's delicate shoulders bare; round arms; breasts emphasised by her dress. Relief coursed through my slumbering state. I wanted to kiss her, hold her close so that she never got away from me again. I put my arms around her and sought out her lips: HORROR; those slithering scarlet lips again, those reddened yellowish stained teeth.

'Will I do, deary?' said the harridan again. Its mouth opened and bawled a banshee laugh. I pulled away in revulsion. It was at that moment that I awoke, sweating, my heart pounding.

I got up, made myself a Millicano coffee and sat on my sofa. The central heating had gone off for the night and I had to go and find a dressing gown. I took a long swig; it tasted good, but then I realised that it would keep me awake; I put it down reluctantly, pushed it away across the occasional table. I had been sleep-dead, but now normality returned to me; I saw that the cleaner had tidied the table; there was now space for the discarded mug.

I chuckled to myself at the nonsensical dream, then shrugged my shoulders because that was the nature of dreams, the absurd, the illogical, the irrational. But then I started to reconsider; was it so irrational? Something must have triggered it. In the dream it was me and Grace, but it was Georgian London that I was lost in. What was that all about? What had triggered my anxiety?

If I had a fear of losing Grace, then it was a strange time for it to manifest itself – it was all water under the bridge; wasn't it? I didn't go back to bed, I dozed on the sofa for a while but sleep did not return to me, there were now too many thoughts swirling in my mind.

I walked to work and was at my desk at six thirty in a deserted history department. I went to my press and took out the next journals.

The Journal of Ginny Farmer

24th September 1793. Corbyn called on me this afternoon and we took tea together. I was anxious, I had struggled with my decision; if he did ask me again, then what would I say? I had changed my mind several times during the week and I was still unsure. I had come to the conclusion that Corbyn was a man that I could share my life with and that I had the skills to make him a good wife. What I was not sure of was Corbyn himself; would those resentments about my past life resurface again and come between us.

Corbyn was very formal when he addressed me on entering and then, during tea, he seemed to want to talk about his latest case, and then he talked politics and then the theatre, there was a new production of Oedipus the King about to be performed at the Haymarket. The conversation had initially been tense, staccato, but now I began to relax because we had that agreement; if he decided that marriage to me was not what he wanted, then we never speak of it again.

The Journal of Corbyn Carlisle

24th September 1793. I called on Ginny this afternoon and we took tea. My heart was in my mouth as I knocked on her door and it was still pounding when Beth showed me in. Ginny was sat in the corner; she looked delightful in a simple loose black dress gathered beneath the breasts, the skirts fanning away charmingly.

I was being so very formal, for what reason I know not why. I took her hand and kissed it gently.

But she played her part. 'Lord Carlisle, your most obedient servant.'

She called for Beth to bring us some tea and cake; I flicked out the tails of my frock coat and sat in the chair beside her.

But I was so feared of asking her the question that had been on my mind all week, in case her answer was to reject me. So I nattered on about anything and everything that came into my mind, it was most uncomfortable. I had played this scene in my head so many times, but now the script was somehow changed and I desperately needed the prompter to get me back to the correct lines.

*

Corbyn stayed for two hours. It was not unpleasant; yes it was, I felt that I needed to loosen my bodice to release me from the restrictions of this conversation. I was upright in my chair, doing everything I could to be charming, but inside I was screaming. I wanted the meeting to end. But then fate took a capricious hand in events.

I called for Beth to remove the tea things as Corbyn was leaving. She came in with a childish grin on her face, looked at me and then at Corbyn.

'Well, as ee asked yer then?' she said.

'<u>Beth!</u> Please?' I pleaded.

'Well as ee or ahn't ee?' she repeated.

'<u>Beth!</u> That's enough. Lord Carlisle and I have an agreement. This is a subject that will never be spoken of again; and that includes you, if you please.'

*

Ginny's maid-cum-friend Beth is a kindly girl, if a plump and dreamy one. She is always willing, but not the sharpest pencil in the servant's box. She has often made me smile the way she addresses people, and her social skills, despite Ginny's efforts, leave a lot to be desired. She always calls me zir, causing me to hide a smile. I sometimes have to look away to Ginny to stop myself from releasing it until after she has left the room when we can then enjoy the humour between us.

Today, however, her wonderful lack of social expertise came to my aid. My meeting with Ginny had come to an end, but I had not found the courage to ask her that question that had so terrified me· Now, as I look back, it is all so illogical; I was afraid of rejection, so I could not ask the question, but by not asking the question I was rejecting <u>her</u>· What a dunderhead I am·

But then this silly girl cut through all that nonsense·

'Well as ee asked yer then?' she said to Ginny·

Ginny, in turn, admonished her, but then Beth looked at me and back to Ginny with bewilderment and naively repeated the question; her naivety is really beyond all comprehension· But it made me realise that I was dancing my usual dance, when I try to take the lead with Ginny I step on her toes· But no more, I thought, and I resolved to put matters right·

'No, Beth is right, dear Ginny,' I said, 'I have come hear to ask you a question and I am as feared as a young subleton at his first skirmish·'

With that I went down on one knee· 'Lady Virginia Farmer, will you do me the honour of being my wife?'

Ginny put her hand to her mouth, and for a moment I saw that she was stunned· Then she leaned forward in her chair and reached out her hand to mine·

'No, Corbyn,' she said, and my heart sank faster than a peregrine diving for a pigeon· 'No, Corbyn, let us be honest with <u>each other</u>, whatever face we may show to the world· Ask me again, but this time ask Ginny, for that is who I really am·'

With relief coursing through my veins I repeated the question as she had bid me·

'Ginny, dear Ginny; will you marry me?'

'Yes, dear Corbyn, I will marry you·'

I leaned over and kissed her passionately· Behind me, that silly wonderful girl, Beth, giggled as she took the tea tray away·

Chapter 44.

I drew a breath as I read that Ginny had accepted Corbyn's offer of marriage. If it had been mapped, a path marked out in signposts, then I had failed to read them correctly; I certainly had looked down the wrong road. I realised that I felt elated, but then that emotion made me consider my folly; I am a historian, I should think like one. Grace is right; I have been reading these journals like a novel. But no matter how much I tried to be dispassionate, that feeling of elation for two long-dead people wouldn't leave.

I decided that it was time to reward myself with a Millicano. I cupped the steaming mug in my hands and then put my feet up on my desk; something that I never do. *Good old Corbyn*, I thought to myself as I contemplated just how courageous he had been. But then I started to think about myself; it doesn't hurt to take a good look at yourself from time to time – oh yes it does, it *hurt*. It hurt so very much; I didn't like what I saw.

As I thought about Ginny and Corbyn, there was an echo of my own previous foolishness. I tried to rationalize it, mused – who among us has not been a fool at times, been the butt of jokes? It stings, but we shrug our shoulders and move on. It didn't work; the echo kept coming back and back the way echoes do.

Then my door opened and, by coincidence, it was Grace.

'What's up,' she said, 'can't you sleep?' her eyes twinkled mischievously.

'Huh?' I said, missing the sarcasm.

She nodded towards the clock on the wall, 'I'm told you were the first in, this morning.'

I looked up at it; it was still only eight twenty-five, 'Oh,' I said, my thoughts still elsewhere, but then added, 'You're here too, do you always start so early?'

'Yep,' she replied, 'so I can be gone before you arrive.'

'Are you serious?' I asked, sitting up again, and spilling the hot coffee on myself. I rubbed the stain on my shirt with my hand involuntarily.

'I am actually,' she said, running her hand through her hair.

That saddened me to think that she had spent so many months trying to avoid me.

'Look,' she said, 'I've spent the weekend going over that transcription again. I'd like to talk through some ideas with you if that's all right?'

'What about dinner tonight? I'll cook. You can come to mine.' Where did that come from? I shocked even myself; it certainly wasn't a rational thought. That twinkle disappeared; I looked and saw there was now suspicion in her eyes instead.

'Is that a good idea?'

'Why not? – Friday night was…' I paused trying to find a word that would not frighten her away, '…productive,' I came up with, but I wanted to say wonderful.

She sighed heavily; I could see that she was unsure. 'You're an odd man, James Postlethwaite.'

'Probably,' I said, nodding my head in agreement. Then I bit my bottom lip in apprehension.

'Well, OK then,' she said, inclining her head in unsure confirmation. She closed the door, but I saw through the glass pane she remained outside for moment, thinking about what she had done.

I put my feet back up on my desk. I think the resulting smile must have been visible for half a mile.

I finished work early, went to Marks and Spencer's and got a couple of bottles of wine and a dine-in meal for two; roast ribs of lamb with mint sauce, with Lyonnaise potatoes and profiteroles to follow. I tidied up my flat and then took a long shower. I put on my best jeans and a good tailored shirt and then set about cooking the meal. Marks and Spencer's, however, had done most of the work, there was no preparation to do and I realised that I had over an hour and a half to spare, with nothing to do before Grace arrived.

I opened the wine and sat before the television; in retrospect it was a mistake. The television just washed over me, I was elsewhere. I had acted instinctively when I had invited Grace; I had been so sure that it was the right thing to do. But now I began to analyse what I had done; realised my impetuosity. All those negative thoughts now returned to me; it was like a jigsaw in reverse, a clear image being taken apart piece by piece, disappearing before me.

Corbyn's words suddenly came back to me. He had said that he was like a sailor who knew his position on the map, but was still lost. I knew exactly what he meant, I felt the same, all of a sudden I was without orientation. I had been so sure that I knew what I was doing, but now all those doubts were back. But then those thoughts of Corbyn began to reassure me; he had felt the same way, but he had overcome it, found just in time that compass bearing to bring him safely into port. I sighed a deep sigh, that dream last night had told me that, deep down, I didn't want to lose Grace, but I had done just that. The events of last Friday had given me one last chance; I resolved to take it.

The meal was in the oven and well underway when the doorbell rang. I had a tea towel tied around my waist like a pinny, but I opened the door without thinking about it. I expected to find Grace leaning against the doorframe; in the past she always was, but she was stood straight, uncomfortable, that suspicion still in her eyes. A little smile flittered temporarily in her eye as she looked down at the tea towel. I realised that I looked domesticated and took it off quickly, throwing it aside over the back of a chair; it missed and slid onto the floor. I left it where it was. Then she looked at my crisp clean shirt and expensive jeans, and that suspicion in her eyes intensified.

'Going somewhere?' she said, using humour as a foil.

'No, I just wanted to get out of my working clothes.'

She seemed unsure, stood in the doorway. I stepped aside, gesturing with my hand for her to come in; she did so, but there was still reluctance in her manner. I realised that it was not going to be an easy night.

'Look at you, and I'm still in my scruff,' she said, looking down at herself, 'I've not been home, haven't even changed.'

I looked down at her. Yes, she was wearing an old pair of jeans, a trendy tear at the knee, and as always, a t-shirt with a witty slogan – this one said, DIP ME IN CHOCOLATE AND THROW ME TO THE LESBIANS. It made me smile, but also gave me the opportunity to shoot a look at her breasts. That first car trip came back to me; I had done the same, noticed them, not large, but prominent, sitting proud on her lean torso. I looked her up and down as if refreshing my memory, this long slender girl, naturally athletic, her natural beauty without make-up; her hair shoulder length, substantial in natural loose curls. And then she ran a hand through her hair as I remembered and I smiled a satisfied smile that she was once again in my flat.

'You'll do fine,' I said, 'then, you always do.'

'What you up to, James Postlethwaite?' her eyebrows knitted as she spoke.

'Wine?' I said sheepishly, avoiding the question.

'Yes, I think I'm going to need it,' she said.

The meal was wonderful, although I think I would probably have enjoyed anything. We did talk about the deciphered chapters and her Master's dissertation as I had promised, but then I started to talk about her, trying to bring the conversation around to us, but each time I tried she deflected the conversation, expertly, elsewhere.

As the hours passed, I began to get apprehensive, I was not getting anywhere. Then she looked at her watch, there was finality in her body language and I knew it.

'Its time I was off,' she said matter-of-factly. She stood and headed for the door.

I was panicked. 'Another glass of wine?' I said, filling up her glass without waiting for a response.

'No, I want to get started on the revisions to my dissertation early tomorrow morning,' she said over her shoulder.

I followed her to the door, but she opened it herself.

'Thanks for the meal,' she said without stopping, hardly looking back, and headed for the stairs without waiting for the lift.

And then she was gone, all was quiet, but the anticlimax was deafening. It all seemed to happen in an instant; I had lost control. I closed the door and leant on it with my back. I thought of Corbyn and Ginny, they had managed to overcome their hesitations, their reluctances, but I had not. I was crestfallen; I had no blundering Beth to help shatter the walls that had been erected between us. And then those awful nightmare images came to me, chasing after Grace through the streets and taverns of historic London. That panic returned to me.

I opened the door and ran down the stairs and into the street. I looked up and down; I couldn't see her. I ran in the direction of where I thought she would catch the bus. I turned the corner, but she was not at the bus shelter. I ran across the street, as it gave me a better view up and down it, but there was still no sign of her. My shoulders slumped in dejection; the cold suddenly ambushed me, I was only in my jeans and a shirt. There was rain on the wind and an icy flurry hit me in the face, stinging my skin.

I set off back across the road, then there she was. Coming out of a late-night newsagent's-cum-convenience store. She was just putting her purse away, looking down, she hadn't seen me.

'GRACE!' I yelled from the middle of the road.

She looked up, but at that moment a bus passed before me, hooting its horn telling me to be careful. I halted my step, startled but still focussed on her. The bus passed me in a red blur; I had a vague impression of illuminated faces staring at me as though I were some madman trying to get himself killed. When it was passed, I saw her looking around confused.

'GRACE!' I shouted again, 'over here.'

She looked up at me, this crazy man in a wet shirt, standing in the middle of the road, my image reflected in the rain puddles. There was now total bewilderment on her face. I ran to her, took her hand, and words just cascaded from my mouth; I don't remember anything that I said, but I think they were incomprehensible. Like many people who spend their time writing words, when you really need them they hide from you: spiteful, mistrusting; you are left only with those that have no meaningful substance. She just stared at me for an age and I felt so impotent before her.

But then she allowed herself a little smile. The corner of her mouth turned up, but mostly it was in her eyes; that was the way she always expressed herself. It was just a little gesture, but it was like an earthquake to me.

'You are a plonker, James; you really *are*, aren't you?' Her words were not the kindest, but somehow they built bridges between us. 'You're soaking, you'll catch your death of...' She didn't finish, left it hanging.

I looked down at myself, saw that I was wet, I shrugged, 'I don't care about that,' I said.

'Well what do you want?'

'I want – no I *need* to tell you something.'

'What, James, what is it?'

And then I said it; without thinking, without composing any words in my mind. The words that I had been denying myself spoke themselves, 'I want to tell you that I love you.'

Again she just stared at me for an age; those normally expressive eyes blank, impassive. My heart began to sink. I suppressed a shudder, looked down at the street between my feet.

'But you were unable to say those words when I wanted you to,' she said, her voice low, hesitant.

'I know; I'm just a stupid man.'

'You are that all right, James Postlethwaite.'

I just looked up at her, pathetic, further words failing me.

'So,' she said, 'you've finally come out of that box you've been hiding in?'

I knew immediately what she meant and I knew she was right. She held my eyes and for some moments we were locked together in unspoken words. It was me that eventually spoke. 'It would seem so,' I said.

She allowed herself a wry smile, took my arm. 'Come on,' she said, 'we'd better get you home.'

I hadn't realised, but I had left the door to my flat open; it still felt warm and inviting though, but I think that was as much to do with having Grace on my arm. She shepherded me to my bedroom and the en-suite bathroom. 'Go on,' she said, 'get those wet clothes off and into a hot shower.'

I did as she had bid me dutifully, and stood a long time under the cascading hot water. It was an elixir, refreshing all my anxieties, and I didn't want to leave in case the elixir was to wear off. When I did get out, I towelled myself vigorously as if to punish myself for my stupidity. I wrapped myself in my robe and went back into my bedroom: Grace was in my bed. The top sheets were across her chest, her long slender arms resting outside, but I could see enough to know that she was naked. She raised her right hand, gesturing me to come to bed, and I willingly accepted. It said more than a thousand words; everything was going to be all right.

I slid in beside her and felt the warmth of her body, she smelt so good, it was intoxicating; we made love. Then we snuggled down and just talked gently, effortlessly for about an hour; I was out of that box and it felt so good to be so. Then she said something insightful.

'Have you just read about Corbyn and Ginny getting married?'

'Err, well yes,' I said, feeling foolish again.

'I thought you might have,' she said knowingly. I could see the mischief back in her eyes, but I didn't care. 'You have another thirty years of journals to get through, you know?'

'Yeah, I know,' I nodded, 'are they as intriguing as these early journals.'

'No, they tend to be more domesticated.'

'So the marriage was a success, then?' I was keen to know if they were happy.

'Oh yes, the marriage was a success, long and fruitful.'

'Tell me about them?' I raised myself up on my elbow, wanting to know.

'Well they founded a dynasty, they had a son and three daughters, a long line of Baron Elloughtons living at Elloughton Park right up to the second half of the twentieth century.'

'Good for them,' I said enthusiastically.

'And when they were more affluent, Ginny called in a young John

Nash who redesigned Elloughton Hall in lavish bold opulent colours, soft furnishings; we have Nash's plans in the manorial records. For the first time, Elloughton Park was resplendent with wallpaper and colour, elaborate classical plaster ceilings running around the rooms, a feminine hand, no longer that severe masculine hall, a place out of time and out of fashion. She also wanted somewhere to display the paintings that Corbyn had collected on his grand tour. Nash ripped out the middle of the hall, made a large picture gallery of it with a glass roof to light it. Do you remember it? It's now the dining room at the hotel.'

'Yes I do,' I said enthusiastically. It was like a line in a song reviving a long forgotten memory. 'So that was Ginny's doing, was it?'

She nodded, held my gaze, but was then hesitant. 'I'm not sure I should feed your fantasy of Ginny,' she said.

'How do you mean?'

'Well, she's my rival isn't she?'

'Not any more,' I said, reaching across and kissing her tenderly.

The kiss lingered, but eventually she brought her hand up between our lips, pulled back to look in my eyes, I think to gauge my intention.

'OK,' she said, 'I'll tell you more of what Ginny did.' I resumed my position on my elbow, my expression telling her to go on. She followed me and held my gaze again. 'She never forgot where she came from; Mrs. Strabane became the cook at Elloughton Park. When her mother's charges grew to adulthood, an apartment was built for her at the hall and she too came to live with them and looked after her grandchildren. She also tracked down her own child; it was a boy, she left him with his adoptive parents, but paid for his education. He later joined Corbyn at Chambers and became a lawyer too.'

'So Corbyn stays within his profession?'

'He does, and rose to be Attorney General.'

'What! – timid little Corbyn, a powerful man?' I said.

'Oh yes, he came into himself, and he was a reformer.'

'That means you can research him through the Law Society?'

'I know,' she said knowingly, 'I've already done it. He was responsible for numerous reforms to the judicial system in the 1820's.'

'I'd like to think that Ginny was in some way responsible for that too, her influence.'

'I *know* she was,' she said. She reached over and cupped my face, there was still that mischief in her eyes. 'I've read it, James – it's in her journal.'

Author's Notes

Journal/Font. I wanted to give the reader the impression that they were reading a journal but not one that would make the reading experience annoying. The selection of fonts to represent these journal entries has, however, proved problematical. There was a lot of guidance on the internet regarding the fonts to use in novel publication but I was unable to find any guidance for fonts to represent handwriting – this was surprising, because, although telling a story through journal entries is unusual, it is not unknown. Additionally Ginny is only semi-literate when she stars and then develops into an educated lady and it would be reasonable to assume that her handwriting developed as well. There are many handwriting fonts available and some do represent realistic handwriting but I felt that they would be demanding over the course of a full novel. In the end, via a lot of trial and error, I have used just one font for Ginny, Segoe Print and MV Boli for Corbyn. Neither are true handwriting fonts – and my apologies for the floating full stops. I hope this worked for you.

The Foundlings' Hospital. I've created Ginny as a child of the Foundlings' Hospital. In fact the Foundlings' Hospital was a London establishment and in 1756, Parliament, in its wisdom, decided that ALL children should be taken in wherever they lived in the country, not just London. So Ginny would have been sent to London and not brought up in Bristol. There was, however, an Orphanage House (or Muller Home as it was known) in Bristol, but this was not opened until the 1830's. I have allowed this inaccuracy for the purposes of the narrative.

Apprenticeships (usually as servants) were organised for the girls at 16 and for the boys (in trade) at 14. Again there is an inaccuracy in the narrative; Ginny would not have been put to service at 14.

William Blake. Blake was born in 1757. I have said that he was only 22 in 1787 when he painted Elloughton Park. He would have actually been 30 and an established poet and painter. I have allowed this liberty.

Elloughton Park. The description is a combination of Stoke Park in Northamptonshire and Wilton House in Wiltshire.

The Coburg Theatre. When Ginny turns to the theatre, she first appears at the Coburg. This would be in 1790, but the theatre was not actually opened until 1818. It is now known as the Old Vic Theatre. Likewise the Sanspareil was not opened until 1806. Generally, Virginia's career at 1791/93 is probably more appropriate to a period ten to fifteen years later.

A Midsummer's Night's Dream. After the puritan era, theatres re-opened in 1660, but *A Midsummer Night's Dream* was only acted in adapted form, like many other Shakespearean plays. It was not performed again in its entirety until the 1840's. I have taken a liberty to include this at 1792 therefore. It is true, however, that through the 19th Century Oberon and Puck were always played by women despite them being male characters.

Maria Elana Viscontessa di Castiglioni is based on **Virginia Oldoini, Countess of Castiglione** (22 March 1837 – 28 November 1899), who was an Italian aristocrat who achieved notoriety as a mistress of Emperor Napoleon III of France.

John Nash (18 January 1752 – 13 May 1835) was a British architect responsible for much of the layout of Regency London. He was at his height around 1810, working mainly for the Prince Regent.

Socket money – is a whore's fee.

Bibliography.

The English, A Social History – Christopher Hibbert. The Early Years – James Boswell The London Journal – James Boswell The Damnation of John Donellan – Elizabeth Cooke Elegance and Decadence (TV series) V & A London Stage Archives Behind Closed Doors: At Home in Georgian England – Amanda Vickery At Home with the Georgians– Amanda Vickery (TV series)

Websites.
British History Online:
www.british-history.ac.uk National Archives
www.nationalarchives.gov.uk

Copy Editing.
With so many thanks to Karl Doughty my copy editor. His invaluable help made this final version possible.